PART FOUR

GUN

Contact details for the author can be found on

www.the realtomfield.com

On Twitter @therealtomfield

Facebook: The Real Tom Field

For Corrine

Standing shoulder to shoulder - Forever

The first person to die was his science teacher, Mr Harper. He slowly walked the halls of the school with tears in his eyes, driven by the intention of walking proudly into the gymnasium to kill all of the jocks who had made his life so miserable for the past two years. As he passed Harper's class, he caught a glimpse of the teacher through the glass panel on the door, and he immediately remembered the ridicule that he had exposed him to in front of his classmates just last week, when he had flunked his test. He felt a rage surge through his body.

He placed the holdall he was carrying on the floor, before carefully unzipping it with two hands, before taking out the AK-47, and the two hand guns that she had provided him with.
He took a deep breath.
He swung the strap of the machine gun over his shoulder and tucked one of the handguns into the waistband of his pants. Clutching the other handgun in his hand, he opened the door to the classroom, walked in, and stood in front of Harper's desk, his knuckles white through the tightness with which he was gripping the handle. Harper looked up at him and went white.

He squeezed the trigger of the gun three times.

The bullets smashed into Harper's chest killing him instantly, the impact of the bullets knocking him forcibly off his chair. As he spun round, the kids sitting at their desks behind him screamed, and a number of them fell to the floor, desperately attempting to become invisible to his eyes which scanned quickly left to right.

But they were not invisible. He saw them all.

He tucked the handgun into his waistband and gripped the AK-47 tightly in both hands. Without any hesitation, and with no particular aim, he lowered the short barrel slightly and squeezed the trigger. The burst of automatic gunfire could be heard throughout the school. Four of his classmates died instantly, two others who were hit in that first burst, would die later that day.

He walked out of the classroom and into the hallway with the intention of heading towards the gym. To his right, he saw two teachers running towards him. He knew Miss Bloom and Mr Keeting well, they had both taught him, and they had both been sympathetic to his inability to mix with other kids. As they got to within twenty feet of him, he squeezed the trigger hard and the volley of bullets stopped them both in their tracks immediately, ripping through them like a knife through butter. He noticed Miss Bloom's white blouse turning a deep crimson red, as she fell to her left and smashed into the lockers that lined the hallway, before Keeting fell forwards, their lives terminated by him just because they were in the wrong place at the wrong time.

He started to move forward along the hallway, stepping over the two bodies of the more likeable teachers, and as he passed over them, he noticed that Keeting was still moving, so he squeezed the trigger hard once again and emptied out the magazine into his torso. He then realised that he had left the spare magazines in the holdall, and so he turned and walked back towards Harper's classroom. A security guard appeared at the end of the hallway heading towards him desperately screaming into his radio, and holding a handgun in his right hand. He threw the machine gun to the floor and grabbed the two hand guns from his waistband.

He then stepped back into Harper's class and closed the door.

The kids inside were crying and screaming at him. He could hear some of them calling his name, begging him to stop, but he ignored them.

She told him that this would happen, and that everyone would suddenly want to be his friend.

He turned and scanned the room.

Josh Gallagher was hiding at the back of the room, using two girls and a boy as a human shield. This was the same Josh Gallagher who hadn't been hiding when he and three other kids had forced his head down the toilet and flushed it last month. He raised both guns and pointed them at the terrified huddle and fired both of them at the same time. The bullets from the gun in his left hand hit the two girls in the chest, and because his right hand was raised slightly higher, the two bullets fired blew the boys head apart. All three of them collapsed like a house of cards in front of him, and

Gallagher's human shield had vanished. He lowered the gun in his right hand slightly and fired four shots into Josh Gallagher's stomach. He died instantly.

Out of the corner of his eye, he caught a glimpse of the security guard peering through the pane of glass in the door, and so he fired both guns towards him, counting as he pulled the trigger. The gun in his left hand ran out of bullets first, and so he dropped it to the floor and clasped both hands around the remaining weapon, and then sent five more shots into the door and then stopped firing. Two seconds later, the guards head appeared through the glass for a brief moment and then ducked out of sight again.

He knew he only had one bullet left.

He lifted the gun to his head, pressed it hard against his temple, closed his eyes and pulled the trigger. Russell Collyfield, just sixteen years old, died instantly.

In Washington D.C., the woman monitoring the police radios in Missouri State heard the news five minutes later. She picked up the phone and dialled a New York number.
'The Missouri Kid came through' she said, before listening to the person on the end of the line and saying, 'I will keep you informed about the other two.'

She then looked across her desk at her colleague sitting opposite and said, 'How close is the kid in Dallas?'

'Just a day or two at most,' he replied.

ONE

Mitchell - Oregon

Ryan Ward and Mike Lawson arrived in Mitchell seven hours after leaving New York. Their Lear jet had touched down at John Day State Airport, where they were met by a guy called Flanagan who had given them the keys to the Ford Taurus that The Old Man had kindly provided for them.

During the hour and a half drive into Mitchell, the bulk of the journey was spent with Ward pretending to listen to the numerous dilemmas that Lawson faced trying to furnish and decorate his new apartment back in New York.

Mitchell was a small town, comprising of only about one hundred houses, and the place where they were heading to was just outside the town, buried deep in the Ochoco National Forest. It was a beautiful place; made up of old buildings that Ward doubted had changed much since the eighteenth century, apart from a new coat of paint every

few years. The drive had taken them past the painted
hills, a sight which he found stunning.

The hills were listed as one of the seven wonders of
Oregon, and their orange and purple colours reminded
him of the bottles that he used to fill with coloured sand
when he was a kid. He told himself that if they had time,
on the way back to the airport, he would get Lawson to
stop the car so that he could get out and take in the
beauty of the view properly for a minute or two.

But their first stop was going to be at the small building
which housed the town's police department.

He knew that the police department only employed four
people, one of them being a civilian who looked after the
departments' admin, and he also knew that the three cops
who worked out of the building were all corrupt and on
the take. And that made them as guilty as the people who
were paying them to turn a blind eye in his eyes.

Lawson pulled the car to a stop outside of the building,
and Ward slowly and deliberately screwed the silencer
onto his Glock until it clicked firmly into place. The only
indication that it was the home of the police department
was a sign to the left of the door which said 'Police',
without the sign, it could have been just a normal house
in the middle of town. They stepped out of the car and
walked casually up to the front door,

'Leave the talking to me,' Ward said.

Lawson nodded.

They walked through the door and into the building.

There was a counter ten feet inside the door which was

unmanned, and beyond it there were three guys in police uniforms.

And four other guys who most definitely weren't police officers.

The four other guys all sported long beards and wore checked shirts and grubby denim jeans.

'Looks like the Beverley Hillbillies are in town,' Lawson quipped.

Ward ignored him.

One of the officers looked up and then slowly sauntered over to the desk. The eyes of the other six guys behind him all eyed the strangers up and down suspiciously.

'Help you?' the officer asked.

He wore a name tag on his uniform which said 'Lester'.

'We are lost,' Ward replied.

As soon as the guys behind the counter heard his British accent, they instantly became more suspicious; three of the four getting to their feet before turning their bodies towards them. Another officer stood up from his chair and walked over to the counter.

He had sergeant stripes on his shirt and a name tag which read 'Parker'.

This was the guy that they were looking for.

'We've been looking for The Church of the Free Spirit for the last hour; can you point us in the right direction?' Ward asked.

'You looking for salvation?' one of the Hillbillies asked.

'Kind of.'

'What's your name?' Parker asked.

Ward knew that Sergeant Dave Parker was working for the Reverend Solomon Tower.

Tower ran a compound which was a paradise for paedophiles. Ward's partner, Eloisa, had put him onto Tower after his vile business had been brought to her attention through her work in child protection at the United Nations in New York. This was not the first time that Eloisa had asked him to deal with someone who abused children on a large scale, and on each previous occasion, he had eliminated the target and destroyed their operation.

This time would be no different.

Nicole-Louise and Tackler, who were his digital hackers in New York, and the most important part of his ultra-lethal team, had discovered exactly how Tower's operation worked, and they had booked Ward and Lawson into The Church of the Free Spirit for two days of cleansing. Nicole-Louise and Tackler had created a fake digital footprint for him that said his name was Paul Homefield, and he was a convicted paedophile. Tower had registered The Church of the Free Spirit with the state of Oregon to give it authenticity. The accounts showed donations regularly being made by donators, amounts that ranged between three to twenty thousand dollars, and on paper, everything looked above board. Tackler had delved into the dark web and found that there were a number of services that Tower offered to paedophiles, and the price of these ranged from three thousand to twenty thousand dollars.

The whole operation was continuous, and although there was no definitive timeline to how long Tower had been running his organisation, Tackler decided it had been at least seven years based on the volume of 'Contributions' that had stepped up over the past five years.

There was no clear indication on how many children were in the compound either, but Nicole-Louise had searched back over the past ten years to find how many young children had gone missing in the surrounding States, and she had found that in that period, thirty-seven young girls under the age of ten had gone missing from California, Nevada, Idaho, Washington and Oregon itself, and she felt reasonably confident that some of those would be in the compound.

The church spent six hours a day teaching the children the way that the Lord demands they should live, and all of the sermons were prepared to brainwash the children into believing that by allowing the strangers who came into the compound to violate them, they were carrying out Gods work.

The Intelligence that Eloisa provided them with had said that when the girls got into their teens, they were married and expected to bare children immediately. There were no records at any of the local hospitals of any births being registered at the compound, so the exact numbers were unclear.

'My name is Paul Homefield,' Ward replied.

Instant recognition seemed to sweep across Parkers face. He knew that Parker was working for Tower because Tackler had spotted someone searching Ward's fake history, and had traced the IP address back to the police station here in Mitchell, and specifically to Sergeant Dave Parker.

One of the Hillbillies stepped forward. He was a big guy, about six two and muscular. He had a definition to him that looked like it had been gained from chopping up logs for ten hours a day. He noticed that his fingernails had black soil ingrained under them, and his hands were dirty.

He stared at them for a moment, staring at Lawson for twice as long as he did him.

Like everyone did.

Mike Lawson was the most stunningly handsome man imaginable. He was six four and muscular and powerful beyond belief. There were very few women in the world who were not instantly attracted to him, and he had the most remarkable, sparkling blue eyes that were impossible not to stare at.

Like everyone did.

But Lawson was also one of the most efficient killing machines on the planet. He had served his time in the British SAS, and he now worked with Ward as part of the most secretive group of government assassins simply known as The Deniables.

Ward himself was a handsome man, very handsome in fact. He was six feet tall, had short brown hair, with chiselled looks, and most women found him attractive. But in Lawson's company, women rarely noticed him.

Ryan Ward was also one of the most efficient killing machines on earth. But what set him apart from the rest of The Deniables was that he was also one of the smartest too.

'You should have been given directions to the church,' the Hillbilly said.

'We have no satnav in our car and no map.'

The hillbilly eyed him up suspiciously again.

'Do you live there?' Ward asked.

'We all do,' the guy said, turning half around and pointing to the other three guys in the filthy denims and checked shirts.

With lightning quick speed, Ward pulled out his Glock and shot the guy in the centre of the face. His head exploded and thin blood sprayed everywhere. Before anyone could react, he had fired three more shots into the centre of the chests of the other three hillbillies. Three seconds later, all four were dead on the floor.

The police officers had made no attempt to move because as soon as Lawson had registered what Ward was about to do, he had pulled his own handgun and was pointing it at the three of them.

'Do you realise what you have just done?' Parker screamed, 'We are officers of the law and this is a police station.'

'We are way, way above the law,' Ward replied softly, 'I'm going to ask you a few questions. If you tell me the truth, I might let you live, if not, I'll kill you. Is that clear?' he asked calmly.

Parker looked down at the bodies on the floor and then at the other two officers who were frozen in fear and he simply nodded.

'How many men does Tower have on the compound?' he asked.

'He did have twenty but now sixteen.'

Ward knew he was telling the truth.

'How many men guard the entrance point?'

'Two.'

'How many young children are on the compound?'

'About twenty,' Parker replied, 'Although three of them are babies,' he said quietly, looking down at the floor as he spoke.

'Is Tower ever alone?'

'No. He always has Mervin and Huey with him. They are his most trusted lieutenants.'

Lawson laughed. Ward glanced at him.

'What?' he asked.

'Mervin and Huey. *Seriously*?' Ward smiled.

'How much does he pay you three to keep everyone away and ensure that his operation runs smoothly?' Ward asked.

Parker paused for a few moments. He didn't want to admit his part in anything, but he had no idea how much Ward knew, and he was sure that he would kill him if he lied.

And so he told the truth, much to the dismay of the other two officers behind him,

'I get four thousand dollars a month, those two get one thousand,' he eventually replied.

Ward raised his gun and shot Parker twice in the face, blowing his head clean apart.

Lawson immediately pulled the trigger on his own gun and fired two shots into the chests of the two officers behind, killing them instantly.

'Call The Old Man and get him to sort this mess,' he said to Lawson as he tucked his Glock back into his jacket, 'Let's go and meet the Reverend Solomon Tower.'

Twenty minutes later, they were pulling over a hundred yards up from the entrance to the compound.

Ward took out his cell phone and dialled the best and most elusive sniper who has ever lived.

The Optician answered immediately.

'You took your time getting here,' he answered.

'We stopped off at the police station,' Ward replied.

'Then let's get this done.'

'Have you checked out the compound?'

'Yes. I'm settled in nicely. Waiting for you to tell me how you want this to go down,' The Optician replied.

'Me and Mike will go inside and try to isolate Tower and his two bodyguards. As soon as you know we are alone with him, you take out every guy who moves.'

'OK. Let's get this done,' The Optician said and the line went dead.

'Drive in Mike, we're ready.' They drove forward to the gate.

There were two guys in the road who promptly moved forward and stopped them; both of them were wearing checked shirts and dirty jeans, and they were both carrying assault rifles. Lawson lowered the window.

'What you boys want?' the guy nearest the car asked.

'Paul Homefield for Mr Tower,' Lawson replied.

The guy unclipped a radio from the side of his jeans and said,

'Paul Homefield.'

'Send him up,' a voice came back almost immediately.

'Follow the road up to the houses in the middle of the compound, and park outside the big white building,' the guy said, as the other guy slowly opened the solid looking wooden gate.

Lawson drove forward and when they were six feet inside, he stopped the car,

'Hey boys, I have a problem,' he shouted out of the window.

The two guys ambled towards the car, and approached Lawson's window,

'What's wrong city boy?' the guy asked when they were about three feet away.

Lawson raised his gun and shot them both, twice in the chest. They fell to the floor, dead instantly.

'I bet they were called Mervin and Huey too,' he said dismissively.

Ward laughed.

They drove into the compound. The road seemed to go on forever. They had gone six miles before the buildings came into view in the distance a mile away.

'As soon as we get Tower alone, take out his two men,' Ward said.

Lawson just nodded.

They reached the buildings a few minutes later.

The white building was pretty imposing when they got close to it. It was well designed; whoever built it had tried replicating the old Georgian style of houses of yesteryear and they had got pretty close to it. It was well presented and had large marble pillars, with a lead roof covering big mahogany front doors, which were well over eight feet tall. There were a number of other buildings dotted opposite the big house, bungalows which were equally as well presented. Ward counted eleven guys around the front of the big building and hanging around the bungalows, and there were seven high end cars parked to the left of the big house. No doubt the client's cars he thought to himself.

'Easy pickings for The Optician,' he said to Lawson.

'I noticed,' Lawson replied, 'We've already killed six of them, the eleven guys out here, and Tower and his two goons inside, make the twenty that we know are here.'

Ward pulled out his phone and dialled The Optician.

'As soon as we are inside, eliminate the eleven guys outside and we will deal with the others,' he said as soon as The Optician answered.

'Understood,' The Optician replied, and the line went dead.

'Let's go and meet the Reverend,' Ward said, and they both climbed out of the car after tucking their handguns firmly into their waistbands.

TWO

The five members of the committee sat around the large mahogany table in the boardroom of the Four Seasons Hotel.

It wasn't a recognised committee.

But it was a committee that had existed for almost one hundred years.

It was a requirement that the people who sat on the committee told no one of its existence, with the exception of the next person who would take their place. Only once over the past forty years had a reporter started poking around after a tip off, and because he only worked for a mid-range tabloid paper, his death went largely unreported and unnoticed.

At the head of the table, the longest serving member of the committee, and the man who was known as the chairman, was halfway through dialling a number on the phone which sat in front of him, when he paused for a brief moment and smiled at the other four members sitting with him. It was a smile of celebration. When he had finished dialling the number, he pressed the speaker button and leant back into the plush leather chair, putting his hands behind his head and interlocking his fingers together, almost as though he was laying on a sun lounger on a hot sunny day.

The ringing tone echoed around the room as the line connected, and then the same female voice who had told him about the shootings in Missouri answered,

'Hello?' she softly answered.

'It's me,' the man said assertively, 'Well done in Missouri,' he added, now with less assertion and more appreciation in his voice.

'Thank you sir,' she replied, sounding very pleased that her diligence and creativity had been recognised.

The beautiful sunny morning in Washington D.C. had just got even better for her. She knew that his satisfaction meant even greater rewards.

'The money will be deposited within the hour,' the man said, 'What is being said on Capitol Hill about the event?'

'They are making the usual noises,' she replied.

'Saying what specifically?' he demanded, the appreciation in his voice now gone.

'The President will be going on TV shortly to condemn the shooting, as he always does. The inevitable questions are being asked by the liberals, and, once again, they are already demanding changes to the constitution and the media are going into overdrive trying to find out as much as they can about this Collyfield kid,' she replied in an efficient tone.

'And what will they find?'

'Nothing at all that they can link to us. That's guaranteed.'

The man smiled to himself and looked around the table. The other four men all looked at him and nodded their delight at what they were hearing.

'And Dallas is almost ready?'

'It is sir,' she replied.

The man sensed an air of doubt in her voice. It made him uncomfortable, and he unclasped his fingers, dropped his arms from behind his head, and leant forward, his elbows taking his heavy weight on the table, and he leant further in towards the phone.

'You have a problem with him?' he demanded, a frown spreading across his face as he spoke.

'No sir. Not with him,' the woman replied.

'Then with what?' he asked.

There was a pause on the end of the line for a few moments.

'Tell me,' he demanded, the pause starting to make him feel uncomfortable.

'Well sir,' she began, with clear uncertainty in her voice, 'Historically, these shootings have been planned a few weeks apart, never a few days. I'm just concerned that people might start looking much closer for links to the shootings rather than at the perpetrators,' she said.

'You said that there is nothing to link us to any of this,' the chairman replied.

'There isn't.'

'Then we have nothing to worry about. Proceed as instructed.'

'Yes sir.'

'Anything else?'

'My contact on Capitol Hill told me this morning that another Senate Committee meeting will be taking place this afternoon, and the shooting has been placed at the top of the agenda.'

'Don't worry about those puppets,' the chairman said, 'They are all empty promises and hot air,' he added, before he pressed the 'End Call' button on the phone and leant back into his chair again.

He looked around the table at the four other men. Three of them looked more than satisfied with what they had just heard, but he noticed that one of them, the youngest and newest member of the committee, had a frown spread across his face.

'What is it?' the chairman asked him.

'Do you think that maybe she could be right?' he asked, 'And that maybe waiting a few weeks might be a good idea?'

'Why?'

'Just in case they do start looking for a link.'

The chairman smiled at him,

'I remember the worry that the first events caused me,' he said, 'I couldn't sleep for weeks, and I was sure that everything was going to be discovered and that I would spend the rest of my life in jail. But do you know what put my mind at rest?' he asked.

The newest member shook his head.

'It was three months after the second event, when everything went back to normal, that I realised that I had wasted months of my life living in blind panic and fear, and I had wasted so much energy, that I promised myself that I would never go through that again. What you feel is normal, am I right gentlemen?' he asked the other three men around the table.

They all nodded instantly, and two of them smiled broadly, almost laughing to themselves about how fearful they used to be too.

The newest member looked around the table and instantly felt reassured.

'Then I am happy to take on board your advice and experience,' he said, and opened his arms wide to bow to the elder's greater wisdom, "Let's get Dallas done," he added with a smile.

All four of the other members smiled with him.

'Gentlemen,' the chairman said as he stood up, 'Anyone for a round of golf, five thousand dollars a hole?'

The newest member stood up first. He played off a handicap of ten, and he knew that taking their money would act as a very rewarding distraction.

Mitchell - Oregon

Ward and Lawson walked up the solid marble stairs and into the house. They noticed how three of the guys in their checked shirts and denims, stopped walking outside and stared at them for a few moments, and then carried on towards wherever they were going. Ward thought to himself that they probably only had about a minute left to live, and that brought a smile to his face for a few seconds. Inside the house there were plush rugs on the floor, and three expensive looking brown leather sofas were situated to the side, end to end. Opposite the sofas there was a desk, an attractive woman in her late twenties sat behind it.

They approached her and he said,

'Hello. I'm Paul Homefield and this is my colleague, James Simmons. The reverend should be expecting us.'

She looked Ward up and down and then looked at Lawson.

He waited for the statutory double take on Lawson's eyes, followed by the inevitable blush and movement of hand to the hair, which all women did when they first set eyes on Lawson, and sure enough, she did all three exactly in order.

Lawson smiled at her and looked away towards the sofas, he was trying to decide if one of them would fit in with the décor in his new apartment, and he made a mental note to himself to research the different colours available.

'Are you here for eternal pleasure?' she asked, a sick smile washing over her face which made Ward's stomach turn.

'Yes we are,' he replied, 'I know that I am going to get immense pleasure from what I am hoping to do.'

'Take a seat,' the woman said, pointing to the sofas, as she picked up the phone on the desk and spoke to someone on the end of the line.

They both walked across to the sofas and sat down.

Outside, The Optician was finishing the countdown in his head from ten to shoot. From his vantage point on top of the bungalow opposite the grand house, he had managed to line up all eleven Hillbillies in his scope over the past fifteen seconds. He had decided to take out the three nearest to him first, as they were only about six feet from the door of the building to his left, and if he killed one of the guys further away; they might have time to escape out of sight.

He wouldn't take that chance.

His breathing was balanced, his hands were rock steady and the count was almost over.

'Three, two, one, shoot,' he mouthed silently.

He squeezed the trigger gently.

The guy nearest the door took the first shot in the side of his head, and as the two standing next to him turned to see what the movement was, He swung his rifle gently to the right, and as the gun was moving, he squeezed two more shots out, both hitting their intended targets in the dead centre of the forehead. Their knees gave way and they all hit the floor in synchronised order, a split second apart, once gravity took charge.

It was as smooth as if he was moving his finger through thin air.

He then swung around his rifle so it was lined up to his right, the four guys on the opposite side of the bungalow were sitting on a small wall, talking and smoking, lined up like tin cans. They were so deeply engrossed in their conversation that they had not noticed their Hillbilly cousins opposite them collapsing to the floor. He squeezed the trigger as he lined up the guy furthest away on the wall, and then swung his arm deliberately and slowly to the right, his eye fixing on the guy's heads through his scope after each fluent movement.

From his four shots he achieved four direct hits to the centre of the guy's foreheads. The force of the bullets knocked them all backwards, and they fell off the wall. It was literally like watching tin cans get shot off at a fairground.

The next two guys were directly in front of him. They were the easiest shots, and to make it a little more challenging for him, he decided to make it blind. In a split second, he lined them up in his scope, moving right to left, and then closed his eyes and squeezed the trigger, moving the rifle back left to right. Two more direct hits in the centre of their foreheads and they hit the floor immediately.

The last two guys were about thirty feet apart.

They had both now registered what was happening, and they were lifting their rifles, more in protection and hope, than attack, as they were looking way too far to his left to know where he was, and so he lined up the guy nearest to the house first and squeezed the trigger softly. He scored another direct hit in the centre of the guy's forehead, and his head exploded much more than any of the other targets he had hit. The last guy raised his gun but before he could fire a shot, he had him in the centre of his scope and had squeezed off his shot. It was a direct forehead shot yet again, and his gun fell out of his hands a split second before he collapsed to the floor.

Eleven bullets had been fired from The Optician's gun.

Eleven Hillbillies were dead.

Eleven seconds was all it took.

As the last guy was hitting the floor outside, three men came out of a door behind the desk and approached Ward and Lawson. The guy in the middle looked like a businessman rather than a reverend. He wore an expensive suit, and he had a set of veneers which were way too white. He was no taller than five feet five, and he had short curly hair which was dyed a ludicrous black colour. There was one guy either side of him.

They both wore checked shirts and grubby jeans.

'His teeth are white man!' Lawson muttered under his breath.

'Mr Homefield, Mr Simmons, I'm the Reverend Solomon Tower,' he said, a sickeningly smug smile spreading across his face as he spoke.

Ward stood up and Lawson copied him. All three men looked at Lawson for twice as long as they looked at him.

'These two guys are unarmed,' Ward said.

Tower looked at him, confusion on his face.

Lawson pulled out his gun and shot the two guys on either side of Tower twice in the chest. The bullets ripped through their torsos', and they both staggered backwards and fell to the floor.

The woman behind the desk screamed, and Ward instantly pulled out his Glock and fired two shots into her chest, killing her instantly. He never differentiated between genders. Evil people were evil people in his mind, although he was always less inclined to shoot women in the face than he was men.

Tower stood on the spot, frozen.

'Outside,' Ward demanded, stepping forward and pushing the silencer hard into Tower's back.

Tower stepped forward and walked out into the sunlight.

'Oh my God!' Tower screamed as he looked out in front of him, and saw seven dead bodies and four sets of feet sticking out over the top of a small wall, 'What have you done?'

'I've done the lords work,' Ward replied, before grabbing hold of Towers hair and pulling him to the centre of the courtyard and then pushing him hard in the back so he staggered a few feet further forward.

Lawson stepped forward and unleashed a solid jab with his right fist and it caught Tower full in the mouth. His expensive teeth crumpled under the force of Lawson's punch, his knees gave way and he fell to the floor, cupping his hand under his chin and trying to catch the veneers as they fell out.

'Look at me,' Ward demanded.

Tower looked up at him, his mouth was now gushing blood and there were tears in his eyes.

He looked terrified.

He looked exactly how he wanted him to look.

'I kill lots of sick animals like you, scum who prey on defenceless kids, but you are the vilest of the vile,' he spat at him.

'Please, don't kill me. I'll give you anything, money? I have lots of money,' Tower begged.

It always came down to money with these animals, he thought to himself.

'I want retribution, an eye for an eye. Isn't that what the good book says?' he asked softly.

'Please don't. I'll stop, I promise.'

'You are way past salvation.'

'What have I done?'

'You've picked on innocent children and destroyed hundreds of lives. You are ten seconds away from death. Tell me what you see now?'

Tower looked up.

He saw a seven-foot giant standing above him, a man with eyes that pierced his own, and he now knew what death looked like. He started to cry.

Ward knew right then that Tower saw exactly what he wanted him to see.

He raised his gun and fired four shots into Towers face, the bullets ripping it apart, and by the time the fourth bullet had impacted, he was now unrecognisable. He fell forward onto the dusty soil and his pathetic frame looked even smaller crumpled up.

'Call the Old Man, and get the F.B.I. social services and State Police here immediately,' he said to Lawson.

'You could have waited ten seconds to kill him,' Lawson replied as he pulled his cell phone from his pocket and hit speed dial.

Ward looked at him quizzically.

'Because I wanted to know where he got those sofas from, they would look great in my new apartment,' Lawson said with a smile.

Ward laughed.

'Make the call so we can go Mike,' he said, and he headed towards the car.

When he reached the car, he pulled out his cell phone and wrote a short text message and sent it to Eloisa.

It simply said, 'It's done.'

THREE

2524 Morgan Street – Irving, Texas

Kyle Newson shut his bedroom door and hurriedly
closed the blinds before turning on his laptop.
He had passed seventeen just a week ago.
He lived with his mother, father and sister in a bungalow
in Irving, and to the outside world; they looked like an
average all American family.
Their home was small but tidy, built of red brick on
Morgan Street, and the outside of the building showed
that it was meticulously well-cared for. The lawn was
neatly cut, and the window frames looked fresh and
white, the result of his father's care in painting them last
weekend.
His father Gary worked as a yardman for a building
materials supplier, and his mother Grace worked as a

customer service clerk at the local supermarket. His sister Sadie was two years younger than him, and she was gradually starting to become more confident and outgoing, due to the fact that she had joined the local gymnastics club a month ago.

To the world, they were a pretty unspectacular family, but they were a nice family, just quieter than most.

The problem with quiet people is that the outside world never really knows them.

Most of the neighbours on the street recognised Kyle whenever he passed them, and he would always respond with a polite 'Hello' to any greeting.

But he didn't talk much.

Kyle's problem had always been that he was overweight. And from the age of four when he had been at preschool, all of the other kids had reminded him daily of that fact.

He had been bullied constantly for the past thirteen years and he had gradually become more and more withdrawn. He had gotten used to the name calling after all these years, and it didn't hurt him so much anymore. What bothered him was the physical violence that the other testosterone filled boys at school subjected him to every day. It was not excessive, little kicks up the backside or punches on the arm, but it was relentless and it wore him down. But the worst part was the way the girls laughed at him.

Like any boy of seventeen, his hormones ran wild, and he felt more and more physical attraction to girls every day. He was desperate to experience physical contact with someone, and he had made more of an effort to try and wear the right clothes and listen to the right music but none of it made any difference.

His mum saved for three weeks to buy him some new sneakers. When he proudly walked into high school the day after she had brought them home, all of the kids laughed at him because they were the cheaper version. One kid, Andy Graves, who lived just up from him on Morgan Street, had trodden in dog mess and then stamped all over Kyle's feet, completely ruining the new sneakers. Kyle ran off to the bathroom and burst into tears, and as he was frantically trying to clean his sneakers, five girls burst in, filming him on their cell phones, calling him 'Dog Boy,' and laughing loudly at him.

He stood still, unable to move, crying uncontrollably. The video was sent through all forms of social media and by the end of the day, the whole school was laughing at 'Dog Boy'.

Kyle Newson had never had one person that he could call a friend.

Until now.

He typed the address of the website that had become his salvation into the address bar on his laptop, and the screen sprung into life with bright, vibrant colours and a blue login box appeared on the right. He typed in his username, 'Spartacus' and entered his password.

The screen switched to a brown colour and he excitedly clicked on the tab that said 'Forums' before typing in the username search for 'MissFit'. He could feel his heart beating as he waited to see if her name would flag up as being online.

She understood him like no one else.

Washington D.C.

'He's online,' the guy said across his desk to the woman sitting ten feet away from him.

Emma Casey looked up at him and said,

'Start gently. Ask him about his day and tell him that you have missed him. In five minutes' time, tell him that you have been thinking about the pact you've made with him.'

The guy started to type.

Emma Casey was thirty-one years old. She had earned a master's degree in psychology at Washington State University and she had intended to forge a career in child psychology for the rest of her life. She had started well, working at a private practice for one of the most exclusive firms in the State. She had worked with numerous children and had outstanding success. One of the children that she had helped was the twelve-year-old grandson of the chairman of the committee.

He had been so impressed by the improvement in his grandson that he had invited her to his sprawling mansion in Michigan for the weekend.

She had just split from her latest boyfriend and she fancied a break, so she accepted.

The chairman had been fascinated to learn how she had managed to stabilise his grandson, and her understanding of his young mind, and before he realised, he had set the wheels in motion for his plan.

He had spent the first part of the weekend trying to find the right time to make the proposal to her, and when he did, she instantly dismissed his idea as insane and illegal, insisting that she wanted no part in it.

That was until he showed her the money that was on offer.

She had spent the last night of her stay at the retreat in turmoil. She knew that the proposal was wrong, completely wrong, but the money that was being offered would set her up for the rest of her life and she would be able to fulfil her dream of going to live on a Greek island, in sun and isolation, at least twenty-five years earlier than she had planned.

In the morning, she had done the right thing and thanked her host for his hospitality, but declined his offer, and he instantly surprised her by doubling his initial fee.

Without further turmoil, or moral or ethical self-questioning, she had found herself accepting his offer immediately.

Russell Collyfield in Missouri had been the latest target and he had come through spectacularly well. She was looking at her new bank account in the Caymans on her screen, and she could not take her eyes off of the balance at the bottom which read one and a half million dollars. Two more targets to go and then she would be four and a half million dollars richer, then she would disappear for the life she had always dreamed of.

She closed her screen and then maximised another. She scrolled back through the conversation that her colleague was having opposite and when she got to the end she said to him across the room,

'I'll take over now.'

'OK. Three, two, one, it's yours,' he replied, and he pulled his hands away from his keyboard in an overly dramatic manner, and then raised them above his head. She looked at the screen and watched as the words appeared in real time as Kyle Newson typed,

She could sense his reluctance and fear as she read what he was saying, and she immediately responded with key words that she knew would get deep into his mind and convince him that what they were agreeing to do was the best thing for both of them.

Kyle would then seem to panic, and so she would change subject for a few minutes to relieve his stress levels, by complimenting him on his character, and how she has never met anyone like him, and how he was the only thing that she could think about.

As soon as Kyle appeared relaxed again, she would go back to their pact and how after they had followed it through, they would live for eternity together and their souls would be inseparable.

After forty-five minutes, she knew without doubt that Kyle was now primed and ready.

She smiled to herself.

She was eager to get this finished, and while she had initially challenged the committee's decision to carry out three shootings so close together, she felt excitement rushing through her body as she knew that there was only one more person to convince.

'The kid in New York, how close do you think he is?' she asked across her desk.

'He's at least two days away,' her colleague replied.

'You need to move quicker. Yesterday he was on course as much as this kid in Dallas. What have you done?' she asked, annoyance rushing through her voice.

'He got spooked by the events in Missouri,' the guy replied, 'They aren't saying very nice things about the Collyfield kid.'

She pondered what he meant for a moment and then said,

'I'll take it over now, you've done the groundwork. I'll get him back on board.'

'Fine with me,' the guy replied, 'You want me to carry on searching for more kids who are right for what we want?'

'No. The New York kid will be fine. Have you arranged for the weapons to be ready in both places?'

'Yes. They are all stored securely and easily obtainable.'

'I want you to write down exactly where they are stored, and where the keys are so that I can get these two up and running. And then because you have done such a great job, you can take the rest of the day off.'

'They aren't keys. They are combination padlocks,' he replied. But he liked the sound of taking the rest of the day off, and so he quickly scribbled down the information and handed it to her.

She read it and then smiled to herself.

'What's so funny?' he asked.

'You've put the weapons in dumpsters?'

'It's the safest place to put them. No one is going to bother smashing open a dumpster to sort through trash,' he replied.

'How very smart of you,' she said without a hint of sarcasm in her voice, 'Well done James, enjoy your time off.'

'That is the first time you have ever used my name,' he said as he tucked his laptop into his bag, 'You must be in a good mood.'

She smiled a warm smile at him.

'See you tomorrow,' he said as he turned and walked out of the office.

She immediately picked up the phone and called New York.

The committee chairman answered on the second ring, 'I'm just off to play golf so you were lucky to catch me,' he answered.

'I'm done with James Novak,' she said.

'Definitely?' the chairman asked.

'Yes. He's just left but he has taken his laptop with him. I have no idea what information he might have on it, so you need to get it back immediately so that there is no comeback at all,' she said hurriedly, picturing Novak melting into the crowds on the street as she spoke.

'Don't panic,' the chairman said, 'I have a man outside watching him. He will be following him now. We will have the laptop back shortly.'

'Do you have someone watching me too?' she asked, suddenly feeling much more vulnerable than she had a few seconds earlier.

'No, of course I haven't Emma, you are almost family,' he replied, and then the line went dead.

James Novak was twenty-nine years old and a graduate of Washington State in computer science. He was an integral part of the plan to begin with, but now he had served his purpose. He walked out of the building on 7th Street NW and turned left, heading towards the parking garage. He walked in through the exit and down to the lower level where his car was parked. He had decided that he would call his friends and see if anyone wanted to shoot some hoops later on.

He was ten feet away from his car when he heard a voice say,

'Is that you James?' and he stopped and turned around to see a guy walking towards him with his left hand extended to greet him.

He didn't recognise the guy, but he looked about the same age as him, and so he raised his left hand to accept the greeting.

As the guy got closer, he did look vaguely familiar.

'I'm sorry, I can't remember your name,' he said apologetically.

'Not to worry,' the guy replied, and he swung his right arm around with lightning fast speed as his left hand gripped Novak's hand, and he jammed an eight-inch serrated knife deep into his side, and the blade ripped through his spleen. The guy then pulled the knife out and jabbed it hard into his left hand side, cutting right through his kidneys.

Novak fell to the floor and the guy pulled him in between two cars so that they were both partially hidden. The guy pulled his satchel from his shoulder and opened it to check that the laptop was there.

It was.

He then dug into Novak's pockets and pulled out his wallet, keys and cell phone, the dying James Novak putting up no resistance, as the life drained from his body, and when he was sure that he had taken everything that he needed, he leant down and slit his throat, making sure that he cut through the windpipe as he moved the blade from left to right.

The guy peered up and looked through the windows of the parked cars.

No one was about.

He then wiped the blade on Novak's jacket and stood up, flinging the satchel over his own shoulder as he did so.

He walked twenty feet away from the body and then lifted the satchel open and dropped the keys and wallet inside, and then removed the battery from the cell phone before dropping them inside too.

He then walked out of the car park and back onto 7th Street NW and melted into the crowds.

He was just another guy on his way to the office.

And James Novak had become just another murder victim of a robbery gone wrong in the nation's capital.

FOUR

DUMBO – New York

Eight hours after Ward had eliminated the Reverend Solomon Tower, he was walking back into his apartment in New York. It was where he felt most at home.
He lived on Washington Street, a neighbourhood in Brooklyn. More specifically, it was in an area that was better known simply as DUMBO. It was a street that had provided the backdrop to a number of iconic movies and pictures. The building was built from red brick, discoloured through years of industrial grime, but it still retained a magic to it. He lived on the sixth floor of an apartment building and when he walked out into the street, a glance to the right gave him the iconic view of the Manhattan Bridge and across the East River the skyscrapers of New York.

It was his one place of sanctuary, the one place where he felt normal.

He had just climbed out of the shower when his cell phone rang. He looked at the caller display.

It was Centrepoint. Or as he was referred to by everyone who knew him, The Old Man.

In truth, he wasn't that old.

His real name was Paul. J. McNair, he was fifty-one years old, and was effectively the boss of the heads of both the CIA and MI6. But he didn't officially exist. He had spent a lifetime taking care of the problems which troubled governments on both sides of the Atlantic. It was he who made the tough decisions, and cleaned up the messes that the politicians weren't willing to risk their political futures over. Over the past fifteen years McNair had built up a core group of lethal, highly trained and supremely intelligent assassins that did what he ordered without question or fear. Known as the 'Deniables,' the group was born out of an attempt to rectify a shambles of a covert operation in Afghanistan which he had put right by selecting the right people.

The Optician was the secret ingredient. He was unique.

The Old Man had always felt that his greatest achievement was keeping all of the Deniables apart so they would never meet, although he wasn't naïve enough to believe that they hadn't at least established some semblance of who the others were. After all they were the best. He always kept the balance right, Five Americans and Five British. That would ensure that both Governments would equally move heaven and earth to keep things moving smoothly, and provide unlimited financial support without hesitation.

Ward answered the phone,
'I've only just got back,' he said.
'I know. I gave you an hour to freshen up,' The Old Man replied.
He had got used to the fact that Centrepoint knew all of his movements. After all, it was he who had provided the transport down to Oregon, and he who would clear up the subsequent mess that Ward had left down there for the police and social services to deal with. He always provided assistance with the favours that he took on for Eloisa, and he believed that having to put up with The Old Man knowing where he was every minute of the day was a fair trade off.

'What's the matter?' he asked.
'Have you heard about the shooting in Missouri?'
He had heard the attendant on the flight mention it to Lawson, but he didn't hear the details.
'Not really,' he replied, 'What happened?'
'A kid went into his school and killed thirteen people, ten of them other kids.'
Ward shook his head. He lived in a world of death, and the truth was, killing another person was easy to him if they were bad, but whenever he heard of kids being killed, he always thought how unfair it was that they could have their lives taken away before they had the chance to fulfil their potential.
'What about the kid who shot them all?' he asked before pausing, 'I take it he took his own life?' he added, answering his own question. They always did.

'Yes he did,' The Old Man replied.

'So what has this got to do with us?'

'That's what I need you to find out.'

'I don't understand,' he replied, 'Surely the local police and F.B.I. deal with these events?'

'Normally they would. But I have intelligence on this that indicates that there is something much more sinister at play,' Centrepoint said in a matter of fact tone.

'Such as?'

'This is the first one of three.'

Ward had stopped being surprised at what The Old Man knew a long time ago. He had carried out numerous missions based on information that he gave him, and he was always invariably right.

'I need a bit more than that,' he replied, 'tell me what you know?'

'I have long suspected that these shootings that define our country are never random,' The Old Man started, now sounding more solemn, 'Certain things never added up. Quiet kids just suddenly flip one day, I get that, but a number of these kids have come from solid families and never gave an indication that they were psychotic,' he added.

He thought about this and he decided that The Old Man had a point.

What invariably happened after these shootings was that friends and neighbours came out of the woodwork saying that the killer was a loner, and they always thought something was off with them, and that they always worried they would hurt someone, and yet none of them had ever done anything formally about it before, or made a complaint, so that took away any weighting that their comments might have in his eyes.

'So what do you know that the rest of the world doesn't know?' he asked.

'I have long thought that these kids were being manipulated into carrying out these atrocities,' he replied.

'For the notoriety or to kill one specific person and hide the fact?'

'No. For financial gain,' he replied.

'I don't understand how that can be possible. Money isn't much use to someone if they are dead,' Ward said, 'So who stands to gain?' he asked.

'That's what I want you to find out. I want you to find out who is behind these acts, hunt them down and eliminate them. I will back you completely on this one. These shootings put a lot of pressure on the Senators on Capitol Hill, and they then dump it on me to sort out,' Centrepoint replied.

'So where do I start?'

'I've commandeered the kids' laptop who carried out the shootings in Missouri.'

'I bet the F.B.I. loved that?'

'If there is a lead, it will be on there. I need you to find it Ryan and find out what else is planned.'

'You said that the shooting in Missouri was the first one of three? You are saying that there are two more to come?' Ward asked.

'That's what the intelligence indicates,' Centrepoint replied.

'Can you send me your intelligence?'

'No point. That is literally all I have. The laptop will be your only lead.'

'And if there is nothing on there? Where the hell am I supposed to start looking?' he asked.

'You are the smart one Ryan. You will figure it out. But I want you to keep me informed of progress.'

Ward already knew where he was going to start. He would get the Laptop sent to Nicole-Louise and Tacklers place. They were the best hackers in the world, if there was anything to find, they would find it, and if they did, he had a point from which he could start.

'Where is the laptop now?' he asked.

'It arrived at Nicole-Louise and Tacklers' five minutes ago.'

The Old Man was always one step ahead.

'If you find out any more from your source, let me know immediately,' Ward said.

'Get moving quickly on this, if there are going to be two more shootings, we have very little time left,' Centrepoint said firmly.

Ward hung up the phone.

Five minutes later he was walking out of the apartment building and hailing a cab to take him to Park Avenue.

Park Avenue – New York

Tackler answered the door to his apartment,

'I want you to tell Lawson to move back to England,' he said as he turned and walked back into the apartment, 'He's driving me mad over his new place,' he added over his shoulder.

Tackler was in his late-twenties and always wore navy blue towel shorts, which came down to his knees, and tee shirts that no matter how new they were, always looked grubby.

Tackler and Nicole-Louise were the most important people in his loyal team. And his team was loyal. It was made up of Lawson, a CIA operative called Gilligan, who was currently out of action after getting shot, and a team of mercenaries run by an Ex-Seal called McDermott. Ward trusted very few people outside of that group.

Nicole-Louise and Tackler knew the real Ryan Ward. They had created his digital footprint, hidden money away for him, and ensured that his back was always covered in the digital world.

'Hello Ryan,' Nicole-Louise said, 'Everything went well in Oregon so Mike told us,' she said as he walked into the living area.

'Thanks to you two,' he said, and Nicole-Louise instantly rolled her eyes at him. She never took his compliments as they were intended, she knew that they were the best, and she didn't feel the need to be constantly reminded of it.

Nicole-Louise was much taller than Tackler. She had long light brown hair and beautiful blue eyes. Ward always thought that Nicole-Louise and Tackler didn't fit together, physically or even characteristically, but in terms of compatibility, now that he knew them so well, they were just perfect for each other. He could never work out how they ended up together in the first place, but he was very glad that they did. Nicole-Louise was outgoing, confident and vibrant and Tackler was much quieter, more methodical and much more serious than she was.

But they were both very, very, very good at what they did.

Their apartment was simple. It had four bedrooms and would fetch a lot of money on the property market, but they didn't use much of it. The lounge was referred to as their living area because apart from the kitchen, bathroom and one of the bedrooms, this was where they spent most of their time. And it was a big living area. It doubled as their work area too.

The living room had two work stations, one on each side of the room, and there were five screens glowing on each station. On a table to Nicole-Louise's right, sat a laptop which had two cables running into it. Ward could see that Tackler had the same image from the laptop on the large screen in front of him.

They were already tearing the laptops memory apart to see what they could find.

No sooner had he arrived when there was a knock on the door. Tackler wearily walked over to the door again and opened it up.

Lawson was standing there, a broad smile across his face.

'Tackler,' he said, opening his arms wide, 'Give me a hug.'

Tackler turned and walked back to his workstation and Lawson stepped in.

'Why are you so happy?' Ward asked him.

'These two, my two favourite people in the world, have sorted everything out with my new apartment. When we got back from Oregon, the decorators and furniture people were in there already. They have said they will all be finished the day after tomorrow.

So can you put me up for two nights?' Lawson asked hopefully.

'No,' Ward replied, 'Get a hotel.'

'Really? You wouldn't put me up for two nights?'

'No I wouldn't. Working with you is bad enough. If I had to spend two nights with you I would end up killing you Mike. It's for your own safety,' he replied without a hint of a smile, before deciding not to wait for a response and walking across to Nicole-Louise's workstation to see what was happening.

'Do you have anything yet?' he asked her.

'Give me a chance Ryan,' she replied, 'I've only just connected it to my system.'

'What are you doing?'

'I'm using some new software that Tackler has developed which can retrieve everything deleted from searches, history, and even find conversations that have taken place on live sites,' she said, 'It's in its infancy, but once Tackler has refined this, it will change internet usage for good,' she added.

'So he will be worth billions?' he said, fully aware that neither of them had any interest in money or success. They had stolen tens of millions of dollars since he had worked with them, all from the profits that the bad guys had accumulated, and they had no interest in keeping any of it for themselves.

'Yes we will,' Tackler replied over his shoulder, 'And we will give it all to Lawson so that he can go and buy a country house in England, and give us a break from his constant talking,' he added.

'I know that feeling well,' Ward quipped.

'I am in the room,' Lawson said loudly, 'Just in case you forgot.'

'OK,' Nicole-Louise interrupted, 'The software is now scanning the hard drive to try and retrieve the data from the most used sites, and then it will automatically pull back any information exchanged on that site, and hopefully, if there are any e-mails or conversations that are related to the shootings, they will come back to life,' she said firmly.

Tackler stood up from his chair and walked across the room to Nicole-Louise's workstation. He put his hand on her shoulder as he leant in, and she put her hand on top of his and squeezed it.

This was a big moment for them both, Ward could see that, and he found himself discreetly crossing his fingers behind Tackler's chair.

Suddenly, Nicole-Louise's large screen kicked into life. Rows and rows of data started streaming down quickly. It was moving too fast to read.

Lists were appearing with dates and times on the left hand side.

On the monitor next to her main screen, sub folders were starting to appear, in alphabetical order. The first folder read, 'Anxiety', the next one 'Boobs' and then 'Character Building'.

'Is this putting them into those folders on its own?' Ward asked.

'Yes it is,' Tackler replied without looking up. Nicole-Louise squeezed his hand tight again.

'It works Tackler. You are the smartest, coolest, sexiest man alive. You are a genius,' she said, excitement rushing through her voice.

At the bottom of the screen, a bar pinged at one hundred per cent.

'That's it,' Nicole-Louise said,' everything that was deleted, intentionally or unintentionally. We now have a copy of everything that was ever on this laptop as well as the information on any sites that were visited,' she added.

She then moved to another screen where all the folders were lined up and clicked on a button,

'Now let's see what site this kid used the most,' she said, and a couple of seconds later, the files had been rearranged by size, the largest file at the top.

'Well, looking at the size of this file at the top,' she said, using a pencil to tap it on her screen, 'He spent eighty per cent of his time on this laptop visiting this site,' she added.

Ward leant forward so that he was closer to the screen.

The folder at the top had a name next to it.

'Are you familiar with that?' he asked Nicole-Louise.

'No. I've never heard of it.'

'What about you Tackler?'

'I've never heard of it either,' he replied.

'I'll open it up, see what's inside,' Nicole-Louise said.

Ward watched as she moved the arrow over the folder and double clicked on the icon that simply said, 'iamalone.com'

'It's been a long day,' Ward said, 'I'm meeting Eloisa at 9:00pm, do you two want to dig around and see what you can find then we can run through it tomorrow morning?' he asked.

'Good idea,' Nicole-Louise replied, 'There is a huge amount of data here that needs sifting through, which will give us both time.'

'Thanks,' he said, he turned and walked out of the apartment, leaving Lawson sitting alone, deep in thought, as to who he could invite over to christen his new bed.

FIVE

Emma Casey sat at her desk feeling anxious. She wanted
these last two shootings carried out quickly so that she
could get on with her life and make a new start. She
looked at her screen, and then down at the time in the
bottom right hand corner, and calculated that 'Spartacus'
had not been online for the last three hours. He had told
her that he had to run a few errands for his mom and that
he should only be gone an hour.
She was now becoming impatient.
She was fully aware that the longer he went without
talking to her, it was more likely that reason and fear
would kick in, and the kid would get cold feet. She
pictured him sitting in his room in complete turmoil and
struggling with his own conscience, which would be
telling him to walk away right now.

She knew that the defining point in the relationship she had been patiently building up with him was now. He would either commit to doing this in his mind, and that would guarantee that he did carry out the shooting, or if he raised questions again, he was never going to come through.

So she had decided to make his mind up for him.

Kyle Newson had given her his email address and she had just sent the pictures of the naked seventeen-year-old girl from Nebraska, whose cell phone Novak had hacked into over five years ago and stolen over a hundred pictures and videos. It was the same girls' pictures that they had used to manipulate Russel Collyfield, and the same that she would also use to entice the kid in New York. They were explicit and graphic. Casey thought to herself that the girl in the pictures would never have to struggle or work hard; she would simply marry into money. She probably had already.

A message box sprung into life on her screen.

Spartacus was back.

'Soz for da delay, my mom added chores to the list,' he wrote.

She hated the abbreviation of words. She believed it showed both laziness and a lack of intelligence, but as most of the teenage world abbreviated everything nowadays, she had to embrace it.

'U get my pics?' she typed.

'They were amazing.'

'When we met again, that is all yours,' she typed.

'U really think dat we will meet in our world of luv if we do dis?' he asked.

'I know we will,' she quickly replied, 'This is our moment to create our legacy. I luv U Kyle, at two tomorrow afternoon, the whole world will no who we R, and then we can meet up again, and no 1 can ever hurt us,' she added.

There was a pause of ten seconds.

This was the moment of reckoning.

Three months of manipulating this tortured soul had come down to his next reply.

A message line appeared that said 'Writing' in the bottom of the box and then the message appeared.

'The whole world will know who we are by tomorrow. They deserve to die, all of them. No 1 will be laughing at us then,' Kyle Newson replied.

She inhaled deeply and then exhaled slowly.

That one reply was worth 1.5 million dollars to her.

'I luv U Kyle,' she quickly typed, and then added, 'U need 2 collect the weapons from the dumpster tomoz morning and pull the trigger at exactly 2pm. I will be doing da same in LA and then we will live foreva.'

'I luv u 2 MissFit,' came the reply.

'Da guns are in a bag in a blue dumpster just outside an empty house on da corner of Compton and Jackson. It has a lock on and da code is 7468. There is a copy of da Koran in da bag, make sure U throw it into da coffee shop b4 U open fire. Then they will blame others for dis and not realize it is about our luv,' she replied quickly.

'I will do anything to spend eternity wiv U. I won't let U down,' Spartacus replied.

'Have U written da code down?' she asked.

'I've just put it in my phone.'

'Dis is da last time we talk until we meet in our world of luv Kyle. I will be doing dis 4 U. 4 us. Swear to me U will not let me down?' she asked.

'I swear on da lives of my folks. I will do this,' he replied.

'Then we are ready my luv. I will meet U in our new world of luv tomorrow just after 2. I will be waiting.'

'I luv you MissFit.'

'I luv U 2 Spartacus.'

The dialogue box closed.

She leant back into her chair and smiled. She knew without a doubt that Kyle Newson was going to see this through. It had been a long day today, but now she was ready to go home and get some sleep. By this time tomorrow, she would be even richer.

Life was good for Emma Casey.

DUMBO – New York

Ward was surprised to see Eloisa in his apartment when he got back. She was standing in the kitchen, preparing food.

'I thought we would eat in tonight,' she said, a grin stretching all the way across her face. She dropped the knife she was using to chop the food and ran across the floor and jumped into his arms.

They kissed passionately and then he lowered her to the floor and just stared at her.

She stared back, deep into his eyes while neither of them spoke.

'With every day that passes you seem to look more and more beautiful,' he said.

'You charmer,' she replied, and then playfully punched him on the arm, 'You go and freshen up while I finish the food,' she added.

'Yes sir,' he said, saluting as he spoke. He kissed her on the lips and then walked through to the bedroom to shower.

Fifteen minutes later, he walked back out into the lounge wearing sports shorts and a tee shirt. As usual, Eloisa looked elegant. She was wearing a black pencil skirt and a white blouse, with her long dark hair up in a bun. She looked every inch the strong, independent, intelligent woman that she was.

The table was already prepared, and she was placing the plates on the two table mats that were laid out neatly opposite each other. Everything looked immaculately presented. Eloisa loved order and control.

He sat down and took a mouthful of the medium rare fillet steak that she had prepared, and he let it dissolve slowly in his mouth.

'This is perfect,' he said.

'Like you,' she replied and smiled, 'Tell me what happened in Oregon?'

Ward slowly explained the events that had taken place. He explained about Sergeant Parker from the Mitchell P.D, the Hillbillies, and The Reverend Solomon Tower and how small he looked.

'What was he like just before you killed him?' she asked.

Eloisa always asked this question. He knew by now that she wanted to know that they had suffered as much as the people that they had inflicted their vile pain upon had.

He explained how Tower had cried and begged, and how he had obliterated his face with his bullets.

A look of satisfaction spread across her face. It was a look that he had become used to.

It was one of the reasons that made him love her. She understood that in the world that they lived in, it took men like him to deal with the evil that existed, and she never, ever saw evil in him, just good things.

'Do you know what you achieved today?' she asked.

'Sure. Another animal who abuses children has been wiped out. I had a good day,' he replied.

'No. What I mean Ryan, is do you actually know what you achieved, relating to what the effect you did today had on real people?'

Ward was confused.

She saw the look on his face.

'What did you do after you had killed Tower?' she asked.

'What I always do,' he replied, 'Mike made a call to The Old Man, and we got out of there immediately. It is always that way Eloisa, we disappear, and you know that," he added.

'Yes I do,' she said and smiled at him, 'And I love you for that, but let me explain what they found at his compound so you know what a great thing you did today,' she added.

'What did they find?'

'They found seventeen children under the age of ten and four babies. They also found four girls who had given birth to these babies and do you want to know the best part?' she asked.

Ward nodded.

'There are thirteen families that have discovered today that their children who were kidnapped, and they had given up as dead, are going to be returned to them. I'm sure that over the next few days, every single one of them will be returned to their families. Just think of that for a moment. Think of the impact that your actions today have had on so many people, in a good way,' she said.

He did think about it for a moment. And he realised that he never thought of what he did in terms of those who would be directly affected by his actions. He was aware that the kids would have been exposed to unimaginable horror, but with the love of parents and the skills of the child psychologists, there was a chance they would recover and lead a normal life.

Those child psychologists were exceptional people who did a lot of good. He knew that.

'You are so selfless,' Eloisa said, interrupting his thoughts, 'You don't do anything for credit, or to make yourself feel good, you do everything just because it is the right thing to do and that is why I love you so much,' she added, and then she stood up, walked around to his side of the table and kissed him softly on the lips once more.

'Actually, that's not true,' he replied as he separated himself from her soft lips for a second, 'I do it so that I can get you into bed,' he added with a smile.

'You only need to ask,' she said and winked at him.

'Can we please go to bed?'

'I thought you would never ask,' she replied, and she took his hand and led him slowly towards the bedroom. They were naked within thirty seconds, he instantly felt glad that he had decided to wear so little after his shower, and that he only had to remove a blouse and skirt before Eloisa was down to her underwear.

He kissed her neck gently as he expertly undid her bra with one hand, and then used his thumbs to pull down her panties as he kissed down to her navel.

He picked her up and carried her over to the bed and laid her gently down, lifting her weight just enough to tense his torso and show the definition of his granite like physique, which excited her even more.

He continued to kiss her body softly all over, from her neck, across her firm breasts and then slowly down the centre of her stomach. He gently moved her thighs apart and kissed along the inside of them, all the way down to her ankles.

'Please, I'm begging. Make love to me Ryan,' she panted.

He climbed on top of her carefully, still kissing the spots that he knew drove her wild as he did so, and then he slowly became one being with her, and their bodies started to move together, in perfect tandem, and as the speed increased, so did the intensity of their kissing. By the time that they had both got to the point of climax twenty-five minutes later, they were both covered in sweat and their naked bodies were sliding perfectly in tandem with each other.

They climaxed together, Eloisa digging her nails deep into his back as she lost control, and the intensity of her orgasm ripped through her body and then Ward shuddered as the last grains of pleasure left his body. He rolled onto his back and she rested her head on his firm chest.

'Oh my God,' she giggled, 'that was unbelievable,' she added.

Ward smiled, a smug smile, and he felt like the greatest lover alive. Eloisa had that gift of always making him feel like the most special man in the world.

And at that moment in time, he felt like the luckiest too.

They woke up together in the morning, her head was still firmly planted on his chest, and he got up and made them both coffee. They never finished their drinks because the urge to repeat the sensation of last night was much more overpowering than their need for refreshment. After they had finished making love, a moment that was equally as good, Eloisa said,

'I'd better shower quickly, I'm going to be late for work,' and she got up and headed towards the bathroom. He watched as the perfect curves on her naked body disappeared out of sight.

And then his cell phone rang.

It was The Old Man.

'Have you spoken to Nicole-Louise or Tackler this morning?' he asked without offering any greeting.

'Not yet. Why?'

'Because I want to know if you are getting anywhere on this?' he added, a surly tone to his voice.

'We found the site that we believe the kid was using, and I'm going over there shortly to see if they have found out anything that might point us in the direction of where we should look,' he replied, 'And I have to sleep sometimes you know,' he added sarcastically.

'I know Ryan, I just don't like knowing that there might be some more shootings over the next couple of weeks and we don't know by who or when.'

'I'll get on it right now,' he said and hung up the phone. He dialled Nicole-Louise's number and Tackler answered.

'Have you got anywhere?' he asked as soon as Tackler had said hello.

'More than that, we have uncovered some things that you have to see to believe,' he replied.

'Like what?'

'We need to show you. This shooting in Missouri was not a one off,' Tackler replied.

'We know that. I told you The Old Man had intel that said it was the first one of three.'

'No Ryan. You don't understand.'

'What don't I understand?'

'We have found something that traces this back to seven mass shootings over the past three years,' he replied solemnly.

'I'll be there in half an hour,' Ward replied and hung up the phone.

SIX

Washington D.C

Emma Casey had spent the last hour talking to 'Late8' online. He was the kid in New York who was going to carry out the third shooting for her, and he was eager to get started. She had spoken with him for an hour every morning for the past two months between 07:00 and 08:00am, just before he went to school. He would be back online at 4:30pm. He always was. She had used her skills to convince him that the world despised him, and by hitting back at those who didn't understand him, the two of them would be free to meet in their new world of love. She used the same story that she had with both Russel Collyfield and Kyle Newson. She was making a pact with him. She would commit an atrocity at exactly the same time as he did, and they would forever be linked together.
It was almost too easy for her.

'Late8' wanted to do it now, but having the gap between the shootings was important. The chairman of the committee was adamant about that.

She was just putting her coat on to go and fetch herself a coffee from the store around the corner when her phone rang.

'I'm disappointed in you,' the chairman said as soon as she answered.

'Why?' she asked, her mind instantly going into overdrive to try and think what she could have done.

'You assured me that there was nothing that could link any of this back to us,' he said sternly.

'There isn't,' she said.

'Then why has someone been poking around getting into the servers you were provided with?'

'I don't understand, firstly, how you would know that, and secondly, there is nothing there to link anything to you,' she replied, her own voice now assertive and stern, 'And Novak was one of the best at what he did. He told me one hundred per cent that no one would find anything and I believed him,' she quickly added.

'Novak was adequate but no more than that,' the chairman replied, raising his voice as he spoke.

'I still don't understand how you know someone has been poking around?' she asked.

'Because we employ one of the best techno wizards around to double check and keep everything clean. You don't think that we would trust you just on Novak's word, surely?' he asked.

She suddenly realised that she wasn't as important as she thought to them. They had someone policing her every move and they had no doubt been following every word that she had typed.

She suddenly felt very violated and very vulnerable.

'You do know that I have put contingencies in place in case anything happens to me. If I get hurt, all of this will come out,' she said in a deliberate and soft voice.

'Don't worry Emma. That is not part of anything. But my concern is that whoever has been poking around might have found something. My guy has now cleaned everything that did exist, and he is ninety-nine per cent sure that it is impossible to retrieve the deleted data that was on the servers, but that other one per cent is what bothers me.'

'Do you know who was poking around?' Casey asked.

'That's the bad part,' the chairman replied, 'Because whoever was looking, is way, way better than my guy, they are completely untraceable, which means whoever they are, they are dangerous.'

'Shall we call off the next two shootings?'

'No. There is very little that they can do with the data they find anyway, and your IP address is unobtainable, my guy has assured me of that so you are safe.'

'Are you sure it's wise to continue with our current plans, just in case?'

'We will continue. I have put an extra three men out on the street to make sure that you are kept safe at all times. The four of them will make sure that you are safe twenty-four seven until this is over,' the chairman said.

She instantly felt reassured and safe again.

'Are they out there now?' she asked.

'They have been following you since 05:00am this morning when you woke up at home, and then to the office. You won't see them, and you won't know they are there, but it is their job to keep you safe.'

She didn't like the fact that people were spying on her, and it made her feel uneasy, but she instantly told herself that she could live with it for a couple more days until this was over.

'Thank you,' she replied.

'Just make sure that today happens at 2:00pm, and then the last one tomorrow by five. Is that clear?'

'Yes it is sir,' was all she could offer as a reply before the line went dead.

Park Avenue – New York

'Whoever bounced this IP address around all over the world is good,' Tackler said to Ward as he sat down in front of his screen.

'But nowhere near as good as us,' Nicole-Louise shouted over her shoulder from her own workstation on the other side of the room, 'I mean, it only took me twelve minutes to figure out.'

'You mean as good as you,' Tackler muttered under his breath.

'Do you want to explain to me what you've found?' Ward asked.

'Don't you want to wait for Lawson? He's on his way over now. I called him after I spoke to you,' Tackler enquired.

Ward sighed. He was impatient and knew that time was in short supply, but he decided it made sense. He didn't want to have to run through the whole thing again with

Lawson when he arrived. As it was, no more than twenty seconds later, there was a knock at the door. Nicole-Louise stood up and opened the door.

Lawson looked shattered.

'Your sleep in your hotel never went too well I take it?' Ward asked as Lawson walked into the room carrying a takeout coffee.

'It wasn't the room, it was the company,' Lawson replied with a smile.

All three of them rolled their eyes and shook their heads. Nicole-Louise did not return to her workstation, she came over to Tackler's side of the room and sat down next to him.

'His new software is incredible,' she said, as she started typing something on the keyboard and pulled up a list of dialogue boxes on the screen, 'It will be worth millions to the right companies. He is so smart,' she added and she playfully poked him in the ribs.

'OK. Here's what we found,' Tackler said, making it plainly obvious that he was deliberately ignoring the compliment, 'The kid in Missouri had been talking to someone called 'MissFit',' he added, pointing to the screen.

Ward leant in closer and looked at the screen. There was a box which held a conversation between 'MissFit' and 'SuperRuss'.

'Start from here,' Tackler said, highlighting a line of the conversation on the screen"

Lawson leant in and they both started to read through the conversation slowly.

'Jesus, she's telling him to do it,' Lawson said.

'If she is a she,' Nicole-Louise said.

They continued reading.

It was all there.

She wanted him to agree to a pact together, and then they would be together for eternity.

'The poor kid never stood a chance,' Ward said, after he had reached the bottom of the conversation where Russell Collyfield agreed to carry out the shootings, 'Look how she is using key words to manipulate him and get him to believe that it is the best thing for him to do,' he added.

'Then,' Nicole-Louise interrupted, 'Tackler asked the question that I hadn't even thought of.'

'Which was?' Ward asked.

'Where did the kid get the guns? He used an AK-47. You don't get them off the shelf at home.'

'Then I started looking for anything related to that,' Tackler said, 'And I found this,' he added, pointing to the screen.

Ward and Lawson leant in even further, the anticipation building.

They read down through the conversation.

'She supplied the guns. Which he collected from a trash can, in a park half a mile from his home,' Tackler added.

'If she is a she,' Nicole-Louise reminded them again.

Ward was quiet for a moment, piecing the whole thing together in his mind.

'I thought that maybe this wasn't the first time they had done this, so I called up the list of mass shootings that had happened over the past three years since the site has been in existence,' Nicole-Louise said, tapping away at her screen, 'And this is what I found.'

Ward and Lawson moved slightly to the left to look at the screen that she had pulled up.

They both read and read again to make sure that they were reading it right.

'Seven of the people who have committed mass shootings logged onto iamalaone.com?' Lawson asked.

'Yes they did. We haven't retrieved the exact data for those people yet, we know that they visited the site constantly in the four weeks prior to carrying out their acts,' she replied.

'How do you know that for sure?" Ward asked.

"Because I hacked into the FBI's' servers and got the data. The web history and IP addresses were all there. Everything I needed to confirm it,' Tackler said

'And you know exactly where this IP address comes from?' Ward asked.

'Yes we do,' Nicole-Louise replied.

'So give us the address and we will go and pay them a visit,' Lawson said.

'You have something much more important to do first,' Tackler interrupted.

'You've found something else, haven't you?' Ward asked.

'Whoever is managing their system realised that we were raiding their deleted data and pretty much wiped everything from the system, so we only have what we managed to retrieve last night,' Nicole-Louise said.

'And what did you find?' Lawson asked.

'I'll show you,' she replied.

She pulled up a dialogue box which contained a conversation between 'Miss Fit' and 'Spartacus', and all four of them read in silence until they had reached the end.

'He's going to carry out a shooting in Dallas today,' Lawson said and shook his head.

'We can stop this,' Ward said.

'You can that one,' Tackler replied.

'What do you mean?"

"I mean now look at this conversation,' he replied.

Nicole-Louise pulled up another dialogue box.

It was a conversation between 'MissFit' and 'Late8'. They read the conversation, once again, all four of them in silence.

'So we know that it will happen in New York but we have no idea when or where. It could be happening right now,' Lawson said.

'Do you have the IP address for the person on the other end of the computer?' Ward asked.

'By the time we had found what was happening and went back in to retrieve it, everything had been erased for good. Whatever might have been discussed after about 8:00pm last night, we won't find because the IP address has been changed, and it is now like looking for a needle in ten million haystacks,' he replied.

'Tell me where the IP address originated from for the site?' Ward asked.

'It was in Washington D.C.' Nicole-Louise replied.

Ward instantly had a bad feeling in the pit of his stomach.

'Political involvement?' he asked with an air of resignation in his voice.

'Not that I can see. All we have is a building address and when I cross-referenced it with the land registers, it is a privately owned company that lets out office space,' she replied.

'Where in Washington is it?'

'2045 13th Street. It's rented under the name of Novak & Co.'

'That's close to The White House,' Ward said.

'Then the chance of those seedy politicians being involved is pretty high, wouldn't you say?' she asked.

Ward didn't reply.

He was working on another theory in his mind. It was a theory that seemed to make more sense to him.

He looked at his watch. It was 07:24am.

'Mike, ring The Old Man and get the jet ready immediately. We should be in Dallas in just over three hours. I want to deal with this myself. And get the local P.D. to get to that dumpster straight away and remove the weapons, and make sure they back off and observe only. I don't want anyone approaching the kid. But if he leaves the house, I want to know where he is at all times. I don't want him out of their sight.'

Lawson took out his cell phone and walked over to the other side of the room.

'This kid in Dallas?' he said after a few moments of silence, 'What is his name and how old is he?'

'His name is Kyle Newson and he has just turned seventeen. Why?' she asked.

'Because we should try our very best to give Kyle Newson a second chance,' he replied.

'I agree,' Tackler replied, 'You read how desperate this kid is. The whole world seems to bully him, and people like you have no idea what that feels like,' he added.

Ward noted the hostility in Tackler's voice.

'You are right, I don't. But what I do know is that locking the kid up and throwing away the key isn't the answer. He isn't ill, he's in need of a friend, and until you lot came into my life, I know exactly how that felt,' Ward replied softly.

Tackler nodded at him and then smiled. He noticed Nicole-Louise squeezing Tackler's hand.

'And anyway,' he continued, 'You might not be the biggest or the toughest, but you are by far the smartest, so don't be greedy, one out of three aint bad,' he added with a smile, patting Tackler on the shoulder as he spoke.

'The jet is ready and waiting now,' Lawson said.

'Send us all of the information you have on Washington, and as soon as we have dealt with the situation in Dallas, we will go there to see what we can find,' Ward said, and he turned and walked urgently out of the room, with Lawson following three steps behind.

SEVEN

2524 Morgan Street – Irving, Texas

Kyle Newson walked out into the bright, mid-day sun, and headed down the path. He stopped and turned around to take one last look at the only home he had ever known. His eyes filled with tears as he thought of his parents and sister, and how he would never see them again, and for a moment, he felt an overwhelming urge to run back indoors and tell 'MissFit' that he couldn't go through with it, but then he remembered the pictures, and the words that they had shared, and he knew that this was his one chance of eternal love and he wasn't going to blow it.

He was feeling sick to the pit of his stomach, and with each passing step that he took; he seemed to be more and more consumed with doubt. By the time he reached the end of Morgan Street, he wasn't sure if he was strong enough to go through with the pact that they had made. And then they convinced him that he was.

As he turned the corner at the end of the street, he saw Mark Cole, a kid that he had known from the neighbourhood his whole life, and one of his chief tormentors. He was helping his dad load some timber into the back of his truck, and as Kyle approached the end of their driveway, he saw Cole nudge his dad and step away from the truck,

'Hey dad, can you smell that?' he said at the top of his voice.

His dad put down the timber that he was carrying and stepped towards the end of the drive.

'Smells like dog crap to me son,' he replied and laughed.

'You got dirty feet again dog boy?' the young Cole asked.

Kyle carried on walking forward, trying his best to ignore them, and then the young Cole stepped out into the sidewalk, blocking his way.

'I said have you got dirty feet again dog boy?' Mark Cole asked.

Kyle ignored him the best he could and tried to sidestep around him. Mark Cole put his arm up and using his forearm, smashed it into his chest.

He felt the tears coming again.

'That's enough Mark,' his father said, 'I don't want him crapping his pants and smelling more than he does already. Help me load this timber,' he added, pinching his nose to indicate how much Kyle stank.

'You were lucky dog boy. Next time I see you, I'm going to beat you to a pulp,' Mark Cole said, and then walked back up his drive.

Kyle continued walking, now totally convinced that his only escape from the torment that he suffered on a daily basis would be to carry out the pact and meet 'MissFit' in their world of love.

He hated the world, he hated everyone in the world so much apart from his own family, and it was glaringly obvious to him, that the whole world hated him too.

He reached the bus stop just as the bus was pulling in. He paid his fare and sat at the front of the bus, two rows in. There were three girls sitting near the back of the bus and he didn't want to go and sit near them, he was sure they would tease him if he did. He felt the anger boiling inside of him, and he wished that Mark Cole and his dad would be sitting in the 'Ground & Fresh' coffee shop where he had decided to carry out the shooting, just so he could kill them too. The bus drove along North Story Road and onto the Airport Freeway. Three more people got on the bus, three kids who were about sixteen. Kyle looked down at the floor and hoped to God that they wouldn't notice him.

They didn't.

They walked to the back of the bus and started showing off to the girls who were already seated at the back. The bus turned onto North Belt Line Road, before finally turning onto Jackson Street. He saw the sign for Compton Avenue and rang the bell. The bus driver pulled the bus over and as soon as the doors were open,

Kyle jumped off and inhaled deeply to try and get some air to his lungs.

He walked to the corner of Compton Avenue and saw the empty house with the three dumpsters outside immediately. He checked behind him, and then up and down the street, and apart from a few parked cars and vans, no one was about.

He walked through the gate and up the path, veering to the right when he reached the end, to move around to the dumpsters on the side of the house. The blue one was in the middle, the large combination lock hanging down off the hasp in the middle.

He walked over to the dumpster and put in the code, 7-4-6-8, and the padlock separated. He removed it from the hasp and dropped it on the floor. He checked behind him again and saw it was still all clear, and so he lifted the lid and peered inside.

It was empty.

He lifted it higher, hoping it was a trick of the light and the bag would be hidden in the shadows but it was still empty.

He turned around again, to make sure no one was watching, and immediately, he saw a man about six feet tall, powerful muscles bulging from under his white tee-shirt, and eyes that were fixed on him, walking up the path towards him.

He dropped the lid and stood frozen to the spot.

The man reached him and stared at him for three seconds and then he said,

'Hello Kyle, my name is Ryan. Come and sit on the step with me and have a chat.'

Kyle Newson burst into tears, just like he had every single day for the past four years.

They sat on the porch steps and Ward waited for Kyle to calm down and compose himself before talking.

'I'm going to jail forever, aren't I?' he said, in between sniffing.

'Do you think you should go to jail?' Ward asked.

Kyle was quiet for a few moments and then said,

'Yes I should. I was going to do something really, really bad.'

He looked down at the poor kid. He desperately wanted to give him a hug, it was obvious that he needed help, not punishment.

'I do bad things all the time to people. Sometimes you have to do bad things to make sense of things,' he said.

Are you like a murderer or something?' Kyle asked, a frightened look washing over his face.

Before Ward could respond, over twenty police officers appeared from behind cars, out of buildings and vehicles, along with a huge, handsome looking man who looked as powerful as the man sitting next to him.

'Are you the police?' Kyle asked.

'No,' Ward replied, 'I'm much higher than the police. You see that big guy standing over there?' he asked, pointing to Lawson.

Kyle nodded.

'He's with me. We are like super government spies.'

'Like the C.I.A?'

'The C.I.A are pussies,' he replied and smiled.

Kyle Newson looked up at Ward with awe in his eyes.

'You sound English? Are you like the S.A.S?' he asked.

'Not me, but he was,' he replied, pointing at Lawson again.

'I'm going to be locked away forever, aren't I?'

'I'm not going to lie to you Kyle, you are in big trouble,' Ward said, 'But not for the reasons that you think you are,' he quickly added.

'What do you mean?' he asked, still visibly trembling.

'I know about MissFit,' he started, 'She isn't real. We aren't even sure if she is a woman or a man.'

'She is real; she sent me pictures to prove it.'

'They weren't her. They were of someone else, and they have been using them for the past three years.'

Kyle Newson looked down at the floor.

'I knew that someone like her could never love a fat, smelly, loser like me. You may as well let me kill myself; I want to die, honestly.'

'So why did you believe what they said?' Ward asked.

'Why? For the first time ever I felt worth something because of her. Everyone despises me, and I'm so tired of the bullying that I want to curl up and die.'

Ward looked down at him and could see the desperation seeping from every pore in his body. He hated himself; he hated every single part of himself.

'On the way over here,' he continued, 'A kid who lives at the end of my street started bullying me and even his dad joined in, calling me dog boy. That's how worthless I am,' he said.

'You are in so much trouble because you are letting them win. You can change if you want,' Ward said.

'How?' Kyle asked, 'How hard do you think it is to motivate yourself when you hate yourself?'

'I'm going to offer you a deal,' he said.

'Like a plea bargain?'

Ward smiled and laughed and then said,

'Actually, it kind of is similar.'

'What is it?'

'You need help with your self-esteem and confidence. You will get counselling for your self-esteem and you will attend sessions daily. I will make sure that I get regular updates about how you are doing, and if you start to slip up at all, I will come and shoot you myself,' Ward said with such seriousness, that Kyle started to shake again.

'My parents are going to be furious,' Kyle said.

'No, your parents are going to be devastated that they never realised how unhappy you were. This will break their hearts, and so it is down to you to win back their trust and reassure them. Can you do that?' he asked.

Kyle Newson nodded and started crying again.

Lawson came walking up the path and said,

'They have a counsellor and a local detective waiting at his house with his parents. The Old Man has confirmed that he is immune from prosecution, but it's your call, and if the kid goes wrong it will be on your head.'

'He won't go wrong, will you Kyle?'

'No I won't, I swear.'

'And you are going to put everything in to working on your self-esteem until you realise what a great kid you are. Deal?' Ward asked.

'I swear, I am so sorry for what I've done.'

'The good thing is, you haven't done anything. So no harm has been done.'

'I'm sorry,' he said again, the tears still streaming down his cheeks.

'Now, there are two more things that we need to do,' Ward said.

Kyle looked up at him confused.

'We need to show the world just how cool you are, and that no one messes with you,' Ward said with a smile.

'I wish,' Kyle Newson replied.

Fifteen minutes later, Ward and Lawson were climbing out of their car outside Mark Cole's house. He was halfway through loading the second load of timber onto his dad's truck. They walked up to the driveway and Kyle followed three feet behind.

'Hey skinny boy,' Ward shouted out to Cole Senior.

He stopped what he was doing and walked cautiously down his driveway. The guy who had shouted out to him had something about him that frightened him, and the guy standing next to him looked like a giant, a very handsome giant too.

'How can I help you Gentlemen?' Cole asked as his son wandered down and stood beside him.

'I kill people for a living. I'm very good at it. Our government pay me a fortune to do it, and I am untouchable. I really am above the law,' Ward said, 'Show him your gun Mike, just so he understands,' he added.

Lawson pulled his handgun out from behind his back and waved it dramatically in front of Cole.

'Young Kyle over there is my friend. He's helped us out a great deal, which makes him a hero for his country. I think they are even contemplating offering him a role at Langley. Do you know Kyle?"

'Hi Kyle,' Cole said, waving as he said it, his son repeating his father a second later.

'You look skinny to me; maybe I should beat you around a bit, just because I can. And in front of your snotty son too, just so he can see what you really are,' Ward said softly.

'Can't we just shoot them both?' Lawson asked.

With lightning quick speed, Ward lunged forward and jabbed Cole senior hard on his Adam's apple. He fell to his knees, desperately clutching his throat.

Ward bent down.

'You think it's OK to pick on a kid. What do you think that says about you skinny boy?' he whispered in Cole's ear.

Cole was too busy trying to catch his breath to reply.

'And you,' Ward said, facing onto Mark Cole, 'You and your friends have picked on him for the last time. If it happens one more time, we will come back and we will kill you, all of your parents, your family and even your pets. Do you understand?'

Mark Cole burst into tears.

'You spread the word about Kyle. He's untouchable. Do you understand?'

'Yes. I promise we'll be nice to him,' Mark Cole said between sobs.

'Good,' Ward replied, and the three of them turned and walked away, got back into the car and drove off.

'That was so cool,' Kyle said.

'One more thing to do and then you can go home,' he said, 'Are you clear on what you need to say?'

'Yes. Is this for real?' Kyle asked excitedly.

'Yes it is,' Lawson replied, 'The Old Man said it is waiting for us now,' he said looking at Ward and smiling.

Forty-five minutes later, Kyle Newson was sitting in his class, a detention already issued for failing to turn up that morning, when the teachers' voice was suddenly drowned out by a chopper landing at the front of the school. Three guys in full SWAT gear jumped out of the chopper and stood on guard, as Ward and Lawson followed them out. The whole school, including the teachers, were looking out of their windows. A minute later, Kyle's classroom door flew open and Lawson and Ward burst through the door, the principal and two other teachers in hot pursuit.

'Kyle, we need your help again,' Lawson said, as every girl in the class swooned when they looked at him.

'I told you guys, I'm done with it,' Kyle nervously replied.

'Please. This is a question of national security, we need you to do one last thing for us and then we will leave you alone,' Ward said urgently.

'This is it,' Kyle said, now fully embracing the role-playing that was taking place, 'Last time, I just want to be a normal kid,' he added as he stood up.

The rest of the class stood open mouthed as Kyle Newson followed Ward and Lawson out of the class.

'We have policies that need to be followed, he can't just leave,' the principal said,

'Listen up idiot,' Lawson said, 'This kid is way more important to our national security than he is to your crappy school, so get lost before I shoot you,' he added, as he started to follow Ward and Kyle who were now jogging.

Hundreds of faces were pressed against windows, as the whole school watched Kyle Newson climb into the chopper with Ward and Lawson, and then the SWAT guys jumped in behind them.

The chopper took off and within twenty seconds had disappeared out of sight.

Three minutes later, they were landing in the park close to Kyle Newson's house, two police officers were waiting to escort him home.

'Your parents and the detectives are waiting for you. They know everything that has happened. They aren't angry, they are sad. Promise me that you will put all of this right?'

'I promise. Thank you,' Kyle said, and started crying softly as he stepped out of the chopper.

'To the airport,' Lawson said to the pilot.

Ward pulled out his cell phone,

'I have an idea,' he said.

That evening, six hours after Kyle Newson was due to carry out an atrocity that was going to shock America; he would receive over four hundred friend requests to his social media account.

He would never cry because he felt lonely ever again.

EIGHT

2045 13th Street – Washington D.C.

'What the hell went wrong?' the chairman demanded in a raised voice.

Emma Casey had frantically been scanning the police radios all over Dallas for the last four hours, and she had heard nothing.

'I don't know,' she replied, with apprehension in her voice, 'I was sure that he was going to do it,' she added.

'Well, he didn't do it, so now you have a big problem,' he spat down the phone, 'The New York kid is going to back out too is he?'

'No. One hundred per cent, he will come through.'

'Then I suggest you find someone else to carry out the third one and convince them to do it quickly. I am paying you for three separate incidents. Not only have you failed on the Dallas attack, you have been compromised. Is the site still active from your end?' She hurriedly opened her laptop and typed in the address.

iamalaone.com was still live.

'Yes. Everything looks as it should,' she replied.

'It is now as secure as you should have made it. Get to work. I want an update in an hour, when you will tell me that you have found another waste of space that is going to carry out the third attack. Is that clear?' he demanded.

'Yes sir,' she replied and before she could say anything else, the line went dead.

'Could they be any more obvious?' Ward asked Lawson as they sat opposite the office Casey was using, drinking coffee.

There were four guys posted outside the building, each of them about thirty feet from the entrance, and each of them failing miserably to look like they weren't meant to be there.

'Amateurs,' Lawson said.

Ward studied each one of them individually. Lawson was right. They definitely weren't former employees of government agencies, or former Special Forces operatives. They didn't even look professional enough to be bad mercenaries. He concluded that they had to be hired muscle. They were the kind of guys who worked the doors of the clubs throughout Washington and were used to brawling.

'Shall we go and see who is working in this office?' Lawson asked, 'Whoever it is must still be in there or these idiots would not be standing around waiting,' he added.

Ward didn't say anything. He just sat there, slowly drinking his coffee, thinking things through, and trying to get three steps ahead of everyone else like he always did.

'I'll speak to myself then,' Lawson said, 'Hey Mike; these cups would look nice in your new kitchen. What do you think?' he added after studying the coffee mug he was holding for a few seconds.

Ward smiled.

'Think about it. Why would we need to go in there?' he asked.

'To shoot the person behind this,' Lawson replied.

'And you think they are in there?'

'Well someone is.'

'I say we sit here, drink our coffee and make the most of the calm before the storm that is going to hit.'

'I've no idea what you are talking about, so I will just follow as usual,' Lawson said without a hint of sarcasm. He had gotten used to Ryan Ward keeping plans to himself a long time ago.

Inside the building, Emma Casey was desperately trying to work on the four people who were visiting the site. She wasn't having much luck.

The first user was a guy with a profile name of 'KingOfTheHoes' and so she ignored him completely. The second one was a girl called 'Venus' and while she knew that girls were less likely to resort to violence, this user seemed to be struggling with her sexuality so she thought she would try and get inside her head. She spent

twenty minutes exchanging messages with her and thought she was making some ground until 'Venus' asked her to send pictures of her engaged in sex acts with other girls, and then she concluded that the user was probably a twelve-year-old kid after cheap kicks.
The third person online was a user called 'Lost247' and their profile picture was of the Statue of Liberty. Initially, this put her off because she was still sure that the New York kid was going to come through, and it would not be an ideal scenario to have two shootings in one city. The aim of this whole plan was to spread fear, not confine it to one place. But she was now getting desperate, and so she tentatively exchanged a few messages with the user, and based on the fact that she had to work hard to draw the information she needed to establish a level of trust between them, she was starting to feel a very small crumb of hope. The fourth user was called 'Killmyself', and when she had enquired why they wanted to end their life, they had responded by asking if she would suffocate them and then shove a stick of dynamite up their ass, she immediately realised it was a total waste of time and muttered to herself,
'I wish you would.'
She decided to turn her full attention to 'Lost247'.

'Two of them over your shoulder are moving,' Lawson said to Ward.
The two guys who had been on his blind side had now moved along the sidewalk and had met in the middle. They were talking to each other, and then one of the guys pulled out his cell phone and made a call. One of the two guys the other end of the street answered his

own cell phone and began a dialogue with his colleague. After thirty seconds, the guy looked at his watch and then nodded urgently.

'They are now heading the other way along the sidewalk,' Lawson continued with his running commentary.

'They've just been given permission to have a break. Let's go and see where they take us,' he replied, as he stood up and threw a ten-dollar bill on the table.

They walked out of the coffee shop and fell in about thirty feet behind the guys. These amateurs were so bad that they never once looked behind to see if they were being followed.

They continued along the sidewalk for five blocks and then they came to a shop and walked in.

'Why would they be going in there?' Lawson asked, a frown appearing on his face, 'You think they are stocking up for the next kid they manipulate?'

Ward watched carefully. They had walked into a shop called 'Tap-Tap Munitions'. He had seen a few of these shops around the country before, so he was aware that it was part of a large chain as opposed to a small back street dealer.

He looked at Lawson and smiled.

'What?' Lawson asked.

'I've just worked out exactly what is happening. It's very clever indeed,' he said.

'What is happening?' Lawson asked.

He ignored the question.

Park Avenue– New York

'They are taking the bait,' Tackler said to Nicole-Louise. Ward had phoned Tackler when he was on the chopper and asked him to see if the site was still live. He asked him to pose as a troubled teenager who felt completely alone and overrun with despair, and to try and engage with whoever was manipulating these poor kids.

It hadn't been hard.

He had chosen the name 'Lost247'.

Tackler's real name was Jeremy Fox. He had grown up in Brooklyn not far from where Ward lived. His father was an accountant and his mother a historian. They were both academics. Tackler was picked on mercilessly at school, he was the geeky kid who always had his nose in a book, and when the bell went to signal the end of the school day, he would run out of the class to avoid the bullies who picked on him daily on route to his apartment. As smart as he was, he could never work out how they always got ahead of him. His chief tormentor was a guy called Francis Gollini, and he would steal his money and punch him every day, much to the delight of the 'Gollini Crew' who followed him everywhere. They were a group of eight local kids, and they were relentlessly cruel to him. He had contemplated suicide at least six times during his last year of high school. When he had left school and gone to Columbia University in New York, to study advanced computer science, he met Nicole-Louise on his second day and they hit it off immediately. Her strength and beauty were his salvation. They grew together, and gradually fell in love together, and now they were moving within a world that made him head and shoulders above the 'Gollini Crew'. He had seen Francis Gollini only once since he left high school, and that was in a coffee shop a couple of blocks away on Park Avenue, about six months ago. As soon as he saw Gollini, he felt sixteen again. He started to tremble and his hands were sweating. Gollini made eye contact with him and Tackler could think of nothing else to say but, 'Hello.'

Gollini had looked him up and down with contempt and said,

'Do I know you?'

Tackler apologised and said he thought Gollini was someone else, and he walked out of the shop, the snort of contempt coming from Gollini was the last thing that he heard.

The fact that Gollini never even recognised him was the most insulting part of it. That man had inflicted a childhood of turmoil on him, and he couldn't even recognise him, he meant that little to him.

Nicole-Louise was the only person on earth who knew the turmoil that he had suffered, and she knew how hard he was finding this work since the discovery of the site, even offering to take posing as a troubled teen off him, but they eventually both agreed that it would be a form of therapy for him to stand up for these kids.

He had thought about asking Ward to pay Gollini a visit on more than one occasion, and he had also thought about hacking into Gollini's electronic life and destroying him that way, but so far, he had resisted the temptation on both counts.

'I've asked her to show me a picture of her,' Tackler said, 'To see if she uses the same one.'

A moment later, the profile picture for 'MissFit' changed to reveal a very pretty girl, wearing just panties and a smile.

'It's the same one we retrieved from the laptop,' Nicole-Louise said.

'And she is nowhere near as beautiful as you,' he said to her.

She leant over and kissed his cheek softly, and sat down next to him, squeezing his leg. She knew how hard this was for him.

Tackler spent the next few minutes explaining how he had no one to turn to, and how he was constantly bullied by a kid called Gollini and his gang.

She asked about his parents and he said that they were out at work most of the time.

He then explained how because he was an only child, when he was at home, he was isolated and he had bad thoughts about killing himself. As Nicole-Louise watched him type, she could see his hands starting to shake. It made her own eyes fill with tears, but she held them back. It was her job to be strong for him now.

'Look at these words,' Tackler said pointing to the screen.

Nicole-Louise leant forward.

'Psychosis', 'Prognosis', 'Frustration', 'Case Study' and 'Neurosis' were all on the screen.

'She's a professional psychologist and a woman,' Nicole-Louise said.

'How do you know she's a woman?'

'Look at these words,' she said, and then pointed at the screen.

'Listen', 'Sympathise', 'Understand' and 'Discuss' were all words that she touched on his screen.

'Point taken,' he replied.

He continued to type, telling 'MissFit' how he hated the world, and he wished that he could wipe out the people who made his life a misery. He then continued to say that he regularly heard voices in his head, telling him to do bad things.

Her response time decreased dramatically. No sooner would he finish a sentence, then she would be typing an immediate reply.

He told her that he had to go as his parents were back and that he would be back on later at midnight if he could.

She said that she would log on too and chat with him.

'Have you found the IP address?' he asked her, as she was tapping away on the keyboard next to him.

'They are good, but not that good,' she replied, 'Of course I have.'

'Same place in Washington?'

'Exactly the same place.'

Tackler picked up his cell phone and called Ward.

He answered after two rings.

'Hey Tackler.'

'You were right,' Tackler said, 'She took the bait. I said I'd be back online at midnight and she said she would wait for me. The IP address matches the building where you are, and so that's where she will be.'

'Are you sure it's a she?' Ward asked.

'Yes we are, one hundred per cent. And she is a trained psychologist too, probably a child psychologist.'
'How are you certain?'
'The words she used, and how transparent it was that she was trying to dig into my mind.'
'And you are sure on both counts?'
'Yes we are,' Tackler replied.
'Then that's good enough for me,' he said, and the line went dead.

In Washington, Ward looked at Lawson and said, 'Let's go inside and see what they can tell us.'

NINE

152 Jane St, Weehawken – New Jersey

Adam Ray had just collected the weapons that 'MissFit' had provided for him. He slid the bag under his bed, and then made sure that the duvet fell all the way down to the floor, so that if his dad walked into the room, he would not see it.

Not that his dad would be sober long enough to notice anything.

He had been due to collect the bag first thing tomorrow morning, but he figured that if he already had it in his possession, then there would be no surprises or problems that would prevent him from collecting it.

He was surprised at how heavy the bag was; although he had yet to open it to see what was inside.

He would do that tomorrow when his dad was at work.

Adam Ray lived in a house on Jane Street in New Jersey. It was a normal, run of the mill house, situated halfway up the street. The only thing notable about it was the fact that because it had no roof, it looked like a square box had been dropped down between the houses on either side. It had three bedrooms, although one of these was full up with clutter, a bathroom, kitchen and living area. It was the type of house that you would walk past a hundred times and never notice it.

He had lived in the house alone with his dad since his mom had upped and left four years ago.

She never even said goodbye to him.

His dad blamed everyone but himself and his drinking for his mom leaving.

Not a day passed without him blaming Adam for his mom running away.

'She always hated you, she thought you were strange,' he would scream at him, more often than not through his closed bedroom door.

He was fortunate that his dad worked long hours, he would leave the house at 06:00am and regularly he would not return home until gone 9:00pm, and so he often never saw him, he only heard him. He had now gone seven weeks without his dad beating on him. It was the longest period that he could remember. His dad was an electrician and he would finish work around 5:00pm, park his van in the drive of the house, and then walk the two blocks to his favourite bar where he would spend four hours drinking solidly, hoping to wash away the resentment that ran through his body every minute of the day. If Adam needed something for school, new clothes, or a few bucks for anything, he would write it down on a note and leave it on the table for his dad. Invariably, he would come into the kitchen after he had heard his dad leave for work, and see a handful of crumpled bills thrown on the kitchen table.

His dad had once said to him,

'I provide for you; it doesn't mean that I have to like you.'

That was the story of Adam Ray's life.

No one seemed to like him.

To look at him, he was pretty unremarkable. He was sixteen years old and about five foot ten in height. He was of average build, with average looks and average brown hair. In fact, everything was average about him, apart from the fact that he had developed a slight stutter the same week that his mom had deserted him, and the kids at school had picked up on it immediately and ridiculed him constantly for it.

So he found it easier not to talk to anyone.

He then had found the website that would bring him into contact with the one person who understood him, 'MissFit'.

He had seen her pictures and she was the most beautiful girl that he had ever set eyes on. She had listened to him and made him feel that what he said mattered. By typing his thoughts for her to see, his stutter was never an issue. He had chosen the username, 'Late8', as 8:00pm was always the time when he started getting anxious, waiting for his dad to return within the next hour in a drunken stupor.

He had explained to her how the other kids at school called him 'Peewee', and due to the fact that he struggled to speak more than eight words before his stutter kicked in, they also called him 'Stammer'. He had told her how the other boys would barge him, or poke him in the ribs whenever they passed him in the hall, and she listened carefully and told him that she suffered the same torment and this made him see that the only way to show them that you are worth something was to hit back.

And hit back hard.

When she had first suggested the idea of the two of them making a pact together, he thought she was crazy. She had asked him to think about it, and he stopped contact with her for two days, but he found himself unable to think of anything but how great she made him feel. He then received an e-mail with graphic pictures of her completely naked, and posing for him, and from that point forward, he belonged to her, and would do whatever she asked. The fact that she was going to do the same thing in Los Angeles, at exactly the same time, meant that they would be bound together forever.

It was a pure love that was going to last for eternity; people would talk about them for years to come.

And the more he thought about hitting back at the world that had failed to give him a happy, decent life, the more determined he had become to destroy as many lives as he possibly could, just like the actions of those who were meant to love, nourish, develop and protect him had destroyed his life, and left him to drown in his own misery.

Park Avenue – New York

Less than five miles away on Park Avenue, Nicole-Louise sat down next to Tackler and said,
'This isn't good.'
'I know",' Tackler replied, 'Whoever wiped everything was either very smart or very lucky.'
'Let's take five minutes and see what we can come up with, away from the screens,' she said as she squeezed his shoulder. She was plainly aware how personal this had become to him, and she had refrained from being her usual self, constantly teasing him, and making everything a competition between the two of them.
They had only managed to retrieve the tail end of the conversation between 'MissFit' and 'Late8', and all they had to go on was a dialogue box which said the following;

MissFit – So do you know where in New York it will be?
Late8 – I have a rough idea, maybe my mom might show her face as this is all her fault.
MissFit – I'm going to kill at least 20. We are going to live forever.
Late8 – I'm nothing without you.
MissFit – I love you AR
Late8 – I love you more
MissFit – I have to go now, my dad is back.
Late8 – I'll be back on by 10. I love you.
MissFit – If you love me as much as I do you, then you will do this for our love
Late8 – I swear to you I will xxx

'We have initials and that's it. Have you any idea how many people there are in New York with the initials AR?' Tackler asked.

Nicole-Louise sighed.

'What?'

'It doesn't matter,' she replied.

'No, tell me, what the sigh was for?' he asked.

'I get how personal this is for you. I understand that it is as much about saving these kids, as it is stopping these atrocities from happening, and I get that you have probably spent the last twenty-four hours thinking about Francis Gollini, but you are losing sight of what you are,' she replied, as she took his hand in hers.

'I was a kid who could quite easily have been manipulated into doing exactly what these kids are doing. It's not their fault.'

'I know that, which is why we will do everything we can to save them,' she replied, and softly smiled at him, 'But right now, you are pissing me off,' she added.

Tackler looked up at her in surprise. He had noticed how she had been supportive and understanding over the past twenty-four hours, and he had appreciated it, but her last sentence came from nowhere.

'You are the smartest, most remarkable man I know. Since we have worked with Ryan we have saved hundreds, probably thousands of lives, and that makes you one hell of a strong guy too. So stop feeling sorry for yourself and do what you do best,' she said.

'Which is?'

'Solve the problem. That's what you are, the best problem solver I know. You have the name of the city, and the initials of the person you are looking for. It's a problem, that's all it is. You solve problems better than anyone I know.'

'I know how these kids feel, I just find it hard not to get dragged back to what I used to be. I can relate to them, I can understand them, and the worst thing is that I can actually feel what they are feeling,' he quietly replied.

'That was back then, way back in the past. You are something much different now. You are the guy I love completely, and my hero,' she said, squeezing his hand even tighter as she spoke.

'I'm your hero?'

'Yes! I have learnt so much from you over the past eight years. I spend every day trying to be as good as you and that is what drives me on. Numbers are my thing, but the thing I admire about you the most is that you can find anything when you put your mind to it. Let me put it another way,' she replied.

Tackler looked at her and raised his eyebrows.

'If you were looking for someone in New York with the initials AR who was going to set a bomb of under the flag of terrorism, what would you do?' she asked.

Tackler pondered the question for a few moments and then smiled.

She smiled back at him, and then leant in and kissed him softly on the lips,

'What do you need me to do?' she asked.

'I need you to get comfortable on your seat right now and then follow my instructions,' he said, standing up and walking over to his own workstation.

Nicole-Louise made herself comfortable and waited for her first instruction.

'Hack into the City records and find out how many people there are with the initials AR,' he said.

Nicole-Louise got to work immediately.

Tackler then hacked into the social services system and carried out a search for the same initials.

A few minutes later, Nicole-Louise said,

'Just over fifty-five thousand.'

'Just over fifty-five thousand people out of a population of eight and a half million, what's that, about one per cent?'

'Zero point six five actually,' she replied.

Tackler smiled to himself.

'Now eliminate those who are female and over the age of say eighteen.'

Tackler looked at his own screen, he had twelve boys with the initials AR who were under the care of social services, or who had been visited by them, and a further forty-seven in foster care.

'Now we are down to eight hundred,' Nicole-Louise shouted over her shoulder.

'Now eliminate those who live at home with only a mom or both parents,' he said.

He looked at his own list.

He had fifty-nine names.

All of a sudden, it hadn't become such an impossible task.

'I told you that you were a problem solver,' Nicole-Louise said.

'What have you got?' he asked.

'I'm down to a list of eight,' she replied.

'Read them out to me?' he demanded.

Nicole-Louise read out the list of names. Not one of them matched with the list that he had in front of him.

'We have sixty-seven names between us,' Tackler said, 'Let's say that we split them and see what we can find,' he added.

'You want me to hack into their school and medical records?' she asked.

'Yes please,' Tackler replied firmly, 'And while you do that, I'm going to hunt for IP addresses.'

'Send me the top twenty-nine names on your list,' Nicole-Louise said.

Tackler split the list and forwarded it across to Nicole-Louise.

'What are you?' she asked him.

'The greatest problem solver in the world,' he replied with a smile.

In the bottom left hand corner of his screen, an icon was flashing. The icon was to let him know that he had a new message from iamalone.com. He looked over his shoulder and saw only the back of Nicole-Louise's head and so he opened the message box.

It was from MissFit and it simply said,

'I am missing you'.

TEN

Tap-Tap Munitions – Washington D.C.

There was a camera facing down over the shop entrance, and both Ward and Lawson made a mental note to make sure that there would be no record of them ever having visited the store as they walked through the door.

The store looked like any other gun store across The States.

It had a tough grey carpet on the floor, and four shelves that ran next to each other in the middle of the room; about eight feet back from the counter. Lawson aimlessly looked at some of the accessories that were on the shelves, and wondered why anyone would want to purchase a mug with 'The World's Greatest Shot' written on it.

There were two other people milling around the store, both guys in their mid to late thirties. They were clearly customers, and probably guys who fantasised about being the next super spy who saves the world.

If only they knew how unglamorous that life really was, Ward thought to himself.

Behind the counter, there was a guy in his fifties who looked like he should be working in a lumber store rather than a gun store, and another guy who was wearing a checked shirt and grubby jeans. He was a big guy and gave the impression that an after work bar brawl was something that he took part in to unwind after a hard day at work.

'What is it with all the Hillbillies in this country?' Lawson said, as he stepped across to the counter with Ward.

'How can I help you guys?' the older guy asked.

Ward looked over his shoulder into the back of the store. He got a glimpse of one of the two guys who had walked in a few minutes ago.

'I want to buy a gun,' he said.

The guy leant down under the counter and pulled out a form, he noticed that one of the customers was walking out of the store.

'You'll have to fill this in first,' the old guy said.

Ward looked down at the form.

There were a number of boxes to be completed.

It asked for Name, address, place of birth, race and citizenship.

It had a separate box for a social security number, but this was only optional, but recommended.

Below the personal information were a number of questions;

Have you ever been convicted of a felony?

Have you ever been convicted of a misdemeanour crime or domestic violence?
Are you an unlawful user of, or addicted to, marijuana or any other depressant, stimulant, narcotic drug, or any other controlled substance?
Are you a fugitive from justice?
Have you ever been committed to a mental institution?

He shook his head. No wonder The States were in the mess it was with such lapse control.
Being raised in The United Kingdom, where there were very few guns on the street, and the checks were both arduous and comprehensive, it never failed to amaze him how anyone could walk in off the street and obtain a gun with such a lapse system. Generally, The Americans got everything right, but the Brits had way outsmarted them on this one.
'What happens after I complete the form?' he asked with genuine interest. He had never had to purchase a gun in his life; every weapon he had ever possessed had been given to him, after rigorous checks had been carried out on the weapon by either MI6 or the C.I.A. He wondered for a moment where The Optician got his weapons from. He doubted very much that he would trust anyone else to select the tools of his trade.
'It's simple,' the old guy replied, 'I then phone the information through to the F.B.I who carry out a background check through the National Instant Criminal Background Check System and that's it. The whole thing won't take me any longer than a couple of minutes,' he added, sounding pleased that he had the opportunity to

demonstrate to a customer just how on top of his game he was.

'What if I don't want a record of my purchase?' he asked.

'Easy. Go to a gun show.'

'Go to a gun show?'

'Yes. They can be sold over the stall at a gun show without any checks. Most States have them, from Vegas to Philly. It's only in cities like here, and New York, where they won't be held, but if you go out further into the State, you'll find one.'

Ward was genuinely interested in this topic. He had no idea that it was so easy to buy a weapon.

'Of course,' the guy continued, 'Our super liberal, idiot of a President tried stopping the loophole that allowed the sale of weapons at gun shows a couple of years ago, with the help of some up and coming Senator who wanted to make a name for himself, but Congress soon put him back in his place,' he added, a broad smile crossing his face, almost as though he was a member of congress who had opposed the bill.

'The right to bear arms I guess?' Ward said.

'Yes sir. No one can take that right away from us. What are you, Australian? I guess things are a bit different down under?'

He couldn't be bothered to correct the guy with his true nationality, so he just nodded and smiled.

The last customer then walked out of the store without buying anything.

He had built up a rapport with the guy, now it was time to start getting what he had come here for.

'What if I want to purchase something different from you and I don't want a record of it?' he asked.

'I'll deal with this Harv,' the big guy said, 'I think you are in the wrong place mister,' he added, eyeing both of them up suspiciously.

'Look' Ward said, 'This is all new to us. I just want something that is untraceable and effective.'

'You heard the man, go to a gun show.'

'I'd rather shop here,' Lawson said, and he lunged forward and grabbed hold of the guy's collar with his left hand and unleashed a massive jab with his right arm, his large fist landing flush on the guys' nose with such force, that his head jerked backwards and forward three times before he slid on top of the counter face first and then fell to the floor, unconscious before he hit the deck.

Harv made a movement towards the side of the counter, clearly attempting to activate the alarm

'Don't do it Harv,' Ward said, pulling out his silenced Glock and pointing it at the old guy.

Harv backed up from the counter.

Lawson walked across to the door and put the latch down, he then slid the sign to 'Closed'.

'If you be quiet Harv, you won't get hurt. It's not you I'm interested in, it's the two guys in the back,' Ward said.

'What two guys?' Harv replied.

'Don't play games, I saw them come in, and I saw them moving around when I first got to the counter. Don't make me shoot you.'

'There's not two guys in the back,' Harv said, desperation in his voice.

Ward raised his Glock and pointed it at Harv's face.

'There are not two guys in the back, there are six of them.'

'Who are they?' he asked quietly, as Lawson walked to the side of the counter and lifted up the hatch to access the other side, as he followed slowly, not taking his eyes or gun off Harv for a second.

'I don't know. They are colleagues of Newman,' Harv replied, pointing down to the unconscious guy on the floor.

'He must work for you, so don't lie to me Harv,' he said.

'Let's just shoot him and be done with it,' Lawson said. Harv went white.

Ward, or indeed Lawson, had no intention of shooting Harv. He seemed like a nice guy who was just doing his job. But installing fear in people was the best way to get what you wanted from them. They had both learnt that a long time ago.

'He doesn't work for me here at the store,' Harv replied, fear running through his voice to such an extent that Ward lowered his gun slightly out of decency.

'So who is he?' he asked.

'Division told me that he was the regional manager and that he would be working out of my store for a few days. I've never seen him before.'

Ward looked down at the crumpled heap on the floor. Newman was most definitely not a regional manager.

'When did division put him in here?'

'Early this morning, I got a call at 05:00am.'

'Who called you?'

Before Harv could answer, a guy that neither of them had seen before appeared from the door that lead through to the back of the store.

He stood still for a split second, glancing between Ward, with his Glock pointed at Harv, the crumpled body of Newman on the floor, and Lawson standing no more than two feet away from him. He opened his mouth to speak, and Ward swung his arm around and pointed the gun at the guys face, and put the index finger of his left hand to his mouth to indicate to the guy that being quiet was his best option right then.

The guy looked at Ward's gun.

He liked using a silencer. It indicated a professional approach, and that frightened people more than anything. Most people looking at a gun with a silencer fitted to it would be sure that the person holding it had killed before.

The guy stood still and simply said to Harv,

'Do not hit the alarm.'

Ward beckoned him to the edge of the counter.

The guy looked nervously behind his shoulder and moved slowly to the side.

'What's this guy's name?' Ward asked Harv.

Harv shrugged, 'I don't know.'

'Who are you?' he asked the guy quietly.

The guy said nothing, just glanced over his shoulder, almost willing for one of the other guys to come out from the back of the store.

'Listen,' he said, moving around behind the counter and stopping two feet away from the guy, just given him enough time to ponder what his next question would be, 'You are so far out of your depth here, the easiest thing you can do is to talk to me. I will kill you just as sure as I will look at you.'

The guy glanced over his shoulder again.

'Your choice,' he said, and he raised his right hand and slammed the butt of the gun hard down on top of the guy's head with lightning quick speed. The sound of his skull cracking echoed around the empty store, his knees buckled and he fell forward.

Unfortunately, he had hit him with such force that his face had smashed hard against the glass of the display case underneath the counter, and the glass cracked The noise twice as loud as the impact of the gun against his skull had made.

'Go,' he said to Lawson, and Lawson walked through the door to the back of the store, by now, Lawson's own silenced handgun was drawn and held out firmly in front of him.

In the back, there was a table with six chairs spread around it and a large number of boxes stacked to one side.

Three guys were sitting at the table, two of them the guys that they had followed to the store, and one other guy eating a burger leaning against the sink.

There were three handguns on the table and one of the guys they had followed in, lunged forward to grab it and so Lawson squeezed the trigger of his gun immediately and pumped two bullets into the guys' chest. Without breaking stride, he continued forward and kicked the table hard, and it flew across the floor, before falling over, the hand guns clanking on the tiled floor as they all splayed out in different directions.

Now the guys had no weapons within easy reach.

'Stay where you are,' Ward shouted before any of them had the chance to move.

They all adjusted themselves in their chairs and sat rigidly still. None of them spoke.

He noticed that the guy eating his burger was adjusting his feet, spreading his weight, like he was seriously contemplating making a lunge for one of them, and so he turned his gun and shot the guy in the kneecap.

He let out a scream and collapsed to the floor, clutching his knee and whimpering. He then immediately studied the faces of the three guys who were sitting at the table, to see how they reacted to what they had just witnessed, and he didn't see any fear.

So he knew instantly that these guys were bad people who had probably done bad things, and that changed the rules for him instantly.

'I don't have time to play games,' he began, 'I will ask you questions, and you will give me answers. If you don't tell me what I want to know, I will kill you, one by one until one of you speak. And believe me, one of you always speaks.'

The three guys looked up at him.

The guy who he had shot in the kneecap was still whimpering and so Lawson turned towards him and pumped two bullets into his side. He stopped moving instantly.

None of the three guys spoke.

'If you are afraid of Newman out there more than you are us, you are making a very big mistake,' Ward said.

None of the three guys spoke.

He raised his gun and pulled the trigger, shooting the guy sitting to his left three times in the face. His head exploded with the impact of the bullets, blood and brain matter sprayed violently out in both directions, covering the two guys sitting next to him. Shooting someone in the face was always the best way to get someone to talk. To watch something that you related to, that you recognised that defined a person, be obliterated in front of your very eyes tended to make you realise just how mortal you were.

While these two guys weren't professionals, they were made of pretty tough stuff, because still neither of them spoke.

And that told him that he had stepped into something very big, and very bad, because if this wasn't working, they were dealing with a different breed of animal.

'Last chance,' he said, pointing the gun at the guy nearest to him, 'What are you doing here in Washington?'

For a moment, the guy looked like he was going to speak; but instead, he just pursed his lips even tighter. Ward pulled the trigger and shot him in the chest three times. The bullets tore through his clothing and he fell to the floor off the side of the chair.

'And then there was one,' Lawson said, smiling at the last guy sitting.

'We are here to make sure that no one gets close to the woman,' the guy suddenly said.

'What woman?' Ward asked.

'The woman who lives out in Silver Spring what's her name? Casey,' he replied.

'Casey who?'

'Just Casey.'

'So why were you outside the office a couple of blocks away rather than looking after the woman?'

'Because that's where she works.'

'You keep watch on her twenty-four seven?'

'Yes, since yesterday.'

'Who do you work for?'

'Newman.'

'Have you been in the military or any other covert organisations?'

The guy adjusted himself on his chair, seemingly reluctant to answer.

'Last chance,' Ward said.

'Yes I have. We all have,' the guy replied.

'Tell me which one?' Ward enquired, sure that the guy was going to say The Marines.

'The Ku Klux Klan,' he replied.

He raised his gun and shot the guy four times in the chest without asking any more questions.

He had been able to piece together a lot more of what was happening now, and he knew that Newman would be able to fill in any gaps he had left.

He nodded to Lawson and walked out of the rear of the store and back to the front, and then stopped in his tracks.

Both Newman and the guy whose skull he had cracked were gone.

And poor old Harv was lying spread-eagled on the floor on his back.

His throat had been cut and he had bled to death in silence.

ELEVEN

57 East 57th Street - New York City

The chairman of the committee had been in good spirits.
He had won every single hole they had played yet again,
and he was just over fifty thousand dollars richer.
The money was small change to him; it was the winning
that mattered. Everything was about winning to him.
He knew that tomorrow afternoon at five there would be
another shooting and he was feeling confident that
Emma Casey would come through with finding a third
shooter, and so he had every reason to feel optimistic.
Then one phone call changed everything.
He listened carefully and barked a few instructions down
the phone and then ended the call.
He rang around to each of the rooms of the other five
members of the committee, and told them to assemble in
the meeting room immediately.

Three minutes later, everyone was there, all of them still in their golfing attire.

'We have a very big problem gentleman,' he said as they all pulled their chairs in and sat down. To a man, they all looked up at him concerned, the youngest member of the committee showing the most panic on his face.

None of them asked what it was; they patiently waited until he was ready to speak.

Eventually he spoke.

'I've just been informed by my man that two British men have been sniffing about in Washington,' he started, 'They paid a visit to the hired hands who have been watching Dr Casey, and these were serious men gentlemen, because they killed some of our hired hands without hesitation,' he added.

'Where was this, in the office building? Are the police there?' one of the older members asked, concern on his face.

'No, there are no police involved and my man Newman is getting the mess cleared up and thankfully, it was not near the office.'

All five of the faces peering up at him seemed to relax.

'So where was it?' another grey haired member in his early sixties asked.

'It was in the Tap-Tap Munitions store two blocks from the office on 15th Street,' the chairman replied.

The youngest member of the committee went white and the other four around the table turned and looked at him, searching for his reaction.

'In the middle of Washington D.C? Can you fix this?' he asked the chairman.

'The first thing to do is to find out who these men are and what they,mm
 want. The timing might just be a coincidence gentleman, two British guys would not be working for the federal government, so it might be totally unrelated,' he replied, 'So the first thing to do is to take a deep breath, calm down and not make any rash assumptions that might lead us to the wrong conclusion.'
'Do you know what they wanted?' one of the members asked.
'Newman himself was knocked unconscious and he only came round to hear them asking what they were doing in Washington.'
'Are you going to make the call to find out?' a middle aged member, who sat at the end of the table asked.
'What can you find out?' the youngest member asked.
'Watch and learn",' the chairman said, 'Watch and learn.'
He dialled a number into the phone that was on the table and put the phone on speaker.
'Hello,' a voice said, a thick southern drawl clearly identifiable.
'Senator, it's me,' the chairman said.
'My friend,' the voice replied, 'My favourite sponsor and donor,' he added with an exaggerated laugh.
'Indeed I am. Now I'm going to call some of that four million dollars a campaign back, in the form of a favour that I need done right now?' he said assertively.
'Happy to help in any way I can my friend, if it's within my power,' the Senator replied.
'This is definitely within your power also in your best interest.'

'Shoot.'

'I need you to make a call right now to your friends in the F.B.I and Homeland security to see if they have any agents operating in Washington around 13th Street, and if so, what are they doing. I need you to make that call right now.'

'I can do that for you my friend.' The Senator replied, 'What's it all about?' he asked.

'I won't concern you with that. What you don't know can't come back to bite you.'

'Good point my friend I'll get on it now.'

'One more thing,' the chairman said quickly before the Senator could hang up.

'Shoot.'

'Find out if any of them are using two Brits to do their dirty work?'

'Brits?' the Senator enquired, 'Why would the F.B.I. or Homeland use British guys as operatives?'

'That's exactly what I want you to find out Senator. Make the call; I am waiting for your response.'

'I'll get back to you within the next ten minutes,' the Senator said and the line went dead.

The chairman looked at the committee members and said,

'Gentlemen, get a drink, this could be a long night.'

Park Avenue - New York City

Tackler typed into the dialogue box,
'I miss you too.'

'Hold it right there,' Nicole-Louise shouted out behind him, 'I'm not letting you do that.'

'What?' he asked.

'I'm mirroring your screen. I know why you are doing it, and how this is eating away at you, and how you want to get to her, but it's not what we do,' she replied, 'We will find this woman for Ryan and he will do the rest. You know there will be only one outcome once he is face to face with her.'

'I want to make sure we get her and she gets what she deserves.'

'Then trust me to do it. I will lead Ryan to her, I promise,' she said softly.

He knew she was right. He would be much more use saving AR than wasting his time hunting her down, and he knew that Nicole-Louise was as good as he was, and she would do equally as good a job of finding 'MissFit'.

'And there is one thing you are completely forgetting,' she said as she walked over to his workstation and put her hand on his shoulder.

'Which is?'

'I want to do this for you. Probably as much as you want to bring her down, maybe more, so let me hunt the bitch,' she replied and she leant forward and kissed him on the cheek.

He tapped on his keyboard and closed the dialogue box.

'She is all yours now,' he said.

'Good. Now tell me where you are with your list?'

'I'm down to fourteen, you?'

'I'm down to fourteen too,' she lied. She had eliminated most of her list and was now down to the last three. If Tackler couldn't find AR somewhere in his group, they were never going to find him. She knew Tackler was not concentrating fully, and he was distracted by thoughts of finding 'MissFit' by the speed with which he was working. She had to shake him out of it.

Tackler became refocussed and reenergised immediately. Ten minutes after Nicole-Louise had told him to concentrate on finding AR; he was down to a list of five possibilities.
'I have five names that we need to follow up, we need to establish what their IP addresses are, and hack into their lives and find if they visit iamalone.com,' he said.
'That's more like my Tackler,' she whispered to herself.
'You take these two I'm sending you, and I'll take the other three. Let's rip every inch of their lives apart and see what we can find,' Tackler said without turning around.
She looked down at the clock, it was almost eleven. If 'MissFit' was waiting, then she must be desperate, she thought to herself.
And that was going to make it very easy to convince her to tell her exactly who she was.
And so she started to type,
'Where do you go to school? I used to live in LA so I know it well.'
Now MissFit would have to lie, and in the process, hopefully give away a big clue towards her identity.

57 East 57th Street - New York City

The chairman put the phone on loud speaker as soon as it rang.

'It's me,' the Senator's drawl echoed around the room.

'What have you found out?' the chairman asked anxiously.

'Well, they definitely aren't F.B.I agents,' he replied, 'And Homeland only have nine Brits working for them in Washington and they are all analysts, so it isn't them either.'

'Then it is just a coincidence?'

'More than likely.'

'Likely isn't enough. I need to know definitively.'

'Well, it's possible that it might be the CIA, they have all sorts of mercenaries working for them that are listed as consultants, but unless what you are doing involves overseas operations, the chances of it being them are virtually zip,' the Senator replied.

This answer seemed to satisfy the chairman and all of the other committee members, with the exception of the youngest member who was still on edge.

'Thank you for your help Senator,' the chairman said, 'Speak soon,' he added, and pressed the button that ended the call.

He looked across the table to the youngest member, 'You can relax,' he said, 'This isn't the first time we have come across a problem doing this and it won't be the last. We will find these two Brits and find out what they want,' he added.

He dialled a number on the phone, clicked the loudspeaker button and leant back into his chair.

After four rings, a voice said,

'I'm here.'

'It's me Newman. Where are you now?'

'I'm back at the apartment.'

'Who is looking after Miss Casey?'

'There were still two guys who haven't left their posts since this morning and I have added four more. No one will be able to get near her, that's a guarantee,' Newman replied.

'So you managed to arrange sufficient reinforcements?'

'Yes I have sir. There are now eleven of us here. And now we know that there are two guys out there who have crossed a line, if they show their faces again, we will catch them and kill them,' Newman replied coldly.

'I need you to talk to them first, find out what they want, what they know and most importantly, who they work for,' the chairman demanded.

'Understood,' Newman replied, 'Two slimy Brits against us won't have a chance in hell now that we know what they look like.'

'Keep me informed of any developments, and find them quickly and then get every last ounce of information from them.'

'Understood,' Newman replied in a determined tone.

The chairman looked around the table,

'As I said gentlemen, this appears to be just a coincidence. I suggest you all get some sleep, tomorrow will be a long day, where a lot of questions will be asked and the media will go into overdrive,' he said.

'Are you really sure that these two Brits are just a coincidence?' the youngest member asked once more.

'Yes I am. But it doesn't matter now. Newman and his men will find them and take care of them. So for the last time, relax.'

The other members of the committee all smiled. They had all experienced the panic that the youngest member was experiencing right then, and over the years, they had all learnt to cope with it. The youngest member looked around the table. He could see their smiles and he found reassurance in the fact that they were all looking at him knowingly.

'I'm sorry,' he said, 'This is just all new to me.'

'We understand,' the chairman replied, 'In fact, I remember your father taking me under his wing and having to reassure me many years ago. It's now my turn to do the same thing to the next generation. The wheels of time are certainly oiled with irony,' he added with a smile.

The youngest member instantly felt better. He knew that he could trust the chairman and the rest of the committee, his father had been very eager to make him understand that before he passed away six months ago.

'Are there any other questions gentlemen?' the chairman asked the rest of the committee.

Each one of them shook their heads.

'Are you sure?' the chairman said, looking at the youngest member again.

'No. I am totally reassured. I know that you have this under control,' he replied.

'Good. Remember, we are talking about two men only. Now we know they exist, they don't have a chance,' he said, before standing up and walking out of the meeting room.

But there were not just two men they had to concern themselves with.

There were three.

As Newman had put the phone down and ended his conversation with the chairman, the centre of his forehead was being lined up in the crosshairs of the scope that belonged to the world's best sniper.

The Optician was in town.

TWELVE

1845 4th Street NE – Washington

The Optician had been in Washington since Ward and
Lawson had landed. As always, Ward had climbed
aboard the jet that The Old Man had arranged to
transport him, and glanced towards the back of the pilot
and co-pilots heads and thought nothing of it. Ward
might have been more concerned if he knew that the co-
pilot had no idea how to fly a plane. It was how he
always managed to stay so close to him. Who really
takes any notice of a co-pilot?
He had collected the red Kawasaki superbike that
Centrepoint had waiting for him when he landed, there
was one held for him in every State in America at the
airports that they always used, and he had used the
tracking system that he had linked to Ward's phone to
follow him. He had been following them every step of
the way since they had arrived in Oregon, where he had

achieved eleven kills from eleven bullets. To most snipers, that would be an achievement to feel proud of but to him, it was a standard days' work.

The only time that he had ever felt more than satisfied with a mission, was when The Old Man had sent him to take out a crime family in Chicago. He had systematically wiped out fifty-one guys, the last person he killed being the head of the crime family itself, and he had managed to do that by firing only forty-seven shots. He thought of Ward as much more than an operative. He had been looking after him for over three years now and he had grown close to him, closer than he had ever been to anyone in his life. Ward knew more about his past than anyone, and why he had become the world class assassin that he had. Ryan Ward had even managed to bring him back into contact with his family.

Prior to protecting Ward, his main objective was to shadow and protect another operative by the name of Gill Whymark. But for reasons that he could not understand, Whymark had gone rogue, and this had disappointed him as much as it had angered him.

He thought Whymark was a better man than that.

But Ryan Ward was a good man, good to the core. When he wasn't running around on missions set by The Old Man, he was wiping out the paedophiles and animals that profited from harming children, and this was something that The Optician took great pleasure in helping him deal with without any hesitation.

Being Ryan Ward's shadow was both his privilege and his calling, he really believed that.

He had followed Ward and Lawson to the Tap-tap Munitions store and when he saw two heavily dazed looking guys run out of the building, he had decided to follow them to see where they would go. That is what had brought him to the elevated position that he was now peering down from, watching the four guys in the apartment across the road. Fortunately for him, and unfortunately for Newman, the apartment block that he had followed them to was opposite a warehouse. It was a red brick building with boarded out windows which were painted grey.

Much to The Opticians delight, there were a set of grey double-doors which were wide open, he assumed someone was using them for access to load or unload a truck, and he managed to slip into the building unnoticed.

He had climbed up the stairs until he reached the top of the stairwell and found the access door onto the roof unlocked too. He had walked across to the left hand side of the building and used his scope to establish what apartment the guys were in. The building they had gone into was a smart looking apartment block that looked like it had been recently renovated. It was painted an off-white colour, which blended in perfectly with the black of the window and door frames. The apartment the guys had gone into was in the left hand corner of the building on the second floor, and from the position that he had now taken up, he was directly across from them. He had counted seven different guys in the apartment and he could have taken them all out already, but he was unsure who they were or what Ward wanted with them, so he thought it would be prudent to ask before shooting the place up.

He took out his phone and pressed number '2', his speed dial number for Ward.

'You are going to tell me you are already in Washington I assume?' Ward said as he answered.

'I'm doing your job for you again. And as there is so much assuming going on, the guys you lost from the ammunition store, I assume that you have unfinished business with them?' The Optician replied.

He heard Ward laugh down the line,

'And I assume that you are looking at them right now?'

'Some of them I am.'

'Some of them?'

'Yes,' The Optician replied, 'Seven of them, including the two guys that you and Lawson failed to deal with properly. I assume that is why they staggered out of the store way before you?'

'Where are they?' Ward asked.

'Shouldn't you be asking where the other four guys who left fifteen minutes ago are?'

Ward laughed down the line again.

'I know where they are. I'm looking at them right now. They are on 13th Street. Seems I'm on my game as much as you are my friend,' he said.

The Optician smiled to himself.

He had watched Ward closely for the past three years and he had never failed to be impressed by the way in which he always worked out the most complex of missions.

'The other seven are in an apartment on 4th Street North East. Do you want me to take them out?' he asked.

'Not yet. I need to talk to the big guy who came out of the munitions store. Once I've spoken to him, they are yours to do as you wish with.'

'I have a question?' The Optician quickly said.

'Ask away my old friend.'

'I know this is about the shooting in Missouri and The Old Man had intel that another one was taking place, but do you have any idea what is going on?' he asked.

'I know exactly what is going on,' Ward replied.

And the line went dead.

Park Avenue - New York City

Nicole-Louise saw the icon flashing in the bottom left hand corner of her screen, notification that she had a message.

She had comprehensively eliminated the last three names on her list over thirty minutes ago, and now she was working with Tackler trying to obtain the IP addresses of the last five kids that they hoped was meant to be the shooter.

She opened the dialogue box.

'I have only been in LA for eight months, before that I had started at Washington State but flunked out because the bitches were all mean to me,' it read.

'I hear you,' she typed back.

She pulled up the screen that she had searched for earlier and looked at the names.

'Have you heard of Carl Legg?' she typed.

'No. Did he go to Washington State?' MissFit replied.

'Yes. He lived on my street.'

'Have you thought anymore about what we were talking about earlier about hitting back at the people who make our lives hell?' MissFit asked.

'I think about it all the time. I wish I had a big gun' Nicole-Louise typed, trying her best to appear flippant rather than eager'

'What if I could get you one?'

Nicole-Louise looked down the list in front of her and decided to take a gamble and skip two of the names.

'Do you know who Josh Maddix is?" she typed.

She watched the screen intently and in the corner of the dialogue box, there was a flashing line that said, 'Writing'. It continued flashing for well over a minute. And then the message appeared.

'He had the right idea. He stood up to them and hit back. He is my hero and someone that I want to emulate. He wasn't psychotic as they claimed. He was all alone, like we are. They failed to help him, and as his last note to his mom said; if they would have cared about him as much as they should have, they would have known how desperate he felt. We are both Josh Maddix, just with different names.'

Nicole-Louise read the message and smiled.

'I've been reading about him and I want to do the same thing. Do you think less of me now?' she typed.

'I've been waiting for a guy like you forever. I feel the same. I think we are soul mates. I have a secret,' MissFit typed.

'Tell me'

'I'm ready to do that and I have the weapons already. But I need someone who make a pact with me so that we can meet in a place I call Forever love.'

'I'm not sure,' Nicole-Louise typed.

'Do you want to see some pictures of how excited this makes me feel?' MissFit typed.

'I have to go to sleep now.'

'Tell me before you go, do you believe in soul mates?' MissFit typed.

'Yes. Are you an only child?' Nicole-Louise typed.

'No. I have two sisters, are you?'

'Yes I am. And I don't think they really wanted me.'

'Then the answer is in the pact.'

'Goodnight,' Nicole-Louise typed and she closed the dialogue box.

She stood up from her workstation and walked across to Tackler. He was in his high concentration zone where he was hacking into the networks of the New York internet providers and his fingers were floating across the keyboard with remarkable speed. She put her hand on his shoulder and he stopped typing.

'Good news or bad news?' she asked him.

'Bad' Tackler replied.

'I've just encouraged a woman to send me naked pictures.'

He smiled at her,

'And the good?' he asked

'I know all that we need to find out who this bitch is, and my guess is that between us, we can find her in under thirty minutes,' she replied and then winked at him.

'What do you know?'

'She is around thirty, she graduated in child psychology from Washington State, and she has probably lived there her whole life. She practiced there for a while and has now dropped off the radar, she has two sisters and finally, she will have one hell of a lot of money in bank accounts somewhere, because she is so devious and cynical, she can only be doing this for money,' she replied in a matter of fact tone. It was the tone that he had grown to love so much over the years.

'How do you know all of that?' he asked.

'Easy. She hadn't heard of Carl Legg but she had heard of Josh Maddix,' she replied.

Tackler looked at her blankly.

'Carl Legg killed nine people in a cinema in Wyoming and Josh Maddix shot thirteen students dead in a school shooting in Kansas.'

'Go on?'

'Carl Legg committed his crime thirty-five years ago. Josh Maddix carried out his shooting only twelve years ago. She would have studied Maddix as part of her degree. And she confirmed that by knowing a hell of a lot about him.'

'And how do you know that she has always lived in Washington?' Tackler asked.

'Because she panicked when I asked her about LA, she said that she had only been there a short while.'

'So how does that mean she has always been in Washington?'

'Because she told me about Washington State after she said she had only been there a while. When people think they are going to get caught out lying, they always revert to a truth and familiarity immediately after. It's human nature Tackler, you know that.' she added with yet another smile.

'Are you laying down the gauntlet?' Tackler asked.

'You bet,' she replied and gently punched him before skipping back to her workstation to begin her search. 'Let's see if we come up with the same name,' he said over his shoulder, as he started to hack into the personal files that were held by Washington State University.

Just fourteen minutes later Tackler had a name. He had not bothered with trying to search for a hidden bank account, that was Nicole-Louise's speciality, and so he continued to stare at the five names that he had left on his list with the initials A.R.
He read down the list.

Andre Roberts
Allan Renshaw
Antonio Riscoli
Aston Routledge
Andrew Rush.

There was no Adam Ray on the list.
Because on all of the records that the city of New York, held, Adam Ray did not exist.
When his father had married his mother, she had insisted on keeping her maiden name so she became Mrs Ray-Watson.
When he was born, he was registered as Adam Ray-Watson.
His father had insisted that he dropped any trace of his mother from their existence and he notified the school that his son now wished to be known as just Adam Ray. They said that they would update the records once the change in Adam's name had been legally confirmed and

his father had never gotten around to doing it. So even on their records, he was still Adam Ray-Watson.

'I've found her,' Nicole-Louise said excitedly, and she jumped to her feet and punched the air.
'I found her five minutes ago,' Tackler replied and smiled at her.
'Without checking her financial records no doubt,' she said.
Tackler ignored her.
'So tell me who she is?' she asked.
'You first.'
'Her first name is Emma,' Nicole-Louise said, and raised an eyebrow, waiting for him to add the surname.
He punched the air and then said,
'Emma Casey.'
'You got very lucky Tackler.'
'It's amazing how often I get lucky,' he said, 'Her financial affairs?' he asked.
"She had one and a half million dollars deposited in an account oversees just yesterday," she replied.
'Do you know where it came from?'
'Not yet, but I will.'
'What's then hold up?'
'Because whoever deposited it hid the trace back quite well, so it will take me a few hours to follow it, but they won't be good enough to stop me from finding it.'
'I know they won't,' he replied, 'Do you want to ring Ryan and tell him, or shall I?' he asked.
She looked at the clock on the bottom right hand corner of her screen and saw that it was almost 01:00am.
'You can call him,' she replied, 'You found her first.'

THIRTEEN

4015 Kennedy Street – Hyattsville, Maryland

Ward and Lawson had watched as Newman's guys collected a woman from the front of the office in a shabby looking SUV. It had off-coloured grey panels, and looked like it was going to break down at any moment. She walked out of the building and was heading for the car park, when two guys approached her and spoke to her, and after a short discussion; she turned and followed them to their shabby vehicle.

'You think she is doing that under duress?' Lawson asked as they sat in the dark blue Ford Taurus that The Old Man had provided for them

'No. She is doing that because she is scared,' he replied, 'Just follow them and see where it takes us.'

They stayed behind the SUV, thankfully, the roads were still reasonably busy for 01:00am, and they managed to sit four cars back undetected.

Lawson wasn't overly concerned about the SUV speeding off and losing them.

Six miles and twenty minutes later, the SUV pulled up outside a house.

It was a quaint looking house on a quiet street. Even in the poor lighting, they could see that the house had a wooden front and was painted a beige colour. There were four trees, and some extensive flowerbeds which obscured the front of the house fully from the road.

Lawson had dropped the lights and pulled into a drive about a hundred yards back from the house when they saw the SUV coming to a stop.

They climbed out of the car and hid behind some shrubs and watched as the woman got out of the SUV and walked into the house.

They couldn't see her clearly, but the moonlight exposed a slim silhouette in a white blouse and grey pants. Two guys walked her up the path and followed her inside, while two others walked around to the back of the house. A few moments later, two other guys stepped out of the battered vehicle and stood as sentries. One of them at the end of the neat drive that was adjacent to the house and the other on the neat steps that climbed up to the porch.

Ward felt the phone on his pocket vibrate. He pulled it out and saw Tackler's name on the screen.

'Hello?' he whispered as he answered.

'Are you in the middle of something?' Tackler asked in response to Ward's hushed voice.

'It can wait. What have you got for me?' he asked.

'I know the name of the woman behind iamalone dot com,' Tackler said, rather bizarrely, he found himself whispering too as he spoke.

'Is she Casey someone?'

Tackler was taken aback for a few seconds,

'Her name is Emma Casey. But how did you know that?' Tackler asked, surprise running through his voice.

'Just a hunch,' Ward flippantly replied, 'What else do you have?'

'She is a children's psychologist and has lived in Washington forever. She has two sisters, and she has deposited one and a half million dollars in the last forty-eight hours. Nicole-Louise is hunting the source now.'

'What are her sister's names?'

'They are called Lyndsey and Brittany. Why?' Tackler said after a few moments.

'It's always good to know.'

'She lives at.......'

'4015 Kennedy Street,' he interrupted.

Ward heard Tackler sigh,

'I'm beyond being surprised by you anymore Ryan. Why don't you tell me what you need to know and then maybe we might be of some use?'

'The source of the money and most importantly, who this A.R. kid is. If we don't find him and stop him, this will all be a waste of time,' he replied.

'Is there anything else?'

'Once we've stopped this kid, there is a lot more but I need you two focussed just on that for now. The other stuff can wait.'

'We are on it Ryan, trust me on that,' Tackler replied.

Ward hung up the phone and slowly screwed the silencer onto his Glock.

'You've probably worked out everything that is happening by now,' Lawson whispered to him, 'Do you want to share it with me?' he asked, as he attached his own silencer to his gun.

'No,' he replied, and he started to move across the road so that he could come at Emma Casey's house from the backyard. Lawson followed two paces behind, still shaking his head in response to his refusal to share what he knew.

But he knew, as usual, Ward would explain everything when the time was right.

They managed to get within thirty yards of the house before they spotted the two guys who were guarding the rear. One of the guys was sitting on a chair on the patio, smoking a cigarette, gazing aimlessly out into the darkness, and the other guy was standing with his back to them, facing the house.

'They aren't the smartest, are they?' Lawson whispered. Ward ignored him.

There was a fence about four feet high that backed on to Casey's yard, and on either side, there was thick shrubbery.

Ward looked down at it, he knew that if they trampled over it that they would make a lot of noise and alert the two guys, and while he was confident that they could shoot the guy who had his back to them with ease, the guy on the patio was a good fifty yards away from them and a handgun, even a Glock, could not guarantee accuracy from that far away. They would hit the target no problem but a kill shot was not a given.

Lawson was thinking the same thing.

Handguns were designed for close combat battles.

'Suggestions?' he asked.

'Apart from jumping over the fence and shouting 'Surprise', I'm drawing a blank' Ward replied without once taking his eyes off the two guys.

'Where is The Optician when you need him?' Lawson asked.

Ward ignored him, he had a great idea.

'Follow me Mike,' he said, and he stood up and sprinted forwards. He trampled over the shrubs and then vaulted over the fence, landing on his feet and then sending his body into a forward roll,

"Surprise!" he shouted, as he faced the house on one knee, and then lifted up his gun and shot the guy on the patio three times in the chest from less than twenty yards away. The bullets smashed into him and knocked him clean off of the chair.

Lawson had been no more than three paces behind him, moving way faster than his immense frame indicated that he was capable of moving, and as the guy with his back to them looked to his left at Ward rolling onto the lawn, he pumped two shoots into the centre of the guys back, and he lurched forward and landed face first into the turf. And then the night silence was shattered by two piercing alarms screaming out.

These guys weren't as stupid as they looked. They were both holding pressure alarms, which were activated as soon as they released their grips on them.

They heard shouting from either side of the building, and then the sound of two sets of footsteps urgently racing towards them filled the split second silence. They were both exposed in the middle of the lawn, and neither of them was stupid enough to stay there. Ward sprinted to the left and dived into some thick shrubbery, while Lawson turned and vaulted back over the fence at the rear of the garden.

Two guys appeared and one was holding a semi-automatic machine gun out in front of him, and then he instantly squeezed the trigger and sprayed the back fence, the wood splintering into a hundred pieces with each bullet that ripped through it. The other guy was holding a handgun, which looked like a Magnum, and he was swinging it from left to right, looking for a target. Ward hoped Lawson was ready.

He lifted his head from above the shrubs and raised his gun; he sent five shots, one after the other in the direction of the guy holding the machine gun. The first bullet smashed into his right shoulder and he let out a scream, the other four followed the same route and smashed into him, the last one skimming off of his shoulder and ripping into his neck, tearing the main artery in two. He fell violently to the left, dead before he even hit the ground.

At the exact same moment that Ward was firing his third shot, Lawson lifted his huge frame from behind the fence and fired four shots directly into the centre of the chest of the guy who was swinging the Magnum around. The force of the bullets knocked him completely off of his feet, and he landed flat on his back, stone cold dead, before he had a chance to fire one shot.

'Let's go,' Ward said, as he headed towards the house. Lawson vaulted over the fence and was beside him within six giant strides.

They reached the back door and looked through the glass window into the kitchen.

It was empty.

Ward turned the handle and walked in. He quickly changed his magazine, while Lawson covered the door and he then did the same for Lawson while he changed his.

They stepped through the doorway that led into the house, Ward leading with his Glock extended in his right hand.

Everything seemed quiet. He stopped moving for a moment and listened, and then used his senses to try and feel where the remaining two guys and Casey were hiding. He felt nothing, his instincts were either not working or they were not in the house. He slowly moved along the hall and peered into the lounge.

It was empty.

And then he could hear the sound of sirens approaching from a distance,

'Mike,' he whispered, 'Ring The Old Man now and get the cops pulled back immediately.'

Lawson nodded and pulled his cell phone from his pocket.

The guy with the machine gun had probably woken up everyone who lived within the surrounding three blocks Ward thought to himself.

The wail of the sirens git closer while Lawson spoke frantically into his phone.

Ward stepped forward and reached the bottom of the stairs, he could now see the flashing lights of the police vehicles lighting up the street outside.

He was impressed with the response time of the local police department, but it was interference that he could do without right now.

He turned and looked out of the window and saw two police cruisers screech to a halt outside.

Then he noticed that the SUV had gone.

'They've left,' he said.

'Not such a great surprise after all,' Lawson quipped in response.

'Has he sorted the police?'

'He says by the time I walk out of the door, they will know who I am,' Lawson replied.

'I'll check upstairs while you smooth it over with them,' Ward said, and as he started to head up the stairs, Lawson opened the front door, stepped out into the flashing lights and slowly closed the door behind him.

Ward reached the top of the stairs and turned left. All of the lights were on. The first room that he stepped into was the bathroom and it was empty. He checked the mirror for steam or condensation and found neither.

He then walked out of the bathroom and into the room next door. There was a bed in there, brass headboard and lots of cushions all over it and on the floor, a bra and some panties thrown on top of a white blouse.

This was Casey's bedroom. She had probably been getting ready for a shower when the machine gun had interrupted her.

He turned around and scanned the room, there were lots of different perfume bottles on a long dressing table, a walk in closet, the door wide ajar, with rows of expensive looking suits hanging up, all the same black colour, at least thirty white blouses on the rail opposite and black shoes lined neatly along the bottom of the rail. He looked across to the other side of the room and saw keys and a purse.

Next to them was a laptop.

The laptop was on.

He walked over to the laptop and looked at it, he moved the pointer until he had called up the menu that said, 'Recent Documents' and he clicked on it.

He immediately saw it.

The second document down was simply called 'Gun'.

He clicked it open and a typed document appeared with just one paragraph in it.

He started to read slowly.

By the time that he had finished reading a minute later, he knew that he was wrong about who was behind this.

But he also knew that he was right about the reasons that it was happening.

All he had to do was find out the 'whom' and he could end this.

He closed the laptop and tucked it under his arm and walked out of the bedroom. By the time he reached the bottom of the stairs, Lawson was walking back in the house,

'Everything is good with the cops,' he said.

Ward ignored him.

'I was wrong Mike,' he said after a few moments deep in thought, 'Well I was wrong and I was right,' he added.

'Well that makes perfect sense,' Lawson replied, 'so I take it we can go home now,' he added.

'I thought that there were Senators behind this, I was sure of it.'

'Are they not then?' Lawson asked.

'No, which is why this makes it interesting.'

'Does it, why?'

'Because my friend, there is only one other group of people who stand to gain from this,' Ward replied.

'Who?'

'I don't know their names yet,' Ward replied.

'Oh God,' Lawson said with a sigh, 'Mr Cryptic is here again.'

'But we will know within the hour.'

'How?'

'Because Casey is going to tell us.'

1845 4th Street NE – Washington

The Optician watched as the SUV turned up and two guys jumped out of the front of the vehicle and scanned the street. When they were satisfied that the coast was clear, one of them opened the rear door to the vehicle and a woman jumped out and ran into the apartment block, and the two guys jogged in behind her. He moved his scope to the apartment in the corner and a minute later, the woman came into view. The two guys who had turned up in the SUV returned to the street with two other men behind them. The two at the front walked to each corner of the building and leant against it, each on the lookout for any approaching vehicles. The other two guys stood outside the entrance to the apartment building, one on either side.

He pulled out his cell phone and called Ward,
'I know' Ward said as he answered, 'The woman is there
and you now have more guys to play with.'
'No. That's not while I'm calling smartass,' The
Optician replied.
'So why are you calling?
'Because The Old Man needs to speak to you, urgently,'
The Optician replied, and the line went dead.

FOURTEEN

Centrepoint did not know why Senator Neville Lockhart had been asking the F.B.I and Homeland Security about two British agents running wild in Washington, and he was hoping Ward could give him an answer that would satisfy him. His sources had told him that enquiries were made direct from the Senators cell phone so it had to be personal.

The Optician had told him that Ward was in the middle of something, and so he had refrained from calling him himself, as he knew that a call at the wrong time in the field could jeopardise an operative's position.

Patience wasn't one of his strongest qualities and Ward stretched his patience to the limit, but he inhaled deeply and then exhaled to calm himself down. For all Ward's inability to keep him updated regularly, as every other Deniable did without fail, his ability to work everything out correctly, and resolve it definitively, far outweighed his frustration, and he had learnt long ago to just accept it. He could not risk anything that would jeopardise another shooting from taking place, those above him would be very unhappy, and so he had been waiting patiently for well over an hour.

And then his phone rang.

He saw Ward's number on the screen and snatched at the receiver,

'About time,' he said curtly.

'What's wrong?' Ward asked, offering no apology for the delay.

'This thing is going political, what have you found out?'

There was silence on the phone for a few moments,

'Political?' Ward asked.

'A long serving Senator has been asking if any agencies have two British guys running around. What do you have on him?'

'What's his name?'

Centrepoint knew instantly that he was telling Ward something that he didn't know, and he felt it offset the frustration that he felt over the lack of contact from Ward immediately.

He ignored Ward's question.

'Is this being instigated from Capitol Hill?' he asked.

'No,' Ward replied.

'Do you know that definitively?'

'Yes.'

'How do you know that?'

'Because I know which organisation that is behind it.'

'Who are they?'

'I don't know yet.'

'Ryan, I can do without the riddles. Tell me what is going on,' he demanded.

'I can't because I don't know for sure yet, but I know why they want it to happen,' Ward replied.

'How do you know?'

'Because the person I'm going to talk to shortly had a list of events and people on a document on their laptop.'

'Who is he?'

'He is a she, and she referred to a committee.'

'Like a Senate committee?'

'No.'

He decided to give up asking questions. Ward knew much more than he was letting on, he always did, and it was obvious to Centrepoint that the best thing to do was to let him get on with it.

'Where are you on this other intended shooting?' he asked.

'I don't know.'

'Why not?'

'Because I'm waiting for you to get off the phone so I can call Nicole-Louise and Tackler,' Ward said sarcastically.

Centrepoint slammed the phone down.

He would just have to wait patiently.

He inhaled deeply and exhaled slowly, and felt himself becoming agitated over Ryan Ward's inability to update him effectively once again.

Park Avenue - New York City

Tackler sighed loudly and then leant back into his chair. He closed his eyes and shook his head. The sun was dawning on a new day, and the bright rays were starting to break into the apartment through the windows.

Nicole-Louise heard the sigh and turned around. She knew what his body language was saying.

He had failed to solve his problem.

'It's none of the five kids you had left, is it?' she asked.

'No.'

'Then we have to refocus on the next problem,' she said.

Tackler stood up and stretched his arms way above his head, trying to push the frustration that he felt out of his body.

'I'm still no closer to finding the source of this money that was deposited in Casey's account. They have some good tech people working with them, whoever they are,' Nicole-Louise said and she stood up herself and mirrored Tackler's stretch.

'What are we missing?' he asked her.

'That's the next problem.'

'Suggestions?'

'Maybe he isn't registered in the State?' she asked.

Tackler thought about this for a few seconds. It made sense.

If the kid lived out of State and was here with relatives, then he may not be on any of the databases that they had hacked in to.

'Going nationwide will take hours just to get it down to a list of possibilities,' he said.

'I don't see that we have any other option. Do you want me to focus on that, and you look for who deposited the money? Fresh eyes on each other's problems might get us a break,' Nicole-Louise said, her words sounding more like an instruction than a question to him.

The cell phone on Tackler's workstation rang.

It was Ward.

'Ryan's calling,' he said.

'I'll get it,' she replied, as she stood up and walked urgently over towards him and picked up the phone. 'Hello.'

'Hey Nicole-Louise, what have you got for me?' Ward asked.

'We've drawn a total blank on the identity of the kid who is planning on carrying out this shooting, and we still haven't established the source of the money to Casey's account,' she replied with disappointment in her voice.

'Forget the money,' Ward said, 'In half an hour, she would have told me who paid her anyway, so I will be able to give you something to go on. The kid has to be the number one priority right now.'

'We know that Ryan. We've been sitting up all night working on this,' she replied angrily.

She was frustrated for Tackler, she knew what this meant to him, and she also knew that it would be eating away inside of him that he couldn't help this kid.

Ward noted her tone instantly and then said,

'How is he coping? Just say we will if he is struggling with the emotional side of this, or we need more to go on if he is OK,' Ward said softly.

'We will,' Nicole-Louise replied.

'Take him out for a break. Go grab a coffee. By the time you get back, I should have some solid leads for you.'

'We'll be OK,' she replied.

'You will, you are the strong one, but he needs to refocus.'

'We are starting to think that this kid might be from outer State. We've been through every possible person under the age of eighteen with the initials AR and it definitely is not one of them.'

'Have a break and then I will see what I can find for you. You are both doing well, keep him going Nicole-Louise, I'm counting on you,' Ward replied and the line went dead.

Tackler was looking at her, trying to gauge from her reaction what mood Ward was in,

'What did he say?' he asked her.

'He said that we have got to go and get a coffee and then come back and go again, and he will see what he can find to help our search,' she replied.

'That's it?' Tackler asked cautiously.

'No.'

'What else did he say?'

'He said that you have got to stop feeling sorry for yourself and get your crap together. He said that you will find who we are looking for if you stop moping around thinking the world is against you,' she lied.

Tackler instantly felt the rage building inside of him as he stood up and grabbed his jacket from the back of the armchair.

'And that was all?'

'No,' Nicole-Louise replied, 'He said if you really want to get even, and let go of your past, stop relying on me, and show that you can stand on your own two feet,' she replied, lying to him again, and looking down at the floor as she spoke to give authenticity to what she was saying.

Tackler threw his jacket on the floor. He felt like he wanted to scream and hit out.

'What are you doing?' she asked as she was putting her own coat on.

'I'm going to find this kid. Forget the coffee. Get back to work, and we will find all kids with the initials AR on the east coast to start with. I'll show him I'm not feeling sorry for myself," he shouted, and then sat back down at his workstation.

Nicole-Louise took of her coat and sat back down at her own workstation.

'I'm sending you a list of States now, you check them,' he barked at her.

Nicole-Louise looked at her screen and smiled. It was a big, happy smile.

Her Tackler was well and truly back in the room.

57 East 57th Street - New York City

The chairman was woken up at 06:00 by his cell phone ringing.

He saw Newman's number on the screen and answered immediately.

'Everything OK Newman?' he asked, his voice sounding dry and broken.

'The house was hit,' Newman replied urgently.

'By whom?' the chairman asked, as he threw the covers back and stood up from the bed.

'I don't know. My guys got Miss Casey out of there as quickly as possible without waiting to see who was shooting the place up.'

'You think it was the Brits?'

'I don't know. But whoever they are, they are dead. They killed four of my men, including my cousin and they will pay for that,' Newman spat back.

'Where is Miss Casey now?'

'Here with us. She is well guarded.'

'She was well guarded at her house. It's fair to assume if they found her house, then they will find you now, so you need to move her. Put her on the phone,' the chairman demanded, suddenly realising that he was pacing backwards and forwards across the floor.

A moment later, a soft voice said,

'Hello?'

'Are you OK Emma?' he asked.

'Not really. This has got completely out of control. Whoever these people are, they know who I am, and I don't think they are the type of people to ask questions. This is your mess, you've put me in this position,' Casey replied angrily.

'Just calm down,' the chairman replied, 'we will keep you safe and everything will work out just fine.'

'I'm finding it really difficult to share your optimism right now.'

'Do you have somewhere safe that you can go?'

'Perhaps,' she replied, 'But I will go alone. I don't want these men with me; I'm not bringing them into my personal world.'

The chairman pondered this for a moment. So far, the only people that had been attacked were Newman's men and it seemed that they were the ones being followed rather than her. It seemed like a good idea.

'Can you get out of the building any other way than through the front?' he asked, 'In case they have guys watching Newman right now,' he added, quickly explaining his logic.

He heard her ask the question to Newman and then she said,

'Yes I can. And he says that he has a vehicle available for me as well,' she replied.

'When was the last time you spoke to the kid who is carrying out the shooting in New York?' he asked.

'Last night.'

And you are sure that he will go through with it?'

'Yes I am, more sure of him than I was of the other two.'

'We need to shut the site down now; do you have any other way of contacting him?' he asked.

'Everything is on my laptop.'

'OK. Can you contact him?'

'No,' she replied.

'Why not?'

'Because my laptop is at my house, and it will be crawling with cops right now,' she said, 'But I know one hundred per cent that he will go through with it.'

'I'm finding it really difficult to share your optimism right now,' the chairman replied, echoing Casey's own sentiments, 'So I just guess that we will have to keep the faith in each other.'

'You will make the payment as soon as the shooting is carried out?' she asked.

'Yes I will. Also any assistance that I can give you in disappearing after that will be guaranteed. But you have to leave immediately Emma; we can't take the chance of anyone finding you.'

'No you can't,' she said and paused, 'because I will remind you again, if anything happens to me, plans are

in place to reveal to the world whoever is behind this,'
she added assertively.
'I would advise against threatening me Emma,' the
chairman spat back.
'I'm not threatening you.'
'Good.'
'I'm threatening all of you, because I know who you all
are,' she replied.

Ward and Lawson were in the car heading towards the
apartment where Newman was holed up,
'This Casey woman needs putting down,' Lawson said.
Ward ignored him.
He was still trying to piece together who the people
behind this were.
'Imagine if someone did that to her kid brother,' he
added, talking to himself rather than Ward. 'She would
soon realise how evil what she is doing is.'
Ward suddenly turned towards him.
'Say that again?' he said.
'Which part?'
'The last part.'
'I said imagine if someone did that to her brother.'
He pulled out his cell phone and called Tackler,
'Have you found the New York kid yet?' he asked as
soon as Tackler answered.
He listened as Tackler explained how they had drawn a
blank but that no matter what, they were going to find
him.
'Is everything alright?' he asked, noting Tackler's offish
tone to his voice.

'Yes,' Tackler replied, 'I've stopped feeling sorry for myself although I still have the chip on my shoulder,' he replied sarcastically.

Ward had no idea what he was talking about, or why he was being so hostile towards him, and so he just ignored it.

'I need something from you and I need it quickly.'

He explained to Tackler what he needed and all he said in response was,

'I'll text you the details now,' and then he hung up.

'Have they found the kid they are looking for in New York?' Lawson asked.

'No. They now have to look into other States but I don't think they are going to find him.'

'So what the hell are we going to do?' Lawson asked.

Ward felt his cell phone vibrate and he opened the message from Tackler.

'What are we going to do?' Lawson said again.

Ward smiled to himself,

'We are going to find him ourselves Mike,' he said, and he leant forward and typed an address into the car satnav.

FIFTEEN

152 Jane St, Weehawken – New Jersey

Adam Ray opened the bag for the first time. He had
heard his dad leave for work earlier and he had taken the
bag out from under his bed immediately. He had stared
at it for the past fifteen minutes, and knew that as soon
as he unzipped it and felt the cold metal of the weapons
against his hands, that this would become real.
It wasn't just his mum deserting him, and his dad
blaming him that made his life so miserable.
It was the relentless bullying and name calling at school
that made him feel so angry and isolated.
The kids didn't care that they made his life hell, bullies
never did, and he had spent a number of hours telling
'MissFit' that carrying out the shooting at his school
would be the best thing to do, but she had convinced him
that their pact would only work if they both carried out
their crimes in a public place away from school. She had
explained how school shootings were common, and that

they had to be different from the others to live in their forever love.

He knew she was right.

With any luck, some of the kids from his school would be where he was planning on going.

Particularly a girl called Wendy Carrington.

She was the one who had encouraged the boys who were desperate to impress her to humiliate him, three years ago.

He had just spent the previous year coming to terms with the fact that his mom had deserted him, when she had told the boys in his gym class to strip him naked and push him out into the gym hall so that the girls could film him on their cell phones.

Wendy Carrington was the prettiest girl in the school and all of the guys wanted to take her out, but first they would have to earn the right.

If Wendy Carrington said jump, they asked how high. Five of them had pounced on him as he discreetly tried to get changed into his gym kit at the back of the changing room, and they had ripped his pants off and punched him and pinched him until he relinquished the grip that he had on his underwear, and then they took an arm and a leg each, and dragged him out into the gym hall and across to the girls changing rooms, where they all rushed out and filmed it as he was dumped on the floor. As he desperately tried to cover himself up, they punched him and slapped his backside so that he moved his hands away from his genitals to protect himself. The girls all squealed with laughter and continued filming, even when he started crying. The ordeal only stopped when the football coach came in and shouted at everyone to stand back.

The five boys, all athletes and popular, only received two after school detentions as a reprimand, and the videos were sent around to almost everyone in the school and he was called 'Peewee' from that day on.

When he told his father what had happened and how he wanted him to complain to the school, he just said that he needed to be more of a man and fight back and stop being a weak and useless person like his mom.

There was not one person in the world who wanted to stand up for him.

People like Wendy Carrington were the worst. They encouraged others to inflict misery and pain on people, and then stood back, all sweet and innocent, like they were good people.

'MissFit' was right when she said that the world was full of people like Wendy Carrington, who gave the order and then disassociated themselves from the pain and miscry that they caused.

It was not the physical pain or name calling that upset him on a daily basis, it was the laughing.

Not a day passed without him having to endure people laughing at him whenever they saw him in the corridor or in class, and as much as he acted like laughing meant nothing to him, each laugh aimed at him cut through him like a knife.

He was a joke.

He was a pathetic, weak joke that his mom didn't want to be around and his father hated.

He knelt on the floor next to the bag and unzipped it slowly until it was fully open.

The first thing that he removed was a book resting on the top.

It was a Koran. He had heard of the book before and knew that it was something to do with religion but he had no idea what. 'MissFit' had said that it was important that he threw the book into the place that he had decided to strike out at. When he asked why, she had said something about it being a symbol of tolerance and hope which he didn't really understand, but she said that she would be doing the same thing, and so he agreed that he would too.

He placed the book on the floor and leant into the bag and lifted out a handgun. It felt quite heavy. Heavier than he thought it would, even though he had never held a gun in his life. She had told him that every weapon that she would provide would be ready to fire, and so he made a point of not putting his finger on the trigger in case he accidentally fired off a shot. He put the handgun on top of the book. Next, he pulled out a long gun. She had told him that it was a sub machine gun, and when he fired it, all he had to do was squeeze the trigger and move his arm from left to right at the targets and it would take out anything in his line of fire. He thought that this was heavy too, so he stood up and held it out in front of him to see how heavy it would be to use, and he decided that he could manage it.

He placed the machine gun on the floor and pulled out another handgun, identical to the first one and he placed that on the floor next to the machine gun.

Below that there were four bullet magazines. Two of them small, which he knew instantly, were for the handguns, and a longer one, which would obviously go in the machine gun.

But as he had no idea how to change a magazine on a gun he decided against bringing them with him, and so he slid them under his bed and covered them in a blanket. He then put the guns and the book back in the holdall and zipped it up. He lifted the bag onto his shoulder, and while it still felt heavy to him, it was manageable.

Today was the day that everything ended for Adam Ray. No more laughing at him, no more bullying, and no more hate from his dad.

For the first time in a good few years, he felt good about himself.

57 East 57th Street - New York City

The chairman had assembled everyone in the meeting room just after seven that morning. A couple of the committee members were irate after being woken so early, and the atmosphere was a little tense as the last member pulled his chair in and sat down.

'I'm sorry to have woken you so early gentlemen,' he began, 'But we have a problem, and we need to invoke our contingency plan.'

'What's the problem?' the next most senior member asked.

'We have a contingency plan?' the youngest member asked.

'There is always a contingency plan, for every eventuality.'

'What is the problem?' the next most senior member repeated.

'Whoever has been sniffing around, has established that Miss Casey is somehow involved in what has happened. But I am sure that they do not know how she might be involved, and I'm more than sure that they are totally unaware of our existence,' he replied, deliberately using a calm tone to his voice to reassure the committee.

There were a few uneasy glances around the table.

'These two British guys again?' one of the members asked.

The chairman nodded.

'And we still don't know who they are?' he asked.

'We know that they definitely don't belong to any official agency, so that means that whatever they are doing, it's not official,' the chairman replied confidently.

'The CIA do things unofficially,' the youngest member said, shifting very uneasily in his seat as he spoke, 'How do we know it is not them?' he asked.

'Because Senator Lockhart would know if it was them. He has very close ties to the C.I.A. as I guess we do too indirectly.'

'So what is the contingency plan?' the next most senior man asked.

'It's a small inconvenience gentleman, that's all. All of you have to vacate your rooms and move to another hotel. We need to distance ourselves from any link to this at all, so I have made arrangements for you all to move to separate hotels.'

'I don't want to move,' the next most senior member said, 'My wife has just arrived and she will get suspicious.'

'That's fine, I will move instead and you can stay here,' the chairman replied, 'We will meet this evening, at a place to be confirmed after the shooting has taken place, and then tomorrow morning, we can all go our separate ways.'

'Who do you think these Brits could be working for, the British government? They might be pissed at us for past events,' one of the members asked.

'No, Lockhart would know. They can't operate on American soil without our knowledge. Yet another plus to our great constitution,' the chairman replied.

'Why can't Newman find them?' the youngest member asked.

'He hasn't found them yet because up until this morning, he hasn't been looking for them. But now everything has changed.'

'How has it changed?'

'Miss Casey has now gone somewhere safe so Newman can focus solely on finding these two Brits and eliminating them. Up until now, protecting Miss Casey has been his priority,' he replied.

'And how confident are you that Newman will find them?'

'I am very confident. Newman might be a little rough around the edges, and you might disagree with his political views, but he is an exceptional hunter. He will find them,' the chairman replied.

The youngest member looked around the table. He could see that all of the other committee members were satisfied with what the chairman had said, and they even looked relaxed about the new arrangements, and so he instantly felt reassured himself.

'So I suggest you all go and get some breakfast and then pack. The details of your new hotels will be sent to your rooms within the hour. Relax gentlemen; this is just a small inconvenience. Everything is going exactly to plan,' the chairman proclaimed.

All of the members got up from their chairs and left the room in silence. In all the years that he had sat on the committee, as both chairman and member, this was the first time that there had ever been any disruption to their plans, and he didn't like it, and even though he had managed to suppress it and hide it from the rest of the committee, doubt was swimming through every vein in his body. He had decided against putting pressure on Casey to make sure that the third shooting took place, and he had already decided that the second shooting would be enough, although he had not shared this with the committee. There would be no point in risking their identities being revealed, and his tech guy had told him that the 'iamalone' website was now completely shut down, and no one would ever be able to find anything relating to it electronically, ever again.

He picked up the phone on the table and dialled Senator Lockhart's number.

'Hello?' the thick southern drawl answered.

'Do you think that these two Brits could be working for the CIA?' the chairman asked.

'It's unlikely,' Lockhart replied.

'But you don't know that definitively?'

'I spoke to the director and he said that they aren't his guys. But they do all sorts of stuff that even he doesn't know about so I wouldn't say with absolute certainty.'

'But someone must know if they are?'

'There is one guy. But he's way out there on his own. I've never even met him, I just know that everyone avoids getting on his radar like the plague,' Lockhart said.

'You are a United States Senator. He can't be more powerful than you.'

'This guy is even more powerful than the president,' Lockhart replied and laughed.

'Who is he?' the chairman asked, more curious than wary.

'A guy called McNair. But if you think that I am going to call him and ask him about any operatives that he may or may not have running around for him, you can dream on. I'm not bringing myself to his attention.'

'I think after all that we have done for you over the years Senator, it's the least that you can do,' the chairman replied.

'Our arrangement has worked both ways, you've probably done better out of it than me over the years, so think carefully before you go down the route of trying to imply I owe you,' the Senator replied, a threatening tone ringing through his voice.

'I wasn't threatening you,' the chairman replied, desperately trying to pacify the arrogant, ignorant and self-centred politician on the end of the line, 'I'm trying to protect everything that we have for the future.'

'Glad to hear it,' the Senator replied.

"So could you please make the call to see if this McNair man knows who they are? Then if he has no knowledge of them, they will be dead within the hour, and we will be home and dry.'

'I'll think about it,' Lockhart replied, 'But I'll think about it after my breakfast,' he added, and the line went dead.

SIXTEEN

1938 Byrd Road, Tysons - Virginia

Emma Casey arrived at her sister's house in Tysons after negotiating the morning traffic out of the city. She wasn't overly concerned about the time her journey took, as she wanted to make sure that her two nieces had left for school before she arrived. She had called her sister immediately after she had spoken to the chairman and told her that she had a burst water pipe at home, and that she needed somewhere to stay for the night while the plumbers did their work.

Her sister, Lyndsey, was a stay at home mom and she gladly offered to put her up, she felt the company would be nice. Her husband Mark had a good job as an accountant for one of the city's larger law firms, and life was looking good. They lived in a nice house on Byrd Road that had white cladding running around the first floor, and brown brick on the ground floor. There was a Stars and Stripes flag flying on a pole at the front of the house, and Casey told herself once again that if her dream was not to go and live on the Med, then this is the kind of place that she would like to live.

She pulled onto the drive and parked the battered SUV that Newman had given her. She walked up to the front door, saw it was ajar and walked in.

'Hello,' she shouted out.

'In here,' her sister's voice replied.

She stepped into the hallway and walked towards the lounge. She stepped through the door, a big smile on her face, and arms raised, ready to extend them to hug her sister.

And then she froze.

Her sister was sitting down on the sofa with a man sitting on the armchair to her left, pointing a gun at her with a silencer attached to it.

'Sit down,' he said.

She turned to run out of the house and turned straight into a giant looking man, with piercing blue eyes, that she felt herself getting pulled into.

'He said sit down. You had better do as he says,' the man said, his English accent obvious to her.

She turned and walked in and sat down next to her sister.

'I'm sorry,' was all she could say as she took her sister's hand in her own.

Ward studied her for a few moments in silence. She was attractive, and she looked like the sort of woman that is a good person. But he had learnt many times over the years that appearances are very deceptive.

'Who do you think we are?' he asked.

'How did you find my sister?' she asked, using all of her psychology training to appear calm and in control.

Ward ignored her.

She kept glancing over towards Lawson, and he could see her eyes trying to establish who was in charge.

'Who do you think we are?' Ward asked again, equally as calm, but not having to rely on training to be so.

'I have no idea,' she replied, 'But I can see you are British.'

'I'm not British.'

She looked at him confused,

'You sound and look it,' she said.

He ignored her.

'I guess I'm your equal in some ways,' he said.

Casey looked at him blankly.

'I don't like her,' Lawson said as he leant against the door frame, with his muscular arms folded.

'Me neither,' he replied, 'I'm debating whether to kill them both now, and then wait for the kids to get home and kill them too,' he lied.

Lyndsey immediately started begging,

'No, no, no, please don't hurt my girls' she said, tears starting to run down her face and desperation running through her voice.

'Why are you my equal?' Casey asked, desperately trying to distract Ward, and get him away from thinking of her sister and nieces.

He smiled at her.

He hated psychologists. They were so transparent and so obvious to him, but to others they were Gods,

particularly in The States, where it seemed to him that having a problem and charging a fortune to share it went hand in hand.

And in spite of the skills that she thought that she had, he knew he was much smarter.

'I dictate this conversation,' he calmly said, 'And my good friend Mike here doesn't like you,' he added, pointing towards Lawson flippantly.

He watched as her eyes darted between him and Lawson. He could see her desperately trying to think of an angle to approach her situation.

'Nothing you read out of your study books will equip you for what is going to happen over the next ten minutes,' he said, 'Attempting to carry out an on the spot psychological profile on me is a waste of time too.'

She looked into his eyes, and for the first time in her professional life, she couldn't make any sense of what she was seeing. She saw goodness and strength, but she didn't see any hate, and he had a look that she could only describe as determined. As his eyes fixed back on hers, she felt fear run through her body, and she shuddered, but she could not understand exactly what she was afraid of. But whatever this man was, she knew for sure that she would have no chance of being able to manipulate him or distract him.

'And there it is,' he said, 'The realisation that I am way, way smarter than you, and also that killing people to me is like you drinking a glass of water. It's a necessity rather than a pleasure,' he added softly.

'I don't know who you are.'

'I know you don't. And I know that frightens you a great deal.'

'I think we should just kill them now,' Lawson said, slowly screwing his own silencer onto his gun as he spoke.

Lyndsey started sobbing harder.

Casey put her arm around her sister and held her tight.

'Why do you think we are equals?' Ward asked.

'I don't know.'

'I'll explain why,' he said and then paused, 'I have lost count of the number of people that I have killed. How many do you estimate Mike?' he asked Lawson.

'Jesus,' Lawson sighed, 'In the last month alone there must have been ten in New York, at least the same in L.A. and another ten of the Russian guys, so that makes thirty, about one a day?'

Ward counted in his head, Lawson wasn't far off, and it surprised him that it was that many.

'Plus,' Lawson continued, 'The scum bags you killed in Oregon, Dublin and London, and wherever else over the past month, when you were on downtime, must make another ten at least,' he said, feigning an impressed look on his face as he spoke.

'So you see,' Ward said to Casey, 'It's my job and I'm very good at it. You are directly responsible for every death in the mass shootings that you have convinced those kids to carry out, probably about the same number as my last month, so that makes us equal killers.'

Lyndsey looked up at Casey,

'What is he talking about?' she asked through her sobs.

'Yes, tell her Emma. What am I talking about?'

'It's nothing Lynds,' Casey replied, 'She doesn't need to be here, you can take me, and I will tell you what you want to know away from the house.'

'You will tell me anyway,' he replied.

'Don't underestimate me if you harm her,' Casey spat, her previous cool demeanour now completely gone.

'Once I am holding my gun in your niece's faces, after I have blown your sisters face clean off, you will tell me.

Everyone always tells me what I want to know,' he lied, 'So you are overestimating yourself Emma. All you are here is just another line of information to me. You will tell me what I want to know,' he said, still using a soft tone of voice.

She looked into his eyes and she knew that he was a killer without any remorse or distinction between who he killed.

He looked into her eyes and he knew that she was going to tell him everything that she knew without another devious threat needing to be made.

Who's the psychologist now he thought to himself?

'Tell him Emma. Tell him whatever he needs to know and tell him now. The girls come before anything,' Lyndsey said as she pushed Casey's arm away from her shoulder.

Ward smiled at her,

'You don't know who we are, but you know why we are looking for you, don't you?' he asked.

Casey nodded.

'Who is AR?'

She looked at him with surprise on her face.

'Don't be alarmed,' he said, 'We know everything, so for each lie you tell me, your sister gets a bullet,' he added, raising his Glock slightly so it was pointing at Lyndsey's kneecap.

'He's a boy called Adam Ray.'

'Where does he live?'

'Just outside of New York.'

'Where?'

'I don't know.'

Ward could see that she was telling the truth.

'Why can't we find him on any lists in New York State?'
She looked at him blankly,
'I don't understand your question?'
'Our people have searched every school and database where someone with the initials A.R. should be, and there is no sign of him. Why? Does he come from out of State?' he asked slowly, lining his gun up with Lyndsey's knee as he spoke for added effect.
'He's always lived in New York, he told me that,' she said urgently.
He could see she was telling the truth.
'So why can't we find him?'
Suddenly, Casey realised why, her look of realisation was noticed by Ward immediately.
'He had a double barrel surname, he told me that. But when his mom left him and his dad, he dropped his mums name, and goes by the name of just Adam Ray,' she said with such excitement, that Ward thought she was even dumber than he thought.
She believed in that moment that was all Ward wanted to know.
He looked across at Lawson and said,
'Call Nicole-Louise and Tackler right now, give them the name and tell them we need an address immediately.'
Lawson nodded and walked out of the room.
'That's a good start Emma. You might survive this ordeal after all,' he said and smiled a warm smile at her.
'Tell him anything he needs to know Em, I mean it,' Lyndsey said.
'Clearly you are the smart sibling,' he said, 'And just so you know, if you need any more persuasion, right now, one of my guys is holding a gun to the face of your other

sister Brittany in Philadelphia, so one wrong answer or lie and your whole family will vanish,' he lied.

Lyndsey started sobbing hysterically, and she turned to her side and slapped Casey hard around the face,

'How can you put us in this position you selfish bitch?' she screamed at her.

'I'm so sorry,' was all that Casey could muster in response.

'Where is he planning on carrying out this shooting?' Ward asked.

'I don't know,' she replied, 'He wanted to do it at his school, but I told him that it had to be in a public place where a cross section of people would be.'

'I found your laptop, and I know the organisation that is behind this, but I don't understand why?' he said, 'I mean, there is no direct and guaranteed gain from it happening.'

'You saw the file called 'Gun'?' she asked.

Ward nodded.

'The information in that file is incorrect. I wrote that two years ago, before I understood the enormity of this. It's not one organisation, it's all of them. It's a committee.'

He thought about what she had just said, he thought about the use of the Koran in the shootings, and how that was designed to prevent fear and panic. He thought about the vulnerability that parents would feel packing their kids off to school, and he thought about the involvement of a Senator and piece by piece, the information fell into the correct order, and he now had a clear and precise picture of exactly what was happening and why.

He leant back in the chair.

'Now I understand the whole thing,' he said calmly, 'I just need the names of the committee and you have given me what I need.'

'I don't know their names, just the most important person.'

'Then tell me from the beginning.'

Emma Casey went on to explain about how she had helped the Chairman's family, and how he had persuaded her to use her skills to manipulate the kids to carry out the atrocities. Her sister sat there listening, open mouthed and shaking her head in disbelief. By the time that she had finished explaining her involvement and what she knew, her sister had stood up and moved across to the chair next to Ward, her disgust clearly evident in her face.

'Is that everything?' Ward asked.

'Yes. I promise. That is it from start to finish.'

'You forgot to mention the money, the one and a half million dollars that was deposited in your account?'

Casey looked down to the floor in shame.

Ward looked at her sister, who was sitting glaring at her, open-mouthed,

'It's always about money and greed,' he said to her, 'At least a terrorist has something to believe in. People like your sister are worse.'

Lyndsey slowly nodded in agreement.

'But anyway,' he continued, 'The money is mine now, I've stolen it, and maybe it can contribute to the funerals of those poor kids who died in Missouri?'

Before she could respond, Lawson burst in through the door,

'We have the address,' he said urgently, 'He's in New Jersey.'

'On your feet,' Ward said to Casey, 'You are coming with us.'

She stood up and looked at her sister who turned away from her.

'You can call the cops if you want, but it will come out that you are guilty by association to your sister, and that will not be a good thing for your kid's future. So think hard about doing that,' he said, 'And if you decide to call them, they won't be able to touch us; we are way, way above the law. So do the right thing for your kids and disown your sister from the moment we walk out of the room,' he added, and then he grabbed Casey's arm and marched her out of the room.

Lyndsey broke down and started crying hysterically.

SEVENTEEN

Washington D.C.

Centrepoint answered his phone immediately,
'I take it you have news for me?' he asked.
'We've found the kid in New York. I need the jet ready.
We are on our way to the airport,' Ward replied.
'And you know what is happening now?'
'Partly.'
'Who is behind it?'
'I haven't got that far into this yet so I don't know. My
only focus right now is stopping the kid from carrying
out this shooting, and then we can hunt those responsible
after that,' he lied.
'Are you still adamant that this whole string of events
isn't politically motivated?'
'Why do you ask that?' Ward enquired, genuine
confusion in his voice.
'Because Senator Lockhart left a message for me to call
him back early this morning.'

'So why is that linked to this?'

'I'm not sure it is, but everyone on Capitol Hill does their very best to steer clear from me. The last time that I had any contact from those in the Senate was when Yeschenko was on the scene, and we both know how that turned out,' The Old Man replied, referring to a recent operation that Ward had conducted in Los Angeles.

'He's the guy asking about me and Lawson?'

'Yes. He's one of those Senators that never courts controversy and he stays well below the radar. I would suggest that if he has had to call me, he is probably involved somewhere along the line.'

'Which State does he represent?'

'Louisiana.'

'How long has he been a senator?'

'Since nineteen eighty-four.'

'And you've got no dirt on him?' Ward asked.

'I've got dirt on all of them Ryan, that's why they avoid me. But his are just the usual unsolicited sexual and bribery rumours.'

'Are any of them proved?'

'He's not important enough to dig to find if they are proven or not. But I will get on that now.'

'I have the woman with me who has been manipulating the kids; I'm bringing her back with me to New York.'

'Bringing her back to do what with her?'

'Help me undo as much of this as we can and to make those behind it pay. The Optician is watching an apartment here in Washington, can you tell him that he can do whatever he wants with the men inside?' Ward asked.

'You know that he will need to be in New York with you, so I'll call him now and pass on your message. As soon as I find out what Senator Lockhart wants, I'll get back to you.'

Ward hung up the phone.

He pressed speed dial and Nicole-Louise answered immediately,

'As soon as Mike called us, Tackler found this kid within two minutes so you owe him big-time Ryan,' she said, without offering any greeting.

He realised why Tackler had been so off with him earlier, and why Nicole-Louise was now making such a big deal of the work that Tackler had done. He cursed himself for not thinking about it earlier. Tackler wasn't cut from the same cloth as people like him, and he imagined that he had spent his whole teenage life being bullied, mainly due to his less than powerful physique, until Nicole-Louise had come into his life and given him the confidence that he needed to grow.

'I'm so sorry,' he replied, 'He was bullied badly, wasn't he? I mean I assumed he was uncomfortable with this because he had been bullied, but I didn't realise how bad it was. Was it more than one person or just one?'

'No. He just found the one name,' she replied, indicating to him that Tackler was probably sitting within ten feet of her.

'Do you want me to kill him?'

Nicole-Louise was unsure if he was serious or not, and so she chose to ignore the question.

'I won't mention anything about that but I need to speak to him, I need his expertise,' he said.

He heard Nicole-Louise passing the phone to him,

'Yes?' Tackler curtly said.

'We are on our way back to New York and should be there in a couple of hours,' he said, 'I need two things from you.'

'Go on?'

'I need to know everything about a Senator called Lockhart from Louisiana. I want you to dig deep and find anything in his past, or financial records, that indicates he's bad.'

'He's a Senator, they are all bad,' Tackler replied flippantly, 'What else?'

'Can you establish where the mass shootings have taken place since nineteen eighty-four until now?'

'Is there anything else?'

'Yes,' Ward replied, 'What have I done to upset you?'

There was silence on the line for a few moments and then Tackler said,

'You told me to stop feeling sorry for myself and get that chip off of my shoulder. It's alright for you Ryan, I doubt anyone has ever frightened you in your life. You think you can just shrug off fear and anxiety if you are normal like me?' he asked. There was hostility in his voice.

Ward knew that he had definitely not said that to him, but he realised straight away that Nicole-Louise had probably told him that he had said those words to get him refocused on finding the kid in New Jersey.

So he played along.

'I'm sorry,' he replied, 'I was under a lot of pressure in the field and I took you for granted. But you certainly are not normal.'

'Hilarious Ryan,' Tackler replied sarcastically.

'No. You are misunderstanding me.' he said, 'You are one of the strongest and most important people that I know, and I would die protecting you both. You are also one of the few people in the world who I call my friend, one of my best friends and sometimes, because you are so good at what you do, and you solve problems for me so easily, I take that as a given.'

There was silence on the line for a few seconds.

'This is just hard for me. It brings back a lot of bad memories,' Tackler replied.

'Do you want me to kill the person in question?'

'Believe me,' Tackler replied, 'I have thought about that so many times over the past few years. I have imagined giving you some misinformation so you take him out, but I couldn't live with that on my conscience, and so I will just have to let it go. But thank you.'

Ward had never been in the habit of killing innocent people, but whoever this person was, a reprimand of some kind, would quell the anger that someone who had tormented Tackler, was making him feel.

'And you are my best friend too,' Tackler said, 'Ouch!' he then screamed, 'Second best friend after Nicole-Louise,' he added quickly.

Ward smiled.

'I'll see you when we are back,' he said and he hung up the phone.

'Tell me something?' he said, as he put his cell phone back in his pocket and turned to look at Emma Casey, who by now was sitting on the back seat of the car with her hands cable tied behind her back, 'How many other shootings have you been involved in?'

Emma Casey did not reply, she just pursed her lips and looked down at her lap.

Ward smiled,

'It doesn't matter how determined you are feeling now; you will tell me. Everyone tells me what I need to know in the end.'

She looked up at him. There were tears in her eyes.

'You are only crying because you've been caught,' he said, seeing the tears run down her cheeks, 'The only thing that will stop your tears, is helping me to put this right.'

'I think those tears are of fear. Fear for her future in jail,' Lawson said, as he sped towards Dulles airport, with little or no consideration for the other drivers on the road.

'She won't be going to jail if she doesn't help me,' Ward said.

Casey darted a look at him and so he continued.

'I have my men rounding up your sister and her kids right now, and Brittany is already in our custody,' he said, and then exaggerated a big smile when she looked into his eyes, 'And here's what I am going to do. I will shoot their faces off, one at a time, and make you watch until you tell me everything that I want to know. As I said, everyone always tells me what I want to know in the end.'

He always found the threat of hurting a person's family to be the most effective way to get them to speak. The reality was, he would never resort to harming an innocent person, and the idea of him ever harming a child was preposterous. But needs must, and right then, he needed to put this all together so that he could ensure that it never happened again.

He felt his phone vibrate in his pocket.

He pulled it out and saw it was a message from Tackler.

He opened it up and a simple bar chart appeared showing where the mass shootings in America had taken place since nineteen eighty-four, how many people were killed and how many were injured.

He looked down the list and saw exactly what he thought he would see. He smiled to himself.

He knew exactly what was happening now, regardless of Casey helping him or not.

'I have just one question,' he said as he turned to face Casey again,

She looked up at him.

'The most recent shooting was in Orlando, I know that was nothing to do with you, the guy who did that was an idealist and a terrorist, so prior to that, last year, do you know where the previous shooting was carried out?' he asked.

'It was in San Bernardino,' she replied.

'Were you involved in that?'

'No. I got involved in this about two months after that.'

'So how do you know about it?'

'Because I was told to study it to make sure.'

'Sure of what?' he asked.

'To make sure that I would not make the same mistakes as the guy who did that, and leave any trace that could lead people like you to me,' she replied.

Ward looked her up and down and shook his head.

'And how did that work out for you?' he asked, as he
turned back around in his seat to face the road just as
Dulles International airport was coming into sight.

Centrepoint's desk phone rang and he knew that it would
be Senator Lockhart.
So he let it ring ten times.
He knew by the fact the phone kept ringing that the
Senator was desperate about something.
He picked it up.
'Speak,' he said curtly, deliberately trying to put the
Senator on the back foot from the start.
'Is that Mr McNair?' Lockhart asked in a thick, southern
accent that immediately irritated The Old Man.
'Yes. Speak,' he repeated.
'My name is Senator Wilson Lockhart; you may or may
not have heard of me.'
'You will already know that I know everything about
you Senator, more than anyone else knows, and that is
why you are nervous about calling me. I'm a busy man,
so tell me what you want?'
'I'm just after a quick favour for a friend of a friend, and
I'm wondering if you could help me with it?'
'What kind of favour?'
'I just want some information. I would appreciate the
help and I will be in your debt.'
'You are already in my debt with the information that I
have on you" Centrepoint said, trying his best to sound
smug as he spoke, 'But tell me what the information is?'
'It's about a couple of guys who are running around
Washington I want to know if you have any idea who

they are?' Lockhart asked, confirming to him that he was involved in this much deeper than initially thought.

'Have you asked the Feds and the CIA?'

'I have, and they say they aren't their guys.'

'Why do you want to know who these men are?'

'I don't know,' Lockhart replied, 'A friend asked me as a favour to see what I could find out,' he added nervously.

'What friend?'

'I respect your need to protect your sources, please do the same for me.'

'But you are the one coming to me for help. It's a simple question,' The Old Man said flippantly.

'It's a friend of a friend of mine. But I don't know why he wants to know,' Lockhart replied, trying his best to distance himself from the chairman, but failing miserably.

'What men are you looking for?'

'Two British guys in Washington.'

Centrepoint looked at his watch and then his screen. He could see that the jet carrying Ward, Lawson and unbeknown to them, The Optician, had taken off eleven minutes ago on their way back to New York.

'I know of them,' he replied, being as vague as he could to see just how much Lockhart wanted to know who they were.

'Do you know what they want?'

'No. They are out of my jurisdiction,' he lied, 'The Brits have their reasons for sending them here, reasons that they don't want to share with us, and we have to respect that. They afford us the same anonymity when we work over there.'

'So, whoever they are, and whatever they want, you have no idea what, but you know of their existence?" Lockhart asked, seeking the clarification that he needed for the chairman.

'In a nutshell, yes,' Centrepoint replied, 'But whatever they are looking for, your friend of a friend, must have pissed the Brits off, and that's never a wise move.'

'Do you know who these two men are?' Lockhart asked.

'Yes I do.'

'Do you know where they are?'

'Yes I do.'

'I would really appreciate you helping me here. If you help me now, you can call in a favour in return at any time you want.'

'I want two favours in return.'

'You drive a hard bargain Mr McNair, your reputation precedes you, but OK, deal, I will owe you two favours,' Lockhart replied, desperation now ringing through his words.

'Their names are Ryan Ward and Mike Lawson. And they are on their way to New York as we speak,' Centrepoint replied.

EIGHTEEN

38 W 31st Street – New York

Lawson's new apartment was above a parade of shops
on West 31st street. For the past two days, the decorators
had been adding the finishing touches, and the rest of
furniture would be arriving any day. The apartment
building had a lot of character. It had a smooth, rendered
front, which gave it an old concrete looking effect, and
the building curved around the corner and reminded
Ward of the coliseum in Rome. The more he looked at it,
the more he was sure that the architect who designed the
building had recently been to Rome himself.
Lawson wasn't best pleased with the fact that Ward had
told him that he would have to secure Emma Casey in
his apartment.
As he pulled the car up outside, he was still complaining,
'It's just wrong Ryan,' he moaned, 'My first night in my
newly decorated place, and I had intended to invite some

of my friends over to christen it, not looking after this piece of trash.'

Casey sat in the back of the car, clearly offended.

'Can't we just shoot her now and dump her body somewhere?' Lawson asked in as serious a tone as he could muster.

Ward looked straight ahead and smiled to himself.

'Just secure her in the apartment and then come back down, we have work to do,' he replied.

'I don't like her,' Lawson said as he opened the car door and stepped out, and then as he opened the rear door to pull her out of the vehicle, he said, 'I'm so frustrated.'

He watched Lawson frog-march Casey into the building entrance. He studied her, she was pretty, and she was sexy, probably the type of girl that Lawson would go for perhaps.

He knew she would definitely go for him, all women, apart from Nicole-Louise and Eloisa, did.

Thinking about Eloisa made him want to talk to her and so he pulled out his cell phone and dialled her number. It went straight to voicemail, and so he left a message saying that he was back in New York and that they would meet up later.

Their next visit was to New Jersey, hopefully to stop AR in time, The Old Man had arranged for the NYPD to watch Adam Ray's house, and they had confirmed that no one had yet left the building, and that he was still inside. Ward then had a thought and so he immediately dialled Lawson's number.

'What?' Lawson answered.

'Bring her back down,' he said and hung up the phone.

Two minutes later, Casey was sitting back in the car.

'Make your mind up,' Lawson said.
'Head over to New Jersey,' he instructed Lawson.
Lawson started the car and pulled away,
'Why is she coming with us?' Lawson asked.
"Because she can talk to this AR kid and tell her that everything she said was a lie, and then if he blows her away, tough,' he replied, 'And I want her to see the real kid behind the name and see what she has created.'
Casey started quietly sobbing once more,

152 Jane St, Weehawken – New Jersey

The journey over to Adam Ray's house in New Jersey took just over 30 minutes. They turned the corner onto Jane Street and they drove past his house slowly. The NYPD were doing a good job of keeping off the streets, and the only clue that something might be happening was a police car parked at the side of the road about a hundred yards up from the house.
'Pull in here,' Ward said, and Lawson promptly responded by swerving the car violently to the right and crossing the road before coming to a stop about thirty yards up from Adam Ray's house.
'The Old Man has definitely cleared this I take it?' he asked him.
'Yes. There is a SWAT team on site and he has informed them that like Kyle, you are making the call here,' Lawson replied.
Ward nodded,

'Wait here,' he said over his shoulder to Casey as he opened the car door and stepped out, Lawson joined him a split second later.

Lawson locked the car and said to Ward,

'This is probably the one occasion that I do advise on knocking on the door and introducing yourself.'

Ward nodded and he started heading back along the sidewalk towards the house.

He noticed the three SWAT guys hiding directly opposite the house immediately. They were crouched down behind a small bush with their eyes glued to the scopes on their guns. The guy nearest to them took his eye away from his scope and looked at them as they approached the path up to Adam Ray's door, and Ward nodded. The guy nodded back.

He raised his head and he saw the heads of four guys on the rooftops of the buildings opposite, and the statutory cable TV van was parked outside the house two doors up from Adam Ray.

No doubt the command centre he thought.

They reached the end of Adam Ray's path and paused for a moment,

'You wait here at the end Mike, let me talk to the kid first,' he said.

Lawson nodded and watched as Ward slowly started walking up the path to meet Adam Ray.

57 East 57th Street - New York City

The chairman had just packed the last of the things into his suitcase when his phone rang.

He saw Senator Lockhart's name appear on the screen, and he was hoping that he had some good news for him. The inconvenience of him having to leave the hotel for new accommodation a few blocks away had put him in a very bad mood.

'I hope you have good news Senator,' he said as he answered.

'I might just have that,' Lockhart replied, 'But first I want something from you.'

'I think I have given you more than enough over the years, don't you?' the chairman asked, as he started to feel a little irked by Lockhart's tone of voice.

'But what I have now is probably more valuable than anything we have ever exchanged, so I think that renegotiation is called for.'

'You know who the Brits are?'

'Yes I do. Their names, and who they work for and also, where they are now,' Lockhart replied smugly.

'What do you want?'

'I want the evidence that you have on the agreement that we made two years ago.'

'That's my security, if I give that up; I've lost my biggest bargaining chip. I haven't made a fortune by being stupid.'

'But that won't be any use to you dead, and from what I have found out, that is a pretty likely scenario.'

'You first,' the chairman said.

'No,' Lockhart replied firmly, 'I want all the evidence that you have on me brokering the arms sale to Samone through the CIA and then we will talk.'

The chairman was in a corner and he didn't like it. He had firm evidence that Senator Wilson Lockhart had sold arms to an African Warlord called Samson Samone, and although he had a long standing relationship with Lockhart, he liked having a little leverage over him.

But right now, his priority was to find the two Brits and stop them getting closer to him.

'Ok Senator, you have my word. I trust that is guarantee enough that I will have it delivered to you by tomorrow morning.'

'Your word is always sufficient Darren,' Lockhart replied.

'Now, tell me what you know?'

'They are two British guys called Ward and Lawson. I have some CIA people digging on them now and they have found out about this Lawson guy, he's ex-SAS, but this Ward guy seems to be a ghost.'

'A ghost?' he exclaimed

'Yes like he doesn't exist.'

The chairman was quiet for a few moments, trying to fathom out why an ex-SAS soldier would be involved with what they had planned.

'But until two months ago, Lawson worked for MI6 in London, now he is no longer on their books,' Lockhart quickly added.

'Are they working for MI6?'

'It looks that way, although out of some warped respect thing, our intelligence bosses turn a blind eye to it and ask no questions. Have you pissed off the Brits?'

The chairman thought hard. Apart from one British guy called Atkins, who dealt with finances, he had not encountered a British guy directly through his business activities in the past twenty years.

'No, I haven't,' he eventually replied.

'Well, they are causing trouble for you for some reason. Are you sure that you haven't tried your game in Britain?'

'No, I haven't. There would be no gain.'

'Then you need to do something about them and quickly before they find you,' Lockhart said.

'Where in Washington are they?'

'They aren't in Washington.'

'Where are they?'

'They are in New York. Isn't that where you are?'

It had to be a coincidence, the chairman thought. Perhaps they had found out who the kid who was going to shoot up New York, and they were trying to prevent that from happening, like they did with the other kid, there is no way that they could get close to him without Emma Casey.

'That's not all,' Lockhart said, 'They flew from Dulles almost five hours ago and they weren't alone.'

'What do you mean, they weren't alone?' the chairman asked, panic setting into his voice now.

'They had a woman with them. And apparently, my man at the CIA. said that his operative told him that she seemed to be a prisoner rather than with them.'

The chairman went white.

'So,' Lockhart continued, 'That concludes our business. I expect you to keep your word and have the evidence with me by tomorrow morning Darren.'

'It will be there,' the chairman confirmed and he hung up the phone.

He tried Casey's cell phone but it went straight to voicemail and so he hung up.

He then called the next senior member of the committee.

'Hello?'

'I need to see you urgently. Are the others still here?'

'No. They all left about half an hour ago. What's wrong?'

'Come to my room, quickly,' he said and hung up the phone.

Three minutes later, the next senior member of the committee was standing inside his room.

'We have a problem,' the chairman said, and then continued to explain the conversation that he had just had with Lockhart in great detail.

'We haven't done anything to risk the wrath of the Brits.'

'I know that. So why would they be trying to hunt us down?' the chairman asked.

'Maybe it's not us they want; maybe it's just the girl or even just you?'

The chairman thought about what he had just heard. Without Emma Casey, they had nothing, and so what he needed to do was to find out what she had told them.

He picked up his phone and called Newman.

There was no ring tone and no facility to leave voicemail, a recorded message just said that the number was not available.

'That idiot is running around Washington while he is meant to be protecting the girl,' the chairman spat,

'She's here in New York and he has lost her,' he added.

'I did advise you against using Newman and his men months ago.'

'That's not helping Kenneth.'

He thought for a few moments and then he said,

'We will carry on as planned. We will wait for the shooting to happen, and then we will convene our meeting as planned at six. I will change the location. At this moment in time, we only have theories, nothing concrete, so let's see what happens. The woman that they had with them might not even be Casey,' he said, the last comment reassuring him to such an extent that he felt back in control once more.

'That's all,' he added, "I'll see you at six. I'll let you know where,' and with that, he turned and walked into the bathroom.

NINETEEN

152 Jane St, Weehawken – New Jersey

Ward walked slowly up the path towards the tatty, red
front door of Adam Ray's house. He had his Glock
firmly placed into the waistband of his pants, and the
only thoughts that were running through his head were
what Adam Ray would look like. He pictured a slight
kid, not too tall, and probably wearing glasses. He was
sure that there would be no need for firearms and that his
presence would be enough to make the kid crumble, just
as Kyle Newson had.

When he had climbed the four steps to the door, he
knocked four times in quick succession and waited.
Through the frosted glass, he could see a shadow appear
for a few seconds and then disappear again.

And so he knocked again.

He turned and looked behind him. Lawson was standing at the end of the path, and he could see that the NYPD police cruisers were now blocking the road off, fifty yards in each direction. The SWAT guys behind the bush were clearly visible now and in a few seconds, he had counted seven uniformed officers who were now gathering on the street.

As he turned back to face the door, out of the corner of his eye, he saw the curtain in the window to his right move slightly.

He cursed the NYPD. If the kid had seen all of the activity on the street, he might panic, and in his fragile state of mind, he might come out shooting or put a bullet in his head.

He knocked once more, the same friendly four knocks in quick succession, and quickly spun around again and using the back of his hand, waved the officers off of the street.

They all either didn't see him, or they chose to ignore him. Whichever one it was, he noticed that they continued walking in the crouched position, with their guns drawn, towards the front yard.

There was still no answer and so he pushed the letter box slightly open and peered through it.

He could see a blue zipper bag on the floor at the bottom of the stairs, and a pair of old sneakers next to the bag, but that was about it.

'Adam Ray,' he shouted through the letter box, 'My name is Ryan. I want to talk to you.'

There was no reply but he could clearly hear movement from inside the house, like a rustling sound coming from the left.

'I know you are in there; I can hear you. You aren't in trouble… yet.'

He waited a few more seconds and there was still no reply.

'MissFit is not real,' he said, sure that he would get a response at the mention of her name.

'She is trying to use you to kill someone that she wants dead, and she is a thirty-three-year-old woman who has taken advantage of your situation,' he continued in as calm a tone as anyone could when shouting through a letterbox.

Adam Ray eventually spoke.

'I don't believe you,' a voice which sounded like it hadn't yet broken, shouted back.

Ward thought back to his conversation with Casey and then said,

'I know that she didn't want you to carry out the shooting at school, and that she wanted it done in a public place. I know she sent you pictures of a girl that isn't her, and I know that she has made a pact with you. But she isn't waiting in Los Angeles, waiting to carry out a shooting at the same time as you; she's sitting in my car fifty yards down the road.'

A few seconds later, he saw Adam Ray for the first time. He wasn't slight in build; he was about six feet tall. He looked like he was carrying only a few extra pounds, he was African American, and he looked like the type of kid that played football and was popular.

He was the exact opposite to what he thought he would look like.

'Do you want to let me in?'

'Are you English?' Adam Ray asked.

He didn't want to add any more confusion to Adam Ray's mind by explaining that he considered himself both British and American so he kept it simple.

'Yes I am,' he replied.

'Are you a shrink or something?'

'No I'm not.'

"So who are you and why are you trying to trick me?"

He was fully aware that Adam Ray was in a fragile place with a confused state of mind, and that by saying the wrong thing, he could set the kid into a state of panic and then he would become unpredictable.

Right now, he had established a dialogue with him and he wanted to keep it as simple and as stress free for the kid as he could.

'I work for both governments. When a delicate situation arises, they call me in,' he replied, 'Right now, my first job is to make you see sense and after that, I have to find out why the people behind Emma Casey want you to do what they are trying to make you to do.'

'Who's Emma Casey?'

'She is the woman pretending to be MissFit.'

He wasn't going to take the risk of lying to the kid; it was easier to deal with Adam Ray's self-denial than it would be to deal with him knowing that he had lied to him.

'You haven't done anything wrong yet. Right now, we are willing to help you. You won't even go to jail. But that is all dependent upon you opening the door.'

'You will arrest me?'

'I won't. But the police will, but I promise they will understand, they know this isn't your fault.'

He watched as the expression on Adam Ray's face softened and he started to look very scared, like the realisation of what he had intended to do had hit home, so he continued,

'The bag next to you, I know what's in it. Pick the bag up, open the door; drop the bag out and no one will hurt you. I give you my word. Then I will put you in the care of the right people.'

Adam Ray's shoulders dropped,

'Will you let me talk to her before they take me away?' he asked.

'Yes I will.'

'Promise?'

'I promise.'

Adam Ray bent down and picked the bag up. Ward could see it was unzipped and he caught a glimpse of a gun sticking out of the top.

'Just pass it out of the door and this is over,' he said, feeling relieved that just as with Kyle Newson, this was going to have a happy ending.

And then in just four short seconds, the whole situation turned into Ward's worst nightmare.

As Adam Ray picked the bag up, a handgun fell onto the wooden floor, landing with a loud thump. He bent down and picked up the gun, holding it loosely in his right hand. He stepped towards the door and Ward caught a glimpse of a guy dressed in full combat fatigues, come into view behind Adam Ray, with his gun raised and his right eye fixed on his scope.

'Stop!' he shouted, 'Back off,' he screamed at the guy behind Adam Ray, and as the last echo of his voice tailed away, he heard four deafening shots ring out.

The bullets smashed into Adam Ray's back and his body arched forward and he dropped the bag and the gun as he let out a sickening scream which was so high pitched that it could only belong to a child.

Adam Ray's body lunged forward and the last thing Ward saw as he peered through the letter box was Adam Ray's contorted face lunging towards the door, and then he heard a loud thump as his face made contact with the wood.

And then for a few seconds everything went quiet.

The silence was broken by people screaming behind him, and he turned to see literally every cop or SWAT guy that was out on the street descending towards the house. Within twenty seconds, there were over twenty cops in the front garden.

'Step back,' a guy in SWAT gear said to him as he reached the steps.

He resisted the urge to smash the guy in the throat as he felt the anger starting to rise inside of him, and he stepped aside.

The door was opened from the inside and he saw Adam Ray's crumpled, lifeless body on the floor. He stood still, looking at the body for a few seconds and then he felt a hand on his shoulder.

He turned to see Lawson standing beside him, shaking his head,

'How can those idiots get it so dramatically wrong?' Lawson asked.

Ward ignored him and looked over his shoulder at the cops, who by now were almost filling the small front yard.

'Who's in charge?' he shouted to no one in particular.

A guy in his early fifties stepped forward.

'I am,' he shouted from fifteen feet away, 'Captain Ronan Gray, New Jersey State police,' he added, in a tone which Ward knew was meant to impress him.

'You received instructions that I was in charge and made all the calls here?'

'Yes, but that went out of the window the moment the kid picked up a gun,' Gray replied.

'How did you know he picked up the gun?' Ward asked calmly.

'Because my SWAT guy told me so I gave him the go ahead to shoot.'

'Who sent the SWAT guy in?'

'I did. I have an obligation and a duty to cover all of the angles. This is my jurisdiction zone.'

Lawson leant into Ward,

'He's just doing his job. However bad he is at it, they are just regular guys doing their jobs,' he said.

Ward respected the work that the police did, in fact he respected all of the emergency services for what they did, even more so after 9/11, but one thing that he had come to learn about the law enforcement chiefs in both America and Britain, was that the people in charge were normally the most inept and inadequate, and they had got where they were by being good at nothing but kissing ass.

He could never respect people like that.

He walked down the steps and across to Gray,

'Which part of you not making any move until I said so didn't you understand?' he asked calmly.

He looked at the other officers who were milling around the garden and they looked visibly shocked. He was sure that well over half of them had kids the same age as Adam Ray, and that knowing he had just been killed by one of their own would not be sitting comfortably with them.

'This is my area. I was instructed to extend you the courtesy of taking control, but as soon as it looked like it was going out of control, I am legally entitled to step in,' Gray replied.

'And then put your face all over the news, saying what a disaster you have averted?' Ward said, 'You are a career cop, no more than that. Every decent, guy here thinks you are incompetent and an ass kisser.'

Gray looked stunned. He was clearly not used to people talking to him in that manner, and he was unsure of exactly who Ward was, other than his bosses boss had instructed that this British guy called all the shots, and he held seniority over the police department.

'I followed procedure,' Gray replied, sounding as though he was trying to convince himself of the fact much more than he was Ward.

Standing two feet away from him, he could see that he was both arrogant and condescending by the way that he held his overweight frame and his arms rested on his hips.

Without saying another word, he swung a lightning quick uppercut with his right hand and connected flush in the dead centre of Gray's throat.

His knees buckled and he fell to the floor, desperately clutching at his throat.

The officers in the garden and even the SWAT guys who were now coming out of the house stood still, unsure what to do.

'He's just doing his job,' Lawson reiterated once more.

'You won't have a job by the end of today,' Ward said to Gray, who now, was managing to get a small amount of air into his lungs, 'I'll make sure of that,' he added, and he walked down the path. As he stepped onto the sidewalk from Adam Ray's house, a cop who was in his late forties, looked at him and winked,

'Well done,' he whispered, 'That is what we have wanted to do for the past six years.'

Ward ignored him.

They headed back towards the car.

'Casey will now tell us everything, even if I have to torture her to get it out of her,' Ward said, 'That poor kid is dead because of her.'

They got to within ten feet of the car and stopped.

The car was where they had left it.

The cops that were positioned near the car and were looking over it when they arrived, were all now in Adam Ray's front yard.

And Emma Casey was gone.

TWENTY

28 West 53rd Street – New York

The chairman had only just opened the mini bar in his room at the Baccarat Hotel when his phone rang.
He saw Newman's name on the phone,
'Where have you been? I've been trying to get hold of you,' he shouted, 'You need to get to New York and quick, I am furious that you have lost Emma.'
'You need to relax a little. You underestimate me and my men and I don't like it,' Newman spat back.
'I think I overestimated you.'
'I have her with me, so get off of your high horse and treat me with some respect.'
'You have her with you? Where are you?'
'Yes I do, and we are in New York already. We let the Brits take her to see what we could find out about them,'

Newman lied, 'As I said, we are much smarter than you think we are.'

'I'm sorry for underestimating you,' the chairman said, relief rushing through his voice, 'Is she safe? What did they get from her?'

'I don't know yet. I only collected her ten minutes ago.'

'Where was she?'

'I'll let her explain,' he said, and the chairman heard her soft voice a few seconds later,

'Hello?'

'Are you OK Emma?'

'Not really. You need to get someone over to my sister's house to make sure that they don't get hurt. Until you do that, I won't tell you anything,' she replied sternly.

'Will the shooting go ahead?'

'No,' Casey replied, 'They found him and they have stopped it. That's where Newman rescued me from. They took me to his house so he could confront me. This has all gone wrong and I need to disappear.'

Under the circumstances, her disappearing was a good idea. He would have Newman kill her, but he knew that she was smart, and if he did, she would have pre-arranged a way of dropping him in it with the authorities and he could not take that chance. He was also slightly relieved that the New York shooting had not happened as well, it would take the heat off of the committee and the Brits, whoever they were, might even run back to London with their tails between their legs.

His thoughts were suddenly interrupted,

'They've stolen my money as well so you need to refund that. It's you and the others they are after, not me, it's the least you can do,' she said.

Under the circumstances, he would have to agree to it, just so he could get rid of her. It was a small price to pay for silence. He was well aware how important it was to keep her sweet,

'That's fair enough,' he replied, 'I'll round it up to two million dollars as a gesture of goodwill.'

'Thank you.'

'I need Newman to bring you to me here at the hotel, so we can go over what you know. I will get him to send a couple of men to your sisters immediately. Is that OK?'

'Yes, that's fine,' Casey replied.

'Put Newman back on.'

'I'm here,' Newman said immediately.

'Bring her to me at the Baccarat Hotel, room 4256. Find out where her sister lives, and get a couple of guys over there to keep an eye on things,' he demanded.

'Will do,' Newman replied and the line went dead.

He poured himself a malt whisky from the mini-bar and sat down in the plush, leather armchair, with his laptop resting on his knees.

He clicked on the company's website and selected 'Missouri' from the drop down menu.

As the screen changed to a sheet with numbers on, he leant back deeper into the armchair, raised his glass to the empty room in a toast and smiled to himself.

Business was good.

Park Avenue – New York

Ward had hardly spoken since he had arrived at Nicole-Louise's and Tacklers apartment. On the journey from

New Jersey, he had called The Old Man and explained what had happened, and how if something wasn't done about Captain Gray then he would kill him himself. Centrepoint had assured him that he would be demoted to a beat cop by the end of the day. He had also asked him to put a couple of men on Casey's sister's house, in the unlikely event that she returned there. He knew that when he had threatened the lives of her sisters and Lyndsey's children, that she believed him, and if she was that important to whomever was behind this, she might insist that her sister is taken somewhere safe.

Lawson tried striking up a conversation with him on numerous occasions, but eventually gave up and decided to let him think things through.

He knew that Ward's mind would now be going into overdrive, trying to piece everything together, and the one thing he did know was that when Ward was under pressure, calm always washed over him, and he seemed to develop a clarity that very few people possess.

Eventually, Ward snapped back into the zone.

'OK,' he said, 'There are three questions that I have that if we find the answers to, we solve this.'

Nicole-Louise and Tackler both sat and stared at him, waiting patiently for any instructions that might be coming their way, and Lawson strode across the room and sat down next to him on the sofa.

'Firstly, Wilson Lockhart is involved, but we don't know why. Dig into his life and find a link to this, however small, there will be something,' he said.

Tackler immediately spun around in his chair and started striking his keyboard furiously.

'Secondly,' he said, pausing for a few moments, 'They knew where Casey was. We need to know how. I believe that they traced her cell phone. Those guys that were protecting her did not seem smart enough, in a technical sense, to be able to set something like that up. Nicole-Louise, trawl through her sister's cell records and find Casey's number and see if you can get a hit on it.'

Nicole-Louise set to her task immediately.

'What's the third question?' Lawson asked.

'I know why this is happening. I worked it out on the way over here, I know who stands to gain, and I know why, so how do we let them find us so that we can confirm it?'

'Who are they?' Lawson asked.

Ward ignored him.

'Do you think that the Ku Klux Klan have a cell in New York?' he asked Lawson.

'Probably, groups like that have people everywhere. They love the old biker and roughneck look. Most of them probably just attach themselves to them so they belong somewhere,' he replied.

'But this isn't about race is it?' Lawson asked.

'No it isn't. But I know why the Klan are involved.'

'Why?'

Ward ignored him again.

'I can help you with that,' Tackler interrupted.

They both looked at him.

'Just last month, I read an article in the Times where they were distributing flyers upstate, the Hamptons and Long Island. I remember it because I thought they had become extinct.'

'So where would they be?' Ward asked.

Tackler turned and got to work on his keyboard.

'Here it is,' he said less than a minute later, 'The Silent Guardians of the Klan. They are a splinter group but they operate from a bar in Hell's Kitchen. Not the sort of place that you would willingly go for a couple of beers,' he added.

Lawson looked at Ward and smiled,

'I'm really thirsty,' he said, 'A nice cold beer is just what I need right now.'

'What's it called?' Ward asked.

'The New Order bar.'

'How subtle,' Nicole-Louise shouted over her shoulder.

'Give Lawson the details. Where are you with Lockhart?' he asked.

'It's all here. Do you want to have a look?' Tackler replied.

They both stood up from the sofa and walked over to his workstation.

On the screen to the left was the official page of the Senator, on the screen in the centre, financial records and a list of committee's that Lockhart had served on.

Ward read down the list of committee's and said,

'What is that one?' as he touched the screen where it simply said, 'Administrative Approval'.

Tackler smiled at him,

'It is something they don't want anyone to know about,' Tackler replied.

'Judging by your smile, you already know what it is?'

'Yes I do. And so should you.'

Ward looked at him blankly.

'Any committee that has approval in the title will be linked to National security. More specifically, it will be related to covert operations. It's not about seeking approval it's about ticking boxes, normally after an event has already occurred.'

'What kind of event?' Ward asked.

'Events that the CIA have already completed, they then water them down and tick them off. I imagine that The Old Man has attended hundreds of these clearing up the trial of destruction that you two leave in your wake,' he replied, his smile even bigger now.

'The Old Man gets approval from Lockhart?'

'No. Lockhart would not be privy to your work. More international operations, I expect.'

'Like oversees missions that we should not be involved in?'

'No. You are getting confused with what you do. This is a committee that is meant to represent clarity. So half-truths will be recorded and they make sure that there is nothing on record that could ever compromise our government.'

'So, you can find out what Lockhart has signed off on?'

'I can, but it would involve hacking into the CIA servers and although I can do it, perhaps a call to The Old Man would be quicker?' Tackler replied.

Ward nodded.

'I have Casey's number but there is no signal,' Nicole-Louise said as she turned around to face them, 'Her cell has either been discarded or is turned off. Hopefully, it is the latter and as soon as she turns it on to make a call, I'll find her.'

Ward nodded at her.

He pulled out his own cell phone and dialled Centrepoint.

'Gray is suspended already,' he said as he answered, 'He will be demoted to an officer by the end of the day.'

'That's good to hear but it is not why I am calling,' Ward replied.

'So why are you calling?'

'Lockhart sits on committees that deal with administrative approval. You know what they are I take it?'

'It's a screen for justification of our actions.'

'Have you ever had to explain yourself to him?'

The Old Man laughed,

'Before Los Angeles,' Centrepoint began, referring to a recent mission that Ward had completed, which resulted in him being given even more power due to the political capital that he now held, 'The only people who I dealt with were the most trusted and powerful Senators. One of them is now dead,' he added, referring to a Senator who had died at Ward's hand.

'We don't exist Ryan. I've never had to explain what we do, only seek funding.'

'So what would Lockhart be signing off on?'

'He's one of the longest serving Senators, so it would probably be the kind of operation that we should not really be involved in, but we have good reasons to get involved for national security reasons.'

'Can you find out for me? I have a feeling that somewhere along the line, there will be a link to the people that are behind this.'

'What makes you think that?' The Old Man asked.

Ward ignored the question.

'Is The Optician still in Washington?' he asked.

'No. He's here in New York. Probably outside Nicole-Louise and Tacklers apartment right now, waiting for you to make your next move.'

Ward had gone way past feeling uneasy that Centrepoint knew his exact movements at any given moment a long time ago.

'Lawson and me are going for a beer in Hell's Kitchen. You can tell him he is welcome to join us if he wants.'

'He doesn't drink on the job.'

Ward smiled to himself. He doubted that The Optician either ate or drank full stop.

'Let me know as soon as you have the information on Lockhart,' Ward said.

'What specifically do you want to know?'

Ward looked around the room; Nicole-Louise, Tackler and Lawson were all looking at him.

'I'll tell you if you give me what I think you are going to find. If I'm right, you'll confirm it to me.'

'I'll let you know within ten minutes,' The Old Man said and the line went dead.

'There is nothing much in his finances to indicate foul play,' Nicole-Louise said as Ward tucked his cell phone back into his pocket, 'He has cash assets of over two million dollars, but you would expect that from someone who has been in politics for almost thirty-five years. To be honest, knowing how corrupt they all are, I would have expected him to have accumulated much more in that time,' she added, clear distain in her voice.

Ward thought about what she had just said and then he suddenly thought of something.

'Does he have any directorships with anyone?' he asked.

'There are no cash payments going into his account from any organisations so I doubt it,' she replied.

'But what if he is not being paid in cash?'

Nicole-Louise looked at him blankly.

'What if he is receiving payment in shares? Let's say that rather than take dividend payments, he builds up a portfolio of shares. Would that show up in his finances?' Ward asked.

She smiled at him,

'Only if he declared them, but as he is a politician, he would be corrupt and dishonest by default, and so I need to look elsewhere,' she replied, before turning back around and got to work.

Ward looked at Lawson.

'Let's go and get that beer,' he said.

TWENTY-ONE

10th Avenue – Hell's Kitchen – New York

Fifteen minutes later, Ward and Lawson were walking into The New Order bar on 10th Avenue. It was much cleaner and more refined than Ward imagined it would be. It looked like any one of the hundreds of bars in New York. It had a long bar that ran two thirds of the way along the right hand side, and there were new tables and chairs spread sporadically around the room. A wooden laminate floor gave the place a clean, fresh feel to it. The only thing that gave a clue to anything being remotely out of place was the type of people that were inside.

The first thing he noticed was that there were no women in the bar. There were at least thirty men inside, all of them eyeing them up suspiciously as they walked in. The second thing was that all of the guys in there seemed to be pumped up with the aid of steroids, and they all seemed well groomed, despite all seeming to wear tee shirts that were at least three sizes too small for them, obviously a wardrobe choice to show their bulging muscles.

Most people who walked into a bar like that saw huge, muscular, intimidating guys. Ward and Lawson just saw a room full of guys that were so bulked out that any speed they once might have possessed, had been well and truly left in the gym.

Big and bulky guys were never very good at fist fights, as long as someone could keep out of their grip; there was a good chance that people of Ward and Lawson's size would put them down with relative ease.

They approached the bar, with Ward leading the way.

'Yes guys?' the barman asked.

'I think we will have two beers please,' Ward said in his clearest English accent, studying the barman to see if there was any reaction.

The barman nodded and stooped under the counter and took two beers from the fridge, removed the tops, and then placed them on the bar. He then moved away to the end of the bar to serve the next customer.

'They obviously haven't put the word out to look for us,' Lawson said.

Ward ignored him.

He was too busy studying the room, trying to select the men most likely to be involved with Newman. As he scanned the room, he noticed a table of four bulky guys staring at them both, so he smiled raised his bottle, tilted it towards them, and took a sip.

They just stared at him.

'If they won't come to us, we will have to go to them,' he said and walked over towards the guys at the table, Lawson stayed at the bar, casually leaning against it. 'Can I buy you guys a drink?' he asked as he reached the table.

'What are you, a faggot?' the guy sitting furthest away from him asked. The other three guys burst out laughing. He had established who the leader of the group was now, so now all he had to do was see if they knew who Newman was.

'He must be a faggot,' The guy sitting closest to him, wearing a pink tee shirt said, 'All British guys are faggots. Isn't that right faggot boy?' he asked, folding his arms and pushing hard against his biceps as he spoke, trying to make the already huge muscles appear even bigger.

'You have something against gay men?' he asked, 'And there's you wearing a pink tee shirt.'

The other three guys laughed at their friend, Ward could see that he was struggling to think of a relevant and funny comeback and was drawing a blank, and so he just said,

'Whatever.'

'I'm looking for someone,' he said, 'I wonder if you guys can help me?'

'We don't help Brits so get lost,' the lead guy said.

'I'm not British,' he replied instantly, 'Why is it that people think I am?'

'What are you then, Australian?' the leader asked.

'I'm as American as you, probably more so. As I said, I'm looking for someone, and I'm sure you would happily help a fellow American.'

'Who are you looking for?' the guy sitting next to the leader asked.

'A guy called Newman. He's from out of town, but he's big stuff down south, and so I'm sure you have heard of him,' he replied.

They all looked at each other blankly. He could see that they had no idea who Newman was.

'Sorry to bother you. Enjoy your drink,' he said. He then turned and walked back to the bar to join Lawson again.

'No luck?' Lawson asked.

Ward shook his head.

The barman returned from serving the other customer and Ward said,

'I'm looking for a guy called Newman. Do you know where he is?'

The guy paused and said,

'People don't share names but give me a description?'

'He's about six feet three, well presented and black,' Ward replied.

The barman looked at him with caution in his eyes,

'He wouldn't be in here,' he said.

'Why not?' Ward asked innocently.

'Because we don't allow niggers in here,' a big guy sitting at the bar to his left said.

'I think he means African Americans,' Lawson interrupted.

Ward tried his best to look puzzled.

'This is a white man's bar. We come in here to get away from the smell they create,' the guy said, 'So I suggest you leave and go to a place where you are welcome.'

'So you are a real Klansman, are you?' Ward asked.

'You won't be told again, you had best leave,' he repeated.

Ward looked at him closely. It was hard to gauge his exact height with him sitting down at the bar, but he was well over six two. He wore a tight tee shirt and clean denims. Ward looked at his hands, they were clean. He deduced pretty quickly that the guy got his bulk from a gym or a bottle, or probably a combination of both.

That meant it wasn't a natural bulk, created in a manual job, where strength is gained over a lifetime of working. So he now knew two things about him. He was not very strong in the brawling sense and way too slow in a fist fight.

Ward raised his hands so that his elbow was level with his ribcage, as if to say that he was taking note of the warning, and then spun his right arm around and slammed the tip of his right elbow directly onto the bridge of the guys' nose. The force of the impact pushed the guy's head back as the noise of every bone in his nose breaking echoed around the narrow bar. He fell backwards off his stool and landed on the floor, his back crunching as it landed, and his feet eighteen inches off the ground, caught in the bar stool.

For a few seconds, the whole bar fell into complete silence.

And then the four guys at the table made their move. The leader, who had been the furthest away was quickly on his feet, and was leading the charge in a few giant strides, Ward was impressed with the speed with which he moved.

But he was more impressed with Lawson.

Before he had finished readjusting his footing, to face the four guys, Lawson had stepped in front of him and unleashed a right hook that landed in the centre of the guys face with such speed and force, that his feet lifted off the ground, and his head shot back and smashed hard into the face of the next guy who was moving directly behind him, they were both unconscious by the time they hit the floor one second later.

That was the first time that Ward had ever seen one punch render two people unconscious.

The other two guys stopped in their tracks.

This was the worst case scenario for two guys who were pumped up from the gym and a bottle. They knew that their size meant nothing to the two guys in front of them, and they would also know that two guys coming into a place like theirs and picking a fight would know how to hurt people badly.

Lawson was still moving forward, and he grabbed the nearest guy to him by the throat and then applied a vice like grip. The guy's eyes started to bulge in a very unnatural way as he flailed his arms around aimlessly, trying to get Lawson to remove his grip.

'Now your friend has a problem,' Ward said to the last guy standing, 'Whether he lives or dies is up to you.'

The guy looked at Ward and for a split second, he could see in the guy's eyes that he wanted to run.

Lawson continued to squeeze his friends' throat harder, and his legs started to violently kick towards Lawson's shins. But the kicks had no affect at all.

'He'll be dead in thirty seconds,' Ward said, 'So you tell me who is the main man in this bar, and my friend here will let him live.'

Without any hesitation, the guy pointed at two guys, who were well into their forties, who were sitting at table situated at the back of the bar, quietly watching events unfold.

Lawson looked at Ward and he nodded to him. Lawson released his grip and the guy fell to the floor, clutching his throat and desperately trying to fill his lungs with air. As the guy was bent on his knees, Lawson pulled his right foot back and swung hard, the toe of his boot smashing hard into the guy's ribs,

'That's for being such a baby,' Lawson said, 'Shall I kill this guy?' he asked, pointing to the last guy standing.

Ward smiled.

The poor guy looked like he was going to pee himself.

'Leave him,' Ward replied as he headed over towards the table where the two guys were sitting.

These two guys were different.

They were totally unfazed by what they had just witnessed, and they didn't look remotely afraid of either Ward or Lawson.

They reached the table.

'I'm looking for someone. I think you two guys can help me,' Ward said.

One of the guys was drinking from a bottle and he said to the other guy,

'Did you hear something Jack?'

'Only a whining voice of a Limey,' Jack replied.

Ward smiled at them both.

He preferred dealing with guys like this.

They were more predictable.

He pulled out the chair and sat down at the table,

'Nice to meet you Jack,' he said, 'I'm Ryan and this is my friend Mike.'

Both guys ignored him.

'I can still hear an irritating noise Colin,' Jack said.

'Jack and Colin, they seem like very British names, don't you think Mike?' Ward asked Lawson, who was now standing next to him at the table.

'They sound like girl's names to me,' Lawson replied.

'Here's how it is gentlemen,' Ward started, 'I'm looking for a guy called Newman and I'm sure that you will know who he is, because he would have come to you for help.'

'Still hearing the noise,' Colin said.

Ward studied them for a moment. He was trying to decide who the more senior of the two men was. Colin had been the first one to speak so logically, it would be fair to assume that he was the main man. But Jack looked more senior to him; he seemed to carry himself in a calmer and less confrontational manner.

In the end, Colin made his mind up for him.

'You are one minute away from getting an iron bar planted in your skull boy,' he said.

Ward moved his hand around to the back of his pants, pulled out his silenced Glock, swung his arm under the table and shot Colin in the knee from less than two feet away.

Colin lurched forward, banging his chin on the table as he did so, and let out a scream, before sliding off his chair to the right and fell to the floor in a crumpled pile.

'You seem like a sensible guy to me Jack,' Ward said, completely ignoring the cries and moans of Colin, as he writhed around on the floor, 'I'm not a fan of your organisation, but if you talk to me and tell me what I want to know, then I will ignore your beliefs and let you live.'

'What do you want to know?' Jack asked, seemingly showing no interest in the screams of his friend, which were getting louder, until Lawson stepped behind Ward and kicked Colin hard in the face, rendering him unconscious.

'I want to know where Newman is.'

'I don't know anyone called Newman.'

He could see that Jack was telling the truth, then he realised that he had asked the wrong question.

'Let me ask it another way,' he said, 'The guy who has just rolled in from out of town, where is he?' he asked.

'I don't know where he is,' Jack replied.

'Wrong answer,' Ward said.

"No, I mean there was a guy who came in no longer than an hour before you. He showed his card and that he belonged to the order in Texas, but I didn't know his name was Newman or where he went?'

'What did he want?'

'He asked if I could provide some muscle if he needed it,' Jack replied.

'And what did you say?'

'I said of course I could. Whether you agree with our politics or not, we have a code that we stick to. We always help each other out in times of need,' Jack said, almost bristling with pride as he spoke.

'He showed his card but it had no name on it?' Ward asked.

Jack laughed,

'It's not like a driving licence with names and pictures on.'

Ward chose to leave the point there; he didn't care what it was.

'Did he say anything else?' he asked.

'No. That was it. Although the four guys I had in mind are not much use,' Jack replied, looking over at the three steroid induced guys who were well out of action and the fourth at the table who was now close to tears.

'Can you get in contact with him?'

'No,' Jack replied, 'He said he'd stop by tomorrow.'

'Are you going to help him Jack, bearing in mind I am only a fraction of the opposition?'

'I have a duty to help him. Sorry, it's just how it is. Our code is everything,' Jack said, almost bursting with pride talking about his code by now.

Ward stood up and looked at Jack.

He didn't like him.

'Let's go,' he said to Lawson, who nodded in return.

Ward turned to leave and then stopped after three paces, turned and fired a shot into Jack's shoulder, the bullet smashing hard into the bone and muscle and knocking him back off of his chair.

'I don't like your politics Jack,' he said.

TWENTY-TWO

28 West 53rd Street – New York

Newman and Casey walked into the chairman's room, flanked by two of his men. He was relieved to see her, despite the fact that he was holding her responsible for things going so badly wrong.

But he was smart enough to know that the best option now was to clear this mess up, and then get it right the next time, when they did it in eight months' time.

'I'm so sorry that you were exposed to danger Emma,' the chairman said, 'But you are safe now, and I will personally ensure that you are kept well out of harms' way in future,' he added, as he walked across to greet her, before hugging her in a warm embrace.

'Is my sister OK?' she asked urgently.

'She's fine. Newman has two of his best men keeping an eye on things, so no harm will come to her, I promise.'

She looked at him suspiciously, but under the circumstances, things were looking much better for her now than they were a few hours ago.

'Tell me what the British guys said to you, and don't miss anything out, I want to know everything that they know,' he said, leading her over to one of the plush leather armchairs.

She sat down, let out a long sigh and then said, 'Where do I start?'

'We know everything up until they brought you to New York,' he replied, 'So start there.'

'When they were taking me to the airport in their car, I heard one of them talking on the phone.'

'Which one was speaking, Ward or Lawson?' he asked.

'I don't know their names, but the smaller one, the less handsome one, was definitely in charge.'

'How do you know that?'

'Because he was ordering the handsome guy around, and he seemed to be calling all the shots and doing all the talking. On the phone I heard him ask someone about a Senator, and if he had any dirt on him or not. He also mentioned an optician, and then he made a second call to someone else, and asked them to find out about a Senator Locksmith from Louisiana,' she said, closing her eyes as she spoke, trying to recall exactly what she had heard Ward say.

'Lockhart, you mean?' he said urgently.

'Yes, that was it. Do you know what he means?'

The chairman was starting to get very flustered.

'Do you know who he was talking to?' he asked.

'The second call seemed more informal than the first one. I would suggest that whoever he made the first call to, was his boss.'

'Think carefully Emma,' the chairman said, 'Can you remember any names that he said during those calls?" he asked.

'It was a bit difficult; I was under the most frightening pressure. He had just threatened to blow off the faces of my sister and nieces,' she said, her eyes filling up with tears once again as she thought about the danger she had put them in.

'What else did he say about the Senator?'

'He just asked how long he had been serving I think.'

The chairman composed himself.

'You have been through a terrible ordeal, go and freshen up in the shower, and order clothes from the shop down in the lobby and put them on my bill. We will talk again once you have freshened up.'

Casey stood up and walked out of the lounge and into the bedroom of the vast hotel suite without saying another word.

The chairman looked at Newman.

'You have to find these two Brits and quickly,' he said, 'They know much more than we thought they did.'

'Now that she is safe,' Newman replied, pointing towards the bedroom door, 'I can concentrate on them.'

'Then get out on the street now, I need to make a call.'

Newman nodded and walked out of the suite.

The chairman dialled the number.

'Are you still in New York?' he asked urgently, as soon as Senator Wilson Lockhart answered.

'Yes, for two more days. Don't tell me that you have a problem with the evidence you owe me?' Lockhart asked.

'It's a bigger problem than that,' the chairman replied, 'I need you to come over to my suite at The Baccarat Hotel urgently.'

'I can't. It will have to wait until the morning. I'm on my way to a charity event in Manhattan, I'm the guest speaker.'

'Then after!' the chairman demanded.

'I can't. I have engagements until gone eleven, and then my wife and I are taking a horse drawn carriage ride through Central Park at midnight to celebrate our anniversary,' Lockhart said, 'It will have to be first thing in the morning.'

The chairman looked at his watch, it was almost seven thirty. There wasn't much that could be done tonight anyway, and Newman might get lucky and find the Brits in the meantime, and the problem would have disappeared, so there was no point in panicking the Senator into doing something rash,

'OK, it can wait until then. Be here at seven thirty, and you can collect your information on Samone, and we can go through a few other things,' he said.

'What is the big problem?' Lockhart asked.

'It's nothing that can't wait.'

'Are you sure?'

'Yes,' the chairman replied, 'Enjoy your carriage ride,' he said and hung up the phone.

Now it was down to Newman.

DUMBO – New York

Ward had decided that there was not much more that they could do without information in his hand, and that would probably not be until the morning, and so he had asked Lawson to take him home.

'What are your plans for the night or should I not ask?' he said as Lawson pulled up outside his apartment building.

'As you didn't tell me until ten minutes ago that we were done for the day, I hadn't made any,' Lawson replied, 'But Chloe and Sasha are only ever a phone call away,' he added.

Ward smiled.

He knew that Lawson was more than likely telling the truth.

'We need a good night's sleep tonight Mike, we are getting close, I need you on top of your game tomorrow,' he said.

'Have I ever let you down?' Lawson asked.

'Pick me up at seven in the morning,' he said as he opened the door and stepped out of the car, closing the door without looking behind him.

He took the stairs up to his apartment, starting to hope that when he got inside, Eloisa would be there waiting for him, like she would often surprise him, but as soon as he opened the door, he could feel that the place was empty before he turned the lights on.

He threw his jacket over the sofa in the lounge and took out his cell phone and called Eloisa. It went straight to voicemail again.

He sighed to himself as he walked across to his kitchen area and he saw a brown envelope on the worktop. It had 'I love you – E xxx' written on it. He smiled to himself.

Eloisa had identified the next bad guy that needed his attention. He touched the envelope lightly with his hand and was going to open it, but decided that he would shower first. He was feeling tired, and as desperate as he was to spend another night with her, he knew that sleep had been in short supply for him lately, and he welcomed the opportunity to get a good night's sleep in. Fifteen minutes later, he was feeling all refreshed after his shower, and he poured a whole pint of orange juice, picked up the envelope and sat down on the sofa. He checked the screen of his cell phone and saw that he had five missed calls from The Old Man.

He opened his phone and called him.

'Is there any reason why you ignored my calls?' Centrepoint asked as he answered.

'I was showering,' he replied bluntly.

'Senator Lockhart knows who you and Lawson are, well your names anyway. But he thinks you are working for MI6.'

'How does he know that?' Ward asked, slightly unnerved that someone knew his name, or at least his assumed name.

'Because I told him,' The Old Man replied.

'Why would you do that?'

'Because the chances of you finding the people behind this seem pretty slim, and so it will be easier for you to get to the bottom of this if they come for you,' he replied.

'Couldn't you have just given him false names?'

'Then I wouldn't know that the CIA checked on Lawson and went into his military records after I told him.'

'If Mike is in any danger, I will not be happy with you,' he said abruptly.

'Relax Ryan,' Centrepoint replied, 'You don't exist, and Mike won't exist anymore in an hours' time either. Nicole-Louise and Tackler are working on that now.'

He felt instantly reassured. Nicole-Louise and Tackler had wiped any trace of him off the face of the earth, and he had no doubt that they would do the same for Lawson.

'So this is more political than you thought,' Centrepoint said smugly, 'A senator involving the CIA to do his fishing for him, that's pretty definitive,' he added.

Ward knew that The Old Man was wrong.

He knew what was happening, and he had no doubt that there might be a political sub plot, but this was not politically motivated from the offset, he was sure of it.

'I need something from you,' he said.

'I don't like where this is going Ryan.'

'It's a bit late for that, but I will just talk to him.'

'You know that after Los Angeles, we cannot risk any more Senator's having accidents,' The Old Man said wearily.

'All I need is a contact number. If he doesn't want to talk to me, then I'll respect his wishes" Ward said with such sincerity, that for a moment, Centrepoint almost believed him.

'I can put the screws on him myself,' The Old Man replied.

'I'm trying to do this the right way for once. I will find him myself anyway, now that I know he is involved, so wouldn't you be better off being involved in it rather than me shutting you out?'

'Seriously,' Centrepoint replied, 'Who speaks to their boss like that?' he asked in dismay.

'Your favourite operative and his team, who have never let you down and fix every problem you put in front of us,' Ward replied.

'I'll give you a contact number and that's all Ryan. I will be monitoring the calls and you will not harm him or even meet him. Do you understand?'

'Yes I do.'

'Why do I not believe you?'

'Look,' Ward said, 'In spite of what you think of me, I'm not completely reckless. I know that if another Senator meets a sticky end, people will start getting suspicious, and if that happens, I know that the focus will fall on you, and therefore us. And I like the way we work just fine, without any interference so you will just have to trust me on this. OK?'

There was a pause for a few seconds and then he said, 'I'll get his cell numbers and have them checked for frequency of use, he will have an unofficial number, like they all do, and I will get that ready for you by the morning, I'm trusting you on this, so don't let me down. OK?' Centrepoint said calmly.

Ward hung up the phone.

He threw his cell phone to the side and picked up the envelope that Eloisa had left for him and opened it.

The first page was a black and white picture of an Asian guy. He studied the guy for a good few minutes, staring at the picture, looking into the guys' eyes. He knew that he was probably going to kill him soon, even before he knew anything about him.

By the time that he had finished reading the file that was contained in the envelope, he knew that he was definitely going to kill him soon.

The guy's name was Zhang Wei. He was a forty-two-year-old Chinese national who had settled in the Chinatown district of Boston. Officially, he was a businessman who owned four mid-range restaurants, but they were just a front, and a money laundering cover. His real business was bringing in young girls from poverty stricken areas of China, and selling them to paedophiles who kept them for as long as they wanted them, or they became too old for their perverted and sick minds. As with all people who ran sex trafficking rings, it was done under the guise of offering a better life to the poor children whose parents saved desperately to pay the extortionate fees that he charged to bring them into America. Those fees were dwarfed by the money that he would charge by selling the children, but greed always took hold of people like Wei and if he could make money twice, he would willingly do so.

What was different about this was that he had a partner, a woman called Yang Li, who was equally as involved as him. There was a picture of her towards the back of the file and she was very pretty, and she looked extremely elegant.

She wouldn't look so elegant once he had shot her three times in the face, he thought to himself.

By the time he had finished reading and then re-reading the file, it was almost eleven. He now knew all that he needed to know about Zhang Wei and Yang Li, and he felt himself starting to wish that he could wrap up this business with Lockhart and Newman as soon as possible so he could make his way to Boston.

He noted the similarity in their names, in another context, he might even find it funny, but as he tucked the file back into the envelope and made his way to his bedroom, he felt a controllable rage gently building up inside of him.

He liked that feeling.

It always told him that something very bad was heading the way of some very bad people.

TWENTY-THREE

28 West 53rd Street – New York

Emma Casey walked back out into the lounge of the chairman's suite, and was surprised to see that Newman was no longer there.

'Where is Newman?' she asked urgently.

'He's gone to find the Brits. And I have the upmost faith that he will find them,' the chairman replied.

'Only if they want to be found,' she replied, barely in a whisper.

'What do you mean by that?'

She paused for a few moments and then said,

'I study people and their behaviours. I read body language, and pick up key words, which give a very accurate indication as to how a person thinks and what they are capable of. That's why you got me involved with this after all, isn't it?'

The chairman nodded his agreement at her.

'These guys aren't your average men. The big guy is probably the most handsome man I have ever seen in my life. Even with tears in my eyes, I felt myself being drawn to him, and hoping that I wasn't looking too dishevelled. I studied him, he is clever, ruthless and there is no limit to what he would do to find out what he wanted to find out. I concluded that he was a warrior. The type of man that someone like Genghis Khan would have had standing next to him all of those years ago,' she said, her voice trailing off as she pictured Lawson once again.

'Newman is highly capable. At the end of the day, ten of his guys against just two of them is a situation weighted highly in our favour. I know that he will find them, and I know that he will have them killed,' the chairman replied, with genuine confidence running through his voice.

'The big guy isn't the problem.'

'Tell me about the other man?'

'I don't think I have ever seen anyone so in control as him in my whole life. I looked for a crack, for a weakness, vulnerability, and there was nothing. I tried to establish what he was thinking as he spoke, and I hit a brick wall every time. He spoke really simply, but all I heard were riddles. And there was something in his eyes. It was the one thing that I could see, that makes me believe that Newman could have a hundred men, and it would make no difference,' she said, shaking her head, almost in resignation, as she spoke.

'What did you see in his eyes?' he asked, now feeling a lot more concerned than he had a few moments ago.

'I saw determination and confidence, like he had been in this situation a hundred times, and he was completely in control of everything. I saw a look that told me he was going to win, like winning was everything to him, and no amount of men, or carefully hidden information will stop him.'

'But he doesn't know where to start looking, and that is the key factor in our favour,' the chairman replied, trying to reassure himself as much as Casey.

'That's not quite true" she said, almost in a whisper.

"Meaning?' he asked, hostility immediately recognisable in his voice.

'Meaning that he found my laptop,' she replied, irritation in her own voice at his aggressive tone towards her.

'Tell me there wasn't anything on there that would directly link any of this to me?'

'Not by name.'

'What does that mean?'

She explained how she had prepared a document that was for her own protection. How she had hidden a hard copy somewhere that no one would ever find. In the event of anything ever happening to her, the document would go to the authorities, and the whole of the committee's plans would come crashing down around their ears. It was her insurance policy.

He knew the document was in existence, she had already told him.

'And he has the document?' he asked.

'No. I initially started to write it on my laptop but Novak told me that wasn't the smartest thing to do, because if you wanted to get rid of me, you could just kill me and steal my laptop. He also advised me against emailing it to anyone, as he knew you had some technical people overseeing what we were doing,' she said, 'So in the end, I took his advice.'

'What did you do?' he asked.

'I did it the old fashioned way, I purchased an old typewriter online and typed it out, and then sent it to the safe place through the mail,' she replied.

He raised his eyebrows. She was right, he had been checking all of her e-mails for the past two years, even her personal ones, and he even had a mountain of sexually explicit pictures that she had sent from her cell phone to a guy in Washington called Tommy Soltan, who she briefly dated eighteen months ago. They were pictures that he had looked over on many occasions.

'So what does he have?' he quickly asked,

'He has one paragraph, that's all.'

'What does the paragraph say?'

'It just says that if anything happens to me, I was involved in a plan to manipulate and arm vulnerable teenagers to carry out shootings across America.'

'And that's it?'

'No,' she said reluctantly.

'Tell me Emma,' he demanded.

'It also said that the man behind it is part of an organisation that has been operational for the past seventy years,' she replied.

'That doesn't seem very damning,' he said, relief in his voice.

'It does with the last sentence added,' she said.

'What does the last sentence say?' he asked.

'This man has innocent people killed for profit.'

Park Avenue – New York

Lawson had picked Ward up exactly at seven as requested, he had even brought along a takeout coffee for Ward to drink on the way over to Nicole-Louise and Tackler.

'Did you sleep well?' Lawson asked.

'Senator Lockhart is involved in this with the CIA somehow,' Ward replied, ignoring the pleasantries, 'We have to find out how,' he added.

'Yes, I slept really well thanks Mike,' Lawson replied, 'What about you?' he asked himself, 'Me? I had both Chloe and Sasha come over, and they gave me a massage and relaxed me until three this morning, and then I slept solidly for three hours, and so now I am raring to go.'

Ward laughed and then shook his head.

'I think I knew that without asking,' he replied.

'So the Senator is involved, do you know what is actually going on? Because after Casey's involvement, I have no idea,' Lawson said.

'Let's see what the Senator says first before jumping to conclusions.'

The truth was, he knew exactly what was happening and why. He had thought about it all morning since he had woken up, and he was hoping that once he had spoken to Lockhart, he would confirm it to him.

'And how are we going to get to talk to him?' Lawson asked.

'The Old Man has given me his number. Not only that, he is in New York right now.'

'So you are just going to ring him up and hope he confesses everything over the phone?'

'No,' Ward replied, 'We are going to pay him a visit, face to face.'

They arrived at Nicole-Louise and Tacklers apartment in under fifteen minutes, the New York traffic was just starting to build up.

'Morning,' Tackler said as he opened the door to the apartment.

'Morning,' they both said in unison as they followed Tackler inside.

'Do you two ever sleep?' Nicole-Louise asked without turning around from her screens.

'Mike doesn't,' Ward replied, 'Did you find anything in Lockhart's finances that can help us?' he asked.

'Doesn't she always?' Tackler said as he headed over to her workstation with the two of them following.

'What you said about payment in shares got me thinking,' she said, 'And so the first thing I did was see if I could find a link to a holding company. I assumed that while Lockhart is probably dumb like all Senators, he would have some smart people advising him.'

Ward was starting to feel a little impatient but he knew how important it was to Nicole-Louise to explain how she solved a puzzle, so he let her continue without interrupting.

'Initially, I found nothing at all. He appeared to be completely clean. Then I thought who would he trust, and so I did some research on his wife and established that she is officially listed as a consultant, but has no educational or practical experience in anything,' she said, 'And yesterday was actually their forty second wedding anniversary.'

Tackler looked at Ward and rolled his eyes. But none of them were going to dare to tell her to hurry up, so the three of them stood there, smiling at her when she turned to make brief eye contact with them to make sure that they were listening properly.

'So then I did some financial background checking on her and she came up completely clean. There was not one cent in her accounts that should not have been there,' she said.

Ward knew that unless one of them asked a question, Nicole-Louise would explain the whole thing step by step, so he quickly said,

'But you found another link to someone else?'

'Exactly,' she replied.

'Who was it?' Ward asked, hoping the question was sufficient to get her to skip straight to the point.

It wasn't.

'I then checked the property ownership records and found that she had sold a house for a massively reduced price ten years ago to a woman called Pamela Boardman, so I started digging on her and found that Lockhart's wife's maiden name was Boardman. It was her sister.'

'So her sister is in on it too?' Lawson asked, equally as desperate to get to the point as Ward.

'No,' she replied.

'I don't understand,' Lawson said.

'Her sister died just under ten years ago, actually a month after she had bought the house.'

Now Ward was confused.

'The house wasn't sold to Pamela Boardman to give her funds for her future or to care for her loved ones in the event of her dying, she was diagnosed with cancer and she had no children or husband,'

'So what was it for?' Ward asked.

'It was to ensure that there was a sufficient amount of money left behind to set up management of her estate, and to control her future earnings. There is one sole beneficiary to her estate,' she replied.

'Lockhart's wife' Lawson said.

'Exactly her,' Nicole-Louise replied and nodded her approval that Lawson had followed her explanation properly, "This is an estate worth three million dollars in hard cash alone, and exempt from a lot of tax laws too,' she added.

'Once you had established where they would hide the money, what did you find?' Ward asked.

'There was one regular payment from a company called Player and Bloom, they were erratic payments, so that got me thinking,' she replied.

'They were erratic in what way?' Lawson asked.

'Some of them were a few thousand dollars they would then jump to over one hundred thousand. So I checked up on Player and Bloom.'

'And who are they?' Ward asked.

Tackler looked at Ward and rolled his eyes again, it was the third time he had listened to Nicole-Louise's revelation this morning.

'They are one of the larger stock brokerage firms on the New York Stock Exchange,' she replied, 'So your initial thought that the money was being disguised in dividend payments was spot on,' she added, turning and smiling at Ward as she spoke.

'Then I hacked into their servers and pulled up the share portfolio for Pamela Boardman,' she continued, as Ward and Lawson bent over to get closer to the screen, 'this is what I found,' she said, pointing to a list of companies that magically appeared after a click of her mouse.

Ward read down the list.

It took a moment for the number of companies to register with him. He was right in his initial thoughts of who was behind this, but he was wrong to the extent with which others were involved.

They were all on it.

'Are they all leaders in their fields?' he asked.

'Each one of them is number one across The States, every single one of them. But then Tackler had an idea and he pulled the whole thing together. Show them,' she said beckoning him towards his workstation.

They all walked across the room and waited for Tackler to sit down at his workstation.

'Then it got me thinking,' he said, effortlessly taking over from where Nicole-Louise had finished off, 'The variation in dividend payments had to be linked to something. The payments were not half year or annual dividends so I looked for a link.'

'And you found one?' Ward asked.

'I sure did, look at this,' he said pointing at the screen.

There was a list of States and next to half of them, a list of numbers.

Ward looked at the list. It was long and comprehensive.

'What are they?' he asked.

'They are all Mass shootings over the past thirty years,' Tackler replied.

'There must be at least seventy incidents there. There haven't been that many,' Ward said.

'Actually, there has. I got caught out the same way. I assumed that a mass shooting was where a huge number of people get killed. That is not the case,' Tackler replied.

'So what is a mass shooting?'

'It is defined as one aggressor who kills at least four people in a twenty-four-hour period,' he replied.

Ward shook his head, the list seemed endless. The world knew that America had a problem with gun control, but he doubted that they knew the true extent of the problem.

'And the numbers next to the States means what?' he asked.

'Dividend payments to Pamela Boardman,' he replied, 'Every one of these payments is one of the higher ones made to the estate, and they follow within four weeks of a shooting taking place.'

Every last part of it, with the exception of Senator Lockhart's involvement, fell immediately into place in Ward's mind.

'I need you to trace this number and tell me where he is right now,' he said to Nicole-Louise and handed her his cell phone, with the message open that Centrepoint had sent him with Lockhart's number.

She took the phone from his hand and walked back to her workstation.

At the bottom of the message below the number, was a note that Ward had added. She read it and smiled to herself. She glanced at him and he winked at her.

'Tell me about the people in charge of these companies?' he asked.

'I'm two steps ahead of you Ryan. Look at this,' Tackler replied and clicked his mouse, bringing another screen into life.

A list of names appeared and Ward read them all slowly.

Darren Hughes
Kenny Hasloff
Charles Andrews
Charles T Dunlop
Peter Cullip

'All CEOs, and effectively owners of their respective companies.'

'Are they the only ones involved?' he asked Tackler

'Yes, I'm sure of it.'

'What makes you so sure?" Ward asked.

'Because every single one is in New York right now.'

Are they all at the same place?'

'That I don't know yet. But I will in an hour or so.'

'I've found him,' Nicole-Louise said over her shoulder. Ward walked over to her,

'Where is he?' he asked.

'Right now he is at The Mark Hotel on 25th East 77th Street.'

'Keep me informed if he moves,' he said and nodded to Lawson, indicating that it was time for them to leave.

TWENTY-FOUR

Fifteen minutes later, Ward and Lawson were pulling up outside the Mark Hotel.

From the outside it looked both elegant and plush. It was a Victorian style building and had a gold trimming around the awning, that stretched over the street, against the black name plate which simply said, 'The Mark', which made it look immaculate. There were two huge Stars and Stripes flying proudly to the left of the awning, a French flag to the right, and a flag that Ward did not recognise next to the tricolour.

His phone vibrated in his pocket.

He pulled it out and saw it was The Old Man, so he ignored it and slipped it back into his pocket unanswered.

'Lockhart knows who we are,' he said, 'So maybe you should go in alone first, to check out what security he might have.'

'OK,' Lawson said and climbed out of the car.

Ward watched as he walked inside and then he pulled his phone out and called Tackler.

'You've only just left, I said an hour,' Tackler said as he answered.

'I've just thought of something. What date was the largest payment made into Pamela Boardman's account?' he asked.

He heard Tackler tapping on his keyboard and then after a pause, he said,

'That's interesting.'

'What date was it?'

'It was in June three years ago.'

'It doesn't correlate to a shooting, does it?' Ward asked.

'No it doesn't, how do you know that?' Tackler asked.

'Let me know when you have the whereabouts of everyone on that list,' he replied and hung up the phone.

Lawson walked into the foyer of the hotel. It had a black and white tiled floor which forced him to adjust his eyes. It looked like a Zebra had designed the place in tribute to his one true love. He was pretty big on interior design himself at the moment, but he didn't get this at all. He approached the reception desk and smiled at the pretty young woman staring at him who was stood behind it. She blushed and tucked her hair behind her right ear, and held her gaze much longer on his eyes than her professional etiquette should have allowed.

'Hello Miss,' he said, after glancing down at her left hand and searching for a wedding band or an engagement ring, and seeing that she did not wear either.

'Hello Sir, how can I help you?' she asked in a clear and concise English accent.

'Where are you from?' he asked.

'I'm from Surrey, you?'

Lawson had grown up in the next county to Surrey, so he jumped on the opportunity to relate to her,

'Wow!' he exclaimed, 'I'm from Guildford,' he said, Guildford being the only town in Surrey that he could think of.

'Oh my God, so am I,' she said excitedly.

Time to change the subject he thought.

'Listen,' he said softly, leaning in towards her as he spoke, 'I'm new to New York and could really do with some company, so if you help me with a little problem I have, perhaps we could meet up for dinner later?'

She blushed again and played with her hair once more, 'What do you need help with?'

'I'm doing an internship with the New York Times, doing a story on Senator Lockhart, and I am desperate for a quote. If you accidentally gave me his room number, and I accidentally knocked on his door by mistake, then that could be the making of me.'

She eyed him up and down. He looked too old to be doing an internship, but she connected with his eyes once more and he instantly knew she would help him.

She scribbled a number down on a piece of paper,

'That's my number, ring me after six tonight,' she said, before turning a thick book towards him and leaving it wide open for him to see.

He scanned down and saw Lockhart's name neatly written in block capitals and next to it, was the number 364.

He smiled at her and said,
'I'll call you later,' and then he headed towards the elevator.
The elevator was empty he stepped inside and pushed the button with number three on it.
Ten seconds later he was stepping out onto a plush carpet. The walls were layered in expensive looking wallpaper, and each door along the hallway was painted in immaculately crisp, white gloss paint.
He strolled along the hallway, looking like he was meant to be there, and reached room 364 without seeing any sign of a security detail, then, without hesitation, he knocked on the door four times.
He waited, and a few seconds later, he heard a deep, heavily southern accented voice shout out,
'Who is it?'
'Hotel security Sir,' he shouted, trying his best to add a generic American twang to his voice.
'One moment,' came the reply.
He wasn't sure what he was going to say. He hadn't expected to get to Lockhart so easily, so he decided to get himself alone in the room with Lockhart and then call Ward.
The door opened and a short, overweight looking man well into his sixties stood in front of him in brown slacks, wearing a white shirt which had the top four buttons undone.
'Can I talk to you inside please sir?' Lawson asked politely, his success at faking an American accent gaining momentum.
'Sure son,' Lockhart replied as he stepped to one side and beckoned for Lawson to walk in.

He stepped through the door and stopped immediately. Before he could react, he felt the barrel of a gun against the back of his head.

'How stupid do you think I am boy?' Lockhart said to him.

Mike Lawson had been one of the best soldiers in his SAS unit. What had made him so formidable was his ability to be ultra-calm under pressure. He scanned the room in front of him slowly.

There were three guys standing to the left, all with weapons drawn, one behind him made four. These guys weren't roughnecks, and they most definitely weren't Newman's men. These guys were professionals, without a doubt. Probably among the most expensive protection that money could buy. He looked at their faces, one by one, and smiled. The three guys in front of him showed no emotion, the guy stepped out from behind him, walked in front of him and fixed his stare on his face.

'I said how stupid do you think I am boy?' Lockhart repeated.

'To be honest,' he replied calmly, 'Really stupid.'

'I'm not the one with four guns pointing at me' Lockhart sneered.

'You may as well be.'

Lockhart stared at him with contempt,

'I'd love to stay and talk, but I have a meeting to attend. My boys will stay with you until your friend comes to rescue you, and then they will get rid of you both,' he said, as he started to do up the loose buttons on his shirt.

'We know everything; you do realise that?' Lawson said.

Lockhart came closer to him,

Such as?'

'We know about Pamela Boardman, and how you are hiding your money, we know how your huge dividends are generated, and my friend may or may not come for me but I can guarantee two things,' Lawson said.

'You don't look like you are in a position to guarantee much at all, but I will humour you, what can you guarantee boy?' Lockhart asked.

'One, I can guarantee that right now, every penny that you have ever made is being stolen and you will never get it back,' Lawson said with a smile.

Lockhart's face dropped.

'You are bluffing boy,' he spat.

'Do you not find it odd that I am so calm and relaxed right now, like I know what's coming?' he asked.

Lockhart looked around the room, panic started to creep across his face. He was tempted to tell his men to kill Lawson there and then, but as corrupt as he was, he would never allow himself to be witness to a murder, and so he put the idea fairly out of his mind in an instance.

'And the second thing I can guarantee is that I'll be the only one to walk out of this room alive once you have gone.'

Lockhart laughed and two of the security guys laughed too.

'Glad you find me amusing,' he said to Lockhart as he watched him put his jacket on,

'Let's go,' he said to the guy who had put the gun to his head, and he strode past him out of the door.

'It's just us five then?" he said to the three other guys.

'Five? This is the part where you tell us that your friend is going to come busting through the door right now and take us out I take it?'

'God no,' he replied, 'He doesn't like me that much.'

'I can see why,' another of the guys said.

He looked at them, slowly, one by one and then he smiled,

'Now I get it,' he said.

'What?' the only guy who had not yet spoken asked.

'You three know each other, and I'm pretty sure that you know already that I was SAS, so that means you are very afraid of me before we even start.'

'You Brits aint so bad,' the guy to the left said, 'They sent some of your boys to train with us once, wasn't at all impressed, they weren't so tough.'

Lawson laughed and shook his head.

'Do you want to know the difference between us and you girls?'

'Tell me big boy?' the guy to the right said.

'We don't want the world to think we are tough. What were you girls, Seals?' he asked.

None of them answered but their eyes told him they were.

'Then you have two problems,' he said.

'We are the ones holding the gun's asshole,' the guy in the middle said.

'You must know McDermott. He's a very good friend of mine; I work with him, Paul, Wired, Fringe, Fuller, Wallace and Lloyd regularly, which means that you are now fighting against them. That should scare you, and appeal to your loyalty to each other, you shoot me, and you may as well be aiming the gun at any one of those men.'

Lawson saw the recognition in the all of their eyes immediately as he mentioned each one of McDermott's team.

'But that's only your smallest problem,' he added.

He could see already that the three of them were losing their appetite for this situation, so he continued.

'It really would be best if you let me walk out of here now, you boys go and earn your money elsewhere, and stay well away from me and the people I work with.'

'We can't do that. Nice try. Lots of people have heard of McDermott and his crew, your words mean nothing,' the guy to the left said, gripping the handle of his gun a little tighter now.

'I wouldn't raise that gun,' Lawson said loudly and with urgency in his voice.

'Listen to this guy,' the guy on the left said.

'Your biggest problem is not McDermott, or me, or even my friend Ryan. Your biggest problem is in the room right now,' Lawson said calmly.

"You aren't so scary SAS boy,' the guy in the middle said and raised his gun in line with Lawson's chest.

Before he had finished his movement, the window shattered, and a 7.62mm smashed into the back of the guys' skull and blew the back of his head clean off. He fell forward and landed flat on his face with a thud.

'That gentlemen, is my friend The Optician, no doubt you have heard of him too,' Lawson said as dramatically as he could.

The other two guys dropped to the floor immediately.

Lawson was just thankful that his faith in The Optician was as strong as Ward's.

'Being on the floor won't help you,' he said and smiled for a moment, 'But throw your guns along the floor to me, and there is a chance that he will let you live, but I can't guarantee it,' he added.

The two guys immediately slid their guns along the thick carpet, both of them stopping a few inches away from his feet.

'On your knees, and hands behind you heads,' he demanded, as he bent down and picked up the guns.

They both responded and did what they were told with urgency.

'What does Lockhart know about us?' he asked them.

'We don't know. We were rushed over from Washington last night to protect him from two British guys, one SAS. That's all we know,' the guy on the left said.

Lawson did not possess Ward's ability to know if people were telling the truth or not, and even though he was studying the guy hard, he had no idea if he was lying or not.

So he did the next thing that Ward frequently did. He raised the handgun and shot the guy next to him, three times in the chest from point blank range. The guy fell back, and his buckled body twisted and he fell to the side, smashing into the other guy.

'He was telling the truth asshole,' the other guy screamed.

'So you say,' Lawson said, and then shot the guy twice in the centre of his chest.

He was dead before his face had hit the carpet.

Three minutes later, after he had called The Old Man to send a clean-up crew, he was walking past the pretty receptionist on his way out of the building.

'Call me,' she mouthed to him.

He checked his pocket, her number was still there. He decided right then that he would call her later.

He reached the car and climbed in.

'Well?' Ward asked.

'Lockhart's gone.' Lawson replied.

'I know I saw him leave with a guy. What were you doing in there?' he asked.

Lawson explained what had happened and Ward shook his head,

'So you didn't ask where Lockhart was going?'

'I never had time.'

Ward pulled out his cell phone and called The Optician, 'That was amusing' he said as he answered.

'Do you have any idea where Lockhart could be going?'

'You are the one on the ground, I was just watching Lawson,' The Optician replied.

Ward hung up the phone.

'You made a right mess of that Mike,' Ward said, 'It's not diff.......' he was interrupted by his cell phone vibrating.

It was Tackler.

'Hello?'

'Would you like to know where Emma Casey is?' Tackler asked.

TWENTY-FIVE

28 West 53rd Street – New York

Emma Casey was sitting on the edge of her bed in the plush suite of the Baccarat Hotel, with two of Newman's men outside in the main suite for company. She was feeling a little more relaxed as she had called her sister five minutes ago, even though Newman had said she was not to use her cell phone, she was relieved to hear that everything was fine, her sister said to contact her in a few weeks when she had time to process the events of yesterday.

Those few minutes were also enough for Tackler to find her location.

She has been awake for the past hour, but had yet to go outside to speak to the two men because they made her feel uneasy. One of the guys, called Hershey, leered at her at every given opportunity, and every time she had spoken to him, he had constantly licked his lips smiling at her. The other guy, Edmonds, had hardly any teeth, and fingernails that were black with grime underneath, which she assumed was the result of years of never having cleaned them.

They were both big guys, muscular and threatening. She imagined that they probably came from the same Southern family somewhere down the line, either indirectly related or through incestuous relationships. The most unnerving part was that she did not feel safe. Even when the two British guys had her in their custody, she never felt in any direct danger, in spite of the threats that the smaller of the two men had made.

They seemed too intelligent to risk jeopardising their mission by focussing their attentions on her.

She needed a drink and was now ravenous, so had called down to room service and placed her order for breakfast. She had heard the door open and close a few moments ago and then one of the guys had shouted,

'Your breakfast is out here.'

She opened the door and walked out into the main suite. Right on cue, Hershey licked his lips and smiled. He was looking at her differently now, he looked more threatening,

'I could have brought that into your bedroom for you,' he said, as he licked his lips again.

She shuddered and ignored his comment.

'The lady thinks she is way too good for us,' Edmonds said.

Casey walked over to the table, which was situated just in front of the large sash window, which took up most of one wall, and sat down.

The breakfast trolley which had been delivered must have had at least five pounds of silver on it. There were tea and coffee pots, cutlery, lids to keep the food warm and a very solid looking, patterned tube with a red rose sticking out gracefully from the top.

'Is it true that you can read people and how they think?' Hershey said, 'Like you can get them to do whatever you want?' he asked.

Casey was smart enough to know that ignoring him would probably provoke them both, and that while he was trying to tease her and make her look stupid, she knew that if she engaged into conversation with him, that he would end up looking ridiculous, and therefore much less threatening, and so she humoured him.

'That's exactly what I can do,' she replied, looking up and flashing him her own smile, as she sipped on her orange juice.

'Can you teach me how to make any woman come to bed with me?' Edmonds asked, and to her revulsion, started picking his nose as he spoke.

Hershey laughed out loudly.

'I could, but it would take a few years,' she replied innocently, her sarcasm lost on both of them.

'You are wrong lady,' Edmonds said as he stood up and walked over to the breakfast trolley. She watched as he started picking through it, making a mental note of everything that he had touched so that she could avoid it.

'You see, I don't need words, I have something much better,' he said.

"'Which is?' she asked.

'You tell me; you are the people reader.'

'Charisma, intellect, hygiene and style?' she asked innocently.

'Very funny,' Edmonds replied as Hershey burst out laughing, 'I have force. I could pick you up now and take you to the bedroom and do whatever I want to you, and you could do nothing about it,' he added, and then smiled a toothless smile at her.

'We both could,' Hershey said, as he got up from the sofa and joined his friend at the breakfast trolley.

She suddenly lost her appetite.

'I don't think Mr Hughes would be very happy, knowing that you were threatening me like this,' she said firmly.

'We don't work for Hughes. We don't even work for Newman. We belong to the Klan, and we have our own code, and our own rules, if you know what I mean,' Hershey said as he grabbed his groin.

She was surprised to hear Hershey say that he belonged to the Klan. She was under the impression that the Klan no longer existed, and that it had been preceded by formal, right wing, political parties.

'You belong to the Klu Klux Klan?' she asked.

'One of the secret orders, yes,' Edmonds replied.

'So how does Newman know Hughes?'

They both laughed at her.

'Who do you think provides weapons?' Hershey eventually replied.

She never had Hughes down as a racist, mainly because his third wife was African American.

'But he can't be a racist,' she said.

'He doesn't care about race. He's a businessman, they tread on everyone, and he has no standards,' Edmonds said.

'So he uses you as muscle in return for giving you guns?'

Edmonds looked at her and sneered,

'For a smart lady, you are one dumb bitch' he said.

'Why am I dumb?' she asked.

'He doesn't give us weapons.'

'I thought you said that he did?'

'No, I said he provides weapons,' Hershey interrupted. She couldn't understand what they were trying to say to her, and she wasn't sure if that was down to their limited intellect or her naivety.

'Maybe if you were naked you might be able to think clearer?' Edmonds asked menacingly.

She ignored the comment, she did not want to give them any encouragement, so she quickly pulled the conversation back to the previous subject.

'Can you just explain to me about Mr Hughes and his involvement with your organisation,' she asked, using the word 'Organisation' to show that she respected who they both belonged to. It seemed to work. Edmonds picked up some toast and sat down on the sofa.

'It's really simple lady,' he started, 'The niggers, the scum who populate every inner city, don't need us to kill them. If you give them the ammunition, they will kill themselves. Hughes makes sure that they get supplies of firearms across the country, and in return, we look after him, and then sit back and watch them kill each other. Thousands of niggers a year are killed, and the hands of the white man are clean,' he added, she noted the irony in his last comment as she fixed her eyes on his disgusting fingernails once more.

'And you transport these weapons all over the country?' she asked.

'No. Hughes has a group like us in every State. You and your liberal world have no idea what really happens out there. As I said, you are one dumb bitch,' he repeated.

She was shocked at what Edmonds had just told her and more than anything, she now felt very vulnerable, anyone who thought like these two men, was extremely dangerous.

'So as I said, Hughes has nothing on us, and no control. We are here to stop you from being killed, and that's all. Now we are here, we may as well have some fun,' Hershey said, and he lunged forward and grabbed Casey's wrists.

He pulled her up hard, her knee knocking the trolley on the way up onto her feet, and a cup of coffee spilt on the floor.

'Come with me bitch!' Hershey spat, and released the grip on one of her wrists and yanked her hair hard and pulled her, screaming, towards the bedroom.

He slammed the bedroom door shut as he pushed her on the floor.

'Now it's just you and me bitch,' he said as he pulled off his dirty, checked shirt.

Casey scrambled to her feet and jumped onto the bed and landed on the other side, trying desperately to sprint past him, but Hershey put out a strong arm and stopped her in her tracks.

'I love a lady who puts up a fight,' he said mockingly. She could smell him now.

He smelt stale and unwashed, and there was something in his eyes that said he wanted her to fight so he could hurt her even more.

He spun her around and wrapped his forearm around her throat.

She screamed and then he put such immense pressure on her that she stopped immediately, and for one split second, she thought that he had crushed her windpipe. She then felt a fist land hard into the side of her stomach and all of the wind was knocked out of her, she fell to her knees.

She felt faint, and was now on all fours, trying desperately to escape the animal. She was waiting for the next punch or kick but it never came. She caught her breath and turned to look up at her assailant.

And saw Ryan Ward standing next to Hershey, with a compressor extending from the end of his gun, which was pushed firmly against Hershey's temple.

'Not that you deserve my protection, but there are certain lines that a man should never cross,' Ward said, and then he pushed the gun hard into Hershey's back and turned him around.

'Outside,' he demanded, leading Hershey out into the main suite, 'Both of you.'

Two minutes later, after she had composed herself, she was walking out into the main suite.

The tall, handsome man was in the room as well he was sitting on the sofa. Hershey and Edmonds both knelt before him with their hands behind their backs and cable ties tightly pulling their hands together. She held her gaze on the handsome guy for a few moments.

'Sit down,' Ward said, beckoning her to the space next to him with his gun.

She sat down.

'They killed AR, do you know that?' he asked.

She didn't say anything.

'So effectively, you killed him, as you put him in that position in the first place,' he continued.

She still said nothing.

'I know everything. I know about Darren Hughes, Kenny Hasloff, Charles Andrews, Charles T Dunlop and Peter Cullip. I know about Senator Lockhart, I know about the CIA and I know about every other manipulation you have carried out over the past few years,' he lied, noting her reaction as he spoke.

He could see that apart from Hughes, she had no idea about the other names that he had mentioned. But he also saw a reaction in her eyes when he said about the other manipulations and so he continued.

'I have to say, it was very subtle,' he said, 'It was only when one of my team pieced it together and explained that a mass shooting can be just four people in twenty-four hours, that we could work out just how many you have been involved in. How can you go from child psychology, where your vocation was to help people, to destroying so many lives?' he asked calmly.

'There were only three other shootings I was involved in before these ones,' she replied,

'What do you know about Senator Lockhart?' he asked, looking for recognition of the name in her eyes.

She shook her head.

He could see that she knew nothing about Lockhart's involvement.

'You two,' he said to Hershey and Edmonds, 'I take it you are Klan members?'

'You don't want to be messing with us,' Edmonds said, trying his best to sound menacing.

Lawson jabbed his heel forward hard into the middle of Edmonds back, sending him face first into the plush carpet.

'Where is Hughes now?' Ward asked.

'He went to a meeting. I don't know where or who with,' Casey replied.

He could see she was telling the truth.

'He was going to rape me,' Casey said, her eyes filling with tears.

'Why did you get involved with Hughes?'

Casey went on to explain about how she had helped his grandson overcome his problems, and how Hughes had enticed her with promises of wealth and a future in the Med. She said that she had somehow been sucked into things by him, and before she knew it, she was in too deep to get out.

'And that's it?' he said, 'You have no remorse about the death and destruction you have left in your wake?'

Casey could see that Ward was smart. She could see that he was much smarter than her, and that the key words that she had tried to introduce when talking to him were being recognised, but also being dismissed for what they were.

So, in the name of self-preservation, she thought she would try a different approach.

'You can use me to get to Hughes and the others and even this Senator. You are clever; I can see that, so I know that you will not cut your nose off to spite your face.'

'What do you have in mind?' he asked.

'I can tell him that I need to see him urgently. That I have some information that someone might be able to find out about his involvement in all of this. He is terrified of anything being traced back to him,' she said desperately.

Ward studied her.

She was pretty and she looked inoffensive, and she even had a warm pull to her that could entice people in, he could see that clearly.

But none of that would ever work with him.

All he saw when he looked at her was greed and evil.

'I have a better idea,' he said as he stood and pointed his Glock at her, 'And bring them along too,' he said to Lawson, 'We are leaving.'

TWENTY-SIX

57 East 57th Street - New York City

The five members of the committee sat in stunned silence around the large mahogany table in the boardroom of the Four Seasons Hotel.
Five men who were part of an organisation that had secretly been run for decades by their forefathers, which was now as close to collapsing as it had ever been.
It wasn't who they were, it was what they represented.
They were all there;

Darren Hughes
Kenny Hasloff
Charles Andrews
Charles T Dunlop
Peter Cullip

Darren Hughes was the chairman.
He was the chairman by longevity.

When the committee was first set up decades ago, it was agreed that the chairman would always be the longest serving member. When Robert Haslof had died eleven years ago, Hughes stepped up by default, as his sixteen years sitting on the committee as a member entitled him to do so.

He was the fourth generation of the Hughes family to sit on the committee.

Hughes was not only the chairman of the committee; he was also the chairman and CEO of 'Gun Shop', the largest supplier of guns in the United States.

Everything was about balance, and one of the perks about being the chairman of this committee was that he could decide who sold and distributed what arms.

'Gun Shop' had been set up by his great, great-grandfather over one hundred years ago. It had grown from a small company in Mississippi to having a shop in virtually every town in The States.

The original role of chairman was to line the pockets of the politicians who would be under constant pressure to review the country's gun laws, to ensure that they continued to maintain every American citizen's right to bear arms.

Seventy years ago, just after the Second World War had finished, the committee at that time realised that their licence to print money had run out, and so they had come up with a number of ideas to ensure that gun sales continued to grow.

Initially, they had become heavily involved with the CIA, in trying to instigate coups and wars in smaller colonies and countries, by giving away firearms for free, but this became way too expensive and the CIA were less than effective in following through on their promises, even though Hughes' great grandfather had been involved in the inception of the CIA in 1947.

Next they had become involved in the assassinations of key public figures. The thinking behind this was that creating discord and anger between social and political rivals, it would unleash an anarchy that escalated out of control and spilled onto the streets, but that failed miserably too.

The death of Kennedy seemed to pull people together, and the anticipated street war that was going to erupt after Martin Luther King was killed, failed to materialise too.

So then they had come up with the idea of using fear to make the public desperate to arm themselves and their families.

Random shootings, at random places across the country, put a lot of people on edge and gun sales surged after each shooting.

For a couple of decades, it was always adults that carried out the atrocities. The sixties, and the willingness of people to embrace their soul's and alternative religions, made it relatively easy to convince people that killing random people would send them to a psychedelic heaven.

Finding the people had been the hard part though. The love and peace movement was not very receptive to violence.

The committee had stagnated for a couple of decades after that, and then everything changed.

The internet was born.

Hughes' father was an innovator and he embraced the new technological age with enthusiasm.

As he watched the internet grow, he noticed that teenagers used it more than any other group, and he had come up with the idea of tapping into those desperate young minds that trawled the World Wide Web looking for a sense of belonging and escapism.

It had taken only three months to sit back and watch as a fifteen-year-old boy in Las Vegas had been brainwashed enough to walk into a diner and kill six people. Profits had soared and the committee flourished.

Hughes' father was staggered that nobody had ever dug deeper into the reason as to why a lot of the people who carried out mass shootings had changed from adults to teenagers.

The shooting that Russel Collyfield had carried out had been worth an extra two hundred thousand dollars of sales to 'Gun Shop' in Missouri alone. That would eventually be multiplied by fifty as everyone who owned a gun in every State, reviewed their own ability to protect the people they loved.

The Ku Klux Klan had first come to the committee forty years ago, initially asking for arms to wage their race war, and they were armed for free, but the Klansmen at the time were a little short of imagination and kept reverting to hanging, and so they were of little use to the committee. Newman was the latest in a long list of high ranking Klansmen who were provided to protect the committee. In the mid-eighties, when political correctness and liberal thinking was born, the Klan became more forward thinking. The committee had suggested arming the African Americans in the inner cities, and they were secretly involved in the birth of the violent street gangs. They gave the poorer, underprivileged teenagers in those inner city areas the ability to make their own narcotics, and they helped create the drug epidemic which swept through the country like a hurricane. Then they armed them with weapons, sat back and watched the shooting and killing start. The panic that ensued in the white, middle-class masses as they turned on their news every night, sent gun sales soaring through the roof.

Once again, Hughes' father had been staggered that no one had actually put any emphasis on where the weapons that these street gangs used were originating from.

The truth was that the committee had been indirectly, or heavily involved in the majority of the violence that took place in America since 1945.

Hughes did not want to be the chairman who presided over the collapse, or indeed the revelation of the committee. And these two British guys appeared to be on a mission to bring them to their knees.

The vice-chairman was called Kenny Hasloff. He was the CEO of Wright & Cannon, the largest handgun manufacturer in the U.S. He was resentful towards Hughes, as they only joined the committee two weeks apart, and but for the fact that his father fought his cancer much harder than Hughes's own father had, he would have been sitting at the head of the table. Hughes knew of his resentment, and the fact that he ignored it made it even worse. He took little victories where he could. That was why he had insisted that he would not move when Hughes had directed them all to go to different hotels yesterday. Every little victory over Hughes mattered to him.

He lived in Oklahoma, on a sprawling ranch with almost twenty horses. His wife, Kathy often gave him suggestions that he would take to the committee, and Hughes would always dismiss them, in spite of them seeming much more rewarding and complex than the ideas that Hughes insisted they followed.

A big part of him wished that Hughes would suffer the same painful disease that his father was struck down with, so that he could take over the reins.

He knew that if he was the chairman, they would not be in the mess that they were in right now.

Charles Andrews was the CEO of Kaleidoscope, the largest manufacturer of rifles in America. Behind Hughes and Hasloff, he was the next longest serving member of the committee, with six years under his belt. He was actually the oldest member of the committee; his own father had lived to ninety-six, and did not step down until three months before his death, even though he offered the committee very little input for the last ten years that he was a part of it. Andrews lived in Alabama, with his fifth wife, and he had fathered sixteen children. With child support and alimony payments, everything was about money to him. Hughes had been good for him, so he agreed to every suggestion that Hughes would make, regarding their latest plan or way forward. He needed the success of the committee to last for at least another eight years until all of his kids were out of his hair and no longer his responsibility. He spoke very little at the meetings that they had, and when he did speak, no one seemed to listen anyway. He was there by default and that was it.

The fourth member of the committee was Charles T Dunlop and he was the CEO of Eastern Imports, the largest importer of guns into The States. He was the analytical one of the group. At every meeting that he attended, he would be constantly updating the others on sales figures and projections, to confirm or undermine what was being said. Dunlop was married to a guy called James Patlock, and the ignorance of the other committee members meant that they tended to ignore him full stop. His father, George, had sat on the committee for twenty two years and all the time that he was alive, he had been married to a typical southern belle called Lucinda. The moment that his father died, Dunlop came out as homosexual, and the committee accepted his place at their table, but in their archaic minds, dismissed his value from day one.

The fifth and youngest member of the committee was called Peter Cullip. He was the CEO of Tap-Tap Munitions. He had only been on the committee for nine months, and when he had learned that the two British guys had visited one of his shops and were asking questions, he had almost run home to Kentucky and turned his back on the committee for good, until the chairman had calmed him down and reassured him that everything would be fine. Now he had the sick feeling in the pit of his stomach once again.

He never wanted to be involved with the committee or even with Tap-Tap Munitions. He had got a first in business from UCLA, and he wanted to work in the financial sector, but his father had insisted that he take over from him when the day came. His father had died just ten months ago and he had sworn to him that he would continue with the family business when he had gone. He had revealed all about the workings of the committee on his death bed, only after Cullip had pledged to keep the family business going, and he was both dismayed and disgusted that his father could be involved in something so evil.

Until he realised the financial value of what the committee did.

Hughes had taken him under his wing and had gone into great detail about their involvement with the CIA and the money that they generated for them. He showed him how the profits were laundered, as the CIA tended to pay using drug money or the illicit profit money that they had generated, and asides from the recorded profit that the companies made, it was at least doubled through the hard cash that passed their way.

Everything had been going perfectly until the two Brits turned up and now, all eyes were on the chairman once again.

'How did they know where she was?' Dunlop asked.

'That's the wrong question,' Kenny Hasloff interrupted, 'It should be how did they know who you were Darren?'

'I'm working on that,' Hughes replied.

'If they know who you are, there is a good chance that they might know who we are,' Hasloff said, raising his voice as he spoke, 'So as chairman, what are you going to do to put this right?' he demanded, looking around at the other committee members to see if they noticed that Hughes did not seem to be taking control of the situation as much as he was.

'And you still don't know who these two Brits are?' Andrews asked.

'Senator Lockhart should be on his way over here now. I'm sure he will have a little more on them,' Hughes replied.

'And if he doesn't?' Hasloff asked.

'Then Newman will find them.'

'I don't have a lot of faith in Newman at all. You said that a couple of his guys were looking after her. Have they gone too?' Hasloff replied.

'We don't know for sure that they have gone, or even that the Brits have them. All Newman said was that he can't get hold of his men and her cell phone is still off. We'll know in the next few minutes,' Hughes replied, trying to speak calmly, but the panic could be heard clearly in his voice.

'How can just two men cause all of this?' Cullip asked. Before he could answer, Hughes' cell phone rang. He picked it up and said,

'Newman?'

All of the committee members stared at him as he said, 'Well you need to find them all and very quickly,' he slammed the phone down on the table.

'So they do have her?' Hasloff asked with contempt in his voice.

Hughes ignored him and picked his cell phone back up.

He touched the screen a few times and then put the phone to his ear.

After ten seconds, he said,

'Senator, it's me. I was expecting you thirty minutes ago. I need you here urgently, so ring me straight back and tell me how long you will be,' and then he hung up the phone.

Hasloff looked at each of the other committee members and noticed that they were all shaking their heads in disbelief at Hughes.

'You seem to have lost control Darren,' Hasloff said, 'I want to table a motion of no confidence.'

TWENTY-SEVEN

Gilbert Pl – Hunts Point - New York City

Hershey and Edmonds had worked out what was happening long before either Casey or Lawson had. As they pulled into Hunts Point, even though they were from out of town, the change in buildings and the people who were on the street, told them both why they were there.
Ward had instructed Lawson to head there, and as they turned into Gilbert Pl, Ward said,
'Slow down Mike.'
They cruised along the street under ten miles per hour, passing the tall and unkempt apartment blocks, which all seemed to be separated by stretches of barren wasteland in between each building.
Ward wasn't only looking for the right place; he was looking for the right people.
Casey was crammed in between the two guys on the back seat, Lawson had attached a cable tie to her wrists, and her hands were now firmly secured behind her back

and with every bump in the road that Lawson drove over, she shuddered as she would brush her shoulders or legs against Hershey or Edmonds.

They had tried to engage Ward in conversation for the first ten minutes of the journey but he ignored them.

He was being smart.

He doubted that the two guys could tell him much more than he already knew, apart from how to contact Newman, and as Lawson had their cell phones in his own pocket already, that would not be too much of a problem, but he still felt that Casey had more to tell him. That is why he made sure that she would get close and personal with her two attackers on the back seat, on the journey to Hunts Point. By the time they got out of the car, he was sure that she would view him as a rescuer rather than someone who was kidnapping her.

'Pull over here,' he said as they passed a rundown apartment block which had a section of wasteland next to it, which he assumed, was where a building once stood.

Lawson pulled the car over to the sidewalk Ward turned and looked at his three prisoners on the back seat. He took a few moments to study each of them, but still could not decide which one he detested the most, although on balance, he concluded that Casey was the most self-centred of the three, and had no twisted belief to cling to, so it would be her.

But for now, she was going to have to wait for her opportunity to beg for forgiveness.

'Get these two out of the car and you stay with her,' he said without even looking at Lawson.

'I'm not getting out here,' Hershey said.

Ward smiled at him.

'Me neither,' Edmonds said urgently.

'Can you access their phones Mike?' Ward asked.

Lawson pulled the two cell phones from his pocket, swiped the screen and they both came up with a digit pad, requesting a numerical code.

'Security pin request,' Lawson said.

Ward raised an eyebrow at Hershey.

'Four sixes,' he said immediately, without any prompting.

Lawson typed in the code and the phone unlocked. Ward looked at him and he nodded confirmation that the code was correct.

'Yours?' he said to Edmonds.

'The same,' he said immediately.

Lawson typed in the code and again, it unlocked.

'Why would you both have the same code?' he asked.

'It's symbolic, that's all,' Edmonds replied.

'Symbolic of what?' he asked

'There are six of us guys who are related. Three sixes is the number of the devil, and so we added another six because you have to have four numbers to unlock it.'

'That's smart, very smart,' he said.

'Yeah, I guess,' Edmonds replied, feeling pretty pleased with himself, in spite of his current situation.

'I was being sarcastic you idiot,' Ward said, and shook his head before turning to the side and looking out of the window.

To the side of the apartment block, where the wasteland started, a group of around ten guys had gathered. They were eyeing the Ford Taurus suspiciously, a couple of the guys strolling along the sidewalk, peering into the car from the other side of the road.

Only cops would stop on their street and stay in the vehicle.

He opened the door and stepped out of the car and Lawson followed. He opened the rear door and grabbed hold of Hershey's arm and yanked him out, Lawson doing the same on the opposite side of the car to Edmonds.

He marched Hershey around to the other side and took hold of Edmonds,

'Get back in the car and don't let her out of your sight,' he said, and Lawson duly obliged, opening the door and climbing back into the driver's seat.

Ward slowly started marching Edmonds and Hershey across the road.

'You don't want to do this,' Edmonds protested, but Ward ignored him.

As he approached the group of guys, three of them peeled off and walked about twenty feet away and then doubled back on themselves, slowly coming up behind him.

He pulled out his Glock, digging it hard into Hershey's back, and approached the group.

'One of you will be in charge, which one is it?' he asked firmly, but in a non-threatening tone.

The guys behind him stopped walking when they were about ten feet behind them.

'Who wants to know?' a big guy in a basketball shirt asked.

Ward ignored him and studied the group.

One of the guys was sitting on some building blocks and this gave him a slightly elevated position to the rest. He knew that this guy would have sub-consciously put himself above the others, without realising, so that the order was kept at all times.

A leader leads, even when he doesn't do it intentionally.

'That will be you,' he said, and smiled at the guy.

A couple of guys to the leader's right, adjusted their feet and put their hands in their pockets and held them there.

'You won't need to pull any weapons on me,' he said immediately and then smiled, 'I've brought you a present,' he added, holding his gaze firmly on the leaders face.

'What do you want?' the leader asked, 'We don't talk to cops.'

Ward smiled at him again.

'Clearly I'm not a cop. My name is Ryan, yours?' he asked.

'What are you then?'

Ward studied him for a moment. He was engaging in conversation, which meant that he was curious to find out what was happening, but there was no trust between them at all.

So Ward decided to tell the truth.

'I'm the person that deals with the bad things, the very bad things,' he said, 'Things the cops or the government can't deal with.'

'He's a bad ass,' a guy who could have been no older than eighteen, standing to the left of the leader said, and most of the group laughed.

'I'm worse than that,' he replied, a stern look on his face, 'I'm the guy who has killed more people than every gang on this neighbourhood put together, and I am allowed to do it. No cops, there is no come back, no accountability, nothing.'

The group all stopped laughing.

Every one of them could see that he was telling the truth.

'You are British?' the leader asked.

'I'm British-American,' he replied, 'Just like you guys are African-American. And that's why I'm here.'

One of the guys to the leader's right pulled out a knife and started to adjust his feet.

'I really wouldn't do that,' Ward said.

'There's eleven of us and one of you. You don't roll into our neighbourhood giving orders Mr Badass,' the leader said.

Ward did a calculation in his head. He had been here about five minutes now; he knew that would be enough time. He looked at the guy with the knife in his hand and said,

'I wouldn't take one step forward if I were you.'

As predicted, the guy was confident in the safety that the sheer numbers of his gang gave him, and so he stepped forward.

A 7.62mm bullet fizzed through the air and smashed into the blade in the guy's right hand, and it shattered into a hundred pieces, the impact of the metal shattering and the bullet hitting its target scorching his hand. The guy screamed and clutched at his hand desperately.

'The best sniper in the world is waiting for the next one of you to move. All of you will be dead by the time you have taken one step. So please, just stay where you are,' Ward said urgently, but still retained a calm to his voice.

'I'm sorry about your friend,' he quickly said to the leader, 'But I'm here to ask for your help and to do the right thing. Can we start again?' he asked.

The leader nodded.

'My name is Ryan and everything I told you about what I do is true. OK?'

The guy nodded. Ward could see that he believed him. He could see that they all believed him, as he watched their eyes darting up, down, left and right looking for where the shot had come from.

'As I said,' he continued, 'I'm sorry about your friend but there is no point looking for the shooter,' he said to the group rather than one person, 'You won't see him. What's your name?' he asked.

The leader looked at him for a few seconds,

'I'm Diamond,' he eventually replied.

'Pleased to meet you Diamond. Tell me, what do you know about the Ku Klux Klan?'

Hershey and Edmonds looked down at the floor.

Diamond immediately realised what was going on.

A guy turns up in their neighbourhood, with two guys trussed up in cable ties, with fear written over both of their faces, and this British guy, who omitted a sense of real danger, was asking them what they knew about the Klan.

'Is this guy for real?' a guy sitting by Diamond's feet said with hostility in his voice.

Diamond put his hand up to indicate that he wanted silence.

'I know that you must have a good reason for bringing those two pussies here,' Diamond said, flippantly pointing at Hershey and Edmonds as he spoke.

'How bad are you and your guys' Diamond?' Ward asked.

"Why do you want to know?"

"Because not only are those two guys real Klansmen, they know the places where the Klan operate out of across New York. Perhaps you know some people who would like to have that information?'

'Where did you find them?'

'I'm in the middle of something big here and I've already killed some of their friends, but these two stepped over a line, and I think putting a bullet in their head is too good for them. I want them to suffer. I've found out just how much they try and keep your neighbourhoods stuck in poverty and misery, so I'm sure that you can issue the appropriate punishment once you have got whatever you want from them,' he replied.

'And what is it that you want in return?' Diamond asked.

'All I want is for you to maybe return the favour to me one day. I'm a street fighter like you. In fact, most of what I do is defending people like you from the greed and arrogance that the powerful people have. I stand up for the guy on the street. I'm telling you the truth when I say that my mission in life is to balance the scales. To hit the greedy who tread all over people like you with everything I have. There will come a time when I need help on the streets, and I trust people like you and your gang, way more than I trust the cops or any government people. We are fighting the same fight,' Ward replied, surprising himself with the passion with which he spoke. He meant every word.

People like Diamond weren't born bad people. They were made bad people by the unfairness and greed of the world.

When he was younger, he always thought that everything that people did was a choice. As he matured, he realised that people like Diamond had no choice. They were born into poverty and had to fight and scrap for everything. No one was ever going to help people like him just because it was the right thing to do.

'You are some badass Ryan,' Diamond replied.

Ward smiled,

'And yet I have enough respect and humility to tell you that I will need your help in the future, and hopefully, by you seeing that I won't tolerate people like these two,' he said, pushing Edmonds hard in the back with his Glock, 'You will get that I see the real picture, and I will fight your corner,' he added.

Diamond stepped down from the blocks and walked forward towards Hershey and Edmonds, stopping about ten inches away. He started into both of their eyes for a good few seconds.

Eventually he spoke to them,

'You boys are going to learn what real pain is. We are going to introduce you to The Hoop Master, he will have plenty to ask you,' he said. 'Take them to the garage,' he added, four guys immediately stepped forward and took one arm each.

'Please, don't,' Hershey squealed, 'I'll tell you everything about Newman.'

'We will find you and we will kill you,' Edmonds spat at Ward as he was marched off.

'They won't have the chance when The Hoop Master has done with them,' Diamond said.

Ward nodded.

'If I need to find you again, you will always be here?' he asked.

'I've been on these streets since I was nine years old. Providing the cops or a rival gang don't kill me, I'll always be here.'

'I'm sorry about your friend's hand.'

Diamond nodded his acceptance of the apology.

'What did they do to step over a line?' Diamond asked.

'They tried raping a woman.'

'Is it the one in the car?'

Ward nodded.

'Are you taking her somewhere safe now?'

Ward shook his head.

'She isn't a Klan member is she?'

'No she is not. She's as bad though,' Ward replied, as he put his Glock into the back of his pants and extended his hand for Diamond to shake,

'Thank you for your help, hopefully we will meet again",' he added, as Diamond shook his hand firmly.

Ward turned and walked away.

'Hey,' Diamond shouted.

Ward turned around.

'So where are you taking her?' he asked.

'I'm taking her somewhere to show her the error of her ways.'

He reached the car and Lawson stepped out.

'That seemed to go well,' he said.

'They were very helpful,' Ward replied.

Lawson smiled. He had a number of contacts back in London who ran with gangs, and he knew that if they understood what you were fighting against, they, like most people, were normally willing to help.

'What are we going to do with her?' Lawson asked.

'I know exactly what we will do and we will do it right now.'

Enlighten me? Lawson asked.

Ward explained where they would go next and Lawson said,

'I'll call The Old Man and make sure it is clear.'

Ward climbed into the car and Casey said,

'What are you going to do with me? I have nothing to do with their political views.'

'I have something very different in mind for you.'

'What is it?' she demanded, fear running through her voice.

Lawson climbed into the car.

'He will have it sorted by the time we get there,' he said to Ward.

'Where are we going?' Casey asked, much louder this time.

'I'm taking you to meet the consequence of your actions.'

TWENTY-EIGHT

152 Jane St, Weehawken – New Jersey

Thirty-five minutes later, they were pulling up outside the house that Adam Ray lived in until yesterday. There was police tape surrounding the entrance to the front yard, and The Old Man had ensured that all NYPD cops had been removed for the next two hours.

'Why are we here?' Casey demanded.

Ward ignored her.

'Bring her with you,' he said to Lawson as he climbed out of the car and headed up the path to the tatty old red door, without once looking behind him.

He knocked on the door four times.

'What do you hope to achieve by bringing me here?' Casey asked.

He ignored her again.

The door was opened a few seconds later by a slight looking man. He looked haggard, and was wearing work clothes.

His eyes were red and he looked dishevelled and badly hungover.

'What do you want?' he asked.

'Mr Ray, my name is Ryan. Can we come in?'

'I'm done with talking to you cops. I told you all that I know. You should find his mother, this is all her fault,' he spat back and went to close the door.

Ward put his foot in between the door and the frame, and his palm hard against it so that it would not close.

'We are not the police, but we need to come in,' he said.

'I aint talking to no reporters neither.'

'We aren't reporters either.'

'Well go away, whoever you are,' Ray said and pushed hard on the door, trying to close it.

Ward used his powerful shoulder to push hard against the door and it flew open. He stepped inside, and Lawson followed, his hand gripping Casey's arm tightly.

'Get out of my house,' Ray shouted at them.

'You will listen to us and then we will leave,' Ward said calmly.

'I'm not listening to anything you have to say,' Ray shouted back.

Ward pulled out his silenced Glock and pointed it at Adam Ray's dad,

'You will stop shouting, you will go through and sit down, then you will listen to what I have to say, and then I will decide if we leave or not. Is that clear?' he asked.

The sight of the gun made Ray freeze immediately.

He raised his hands in surrender.

'Now, where can we sit?'

'Through here,' Ray replied, and he walked up the hall and turned left into a lounge, with Ward following and Lawson, still gripping Casey's arm tightly, two steps behind.

There were two shabby sofas in the lounge, one of them with misshaped cushions that had been wedged back into their original place but looked distorted.

Ward was sure that Ray probably passed out on the sofa most nights in a drunken stupor and that was why the cushions were so out of shape.

Ray sat down on the sofa which was not distorted and Ward sat opposite him. Lawson then pulled Casey down next to him. He then stood behind them both.

'What do you want?' Ray asked, speaking with much less hostility now that Ward had his gun pointed at him.

'Do you know why your son got involved in what happened?' he asked.

'Because his mum messed with his head when she ran off and left us alone.'

Ward knew the background of the manipulation that Casey had carried out on Adam Ray, but he did not realise the extent to which his father had contributed to the young boys' state of mind until that moment.

It made him want to fire three bullets directly into Ray's face. But he inhaled deeply and composed himself.

'I meant how he came to have the weapons, why he was going to carry out the shooting, and who convinced him to do it?'

'It was one of those crazy religious preachers,' Ray said.

'What makes you think that?'

'He had a copy of the Koran.'

'What if I told you that it was just a smokescreen to create more fear and panic?'

'I never knew what went through that kids' head. He was never right,' Ray replied.

'He was what you made him. You are a pathetic excuse of a father, and if anyone should be lying dead on a slab, it should be you,' Ward said, 'I came here with the intention of giving you the whole story, hoping that it would bring some peace to you, but I can see that the only person that you care about is yourself.'

The comments seemed to throw Ray for a few seconds. Ward watched as he was trying to make sense of how the events could in any way be his fault.

'So you will keep quiet and listen very carefully, and stop acting like you are the victim here.' Ward said.

Ray was visibly shocked by Ward's attitude towards him. Men like him always were.

Aggressive men like Ray were used to people trying to avoid confrontation with them. He had probably spent a lifetime of talking down to people and realising that they found him intimidating.

Ward could see that he was nothing but a bully and he hated bullies.

'Your son had no one to turn to and so he went online and found someone who would listen to him. That's all he wanted, someone to listen to him and to understand him. Do you think that is too much for a teenage boy to expect?' Ward asked.

Ray shook his head. It was the first time that anything resembling shame or sadness had been visible in him.

'So he found this website where someone listened to him and the person who listened to him was this woman,' he added, pointing at Casey.

'Her?' Ray said, 'She isn't a teenage girl. The cops told me that he had been involved with a teenage girl.'

'The cops told you what they were told to tell you,' he replied, 'Now I want her to tell you exactly what she did to convince him to go shooting people.'

'What are you hoping to achieve by doing this?' Casey asked Ward, without once looking up from the floor.

'I'm hoping that you don't make one mistake, tell one lie or leave one thing out, because if you do, one phone call and your whole family gets wiped off the face of this earth in about two minutes flat,' he lied again. 'And don't think the little protection that Hughes has put on your sister will help, my men are professionals,' he added, assuming that Casey would have begged Hughes to have someone watching her sister.

His gamble paid off.

He could see in her eyes as she looked up at him that was exactly what had happened. Now she knew that he was on top of everything.

'OK,' she replied, 'where do I start?'

'Tell him why his son was on there in the first place. Tell him why he felt so alone that he was desperate for someone to listen to him,' Ward demanded.

Casey looked at Ray.

The child psychologist in her knew that he was to blame for Adam Ray's vulnerability in the first place. The survivalist in her was thinking how she could put all the blame on him to work a way out of this for herself.

'Your son needed you when your wife left, but you turned your back on him. He told me how you spoke down to him, how you made him feel inadequate. He even told me that when he was stripped at school and constantly bullied, he tried talking to you about it all you told him was to man up. You blamed him for your wife leaving, and not once did you look at yourself. You are a pathetic excuse for a father and also a husband too,' Casey said.

Ward saw right through her immediately.

She was trying to make it appear that she really cared for Adam Ray, and that somehow, she was as much a victim in all of this as the teenager had been.

But he wanted Ray to hear the truth and so he played along,

'Tell him the impact that his actions had on his son,' he said, speaking softly, and even aiming a half smile at her for added effect.

'He needed love when your wife left. Not your anger and blame directed at him. The day she walked out of the door, you walked out on him too,' Casey said.

'That's not true,' Ray spat back, 'I gave him everything. I gave him money whenever he needed it, and I made sure that he never went without.'

'But you never gave him an ounce of love, support or understanding. What I did was wrong, but I'm not a lot different to Adam Ray,' Casey replied, going in for the defining point which she hoped would convince Ward that she wasn't as evil as he thought, 'I was manipulated into this too by greedy, powerful men, who made me feel that I was in a corner, and the only way to escape was to agree to do what they told me to do,' she added, and then she looked at Ward to gauge a reaction.

He raised his eyebrows in mock realisation, like he had never thought of her being similar to Adam Ray, and this seemed to encourage her further,

'Do you know,' she said, lowering her voice to a soft and gentle tone, 'He hated his mom for what she did to you, and he loved you, and wanted you to be proud of him, and to grow together so that her running away would not beat you. But you failed him. You let her rip you both apart. Even now, you are seeking comfort in a bottle and refusing to take any responsibility. Doesn't Adam Ray deserve to have you take some responsibility now?'

Ray's eyes filled with tears.

He had been in denial so long that being mean to Adam Ray had become second nature to him.

He started to sob,

'I loved him, more than anything, or anyone, in the world,' he said through his sobs, 'It was just every time that I looked at him, I saw her.'

Ward felt genuinely sorry for the guy.

Not for the grief and pain that he was feeling right then, he felt that Ray deserved to feel every bit of pain that was ripping through his body, but for the fact that he had lost the last link that he ever had to his ex-wife.

He basically had nothing left.

'So she jumped on that loneliness and convinced Adam Ray to carry out an act that would have made another fifty parents go through what you are feeling now,' Ward interrupted, 'What do you think of her?'

Ray looked at her up and down.

Ward could see a rage building in his eyes.

It was exactly what he was hoping he would see when he knocked on Ray's door.

'She can try and put this on me, and she is right in the way that I turned my back on him and I hate myself for that, and I don't know how I will continue to go on without him here. But what she did was beyond evil. My actions were down to self-pity and anger, and I will have to try to live with that. She took my poor kids pain and turned it into a weapon just because she wanted to. I hope she dies.'

Casey was visibly shocked. She thought she had control of the situation up until a few moments ago, now she could see everything slipping away from her.

'You think she deserves to die?' Ward asked.

'Yes she does.'

He paused for a moment, looking down at the floor and then he suddenly looked up at Ward,

'I want to know something,' he said.

Ward nodded at him.

'Were there any others apart from my Adam she made do this?' he asked.

Casey looked at Ward, her eyes begging him to say that there were no others, and that this was a one off.

'Yes there were,' he replied, 'There were others who actually carried out the killings she had convinced them to do,' he added softly.

'You sick, evil bitch,' Ray shouted at her, standing up as he spoke, 'You should die!'

Casey leant in towards Ward, trying to find some form of protection from Ray's rage, which had now transferred into his body, his arms became rigid and he clenched his fists.

Ward stood up and moved away from the sofa, leaving Casey sitting all alone and exposed.

He walked around and stood next to Ray.

'Do you want punish her?' he asked calmly.

'I am going to beat the bitch to death,' Ray replied, transferring the weight from his left leg to his right leg, in an agitated hopping motion as he spoke.

Ward took his Glock and put it firmly into Ray's hand, 'You have one free shot. One bullet and you will be exempt from prosecution, and I will get it fixed so that no one will ever know that you have killed her. Do you think that you owe it to your son to finally stand up for him, and hit back at the one person who destroyed him more than anyone else?' he asked.

'Please, don't. I beg you. None of this was my doing,' Casey pleaded, her own desperate sobs now echoing around the room.

Ray raised the Glock and without any hesitation, he squeezed the trigger of the gun.

The bullet smashed into her chest from four feet away and forced her body back into the distorted cushions, before her body tipped to the right. The blood soaked through her white top immediately, and Ray stood frozen to the spot, his arm extended and the gun still pointing at her.

Ward gently pulled his fingers apart and took the gun from him.

Casey was in a bad way but she was still alive.

He knelt down on the floor so that his eyes were level with hers.

'That is the consequence of your actions,' he said quietly, 'Not only that, but both of your sisters and your nieces were killed by my men ten minutes ago. So the scales are balanced a little better now,' he lied.

He wanted the last thing she heard to be that her own family had been destroyed, like all of those poor people who had been affected by her actions.

He raised his gun and fired two more shots into her left temple. Her head exploded, blood, bone and brain matter covering the sofa.

Ray just stood still, unable to move.

'Make the call Mike,' Ward said, and Lawson stepped outside of the room to call The Old Man for a clean-up crew.

He looked at Ray.

Tears were streaming down his face and he could see the devastation that he was feeling.

But he was still partly to blame.

Someone had to stand up for Adam Ray against everyone who had destroyed him.

He spun around and punched Ray hard in the centre of the stomach with an uppercut which felt like a sledgehammer.

Ray fell to the floor, the wind knocked out of him.

'You failed your son. Your punishment is to live with that. That punch was for him,' he said.

Ray heard every word clearly, despite struggling for breath.

'He deserved better,' Ward said, and he walked out of the room.

TWENTY-NINE

152 Jane St, Weehawken – New Jersey

'Do you think he really takes any responsibility?'
Lawson asked as they pulled away from Ray's house.
'I'm not sure. I think he does right at this moment, but
once he loses himself in the bottom of a bottle later, he
will probably blame his wife, Casey and everyone but
himself,' Ward replied.
'That poor kid,' Lawson said and shook his head.
'Pass me one of the cell phones we took from Newman's
guys.'
Lawson dug into his jacket and pulled out a cell phone
and passed it to him.
He entered the code, four sixes, and scrolled down the
contact list until he found Newman's name and number.
He pressed dial.
Three rings later, Newman answered,

'Jesus Hershey, where have you been? I've been trying to get hold of you all morning,' he answered.

'They are both dead. Beaten to death by a group of rather helpful gangbangers down in Hunts Point,' Ward replied.

There was silence on the line for a few seconds.

'I was half expecting you to hang up because you are scared,' he quickly added.

'You don't frighten me boy. This isn't England.'

'It certainly isn't. If it was, I'd be blowing your face off right now. But travelling from A to B takes much longer here.'

Newman said nothing.

'Your boss is going to die today, and there is nothing you can do to stop it,' he continued.

'You think?'

'I know.'

'Maybe you and me should meet up and have this conversation face to face,' Newman said, trying his best to goad Ward.

'Sounds like a good idea to me. I'm heading back into New York now, I'll ring when I get there,' he said and hung up the phone.

He took out his own phone and called Nicole-Louise and Tackler.

Nicole-Louise answered.

'Do you know where all of those CEO's on that list are right now?' he asked, without offering any greeting.

'We have been following them. They were at the Four Seasons, but now it looks like they have all gone to separate hotels,' she replied.

'I want you to keep tabs on their movements at all times,' he said, 'Shortly we will be paying each of them a visit.'

'We are on it, don't worry, we won't lose them.'

'And the other thing I asked you to discreetly find out?' he asked.

'I have everything that you need already.'

'Thanks Nicole-Louise,' he said and hung up the phone.

'What's the other thing that you had her discreetly find out?' Lawson asked.

Ward spent the next five minutes of the journey explaining to Lawson what he had Nicole-Louise working on, and when he had finished, Lawson said, 'How do you keep so many things running around in your head at the same time?'

'How do you keep track of all of the women in your life?' Ward retorted.

'Fair enough,' Lawson replied.

They both laughed.

His phone vibrated as he held it in his hand, and he saw it was The Old Man,

'Hello,' he said, after letting it ring seven times just to make Centrepoint feel irritated enough to be slightly off guard.

'Have you approached Senator Lockhart at all?'

'Not yet. He is on the list though. Why do you ask?' Ward replied.

'Because I have found out the extent of his involvement with the CIA, the people you are hunting, and it is a complete mess.'

'How much of a mess is it?'

'A big enough mess that after you have cleared up this mess, you are going to have to go straight onto dealing with what I've just uncovered,' The Old Man replied.

'Surely I am due some time off?' Ward asked.

'No doubt you will be running around for the lady in your life first, and I am supportive of that, and make whatever resources you request available, but that is your downtime. How you chose to spend it is up to you.'

'You aren't exactly going to win employer of the year,' Ward said.

The Old Man ignored him.

'So give me the short version of Lockhart's involvement,' Ward asked.

'What do you know about Sudan?'

'I know that the South is oil rich, and that the CIA supported a lot of the power crazed generals out there, and they don't have the control over them they anticipated having. But everyone knows that, didn't one of the current criminals going for The White House say something like, a little bit of something is better than a little bit of nothing or something similar?' Ward asked, reiterating his belief that all politicians are criminals without exception.

'But you probably aren't aware how involved the CIA has been?'

'Not specifically.'

'Have you ever heard of Samson Samone?'

Ward had heard of Samone. Surprisingly, it was Lawson who had told him about Samone a few weeks back, when they were talking about who the most ruthless men in the world were, and while Ward had said it was the

Columbians, Lawson had just touched on a Sudanese warlord called Samone who did inexplicable things.

'Yes I have, he's the warlord. Don't tell me that they put him in power? He controls a route through to the oilfields in the South.'

'Yes they did. The idea was to secure the route of access for certain American companies to get at the oil,' The Old Man replied.

'So how does Lockhart fit in?'

'He brokered the deal between the CIA and Samone to arm him and his men, so that he could take control in the first place.'

'And let me guess, the five big companies all made a hefty sum out of it?'

'And so did Lockhart. We can't find a trace to any money yet, but we will,' Centrepoint said.

'Nicole-Louise and Tackler have already found some. It's not cash, it's paid in share dividends to a dead relative whose estate they control,' he replied.

'But that is not the problem.'

'What is?' Ward asked.

"Samone has decided that he no longer wants to cooperate with the CIA and he wants the wealth himself. It's turned into a right mess. He's now targeting American nationals working out there and killing them,' The Old Man replied.

'How did you not know about this before?' Ward asked, 'I thought you knew everything.'

'Of course I knew about it, but I did not put any importance on it until I started digging into Lockhart. We've been involved covertly there for decades; we were involved in the incarceration of Mandela for God's sake. Everyone on Capitol Hill knows that we are involved over there, they just chose to ignore it.'

'So Lockhart cosied up with the gun companies and he probably has friends on the Senate Committee's that review our gun control laws and makes sure that nothing ever changes?'.

'That's pretty much it. But this problem in Sudan is much bigger than what we are dealing with now'

'Not to the parents of those kids in Missouri who went to school and never came home it isn't,' Ward replied sarcastically.

'We need to know what Lockhart knows before we do anything to him. It's really important that you find out, is that clear Ryan?' The Old Man asked sternly.

'You've already told me not to kill him.'

'Are you going to see him now?'

'Not yet.'

'Why?'

'Because I need to finish this before I see him. I have to see some Klansmen first.'

'You mean the Ku Klux Klan?' Centrepoint said in astonishment, 'How are they involved?' he asked. Ward ignored his question.

'I need you to make an appointment with Lockhart for me. Mike met some of his men, but you already know that because I'm sure that The Optician told you what happened. I will find him anyway if I hunt him, you will just be saving me some time.'

'I'll see what I can do. Do not do anything to Lockhart until I get back to you,' The Old Man said.

Ward hung up the phone.

'Were you talking about Samson Samone?' Lawson asked excitedly, the recent conversation that he and Ward had shared still fresh in his own mind.

'Yes, can you believe that? The Old Man wants us to deal with the problems that the CIA has caused.'

Lawson went quiet for a moment.

'What's wrong?' Ward asked.

'He can't seriously be contemplating sending us over there? That is special forces territory, and while I'm sure that me and you might be OK, even Mac and his boys, even that won't be enough to deal with what he will throw at us,' Lawson replied.

'Let's deal with it if and when it happens,' Ward replied, 'Right now, we have a meeting to arrange with Newman.'

He picked up Hershey's cell phone and called Newman. He answered on the third ring.

'I thought you had got scared and run off English boy,' Newman said as he answered.

Ward sighed,

'I'm not English Einstein,' he replied, 'Do you want to tell me where you are now?'

'No need for you to know my location, we can meet on neutral ground.'

'You sound scared to me Newman. How many of your boys have I killed so far? Is it eight or ten? I have no idea, I've lost count. That must eat away at you,' Ward said calmly.

'You can see how much it eats away at me. Get yourself over to Hell's Kitchen and call me when you are there.'

'What makes me better than you is that I am not dumb. There's what; twenty of you? There are only two of us, so I make the call where to meet. You need me more than I need you. I can walk away now and never give you another thought but you are stuck, your boss Mr Hughes is screaming at you to get me, so you have to do what I tell you to do, or you will just have to wait until I find you, if I can be bothered. You see Newman, you really aren't important to me; I'm offering to meet you just so I can kill you. All you are is a little bit of sport, a little bit of light relief for me and my friend.'

'Bring the girl,' Newman demanded.

'The girl is dead. I shot her in the head. Once she had given me everything that she had on Hughes and the involvement of your groups, I had no further use for her.'

There was silence on the end of the line.

Ward wasn't sure if he was communicating what was being said to someone else or if he was weighing up the pros and cons of actually turning up for a showdown with him.

What he had said was partly true. He didn't have much use for Newman. His aim now was to find the committee members and Lockhart, and distribute the relevant justice to them.

But he figured that if he could remove Newman and the majority of his men before confronting the others, it would make the final part of this operation much more straightforward.

Without Newman and his men, they would not encounter too much resistance.

'Where do you want to meet?' Newman eventually asked.

Ward thought of an appropriate place to meet for a few seconds.

He wanted it to be in a relatively public place but far enough away from the streets to avoid any innocent people getting hurt. He initially thought of meeting close to the Yankee Stadium, but then remembered that even when the Yankee's weren't playing, huge numbers of tourists went along to visit the stadium, and so he dismissed that immediately.

And then he smiled a big smile to himself.

He knew a place well that he had been to before. It was secluded and it was so beautifully ironic.

'I know where to meet.'

'Do you want to tell me?' Newman demanded.

'There's a place called Revolution books. It is on the corner of a building block. At the rear, there is some wasteland where there used to be some lock up garages, you can meet me there, in half an hour,' Ward said, waiting for Newman's next question.

'How about give me the address,' Newman said sarcastically

'Drive up 121 West 132nd Street, and then turn onto the next road,' he said, waiting for the next question.

'What road?' Newman asked, right on time.

'It's on Malcom X Boulevard,' he replied and hung up the phone.

THIRTY

433 Malcom X Blvd – New York

Less than ten minutes later, Lawson was pulling the car to a stop at the back of revolution books on Malcolm X Boulevard. Ward knew that the chances of Newman being close by were very slim, and he wanted to get there first and check out the lay of the land, mainly to make sure that nothing had changed since he was last there.

He stepped out of the car and looked out at the wasteland.

It was exactly how he remembered it.

Lawson had laughed when he had heard Ward tell Newman where to meet.

The Brits were big on irony.

He took out his cell phone and called The Optician.

'Are you following me?' he asked before The Optician could greet him.

'I'm looking at you right now,' The Optician replied, a slight jumpy tone to his voice, like he was jogging.

Ward smiled to himself.

'You are now getting yourself into position I take it? There's a guy turning up with possibly up to twenty guys with him. You can take as many of them as you want, whenever you want, you don't need to wait for my signal, but leave the main man to me and Mike. Is that OK?'

'Whatever you want my friend. The Old Man has told me that these guys are in the Klan. Is that right?' he asked.

'Yes it is,' Ward replied.

'I hate those people. They killed an old colleague of mine down in Mississippi and they never caught them,' The Optician said.

'Well your luck is in today, these boys are all from Mississippi, my guess is that one or more of them would have been involved in that,' Ward lied.

'Then I will enjoy this,' The Optician replied and the line went dead.

'How many people do you think that he has killed over the years?' Lawson asked.

Ward thought about this for a moment.

He started counting the number up from the first mission that he had worked with The Optician, but when he hit thirty people by the time he got to their fourth outing together, he gave up.

'It's a frightening number,' Ward replied, and shook his head at the thought.

Killing to Ward held no emotional attachment. Most human beings can't live with taking another life, but he had conditioned himself over the years to accept that for every person that he killed, he had probably saved at least ten lives in the process, and so he saw it as morally correct.

Which to an extent, it was.

'Where shall we set up?' Lawson asked, interrupting his thoughts of The Optician.

He looked around at the wasteland.

It was an open space; the building that once sat on the plot would have been very big.

He stepped out of the car and leant against the hood, Lawson joining him immediately.

'It's a pretty open space, what do you think?' Lawson asked.

Ward smiled to himself.

He felt completely safe knowing that The Optician was watching over them, and he knew that he would start taking Newman's guys out before they could fire a shot at them. He also knew that if they stayed exactly where they were, they would have to come out into the open to approach them. Newman would have been told to find out exactly what he knew; he was sure of that.

He could bring his twenty guys; he knew that he would be safest where he was.

'Here will do,' he replied.

'I just knew you were going to say that,' Lawson replied.

As it was, twenty minutes later, Newman turned up with only eleven men including himself.

They watched as first a silver BMW turned up, and stopped fifty yards away from them, and five guys stepped out, and a few moments later, a black SUV rolled to a stop behind the BMW, and six guys were standing outside of it almost immediately.

Ward recognised Newman from the 'Tap-Tap' shop immediately. He was a big guy.

The other ten guys with him all looked the same in two different ways. Five of them were muscular, too muscular for their gym strength to be effective, and the other five guys looked like they had all slept in the woods overnight. They wore tatty jeans and dirty checked shirts.

There was an initial stand-off while Ward and Lawson watched some of the guys arm themselves with baseball bats and the rest pulled out handguns.

They weren't going to be able to shoot them from that far away.

'What sort of idiot brings a baseball bat to a gun fight?' Lawson asked.

Ward ignored him and stepped forward about ten feet, still within relatively safety, and he beckoned towards Newman and then put his hands into his pocket to appear non-threatening.

Newman snarled at him he then said something to a guy holding a gun on his right, the guy peeled off to the side of the wasteland.

He had taken no more than eight steps when The Optician began a stunning sequence of shooting.

On his eighth step, a red mist sprayed from the guy's head and his body contorted into a position that made him look like he was going to roll forward for a moment, before springing backwards and landing on his back. His second shot took out the guy standing two feet away on Newman's left hand side, the 7.62mm bullet smashed directly into the centre of the guys' forehead, hitting with such impact that his legs kicked off the ground and the back of his head smashed hard into the fender of the BMW as he fell to the ground.

Shots number three and four were fired a split second apart. The first bullet hit the guy just over Newman's right shoulder in the centre of his forehead and his knees gave way with minimum fuss, as the blood sprayed from his head. The same could not be said of the fourth guy. As the bullet smashed into the centre of his forehead, his head exploded, his shattered skull and brain matter sprayed everywhere, almost in a three sixty loop. The guy seemed to stay on his feet longer than he should have, as his brain waited to shut down, and then he wobbled and fell to the side, landing face first on the rocky floor.

Ward stood still, staring straight ahead at Newman. And still with his hands in his pockets.

The fifth and sixth shots went exactly where Ward was expecting them to go.

The fifth shot smashed into the forehead of the guy holding a gun to Newman's right, and he toppled backwards and fell into some fencing, the old fence breaking his fall as he landed.

The sixth shot was for Newman.

The bullet smashed hard into his left kneecap and he yelped loudly, and fired off two shots towards Ward and Lawson as he fell to the floor.

He missed them by at least thirty feet.

He let go of his gun and used both hands to grasp his knee and pull it up towards him, desperately trying to stop the pain that was like nothing that he had ever experienced before. Ward took a moment to smile to himself.

Now all that was left were five guys who had come to a gunfight holding baseball bats.

The muscle men had just about registered what was happening as the seventh, eighth, ninth, tenth and eleventh shots hit their intended targets within a split second of each other.

Shots seven and eight hit their targets in exactly the same fashion as the other guys who The Optician had taken out, the bullets smashing hard into the centre of their foreheads and blowing their skulls apart, and they both fell backwards in perfect harmony, almost as graciously as a couple of synchronised swimmers.

Then Ward figured that The Optician must have gotten bored, because on shots nine and ten, he mixed it up a bit. The ninth shot hit the muscle guy in the left side of his chest, the bullet ripping through the steroid induced muscle with ease, and tearing his heart apart like a jagged blade would, and his arms sprung up to the side and he fell back without making any other movement. The tenth shot hit the guy next to him directly on the temple on the left hand side of his head, as he turned, almost in slow motion to watch his gym buddy ceasing to exist. The bullet tore through the tissue and exited the other side, the guy's knees gave way and he collapsed to the floor before the bullet had smashed into the wall of the building behind him after leaving his head.

That left one more shot.

The last muscle guy was a good twenty feet away from the rest of the group, and he was starting to sprint for the safety of the rear of the SUV.
He never made it.
The Optician fired a deliberate shot that tore into the guys back and ripped his spinal cord apart, and when the speed that he was sprinting was added to the force of the impact of the bullet hitting him, he jerked forward and fell to the floor, landing face first against a big concrete rock with such force that it ripped the whole front of his face clean off. He was dead by the time he had slid down the rock and onto the dirty floor in a crumpled heap.

'The frightening number has just got bigger,' Lawson quipped.
Ward ignored him and he started to walk across the wasteland towards Newman, noting that his cries of pain were getting louder with each step he took. By the time he had reached Newman, the cries had stopped and he was frantically scurrying for his gun which had landed a

few feet away from him. As Newman reached the gun and went to wrap his fingers around it to grip it, he stamped hard on his hand with the heel of his boot. Newman screamed again and moved his hand back in towards his body.

Lawson leant down and picked Newman's gun up and then said,

'What sort of idiot brings guys with baseball bats to a gunfight?' and then he kicked Newman hard in the ribs for good measure.

Newman groaned and then looked up at Ward.

He saw a seven-foot giant standing over him, with eyes that installed a fear in him more than he had ever felt before, and it frightened him to such an extent, that he momentarily forgot about the pain of his shattered kneecap coursing through his entire body.

Ward studied him for a moment, when he was satisfied that he could see the fear in Newman's eyes that he wanted to see, he said,

'What I don't get is why?'

Newman looked at him blankly, in between wincing in agony,

'Why what?' he asked.

"Why you would bring a fight to me in spite of you knowing that we are in a league way, way above yours?'

'It wasn't about you.'

'What was it about then?'

'It was about keeping our fighters armed and protected,' Newman replied, 'I'm in agony, I need help. Call me a paramedic and I will tell you whatever you want to know,' Newman begged.

'No paramedics,' Ward replied, and he raised his Glock and fired a shot into Newman's left thigh. The bullet tore through the muscle and blood started to pump slowly from the gaping wound.

Newman screamed in agony again, and stopped clutching his knee and moved his hands up to the new wound and pushed down hard. He was smart enough to know that if he did not stem the flow of blood, he would bleed out and die very quickly.

'I will call you a paramedic if you answer my questions truthfully,' Ward said, 'And if you lie to me, I will put a bullet in you for every lie, but I will not kill you outright, I will wait for you to slowly bleed to death in front of me. Your hands can only cover two wounds at one time, the next one, if you lie to me, will give you a real problem. Do you understand me?'

Newman nodded at him.

He knew that he was going to tell him the truth.

'What do you mean by keeping your fighters armed and protected?' he asked.

'Hughes supplied every order of the Klan in the Southern States with weapons, so that we can arm ourselves against the Negros and Jews who want to take over our country,' he replied through gritted teeth.

Ward had no time for ideologists. He had dealt with so many of them, from so many different cultures over the years that, while he once respected anyone who firmly believed in something, he had come to realise that brainwashing is brainwashing.

And that's all politics and religion really was.

'Where is Hughes right now?'

'He's at the Baccarat Hotel.' Newman replied without any hesitation.

He knew that he was telling the truth.

'Are the other men with him, the other CEOs?'

'He moved them all into completely different hotels so that you wouldn't find them together.'

He knew he was telling the truth.

'Did you know about the planned shootings and the kids involved?' he asked calmly.

Newman looked up at him; the pain was now clouding his vision,

'No I didn't,' he replied, 'I knew we had to protect a woman but I didn't know why.'

Ward knew that he was lying.

He was going to kill him right then for Kyle Newson and Adam Ray, and he wanted to tell him they were the reason that he was going to die, but then he remembered something else and so he decided to save their names until he came face to face with the men behind the whole thing.

'Do you remember Harv?' he asked.

Newman looked at him blankly.

'Harv, he was the old guy?'

Newman still looked confused.

'He was the old guy that you killed in the 'Tap-Tap Munitions' store,' Ward said softly, 'And the fact that you can't even remember him shows that you are scum Newman. Black, White, American, Jewish, none of them mean anything to you.'

He could see Newman trying hard to think about Harv, and a slight light of recognition started to spread across his face.

He hated the fact that a guy like Newman could kill an ordinary, hard-working guy like Harv, and that it would mean so little to him, that he would have to think hard to remember him.

'I'm going to rip everything apart that you belong to,' he said, 'And after that, I am going to take a group of my black colleagues, and hunt down every woman in your family and then I'm going to let them loose on them,' he lied.

Newman wanted to respond but Ward never gave him the chance.

He raised his Glock and pointed it at Newman's head, 'After all,' he said calmly, 'Isn't that what you would expect from Negros? You think they are all animals. But this time, they have well and truly won. They are laughing at you. Take that to hell with you,' he added and then he fired his gun, four times at Newman's head. The bullets literally blew his head apart.

By the time that the fourth bullet had hit, there was a four-inch hole in the centre of his face and an equally big hole in the top of his skull.

'Seriously,' Lawson said, as the ring of the last shot disappeared, 'Who brings a baseball bat to a gunfight?' Ward laughed.

'I take it we are going to the Baccarat Hotel now?' Lawson asked.

'No,' Ward replied, 'I need to make a call first, and then we will hopefully be going somewhere completely different.'

THIRTY-ONE

Park Avenue– New York

The phone rang in Nicole-Louise and Tacklers' apartment, as she looked at the screen and saw Ward's name in bold letters, Nicole-Louise said,
'You found him, you can tell him.'
Tackler reached over and picked the phone up from the coffee table.
'Hello Ryan,' he answered,
'Hey Tackler,' Ward replied, 'Everything good?'
Tackler noticed immediately that this was different.
Ward was never one to exchange pleasantries over the phone; every second that he spent in the field was too precious to him for that, so Tackler instantly knew that he was being subtle.
He wasn't sure if it made him feel angry or happy.

He felt angry because this whole mission had highlighted his past, full of bullying and insecurity, but he also felt happy that Ward was looking out for him as a friend.

'I'm not that pathetic guy anymore,' Tackler said defensively.

'I'm going to tell you something,' Ward replied, 'There's nothing wrong with being vulnerable at times. It happens to me a lot.'

The revelation surprised Tackler. He doubted very much that Ward had ever been frightened, or felt vulnerable in his life. Tackler saw him as a machine. He was a good guy, with good morals, and the thing he admired most about him was that he always stood up for the little guy, but he doubted very much that Ward ever felt vulnerable.

'So what makes you feel vulnerable Ryan?' Tackler asked sarcastically.

There was a pause on the phone for a few moments and then Ward said,

'I get lonely Tackler. I crave normality. I want me and Eloisa to live normal lives and my vulnerability is that I am frightened that I will never have that, and sometimes that gets me really down. I look at what you and Nicole-Louise have and I am envious.'

Tackler had no idea how to respond, so all he could say was,

'And how do you cope when you feel vulnerable?'

Ward laughed softly down the phone and then said,

'I do what all little boys do, I run home to see my mother for a cuddle and a good meal.'

Tackler knew that he was telling the truth.

When he set up his new identity, Ward had insisted that his mother was put in a safe place first, and that any link to her through him could never be traced.

Ward had grown up in England, but his mother was from Ireland originally, and Tackler had used money that they had stolen from a corrupt South African family to set his mother up with a new life in her place of birth, County Cork in Ireland.

He also knew that Ward frequently visited her and would only ever call her from a call box.

He realised at that moment that the shame and vulnerability that he had been feeling affected everyone at some point in their life.

'Well my parents aren't quite as reassuring or interested as your mom,' he said and laughed.

"'We are your family Tackler. Anything that affects you, affects us. Anyone who hurts, or indeed has hurt you in the past, is attacking us. To be honest, having me, Lawson, McDermott and the boys, also The Optician standing shoulder to shoulder with you, probably makes you the worst guy on the planet to bully or pick on.' Ward replied.

Tackler felt a warm glow all over his body. He had never felt that he belonged to a real family until now. He looked across at Nicole-Louise and she smiled at him warmly.

He knew right then that what he used to be, had long gone.

'There was this guy at school called Francis Gollini,' Tackler said, 'And he made my life…"

'I know about Gollini,' Ward interrupted, 'But right now, we have more pressing matters. Where is Senator

Lockhart?' he asked in his normal rushed and assertive tone, which made Tackler wonder if the previous part of the conversation had taken place at all.

'He's at the Greenwich Hotel on Greenwich Street. He had an engagement there which finished an hour ago and it looks like he is settling down for lunch,' Tackler replied.

Hughes and the other guys on that list, do you know where they all are?'

'Yes we do. Nicole-Louise is keeping tabs on them all.'

'We know that they operate some sort of committee, who is likely to be the youngest one?'

'That would be Peter Cullip. He is the CEO of Tap-Tap Munitions.'

'So that's why he was bullied into letting Newman's men use his store as a base,' Ward replied, 'They are all in different hotels, I want to know where they are, starting with Cullip.'

'Actually, they are not all in different hotels, two of them are together.'

'Just tell me where they are, and if they move location. And I want you to steal as much money as you possibly can from them,' Ward replied.

'I'll get Nicole-Louise on the money immediately, and I'll send you the information on their whereabouts as soon as you hang up.'

Ward hung up the phone.

377 Greenwich Street – New York

Greenwich Street was about twenty-five minutes away from Malcolm X Boulevard, so it gave Ward the opportunity to call Eloisa.

He pressed dial on his speed dial, and to his surprise, she answered.

'Hello you,' she said, 'Sorry I did not get back to you last night; I'm working on a new case that has landed on my desk, and we didn't finish until the early hours of this morning. But I'm free tonight and I'm hoping you will take me out to dinner.'

Ward smiled.

He knew that everything would be resolved by tonight and he could spend some quality time with her.

'I got the envelope,' he said, 'So tonight can be all about us. No work, just us.'

'That sounds perfect Ryan. I love you so much and I want to be close to you.'

Ward instantly felt butterflies in the pit of his stomach. Only she could make him feel that.

'Have you heard of a guy called Samson Simone?' he asked.

There was a pause on the end of the line for a few moments.

'Of course we have Ryan. But that's not for you to get involved with, that's way too big for you. Leave that to the governments of the world to sort out. I mean it, is that clear?' she asked, sounding anxious as she spoke.

'Understood Ma'am,' Ward replied, 'What time will you be home?'

'I'll be at yours by seven thirty, don't be late,' she said, 'Or I won't do that thing you like,' she added with a chuckle.

Ward felt himself becoming instantly aroused.

Only she could do that to him.

'I'll be waiting, don't you worry about that,' he replied.

'I love you,' she said and hung up the phone.

Lawson looked across at him, he went to say something but Ward said,

'Don't!'

Twenty minutes later they pulled up outside the Greenwich Hotel. It was meant to be one of New York's top hotels, but from the outside, he wasn't impressed with it. He felt it looked more like a building that housed offices rather than one thousand dollar a night rooms.

Lawson parked the car on North Moore Street opposite a parking garage, and they walked around to the front of the hotel and entered through the main doors.

There were two pretty women behind the reception desk, and they both fixed their eyes firmly on Lawson as they approached the desk,

'They seem to be under your spell Mike, find out where Lockhart is,' Ward said quietly.

Lawson approached the desk.

'I have a dilemma,' he said, 'You are both beautiful, and I don't know which one to ask for help,' he added then smiled.

Both of the women blushed and did a double take on Lawson's eyes again.

They were both in their early thirties by Ward's estimation. In the end, the decision was made for Lawson when he spotted the engagement ring on one of the women's finger,

'Some lucky man beat me to it,' he said to her and smiled, 'but you seem ring less,' he added, moving the few steps that brought him directly opposite the other woman. The woman with the engagement ring moved over to the left to help another guest, looking disappointed in the process.

'I need your help,' Lawson began, 'I've been sent here to carry out a short interview with Senator Lockhart which will get me the promotion I have been after for two years. The problem is, I left my appointment sheet with his room number on at the office, and if I ring my boss to ask for it, he will more than likely, tell me to come back to the office so he can fire me.'

Ward could see the willingness to help Lawson written all over her face.

'I shouldn't pass on any guest information,' she said.

'Even if it means I'll lose my job?' Lawson asked

She looked deep into his eyes once more so he went in for the kill,

'How about if you give me his room number, I will give you my number, you call me when you finish work, then I take you out for dinner, as a thank you for saving my job?'

She smiled at him.

'Your number?' she asked, 'And I'm Charlene,' she added, pointing at her name plate.

Lawson pulled out a card and gave it to her.

Ward caught a glimpse of it, and could see it was just a card with a number stamped on it in the middle.

She took the card and said,

'Four thirty-one,' and smiled at him.

'Call me later Charlene,' Lawson replied.

Because he had already decided that he would try to convince her later to join him and one of five of his recently acquired new 'Friends' on a threesome date.

They walked off towards the elevators.

'You actually have printed cards with your real number on them?' Ward asked in dismay.

'Of course I have' Lawson replied as they stepped into the elevator, 'Women love the mystery of it.'

Ward shook his head as Lawson pressed the button for the fourth floor.

They stepped out of the elevator when the doors opened, and immediately saw the guy standing guard outside room four thirty-one.

He definitely wasn't Secret Service; Ward was in no doubt that he was one of the hired hands that Lockhart had called in.

They walked down the corridor towards him, without making any eye contact with him as they got about ten feet away, the door to Lockhart's room opened and another guy walked out, shutting the door behind him with his back to them.

He turned around.

It was the same guy who had walked out of the room with Lockhart at The Mark Hotel, the guy who had pushed the barrel of his gun into Lawson's back.

He recognised Lawson immediately.

Ward noticed the look of recognition on Lawson's face, without a second's hesitation, he sprinted forward, with an electric burst of pace, before either guy could react, he unleashed a right hook from his side, as he pushed forward with his left foot, and his fist connected squarely on the nose of the guy who had just come out of the room. He turned to face the other guy who had been standing guard, as he looked at him, he saw the guy was slowly starting to raise his hands above his head.

Ward looked around and Lawson had his handgun drawn pointing directly at him.

He then looked down at the guy on the floor, he was not moving. He stepped over to him and kicked him hard in the ribs.

The guy groaned.

He was pleased to see he was alive he didn't want to kill any guy who was trying to make a living guarding people like Lockhart, particularly guys who used to be in the forces.

'How many men are in there with Lockhart?' he asked the guard quietly.

'He was the only one. There are only two of us. The rest are somewhere else,' the guard replied.

'The rest are dead,' Lawson interrupted, 'They were all dead on the floor of the room in the Mark Hotel when I last saw them.'

'You two are the Brits,' the guy said, suddenly realising what he was faced with, 'I have a wife and a kid. I'm just trying to earn some money so that I can get my kid through college when he is older. My service pension doesn't pay me too much, and I am unemployable in any other industry, I have no skills.'

Ward could see by the desperation on his face that the guy was telling the truth.

'Take your friend and disappear, go back to Washington or wherever you live, and forget you ever heard about us or saw us. Can you do that?' Ward asked.

'Yes I can,' the guy replied.

Once again, Ward could see that he was telling the truth.

'We don't want to kill you, but we will without any hesitation, and we will never give you another thought again. At the moment, you are a normal guy we are cutting a break to, if you try coming back with any other guys, you become our enemy, and you really don't want that. Do you understand?'

'Yes I do. I know when to cut and run. We are gone and you will never see us again,' the guy replied, and he moved over to his colleague, who was just about coming around, and helped him gingerly to his feet.

'I should shoot you in the head right now for putting your gun into my back, so this really is your lucky day,' Lawson said to the guy who was desperately trying to coordinate his feet as he regained full consciousness.

Both of them ignored him.

They watched them both stagger down to the end of the hall until they reached the door which led to the stairway, and a few seconds later, they were through the door and out of sight.

Ward looked at Lawson and nodded, and then he stepped over to Lockhart's door and knocked four times.

THIRTY-TWO

Park Avenue– New York

Nicole-Louise could find money hidden anywhere. It was her forte, her speciality.
She had established that the committee members had a combined personal wealth of almost one hundred million dollars. And that was excluding the net worth of their five companies which would, with current turnover values taken into account, push them close to a billion dollars.
'These people are obscenely rich, and all on the back of misery,' she said, 'Look at these personal accounts.'
Tackler walked across to her workstation and looked at the sheet she had on her screen.
Their current cash values were staring back at him;

Darren Hughes - $33, 952, 450
Kenny Hasloff - $ 27, 527, 691

Charles Andrews - $ 13,684, 600
Charles T Dunlop - $ 11, 834, 704
Peter Cullip -$ 9, 525, 857

'Do they have any other money stored away?' Tackler asked.

'No, that's everything. The figures you are looking at are a total combination of all of the accounts that they have. Eighty per cent of them were off shore, but it was easy to find them all.'

'How did you find them so quickly? I mean, even for you, it was only half an hour ago that Ryan asked for the information,' Tackler replied, genuinely impressed.

She smiled at him and then punched him on the arm. 'What?' he asked.

'I started digging yesterday, and if you weren't in such a state of misery you would have noticed.'

'I've not been fun to be around, have I?' he asked ruefully.

'No, you haven't,' she replied, 'you are also as dull as anything when you are like that.'

'I'm sorry,' he replied, and he leant down and kissed her cheek, 'It just brought back memories of Gollini and the torment that the douche put me through.'

'Well we can put that right,' she said.

'How can we?'

'That can wait, but right now, we have a lot of money to steal. Fancy a race?' she asked.

'You take the top two, and I'll take the bottom two, and the winner gets to take this Andrews guy?' he asked enthusiastically.

'Exactly the same as I had in mind.'

'Send it over,' he said as he turned, heading back towards his own workstation.
'It's already there,' Nicole-Louise replied before starting to tap furiously on her keyboard once again.

377 Greenwich Street – New York

Senator Neville Lockhart opened the door shortly after Ward had stopped knocking.
And immediately took a short jab to the throat before he could even speak.
As he wheeled back into the room, clutching his throat, Ward and Lawson stepped through the door, Lawson closed the door behind him.
Lockhart's wife screamed, so Ward pulled out his silenced Glock and said,
'One more noise and I'll blow your husband's head off.'
She stopped screaming immediately,
'You are the two Brits,' she stuttered as she threw an anxious look at her husband, 'He is a United States Senator, and you are going to create an international incident if you don't turn around and walk away right now,' she added.
Ward walked past Lockhart, who was now slowly starting to get back some control of his breathing, standing directly in front of her.
Then he punched her hard in the stomach, knocking her off her feet, forcing her to fall backwards on the sofa.
'And you've just told me that you are aware of everything that is going on, as I know that you already launder the money through your sister's estate, that

makes you as responsible as he is for all the people that have died,' he said softly.

'Keep your hands off of her,' Lockhart screamed through his gasps.

Lawson stepped forward and cuffed Lockhart around the ear with his open palm,

'I told you that I would walk out of that room alive,' he said.

Lockhart ignored him and looked at Ward, who in turn, stared back at him, with no emotion on his face at all. This unsettled him much more than his curiosity to find out how Lawson had walked out of the room at The Mark Hotel. Before he could pull himself away from the glare of Ward's eyes, Lawson pulled him off the floor with one strong hand and shoved him hard in the back towards the sofa.

'Sit!' he demanded.

Lockhart sat down immediately like an obedient dog.

'Are you OK?' he asked his wife.

She managed to nod at him.

Ward sat down on the armchair which was directly opposite them, with only a small coffee table separating them.

'I am a United States Senator,' Lockhart said, his breathing sounding relatively normal now, 'Our government will not tolerate this. There are people in Washington who know who you are, and they will find you. I have contacts in the CIA and they can find anyone or anything they want,' he added, trying his best to sound assertive and in control, despite the fear that Ward could see all over his face.

'You haven't even considered the fact that it was the people in Washington who sent us, have you?' Ward asked softly.

'What people are you talking about, who?' Lockhart's wife asked, now seemingly over the punch she had taken to the stomach.

Ward smiled at her,

'Who is in charge here, you or him?' he asked.

'Do you understand the trouble that you are in? There are powerful people in Washington, way above politicians who have our backs,' she replied.

'You aren't getting it lady,' Lawson said, 'We have been sent by the people, who are above the people, who are above the people that you are referring to.'

'Keep quiet,' Ward eventually said to Lockhart's wife, 'I'm going to ask you some questions. It's not preferable that I kill you, after all, regardless of how much of a scumbag you are, we have just recently killed some Senator's in California, so I am going to ask you some questions, and if you tell me the truth, I will walk away. Do you understand?' he asked, sounding like a parent talking to a child.

'That was you?' Lockhart asked, panic running through his voice now.

'Do you understand?' he repeated.

Lockhart nodded enthusiastically to him.

He was all about self-preservation, all of the cowardly and greedy politicians were.

'Why did you arrange for arms to be sent to Samson Simone?' Ward asked.

Lockhart went white, and his wife looked at him in panic.

'I'm asking you, not her,' he said.

Lockhart bit his bottom lip lightly, it was telling him that he was either going to lie, or deny any knowledge about Simone.

So he thought he would help him.

'Three years ago in June, you arranged, through a CIA contact, to provide arms for Simone to overthrow an elected leader. You went to Darren Hughes and he helped you deliver on your promise. He gave you a huge amount of arms, a lot of them faulty or second hand for no payment. You then sent the weapons to Simone, the CIA paid you handsomely for them, and you pocketed all of the money. So we know why you had the one mammoth payment to your sister-in-law's estate through shares.'

Lockhart's wife started looking really agitated.

'But that is not why you are actually sitting opposite me and why I'm deciding if I should kill you or not. So to help me make my mind up, am I right about Simone?' he asked.

Both Lockhart and his wife nodded.

'He can't hear you,' Lawson said.

'Yes,' they both said in unison.

Ward could see that they were both telling the truth.

'Hughes then continues to pay you shares, and they line up with events that he and his committee orchestrated. Tell me why, but be careful what you tell me, because I already know the answer and if you lie, I will shoot you here and now,' he said.

'It wasn't his doing,' his wife interrupted, 'He got involved by passing certain legislation on the Senate Committee's that he sits on, minor committee's I stress, in return, they refused to make any changes to our current gun laws. Then Hughes gave us shares as a thank you.'

'And the committees were always called after a shooting took place?'

'Yes,' Lockhart replied.

'And they kept the events away from Mississippi so that you wouldn't have any pressure put on you by your voters?'

They both shifted uncomfortably on the sofa, telling him that was exactly what they had agreed.

He studied them again, carefully; it was becoming more and more apparent to him that Lockhart's wife seemed to be the one making the decisions.

'Do you know who sent me?' Ward asked.

Lockhart shook his head.

'It was the families of all of the innocent people you have directly been involved in the killing of. What do you think they would do if they were sitting where I am now holding a gun?'

Lockhart started to panic, his breathing got heavy, and he started to grind his fingertips together.

'What do you think they would do Mike?' he asked Lawson.

Lawson stepped forward and sat on the arm of the sofa and then he leant down towards them both,

'We had to go and see two kids to stop them from killing innocent people,' he said, 'One of them we got to in time and the poor kid was all alone in the world. The other one got killed before our very eyes. They were just boys, little kids, and you happily got involved in destroying their lives, also the lives of hundreds of other innocent people, probably thousands, so if they were sitting here, they would probably want to do what I want to do now, which is pump three bullets into your face,' he added, calmly and menacingly.

Ward had never seen Lawson act in such a threatening manner before and it impressed him.

'I can give you names,' Lockhart said, 'Names of other Senators who have additional incomes from less than reputable means.'

'I already have them,' Ward replied, 'How long have you two been married?' he asked.

They looked at him blankly.

'Forty-six year's yesterday' Lockhart replied, 'Why?'

'There's a kid called Adam Ray who will never get married and have kids. He lived a short life full of misery, he was a better person than you two have ever been capable of being. How much do you love her?' he asked.

'I don't understand,' Lockhart replied.

'It's a simple question. You've been together for forty-six years', how much do you love your wife?'

'I've always loved her, since we were kids, why?' Lockhart asked, confusion running through his voice.

Without another word, Ward raised his Glock and shot her three times in the face.

The first bullet hit her directly in the right eye and ripped the tissue apart, the second smashed into her nose ripping it clean off, and the third bullet hit her in the forehead.

Bone and gristle sprayed everywhere covering Lockhart. Her head was forced violently backwards then she rolled to the side.

Her face had gone.

Lockhart let out a scream and pulled at her arm desperately trying to get her back into an upright position. Her body was still jerking, giving Lockhart the false impression that she was still alive, but Ward had seen enough dead bodies to know that they were just the last signals being sent from her brain before it shut down.

Lockhart burst into tears and started hyperventilating. Ward stood up and walked over to the sofa.

'Look at her and now tell me that all money you have made has been worth it. Was it worth it Senator?' he asked.

'You bastard,' Lockhart screamed.

Ward grabbed hold of Lockhart's hair and pulled him off of the sofa and threw him to the floor.

Lockhart looked up at him his sobs stopped instantly and he went white.

He was looking into Ward's eyes and they were screaming at him. There was no emotion to them, but there was a message coming from them that he couldn't decipher. This British guy looked about seven feet tall to him, and right then; he was the most frightening sight that he had ever seen in his life.

'Please, don't,' was all he could manage to say.

'Surely you don't want to carry on living without the great love of your life Senator?' Ward asked softly.

'We have family, please, don't kill me,' Lockhart begged.

He looked as pathetic as Ward wanted him to look. He had residue running from his nose down to his chin, he was shaking with fear, and he looked terrified.

He looked every single thing that he deserved to look. Now Ward had one more thing to say.

'In a few minutes we are going to walk out of this room. When we leave, we are heading down to Mississippi to kill your family, every single family member we can find, from your siblings to your grandchildren, before we kill them, we are going to tell them everything you have done and that is why they are about to die,' he lied.

This part was always important to him.

He didn't want someone that had carried out evil acts to die with an air of resignation; he wanted them to die with a fear of what was yet to happen as a direct result of their actions.

'I'm a Senator,' he pleaded.

Ward raised his gun and fired three shots into Lockhart's face, they hit in an almost identical fashion to the bullets that had killed his wife.

He was dead by the time he fell forward off the sofa smashing what was left of his face against the coffee table.

They looked at the two dead bodies for a few moments and then Lawson said,

'Shall I call The Old Man?'

Ward knew that Centrepoint was not going to be happy, in fact, he knew that he was going to be furious, but the Lockhart's had gotten what they deserved, and he knew that he could live with that, no matter what The Old Man said.

'Yes Mike, call him but don't tell him about the wife just yet, let him find out about that through the clean-up crew.'

He pulled out his own phone and looked at the message from Tackler that was giving him the whereabouts of the committee members and Cullip's name was at the top of the list.

He read the message again and then said,

'Stop!'

'What's wrong?' Lawson asked.

'Can you sweet talk the receptionist again?' he asked.

'Why?'

'Because Peter Cullip is staying here at the Greenwich and there is no point in having to call two separate clean-up crews is there?" he asked.

Lawson smiled at him,

'Give me a minute,' he said he then flashed his mesmerising smile, 'I'm sure Charlene will help me,' he added as he walked out of the room.

Ward looked down at the dead bodies of the Lockhart's once again,

'That was for you Adam Ray,' he whispered to himself,

'Now rest in peace.'

THIRTY-THREE

377 Greenwich Street – New York

Lawson knocked on the door five minutes later and Ward opened it after looking through the security spyhole.

'Charlene has been most helpful,' he said as he walked into the room and Ward closed the door.

'He's still here?' Ward asked.

'In room three twelve,' Lawson replied.

'Let's go.'

They walked out of the room, Ward taking one last look at the bodies of Lockhart and his wife before closing the door, and it gave him a great sense of satisfaction that he had in some small way paid back the misery that they had been partly responsible for inflicting on so many others.

They walked down the hall to the same steps that Lockhart's guards had used, and they started the descent to the third floor.

'Can I ask something?' Lawson asked.

'Providing it's not about interior design or sex, feel free.'

Lawson smiled,

'Actually Ryan, it's a serious question and something that has been bothering me,' Lawson said with an unusually serious look on his face.

Ward stopped walking and turned to him,

'What is it?' he asked.

Lawson carried on walking two more steps until he was past him and then he turned so that their eyes were on the same level.

'You aren't seriously thinking of going to pick a fight with Simone, are you?'

'Why do you ask that?'

'Because I've been into Sudan on secret missions with the best soldiers in the world when I was serving, and it was the only time that we called for an extraction before we achieved our objective. You can't win there Ryan, not without air support clearing the way for you and no government will authorise that.'

'Is this the frightened Mike Lawson talking?' Ward asked dismissively.

'No, it's the smart Mike Lawson talking.'

He looked at Lawson and smiled,

'We will discuss it again when we have finished this, one job at a time Mike.'

'Also,' Lawson said as Ward walked past him and started descending the stairs, 'Do you think beige goes better with brown or black?'

Ward laughed for the tenth time that day at Lawson's brilliant sense of humour.

They came out of the stairwell and onto the hall of the third floor.

The near side room to them was three zero five, and so they turned right and reached the door that had the numbers three, one, two in the centre in bold, brass numbers.

Ward knocked four times in quick succession.

The door was opened by a guy in his early thirties who looked totally inoffensive.

'Peter Cullip?' Ward asked, adding an American accent to his words.

'Yes sir,' Cullip replied, 'How can I help you?'

Ward reached behind his back and pulled out his Glock, 'You are going to invite me and my friend inside, and then you are going to tell us a detailed story about the committee,' he said.

By the time Cullip was sitting down on the sofa in his hotel room, he was shaking badly and his face had gone completely white. Ward sat down opposite him studying him carefully without speaking, and Lawson pulled his gun out and changed the magazine for additional effect. Cullip looked as though he was on the verge of passing out, and so Ward started to speak,

'Do you know who we are?' he asked.

Cullip took a few seconds to compose himself, swallowing hard,

'You are the two British men,' he replied, the sound of fear and panic clearly evident in his voice.

Ward always found that people who were as scared as Cullip were always the hardest people to read. The expression of fear took over their whole face, and their voices shook so bad, it was hard to tell if they were telling the truth or not. Most bad guys he ran into tended to try to be defiant, but Cullip was a complete wreck.

'But do you actually know why we turned up in the first place?'

'Because someone, somewhere, pissed of the British government and they sent you to fix it,' Cullip replied.

This was a positive start he thought, they actually still had no idea why they were after them.

'We don't work for the British government,' he replied, 'We work for the American and British governments. Someone high up got wind of what you had been doing, they sent us to bring you down, with no questions asked.'

'I never wanted to get involved in any of this, I wanted to forge my own career, but my dying father made me promise him on his death bed that I would take over the family business,' Cullip replied.

Ward could see that he was telling the truth.

'Hughes makes all the decisions?' he asked.

'He did but there was a vote of no confidence in him.'

Ward looked at Lawson, and Lawson shrugged his giant shoulders to indicate that he had no idea why they would change the decision maker all of a sudden.

And then he realised.

'It was because of us and his inability to find us and eliminate us wasn't it?' he asked.

Cullip nodded.

'Who is in charge now?'

'Kenny Hasloff.'

'Who is he?' Ward asked, unable to remember which business he ran.

'He is the CEO of Wright & Cannon. We voted him on to replace Mr Hughes after he couldn't find you two,' Cullip said wearily, 'I didn't want any part of this so I tried to back out,' he added.

'When did you try?'

'After you foiled the shooting in Texas.' He replied. Ward nodded,

'Was that the moment you decided you wanted nothing to do with it?' he asked.

'Yes. I wanted to walk away, but Mr Hughes insisted that I stayed,' Cullip replied, his voice less shaky now but still full of nerves.

'We have a problem,' Ward said.

Cullip looked at him.

'Right now, I'm deciding whether to let you live or die,' he started, 'I was starting to believe that you had gotten into this out of a sense of misguided loyalty to your father, which while the wrong thing to do, was still sort of admirable. Family is important; I understand that as well as anyone.'

Cullip looked at Ward and he noticed a sense of hope flicker in his eyes.

'But then you and said the wrong thing,' he said abruptly.

'What?'

'You said after we foiled the shooting in Texas.'

'But it's the truth, I did,' Cullip protested.

'But that was the wrong thing to say,' Ward replied, 'What would have been the right thing to say Mike?' he asked Lawson.

'You should have said after the shooting in Missouri, then we would have known that you genuinely had regret over your involvement in this,' Lawson replied firmly, 'And you really don't want to be saying the wrong thing to my friend, He doesn't respond well to lies.'

'With that in mind,' Ward interrupted, 'You are now going to do something for me and if you get it right, you will live.'

'What do you want me to do, I'll do anything,' Cullip pleaded.

'Wait here, I need to make a call,' he said as he stood up, and walked out of the room.

'You really should do whatever he asks,' Lawson said to Cullip.

'I will, I promise.'

Lawson sat in silence for the next few minutes, just staring at Cullip, trying to make him feel as uneasy as he possibly could.

Ward came back into the room and sat back down opposite Cullip.

'Within the next couple of minutes, your personal bank account is going to swell to almost one hundred million dollars,' he said, 'Our hackers are moving it all out of the accounts of the other committee members into yours. You are a very rich man Mr Cullip, how does that make you feel? After all, wasn't this all about money and power anyway?' he asked calmly.

Cullip looked confused.

Ward could see that he was trying to work out what was going on but was failing miserably, so he explained.

'Don't get too excited, you won't have the money very long,' he said.

'The money is for you?' Cullip asked.

Ward smiled and Lawson laughed,

'If we wanted the money, we would have just taken it you idiot,' Lawson said, 'This guy is so stupid I bet it was his idea to bring the baseball bats to the gunfight,' he added.

Ward laughed.

Cullip had no idea what Lawson was talking about.

'No Mr Cullip. You are so overcome with guilt at the senseless violence and murder that your ammunition has caused, that you decided to take your vast wealth and share it all with the families of the victims of senseless mass shootings. Do you know how many there have been over the past twenty odd years?' he asked.

Cullip shook his head.

'There have been well over seventy. Let's call it seventy-five. At an average of eight people per shooting, what does that make per family Mike?' he asked Lawson.

Lawson started to do the calculation in his head and then Cullip said,

'About one hundred and sixty-five thousand dollars per family.'

Lawson shrugged.

'You see, our people have compiled that list, and that's a lot of lives that your committee has ruined. Explain something to me, what happens when one of the committee retires?' Ward asked.

'No one retires.'

'So what happens?'

'They view the position as an inheritance, like a birth right, as I said; I had no choice but to join them.'

'Do you have children?'

'No I don't.'

'Wife?'

'No.'

Wards phone vibrated in his pocket. He took it out and saw he had a text from Nicole-Louise that simply said, 'Completed'.

'The money has gone,' he said.

Cullip said nothing.

'Do you know who Harv was?' he asked.

Cullip looked at him blankly.

'The question requires a simple yes or no answer.'

'No I don't,' Cullip replied.

'He was an old guy. He ran one of your stores, you know, the store where Newman was allowed to set up base. Newman didn't remember him either.'

'That wasn't me,' Cullip stuttered, 'Hughes forced me to allow Newman and his men to use my store, I tried resisting, but he told me that I had to allow it because the committee had agreed it,' he said.

'That part doesn't bother me; I'm not interested in that. Harv was a good guy, he was helpful to us,' Ward said.

'I liked Harv too,' Lawson said.

'Yet you didn't even know he existed, he was just a run of the mill employee, a name or a number to you. Newman killed Harv, and all the old guy was doing was his job to earn more money for you. Do you want to know what I resent about people like you?'

Cullip didn't respond.

'I resent the fact that when you strip away your position and your money; you are weaker than normal working people who have to fight for everything. You were almost in tears the moment that you saw my gun, and you have sat there like a frightened child from the moment that we sat down. You have nothing. You are nothing. You CEO's are all the same, I've met lots of you, you think business power can make you strong but it can't. Look at you, look how pathetic you are. You look like you are on the verge of crying,' Ward said through gritted teeth for added effect.

Cullip started crying.

Not just a few tears, he started crying and shaking violently.

He then he started to pee his pants.

'For God's sake, have some dignity,' Lawson shouted at him.

'How do you want to die?' Ward asked menacingly.

Cullip started hyperventilating.

It would have been easy to feel sorry for Cullip looking at him, rocking backwards and forwards on the sofa, but then Ward pictured hundreds of parents, wives, children and siblings reacting in the same way when they had discovered that one of their loved ones had been killed in a shooting when they were just going about their everyday life, or having a meal, or just out having fun, and he felt no pity for Cullip at all.

This guy was the worst kind of evil. He blamed others for the misery that he had been a part of and genuinely, deep inside, he didn't think that he had done anything wrong, just because he raised a feeble protest.

Ward looked at Lawson and nodded.

Lawson looked back at him and mouthed, 'Me?' and Ward nodded again.

He wanted to watch Cullip die from a different angle than usual, he wanted to be the witness rather than the executioner, because he wanted to see what Harv would see if he was looking down on them right now.

Lawson walked over to the sofa and stood in front of Cullip.

'Please, please, I'm sorry, I'll fix it,' Cullip begged

'No you won't,' Lawson replied and he squeezed the trigger on his silenced gun, three times, all three bullets smashing into Cullip's chest and heart.

He died instantly.

'Now you had better call The Old Man,' Ward said, 'Tell him to ring me as soon as you are done with him. I'll wait downstairs,' he added, and then he stood up and walked out of the room.

He headed towards the stairwell and pulled his phone out and dialled Nicole-Louise.

'Hello Ryan,' she answered.

'How did you get on with the other thing that I asked you to do?' he asked.

'I have it all, everything you need.'

'And are you OK with it?'

'I'm more than OK with it.'

'Let me know if any of the committee members move from their current location,' he said and then he hung up the phone and made his way down the stairs.

THIRTY-FOUR

377 Greenwich Street – New York

Ward stood on Greenwich Street and observed the people moving around. He noticed that everyone was walking with urgency, like they had somewhere important to get to, and he wondered if he would ever get to a point in his life where he would be able to take things at a leisurely pace. Such was his focus and drive when he was embroiled in a mission that he rarely felt tired on a job. For the first time, as he watched the bankers, lawyers and other people in their suits rushing around, he realised that he was not that different to those people after all. The only difference was that while they closed a deal with a signature, he normally closed his with a bullet.

It was a thought that gave him comfort.

He felt his phone vibrate in his pocket, interrupting his observations, he saw Centrepoint's name on the screen. For a couple of seconds, he thought about ignoring the call but he needed to talk to him more urgently than he needed to avoid a lecture.

'I had no choice,' he said as he answered.

'I'm not happy with you Ryan,' The Old Man said in a louder than normal voice, 'He's a Senator for God's sake. We spoke about this after Los Angeles. Do you realise the complications in trying to cover this up?'

'He was rotten to the core and you know it. I think you are angrier with yourself for not knowing that Lockhart was involved in arms sales with the CIA and they hid it from you,' he replied, not appreciating being spoken to as though he was being lectured, sounding defensive as he spoke.

'You can't keep running around killing whoever you decide to kill after I have told you to steer clear. I give you more than enough scope to do your job, much more than I give anyone else, so it would be nice if now and again you could give me the same trust and respect back. Am I being unreasonable?' he asked, his tone softening now.

Ward knew that he was right.

He imagined The Old Man hunched over his desk in Washington, his head in his hands, now faced with yet another problem created by his hand.

'I'm sorry. I had every intention of letting him live, but he showed such contempt for the people that had suffered, that he somehow pushed me over the edge. I know this has created a problem for you, and next time, I won't kill anyone of political value without clearing it with you first,' he replied, trying his best to sound genuine.

'You only killed him as a last resort?'

'Yes,' Ward replied, 'I was halfway out of the room when he started threatening me,' he added, now feeling pretty sure that The Old Man was buying into this version of events.

'So why did you kill his wife as well?' Centrepoint asked.

He decided to cut his losses there and then. He knew that The Old Man wasn't buying into it at all.

And so he did what he normally did.

He ignored the question and changed subject.

'How deep does this thing with Samson Samone go? Have you established who was involved at the CIA?'

'It is a much bigger mess than I thought I had four people removed from their posts today as a direct result of their involvement,' Centrepoint replied, much to Ward's relief, moving away from the subject of Lockhart, 'You are dealing with the people who provided the arms, so there is deniability there, but this wasn't sanctioned directly by the people on Capitol Hill, this was about senior operatives deciding that they would instigate change, now that it has all blown up, they have just walked away from it.'

Ward could hear him sigh as he finished speaking.

'And they've now dumped it on your desk to sort out?'

'I'm not sure I can. Sudan isn't The States.'

'I needed to speak to you urgently for something,' Ward said.

'I worked that out. There had to be something you needed badly to request a call, rather than call yourself, when you knew you were firmly in my bad books,' Centrepoint replied.

'The people who are on this committee will all be dead within the next couple of hours. Can you intervene and make sure that the people who take over their companies never reinstate this committee and that you get some sort of control over what they are doing. You know how greed works. As soon as people realise that there is an opening, someone else will see an opportunity.'

'What makes you think that it will be reinstated?' Centrepoint asked with genuine curiosity in his voice.

'Because I have had a feeling from the moment I realised what was happening that there was someone else pulling the strings from higher up,' Ward replied.

'Why?'

'Think about it. The moment I found out about Samone, I realised that there had to be someone heavily involved from both high up in the government and the security services. Taking control of the drug trade, sex trade or even the news is one thing, but taking control of a country is a whole different ball game.'

Centrepoint was quiet for a few moments and then said, 'That's what I've been looking into the past twenty-four hours. I'm impressed Ryan, are you trying to take my job from me?'

Ward laughed,

'And put up with people like me? No thanks.'

'I will do what I can to make sure the people who take over these companies will be under our direct control and we will monitor them,' Centrepoint replied.

Ward felt more in relaxed now.

He was always in control face to face with the bad guys, but he was fully aware that there was a whole world of corruption and greed which drove everything in Washington D.C. that he knew nothing about, and Centrepoint was a genius when it came to playing the power game moving politicians around like chess pieces.

He was now sure that once he had eliminated the entire committee, he could walk away knowing that The Old Man would ensure that it would never resurface.

'Lockhart deserved to die,' he said after a moment's pause, 'However much grief it has caused you, I couldn't let him live. You understand that, right?'

'Just get this finished Ryan because I am working on a way to explain to the world how this has all happened. They will notice when all of the CEO's of the biggest arms companies in America, and our longest serving Senator all die within a few hours of each other. But of course, you don't concern yourself with that.'

Ward decided to end the conversation there rather than get into a discussion about the fact that if he had his way, the world would be told the truth.

'I'll finish it,' he replied and hung up the phone.

He turned around and looked into the hotel reception. Lawson was talking to Charlene, and he caught a glimpse of Ward looking at him, so said a quick goodbye and walked out onto the street.

'It turns out that Charlene has a roommate who is a pole dancer,' Lawson said.

Ward shook his head.

'And she is also willing to....'

'Let's go Mike,' he interrupted, and he started to head back towards the car.

'Where are we going?'

'I am going to Spring Street,' Ward replied.

'What about me?'

'You are going to Thompson Street which is a few minutes away.'

'Why?'

'Because I am going to take out Charles Andrews and you are going to eliminate Charles T Dunlop. The hotels are close to each other, so we can save time. That's if you think that you can cope on your own?'

'Without you holding my hand?' Lawson enquired, 'I'm not sure. Can we keep in contact via cell phone throughout?'

Ward laughed.

They jumped into the car and drove the seven minutes to Spring Street.

'Meet me back here in thirty minutes,' Ward said as he stepped out of the car.

246 Spring Street – New York

Ward stood on the street and looked up at the Trump Soho New York Hotel and smiled to himself. His first impression of the building was that cleaning the glass that adorned it had to be a full time job. He thought it was a very flamboyant in your face building and he thought it reflected the owner very well indeed. He walked inside and approached the reception desk. There were two guys busily tapping on keyboards behind the counter.

'Hello Sir,' the guy to his right said as Ward rested his hands on the counter, 'How can I help you?' he asked. He could see by the guy's badge that his name was Rory.

'Can you ring through to Charles Andrews and tell him that he has a visitor please?' he asked pleasantly.

Rory looked him up and down for a moment, and then he could see that he had decided that although he was unsure about Ward's appearance, his crisp and polite British accent had swayed him.

Rory looked at the screen and picked up the phone receiver on the desk,

'Who should I say is here,' he asked as he punched in a number that Ward was unable to see.

'Tell him that Kenny Hasloff is here and I need to see him urgently.'

Rory nodded as he put the phone to his ear.

A moment later, Rory said,

'Sorry to bother you sir but you have a visitor,' still eying him up and down.

'Mr Kenny Hasloff,' he then said, clearly in response to Andrews asking who it was.

'Very well sir, I'll send him up now,' Rory said putting the phone down,

'Room six, four, seven,' he added, smiling at Ward, relieved that he had made the right call, and his guest knew the man who had come to visit him.

'Thank you,' he said, heading across to the elevator, where he saw two young women with their arms around the shoulders of a guy taking selfie's with their cell phones, while an older woman, who Ward assumed to be the guys' wife, stood to the side smiling patiently. The girls walked off as they waited for the elevator, excitedly looking at their phones, and they both came and stood next to him.

The doors opened and Ward said,

'After you,' and ushered them into the elevator.

They walked inside and the guy said, 'Floor?'

'Six.'

Ward recognised the guy.

He was a movie star and a very well-known one, while he was not big on movies, he knew who this guy was because he had played the main character in a franchise about a CIA agent who had lost his memory and was hunting down the bosses who had betrayed him. Ward had watched the movies, if nothing else but to see how close to the truth they were, while he thought the frantic pace of the movies summed up the speed of which they really worked very well, there were way too many fist fights and car chases for it to be authentic. The bosses were not like The Old Man.

'Enjoying New York?' the guy asked.

'It's lovely,' he replied, 'Although the traffic is awful. No chance of going faster than five miles per hour here,' he added, resisting the urge to make a reference to the fist fights.

The guy smiled,

'Are you from England?' he asked.

Ward nodded.

'I guess everything seems like it's moving at a hundred miles an hour to you here?'

Ward nodded,

'Yes it does,' he replied, 'You know what us Brits are like, we like to take things slowly and calmly,' he replied.

'I think you have got it right and we have got it wrong,' the guy added, both he and his wife smiled at him.

He seemed like a nice guy, and Ward liked him instantly. He had no airs about him. He seemed modest.

The last movie star Ward had met, he had shot in the face, so it was refreshing to find that this guy was just a normal guy with no arrogance about him.

He thought how ironic it was that this guy had made a fortune playing at being everything that he was, even though the fist fights and car chases bordered on the ridiculous.

They reached the sixth floor and the elevator stopped. 'Enjoy the rest of your stay,' the guy said as the doors opened.

'Thank you,' Ward said, 'Nice to meet you,' he added, and he stepped out of the elevator and saw room six four seven, directly in front of him.

56 Thompson Street – New York

Lawson pulled up outside the Sixty SoHo Hotel and found a parking space directly opposite the entrance. It looked more like an apartment block that a hotel to him. The only thing that indicated it was a hotel were the two valets standing outside under the burgundy awning with 'Sixty' written in bright white letters on it.

He crossed the road and walked under the awning into the reception area.

He noticed there was a stern looking, middle aged guy behind the desk and he approached him with a big smile on his face.

'Hello Sir,' the guy said, doing a double take on Lawson's eyes as he spoke.

'Hello, I need to see Charles T Dunlop urgently,' Lawson replied.

'Room number?' the guy asked.

'No idea,' Lawson said, 'But if you call up and tell him that he has a visitor, he will definitely want, to see me.'

'Your name?' the guy asked.

'Kenny Hasloff,' Lawson replied, he turned around to watch the pretty and elegant woman walking from the elevator to the hotel bar. She caught a glimpse of him looking at her, and for a moment, she almost stumbled in her tracks, caught in two minds whether to continue in the direction that she was heading in, or to take a detour towards the reception so that she could strike up a conversation with him.

'He says go up sir, he's in room four twenty,' the guy behind the desk said.

'Thank you,' Lawson replied, without even turning around to look at him, he headed across to the elevator quickly before the doors closed.

He stepped inside and pressed the number four, he instantly smelt the perfume of the woman who had just stepped out of the elevator. He saw her turn to smile at him through the last gap in the doors as they closed.

Ten seconds later he was stepping out of the elevator and saw the room numbers going up from right to left as he stepped into the hall.

He turned left and walked past ten doors on his right before reaching door number four twenty.

He knocked on the door, four times.

THIRTY-FIVE

56 Thompson Street – New York

Mike Lawson, despite his apparent lack of concentration and constant humour was as good a killer as Ward, if not better. Lawson had in his armoury something that Ward did not necessarily possess.

Lawson had the ability to beat any man to death.

He had done it on many occasions.

He was unbelievably powerful and strong, much more powerful than his giant, muscular six foot four frame even suggested he was.

He was a freak of nature.

He was so impossibly strong that when he hit someone with all of his force, it was akin to being hit by a forty-pound sledgehammer, and he would rattle any man's brain with one punch.

He had walked past four people in the hall on the way to Dunlop's room, and he had decided as soon as he stopped knocking on the door of room four twenty, he was going to beat Dunlop to death.

Dunlop opened the door five seconds after he had finished knocking, his face turned from a smile to a frown when he saw Lawson's giant frame filling the doorway.

Dunlop was no taller than five foot five and he was extremely overweight.

'Can I help you?' Dunlop asked.

Lawson leant forward and unleashed a jab into Dunlop's gut, and he doubled over instantly, he then used the palm of his left hand to push hard against the top of Dunlop's head, he pushed him back into the room before stepping inside and closing the door.

Dunlop was gasping for air, the single jab which Lawson had only applied about twenty per cent of his power to, made him feel like he had been hit by a truck.

He stood still, with no emotion on his face, waiting patiently for Dunlop to get his breath back.

He had to wait longer than he thought.

Dunlop was the kind of guy who would walk up a flight of stairs and have to sit down for ten minutes to recover; he was so out of condition.

After a few minutes, Dunlop managed to pull himself into a three quarter upright position.

'I need to sit down,' he said.

'Do you know who I am?' Lawson asked.

As soon as Dunlop heard Lawson's accent, he knew.

'Whoever you are, you have the wrong person,' he said.

'You are Charles T Dunlop; I have the right person.'

'No, that's not me,' Dunlop replied, 'I am his assistant.'

In spite of Ward underestimating how smart Lawson was, he was never going to fall for that.

'Then I may as well kill you now,' he said calmly, 'You have seen me now, and I have been told to get some information from Dunlop that's all. He won't go to the cops but you will, so you are in the wrong place at the wrong time.'

'I am Charles T Dunlop really.'

'So I'll ask you again, do you know who I am?'

'You are one of the Brits who were looking for Darren Hughes,' Dunlop replied.

'Where is he?'

'He's at the Baccarat Hotel.'

'We have got to the bottom of everything. How can you sacrifice so many innocent people just for money?' Lawson asked, despite already knowing the answer.

'It wasn't a choice, I got put on the committee by default I never wanted any part of it.'

'What do you know about internal organs?' Lawson asked.

Dunlop looked at him in confusion.

Lawson rolled his eyes, in that moment; he knew why Ward was constantly rolling his eyes at him when he mentioned sex,

'It's a simple question.'

'Not much, I know about the main ones, your heart, kidneys, lungs and liver and so on,' Dunlop replied.

'Good,' Lawson said, 'Because in a few moments, I am going to hit you so hard that I will damage every internal organ that you have, and you will feel a pain that you never thought possible, and then I will sit here and watch you die. It will take about ten minutes, and the last thing you will see is me smiling at you.'

'Please, don't hurt me, I'll tell you what you want to know.'

He was actually disappointed at how pathetic and weak Dunlop was.

'Pull yourself together,' he said, 'Try to die with some dignity, I'm embarrassed for you. What's wrong with you?'

'I don't want to die,' Dunlop said, his voice becoming louder, a fact not lost on Lawson, conscious that the other guests in the rooms either side might hear Dunlop shouting.

'There is one thing?' Lawson said.

'Anything, I'll tell you anything.'

'What would be the best colour for blinds to match in with a hardwood floor which is stained an oak colour?' Dunlop pulled himself completely upright and then said, 'Sorry, I don't understand.'

'Not to worry, I'll ask Nicole-Louise.'

Dunlop had no idea what this giant of a man was talking about.

But it didn't matter.

Lawson was bored with talking.

In his head, he challenged himself to kill Dunlop with three hits.

He unleashed a right handed uppercut with all of his weight behind it and his huge fist connected with Dunlop's ribs, smashing through his rib cage splintering the bones like a brittle candy. Lawson was hoping that one of the bones might pierce Dunlop's heart.

The force of the punch lifted both of Dunlop's feet at least six inches off the ground, he fell backwards, against a small table which was next to a chair, the force of his excessive weight breaking it like a twig.

Lawson looked down at him, he was groaning, quietly, but he wasn't dead.

He was a little disappointed; he felt it was a good punch. Now he was challenging himself to finish it with the next hit and he knew how he was going to do it.

He was sure that he would not need a third attempt.

He bent down and pulled Dunlop up so that the middle of his back was resting against the cushion of the chair, and because of his weight, it was awkward putting his bulk into the correct position.

He eventually managed to set Dunlop up exactly the way that he wanted. His arms were down by his side and his chin had dropped forward onto his chest.

He was barely conscious and he was struggling to breathe, and he was starting to gargle. Lawson knew that one of the ribs must have pierced a lung.

But his injuries would take much more than ten minutes to die from, so he resisted the temptation to wait, just so he could tell himself that he killed Dunlop with one punch, and so he stood upright and stepped back about three feet.

He then raised his foot and stamped forward, smashing the sole of his boot hard against Dunlop's face.

As he connected and he felt the resistance of Dunlop's neck bone and muscle, he followed through with the movement and pushed harder, almost like a double push, he felt Dunlop's neck break immediately and his head fell back into an unnatural position.

He died instantly.

He stood over Dunlop for a few seconds and then checked for a pulse just to make sure.

Dunlop was most definitely dead.

He smiled at the crumpled body then simply turned and walked out of the room back into the hall.

246 Spring Street – New York

Charles Andrews was much more vigilant and aware of the position that he was in than Charles T Dunlop. As Ward knocked on the door, he looked through the peephole in the door and didn't recognise Ward.

'Who are you?' he demanded.

'I'm one of Newman's men. Mr Hasloff is waiting downstairs, we have to leave immediately,' he replied, feigning a southern accent as best he could.

It worked.

Andrews unlocked the door,

'What's wrong?' he asked urgently.

As soon as the door was open enough for him to walk inside, he pulled out his silenced Glock and said,

'I'm wrong.'

Andrews made a desperate attempt to push the door shut but Ward was too strong and too fast, and by the time he had a grip on the door, he was two steps inside.

He shoved Andrews hard in the chest with his left hand, causing him to lose his balance. Then he fired one shot into Andrews left thigh.

Andrews yelped and fell backwards, clutching at his thigh as the pain of the bullet tearing through his muscle kicked in.

He took two more steps inside, closing the door.

'You've shot me!' Andrews screamed, louder than he would have liked,

'If you make that much noise again, I will shoot you once more,' Ward said calmly, 'It's a flesh wound for God's sake, what's wrong with you?'

Andrews used the palm of his hands to push himself back along the carpet on his backside until he was leaning against the black leather sofa that was on the left side of the room.

'Are you comfortable now?'

'I can't believe you shot me,' Andrews replied through gritted teeth, the pain starting to subside slightly now, as much to do with Ward saying that it was just a flesh wound as the burning sensation easing off.

He stepped over Andrews legs and sat down in the armchair opposite the sofa.

Andrews didn't look as scared as he thought he would, then he realised that Andrews did not believe that he was actually going to kill him.

'You've miscalculated a lot of things Mr Andrews,' he said.

'But I got a lot more things right,' Andrews replied.

'No, you got everything wrong. You still don't know what's going on here, do you?'

'Are you going to enlighten me boy, is that why you are here?'

Ward smiled at him.

'You got it completely wrong when you thought that the British government wanted rid of you.'

He could see the curiosity shining in Andrews's eyes.

'So who was it?'

'It was Darren Hughes. It's always been him. He wanted everything and now he has it,' he lied.

'Hughes?'

'Yes. I'm amazed that you were too stupid to see it.'

Ward could see Andrews trying his best to piece everything together.

'So Kenny got wind of this so that's why he called the vote of no confidence and has taken over. He found out what Darren was doing?'

'Something like that,' he replied, 'You know that we have taken all of your money I take it? Every cent that you personally had has now gone, you have nothing left.'

'You aren't making much sense boy, and to be honest, you don't scare me. I've been brought up amongst tough, southern men, and if you think I could be afraid of you then you are seriously mistaken.'

Ward laughed.

'You find that funny boy?'

'I find it more sad than funny.'

'I suggest you leave now,' Andrews said, bizarrely thinking that he was in control of the situation.

'I can't leave,' Ward replied.

'You can stand up, turn around, walk out the door and if you get out of the country quick enough, you might live another day.'

'No, I mean I can't leave without getting what I came for?'

'You won't get anything from me boy,' Andrews said, appearing to be growing in confidence by the second.
'You won't be giving it to me, I will be taking it,' he said, still using calm, polite tones.
'You will take nothing from me boy.'
He stood up and pointed his Glock at Andrews; he was amazed that he still didn't comprehend what was happening. He was either very brave or very stupid.
It turned out he was stupid.
He stepped over to him and said,
'I'm going to kill you right now. What I then need is a photo which I am sending to my friends who are going to wipe out your children,' Ward said, taking a gamble that someone so arrogant and self-centred would not have a wife, 'But we want them to see you dead, your body ripped apart and your face torn to shreds by the three bullets I am going to fire into it,' he added, calmly and clearly.
Andrews' whole demeanour changed.
So he squeezed the trigger gently and shot him in the left shoulder.
The bullet smashed into his collarbone and he screamed again, this time louder.
He took two more steps closer to him so that he was virtually standing over him.
'Look at me,' he demanded.
Andrews looked up at him and he looked petrified.
In spite of the pain that he was feeling, he found himself trying to pull away from the eyes that were staring down at him but he couldn't. They were telling him that he was going to die and that somehow, there would be much worse to come after that.

'Please, I'm begging you, don't hurt my children,' he pleaded.

'Hurt them? We are going to kill them and your grandchildren,' Ward lied, taking another guess that, because of his age, Andrews would have grandchildren by now.

'Please, I'm begging you,' Andrews said and the tears started to run down his cheek.

He was now satisfied that Andrews was feeling what he deserved to feel. They were way short of the number of tears that the victims of the shootings he had been involved with over the years had shed, but they were still tears.

'You have nothing old man,' Ward said, 'And you leave no legacy either, your family, wealth, company, all of it, gone. I've taken everything old man. Take that with you,' he added, and then he fired three quick shots and obliterated the face of Andrews to such an extent that he had a three-inch gap where his nose once was.

He looked at his overweight, lifeless body and he smiled. Andrews got what he deserved and assuming Lawson had taken care of Dunlop, they only had two more committee members to take care of.

The end was in sight, by the end of the day, not only would the committee cease to exist, the one thing that had bothered him more than anything through all of this operation would be put right.

Comprehensively and definitively put right.

THIRTY-SIX

Park Avenue – New York

Just as Ward and Lawson were making their way over to
the Four Seasons Hotel to eliminate Kenny Hasloff,
Nicole-Louise and Tackler were depositing one hundred
and fifty thousand dollars into the bank accounts of all
the people they had so far traced, who had been directly
affected by the committee's actions.
'Are you sure about this?' Tackler asked.
'It's the right thing to do Tackler, wouldn't you want to
know. Look at those four people, look what they have
lost. It's the right thing to do. Everyone else still gets one
hundred and fifty,' Nicole-Louise replied.
'And you are OK doing it?'
'Yes I am,' she said.
Tackler walked across to her and sat down next to her.
'How did I ever end up with someone as perfect as you?'
he asked her.

'That's easy,' she said without hesitation, 'You are the cream to my coffee, the ying to my yang, the right side of my heart, my equal, my strength and my meant to be.'
'God, from such shitty beginnings, I have ended up with more than anyone,' he said and kissed her on the cheek.
'Plus you make me look good when we have a problem to solve because I always win.'
'Because I always let you,' he replied, and then he kissed her softly.

In Missouri, Sandy Harper was saying goodbye to the latest neighbour who had called around to offer her condolences.
Everything had gone from perfect to hell in the past week, and she did not know how she was going to carry on.
Her husband Matt was a science teacher, a very good science teacher, and that kid who had walked into his classroom last week and taken his life, had not only taken away her husband, that kid, and she couldn't even say his name in her head, had taken away the father of their fourteen-month old daughter, Joyce.
She was angry and she was scared, scared of the future. None of the words that people were saying to her were making the pain seem any less, and she now had the worry of trying to raise their daughter alone, meaning her own job as a cashier at the local bank would have to be sacrificed.
She had been with Matt since they were sixteen. Neither of them had ever set the world alight, and they kept themselves pretty much to themselves. They were simple people in the fact that they never took grand vacations or

drove expensive cars, money was too tight for that, but they had saved and got a mortgage on a small two-bedroom bungalow, which they called home.

Now she was terrified that she would not be able to afford the repayments, and that her and Joyce would be homeless.

The funeral was going to wipe out her savings, and the school were being vague about any insurance pay out. She was starting to feel as desperate as she was heartbroken.

And then her cell phone rang and everything changed. She did not recognise the number, other than it was a cell phone number, but she thought it might be the school calling about insurance and so she answered it.

'Hello,' she answered softly.

'Is this Sandy Harper,' the woman's voice on the end of the phone asked.

'It is she.'

'My name is Nicole-Louise and I work indirectly with the finances of big corporations and I am aware of the events of last week,' she said softly.

Sandy's heart sank, and she felt panic rushing through her body to such an extent that she could hear her heart beating in her ears.

'But don't panic Mrs Harper, I'm not calling to ask for anything, I'm calling to make sure you understand why you have received what you have received,' Nicole-Louise said.

'I don't understand,' Sandy said.

'Do you have a device to hand where you can see the deposit that I have just made into your account?'

'I have a laptop but what is this about?'

'Please have a look at your account Mrs Harper,' Nicole-Louise asked softly.

Reluctantly, Sandy Harper refreshed the page for her account; she had been looking at it almost in tears an hour ago.

She put in her password details and saw the balance at the top of the screen. And she was instantly suspicious. 'I'm not that naive, this is a scam. How can you be so heartless?' she said and started to sob.

'Please Mrs Harper, just listen to me. If I'm smart enough to put that money into your account so that it can't be traced, I am smart enough to scam you without calling you to notify you. I was instructed to take that money from somewhere else, and you need it. It is your money now, and you would struggle to get rid of it, however hard you tried; the bank will just tell you the same thing. It is your money,' Nicole-Louise softly said, conscious of the fact that this was a massive shock to her.

'Who instructed you, where did it come from?' Sandy asked, still not believing this was real.

'The people I work for. Think of them as good Samaritans. The money has come from a weapons company. It's time they had to pay their dues. You have suffered the cruellest and unkindest of agonies, and we decided to make sure that you and Baby Joyce will not suffer as a result of greed and twisted laws.'

'Is that number right?'

'Yes it is,' Nicole-Louise replied, 'One million dollars,' she added, 'That will make sure that you are both provided for and that you and Joyce can just concentrate on rebuilding your life.'

'But why did you choose us?' Sandy asked, 'There were lots of other people who will suffer as a direct result of what that animal did.'

'But you are the only one who struggles to stay afloat and has a fourteen-month old baby,' Nicole-Louise replied.

'I'm struggling to believe that this is real.'

'Of course you are, you would be naive not to, but here's what I suggest you do,' Nicole-Louise replied and then paused, 'Leave the money for a week, a month, however long you want but it will not move. Then when you start spending it, you will see that there is no fall out or contact from the bank then in time, you will see it for what it is.'

'And what exactly is it?' Sandy asked.

'It's the right thing to do,' Nicole-Louise replied.

'Who are you? Good Samaritans don't exist.'

'Are you sure? Your husband devoted his life to teaching kids, making their lives' better, giving them a good chance to have a decent future, all of that for a paltry salary that meant you could just about survive. You need to look closer to home to see that your husband was a Good Samaritan himself.'

Sandy could hear this woman who had called out of the blue, who had just told her that she was giving her a million dollars, was struggling to hold her voice together.

She knew then that this was completely authentic.

'I don't know what to say,' she said as her own tears started to fall once more, but this time they were tears of relief.

'You don't need to say anything. I just wanted to put your mind at rest,' Nicole-Louise said.

'Thank you, thank you, thank you,' Sandy said.

'Goodbye Mrs Harper,' Nicole-Louise replied and the line went dead.

Four years ago, in South Central, Los Angeles, a street war had erupted over two killings which rival gangs had blamed each other for, but had actually been instigated by the committee, through Newman. They had subsequently arranged for extensive arms to find their way onto the street and sat back while all hell broke loose.

Over a seven-week period, twenty-three people died. Twenty-two gang members and one innocent victim.

Tray Lindon was a good kid who was studying hard at school, with aspirations to move onto college and then university. He avoided the areas where the gangs met so he made his way to and from school as quickly as he could to avoid any contact with the gangbangers.

Tray was fifteen years old.

Tray's mom was called Elina and she worked as a nurse at a nearby hospice. She had raised Tray alone since he was five after his father got incarcerated for drug offenses for the fourth time so she threw him out. He had willingly gone, never to be seen or heard of again.

Tray was rushing home from school one day when two older guys ran past him at speed and then a car skidded around the corner and three guys hung out of the windows shooting the two runners dead in front of him. Tray froze to the spot and one of the guys in the car; sure that Tray would tell the cops who had did it, opened fire on him with an AK-47 and seven bullets ripped into his small, young body, killing him instantly.

After a year grieving, Elina set up a local club to help the local kids escape the clutches of the gangs, she firmly believed that if she could save one kid from joining the gangs, then she had done the right thing by Tray.

Three years later, Elina had prevented over one hundred kids from joining the gangs, and the local community all supported her efforts through donations and providing free equipment.

But the group were struggling. The government would provide no funding, and there was still the problem with local politicians not having enough votes to gain by supporting the programme, and so they were now relying solely on handouts to survive.

And then her cell phone rang.

'Hello?'

'Is this Elina Lindon?' Nicole-Louise asked.

'Who wants to know?'

'My name is Nicole-Louise; can I have five minutes of your time?'

'What about?' she asked curtly, assuming that this was yet another call relating to a stoppage of the support given.

'About doing the right thing,' was the reply.

'I always do the right thing honey; I think it's others that don't.'

'Well perhaps I can change that,' Nicole-Louise replied.

'I'm listening.'

'Do you have a device to hand where you can access your personal bank account, the one ending four, four seven?'

'What is this, a scam? How do you know my account details?'

'Just have a look at your balance please.'

Elina slid open her iPad and connected to her online bank.

'What's this about honey?'

'Have you checked it?' Nicole-Louise asked.

'Not yet.'

'You lost your son Tray four years ago and you have devoted your time to helping other kids not to get pulled in by the gangs. I can see…..'

'Holy shit, is that what I think it is? Is that genuine?' Elina interrupted

'The million dollars?' Nicole-Louise asked.

'Yes, the million dollars!!' Elina exclaimed.

'Yes it is. Do you want to know where it came from?'

'You bet your life I do honey.'

'We stole it from the gun companies. It is untraceable; they will never be able to trace it back to you.'

'Why would you help me though?'

'Because I know that you will use it for good, to save more lives and help more kids. Am I right?'

'You know it.'

'Then look at that as a memorial to Tray.'

'Tell me something, what makes someone like you help someone like me?'

'Goodbye Mrs Lindon,' Nicole-Louise said and hung up the phone.

Over the next twenty minutes, Nicole-Louise made two further calls. One to a man called Winston Edgewood who lived in Ohio. Winston had lost his daughter

Precious when a guy had walked into a bar and started randomly shooting women.

She had been sitting at a table with her mother, celebrating her 21st birthday.

Both of them died instantly.

Winston had donated all of their organs to people who were desperate for them, and between the two of them, they had given six other people the opportunity and gift to live a longer and healthier life.

The second call was to a guy called Andy Poulter.

He had lost his wife and daughter when a seventeen-year-old kid had run amok in a shopping mall, killing seven people. His daughter was only four years old.

He had since campaigned heavily for a tightening of the nation's gun laws, and while he had yet to make any progress, his quest was starting to make good ground and he was starting to gain more and more support.

By linking the exchange of money and finding part of the shooters internet usage, Nicole-Louise had been able to establish that the shooter had received the same set of naked pictures that Emma Casey had sent to all of the other kids that she was manipulating, and so she was more than sure that Andy Poulter had lost his wife and daughter just because the committee had decided that it was time for another shooting.

Both of them took very little convincing to receive the money in good faith.

After she had finished talking to him, Nicole-Louise sank back into the chair, inhaled deeply and let out a long sigh.

Tackler had listened to all four conversations on loud speaker.

'Everyone is a victim in this,' she said as Tackler held her hand, 'Those poor kids who were convinced to do awful things because their lives were so worthless, that the only way they could escape was by carrying out an atrocity, the victims and their families, and the families of the shooters, who have to carry around the guilt of knowing that they not only did nothing to prevent it from happening, they didn't even realise that their loved ones were so desperate,' she added.

'Everyone is a victim but the powerful and the greedy once again you mean,' Tackler replied, 'They always get away with it, sure, Ryan can take out one group but is he really making any progress? Another one just appears. The strong will always come out on top, who is going to hold the Francis Gollini's of this world to account?' he asked.

Nicole-Louise squeezed his hand and smiled at him. It was a big, warm smile that lit up the room.

'I want to talk to you about Francis Gollini,' she said.

THIRTY-SEVEN

57 East 57ᵗʰ Street - New York City

Kenny Hasloff had insisted that he would not move from his room at of the Four Seasons Hotel because his wife had arrived to take in a shopping trip in New York, and he did not want her to get suspicious as to why he suddenly felt the need to move.

She didn't like the fact that he spent time with Darren Hughes as it was.

She never really understood the complexities of the business world, and she blamed Hughes for introducing her husband to the world of prostitution and debauchery that he now moved in.

Just because she didn't understand business, she wasn't stupid.

She had seen all the signs, the text messages, the new clothes and change of aftershave, and then she had seen all of the evidence.

She had hired a private detective to watch over her husband when he was away on one of his 'Committee Summits' as he called them, and in the space of eight days, he had collected enough evidence to prove that he had been with four different women.

She had yet to use the evidence through the divorce courts or even confront him with it. She turned a blind eye to his philandering because what else could she do? She had no close family apart from her children, and they had all moved on, and she had very few friends. Her day was spent either shopping, or at home instructing the maids on what room to move the furniture around in next.

She was sitting in their suite when there was a knock at the door.

Her husband was in the other room with the door closed, whispering into his cell phone, no doubt talking to another floozy she had told herself.

She stood up from the sofa, walked across to the door and opened it.

There were two men standing there, one who looked handsome yet menacing, and a man behind him who looked like a giant but possessed the most remarkable, sparkling blue eyes that she had ever seen in her life.

Ward was surprised to see a woman opening the door. He was sure that Hasloff would be inside alone.

He raised his silenced Glock and pointed it at her face, 'Make one noise and I will blow your face off,' he calmly said as he stepped into the room, with Lawson following and closing the door behind him.

'Who are you?' Ward asked.

'I'm Abigail Hasloff' the woman replied quietly.
'Kenny Hasloff's wife'
She nodded back.
'Where is he?'
'He's in the bedroom there,' she replied, pointing to the door that was closed, 'What is this about? A robbery?' she asked, still showing a calm that impressed Ward.
Lawson walked across to the bedroom door and Ward raised his hand, indicating for him to stop.
'Go and sit down over there please,' he said, nodding towards the sofa.
Abigail Hasloff duly turned and walked across to the sofa and sat down, keeping her back straight and her hands, palms down, on her knees.
Ward sat down on the matching sofa was opposite her, He studied her for a few moments, and she looked back at him with equal curiosity, but no fear.
He realised that she had no idea who they were, and no idea why they would possibly want to speak to her husband. But most impressive of all, she was waiting patiently to discover the answers.
'Mrs Hasloff,' he said, calmly and deliberately, 'I'm a good man who has to do bad things to put things right. I'm here to kill your husband for the terrible things that he is responsible for, and I need to know if you are a part of what he has done.'
'And if I am, you will have to kill me too?' she asked, completely unfazed by the threat of imminent death.
'Unfortunately, yes.'
He looked up at Lawson who looked back and shrugged, it was rare to meet a woman who was so matter of fact about things faced with a gun pointing at her.

'So why don't you tell me who you are?' she asked.

'My name is Ryan and this is Mike.'

'You are English?'

'Yes we are.'

'And why would two English men want to kill my husband? I can't imagine that his company does much work over there?'

'We are representing the U.S. government today. And your husband has done some very bad things. We are shutting everything down, but there is no way that he is going to leave this room alive today.'

'Is Darren Hughes involved?' she asked.

He looked at her. She genuinely had no clue about any of this.

Which Ward realised made this a difficult situation.

He would never kill an innocent person, at worst he might beat them around a little, but he had to take into account that there would be questions asked when all of these CEO's were announced as being dead, and he had to establish if she could be trusted not to say anything, or he should bundle her into the bathroom, cable tie her hands together and leave her for the clean-up crew to sort out

'What has he actually done? Apart from cheat on me regularly and constantly act secretive, what could be that bad?' she asked.

He looked into her eyes. There wasn't any fear or even an air of resignation showing in her eyes, but there was a steely determination, like she had to know the truth.

So he took the gamble.

He spent the next few minutes explaining everything to her. He told her about Kyle, Adam Ray, Emma Casey, the Klan, and the Missouri shooting, and about arming Samson Simone. When he had finished speaking, he noticed her eyes filling with tears.

'Oh my God, all of those poor innocent people and those parents who have lost their children,' she said and she put her hand to her mouth.

She knew nothing; Ward could see that clearly, it was so obvious in fact, that even Lawson on the other side of the room said,

'She doesn't know anything.'

He nodded at him.

'There will be questions when he dies. We can sort out the police side of it, but friends and the media might ask questions. You have children, your reaction was that of a parent, not a cheated upon wife, if you want to protect them, you have to walk away and never breathe a word of this day to anyone.'

'We have three children,' she replied, 'And four grandchildren.'

'He's not treated you very well, has he?'

She shook her head,

'That's the understatement of the year,' she said.

He could see that she was just another victim that Hasloff had left trailing behind.

'You can walk out of the door now, there is no need to witness any of this,' he said.

He liked her, she seemed like a dignified and decent woman, in some ways, and she reminded him of his own mother.

'I just need to know one thing from him?' she said, confirming her innocence by not making a run for the door immediately.

'What is it?'

A couple of minutes later, Ward looked at Lawson and said,
'Bring him out,' Lawson pulled on the door handle and stepped into the bedroom with his handgun raised.
Hasloff dropped his phone and screamed.
Lawson took three giant steps forward and grabbed him by the collar of his shirt and yanked him towards him and pushed him hard in the back towards the door. He then turned to follow him, making sure to end the call on Hasloff's cell phone which, going by the call display, was to someone called 'Harriet'.
'Sit down there,' Ward said as Hasloff stumbled into the suite.
'It's you two, the Brits. Where is my wife?' Hasloff stuttered.
'She's in our van downstairs. I'm going to ask you one question. It requires a simple yes or no answer. If you tell the truth, I will let her live. If you lie to me, my friend there,' he said, pointing to Lawson, 'Will go downstairs and put a bullet in her head. Do you understand?' he asked calmly.
Hasloff nodded at him.
'Were you directly involved in the committee that sponsored the manipulation of people to carry out the massacre of innocent people? It requires a yes or no answer.'
He could see that Hasloff was weighing up his options, and so he raised his Glock and pointed it at Hasloff's head.
'Yes or no?' he demanded.

'No.'

Ward shook his head,

'There's your answer Abigail,' he said loudly, and Abigail Hasloff stepped out of the adjoining room and walked across to him and slapped him hard across the face.

With no tears or tantrum, she said,

'I knew you were heartless, but I never knew you were a coward.'

She then turned and looked at Ward,

'I won't say anything; do what you have to do to him.'

She then turned back to Hasloff and said,

'These men have our children and grandchildren held captive. If you don't give them what they want, they will kill them. For once in your pathetic life, do the right thing,' and she lunged forward and slapped him hard around the face again, and then she looked down and spat in his face.

And then she grabbed her bag, and walked out of the room, slamming the door behind her.

'Don't hurt my children, please,' Hasloff begged.

'You were going to have your wife killed to protect yourself, which kind of says what type of man you are. She's right, you are a coward,' Ward said.

Lawson stepped forward and cuffed him around the ear. From a normal guy, a cuff around the ear would leave a short ringing sound in the ear, receiving a cuff around the ear from Lawson was like the bells of Big Ben going off in your ears,

'There is nothing worse than a coward,' he said.

'Tell me what you know about the Samson Simone deal?' Ward asked.

'What do you mean?'

'I mean tell me the committee's involvement.'

'We provided second hand arms to the CIA, most of them were pretty useless and not very accurate. Guns, like people, deteriorate with age. We charged a full price and we flooded the region with weapons so that Simone could take control. All we did was make money, it was Lockhart and the CIA who were behind it,' Hasloff replied.

This lined up with what Ward already knew, what Hasloff had failed to say was that they had made an incredible amount of money selling useless goods.

'Who is the chairman of your committee?'

Hasloff delayed his response, he had no idea how much Ward already knew.

'Darren Hughes is,' he replied.

Ward looked at Lawson,

'Make the call to Mac. Get the oldest one of his children killed first and have them send a picture to us,' he said. Lawson promptly pulled his phone out and pretended to make the call.

'Please, don't,' Hasloff begged, 'It was Hughes up until yesterday but we voted him out. We wanted to put a stop to this madness,' he added.

'More lies,' Ward replied, 'Mike, tell him to take out the youngest grandchild too. I can do this all day Hasloff, until they are all gone, and then I will kill you anyway. We've taken all of your money, we have killed Newman and his crew, and we would have killed all but one of your committee by the time we leave here, so three children and four grandchildren means you have got five lies left to tell and at the speed you are lying to me, that won't take too long,' he added calmly.

'No more lies, I promise, just please don't hurt them,' Hasloff begged.

'Then start talking,' Ward demanded.

'I raised a vote of no confidence in him because I could see that you two were tearing the committee apart. The other members agreed, and so we made him step down but he is not going without a fight. He still thinks that he can beat you.'

'How can he possibly think that?'

'Because he says that he has someone on his side that is very powerful that he can protect him.'

'You mean Lockhart?' Ward asked.

'No, I asked that and he just laughed at me, and then said Lockhart had no power.'

'You believed him?'

'Of course not, he would say anything to keep hold of the chairmanship. I'm sure he and Lockhart kept lots of secrets from the rest of us, and Lockhart will run away blameless as usual I expect.'

'Lockhart is dead, we killed him, and his wife,' Ward replied.

'You killed a United States Senator?' Hasloff asked in disbelief,

'We've killed lots of them actually, we are rather good at it,' Lawson said from the other side of the room.

'That's impossible,' Hasloff said.

'Is it as impossible as the U.S. government helping us to cover it up?' Ward replied, 'Now for my next question, in fact, my next two questions, and I want the truth, because these are the two most important questions that I am going to ask you. Do you understand that?' he asked. 'I won't lie to you, I promise, the love between my wife and I died a long time ago, but my children and grandchildren are the most important people in my life and I will do anything to save them,' Hasloff said, now shaking as he spoke.

'Most important people in your life after yourself, you mean?' Ward said.

'I won't lie, I swear.'

'My first question,' Ward said, leaning forward to the edge of the cushions as he spoke, and aiming the end of his silencer in line with Hasloff's kneecap, 'Do you know who Kyle Newson is?'

Hasloff was straining to think who that could be but he drew a blank, in the end he said,

'I've never heard that name before; I have no idea who it is.'

Ward squeezed the trigger of his gun and a bullet smashed into Hasloff's right kneecap, shattering it into a hundred pieces, like an eggshell crumbling. He screamed and fell to the left, before rolling onto the floor and less than five seconds later, he was crying like a baby, screaming in between exaggerated sobs.

'My next question,' Ward replied, 'Do you know who Adam Ray is?'

Hasloff was screaming so loudly that he never heard Ward speak, and so Lawson bent down and pulled him up, one handed by his hair, so that he was at eye level with Ward.

'I asked do you know who Adam Ray is?' he repeated.

'No!' Hasloff screamed, 'I've never heard of him.'

Without looking down, Ward squeezed the trigger again and a bullet smashed into Hasloff's left kneecap and Lawson let go of his hair and he crumpled to the floor.

'Look at me,' Ward said.

Hasloff looked up at him.

He saw the devil.

He saw a seven-foot giant glaring down at him with eyes that were burning right through him.

He saw the devil in his physical form for the first time in his life.

He saw everything he had ever done wrong and he heard the screams of every person that his committee had killed.

Ward could see that Hasloff was seeing everything that he needed to see.

He pulled the trigger hard, three times and blew Hasloff's face apart.

Lawson tilted his head and raised his eyebrows at the way Hasloff's head seemed to sink in as it jerked back, and they both watched the last breath leave his body.

'Call them in Mike,' Ward said, 'We then have two more calls to make and then we are done for the day and you can meet Chantelle, her friend and whoever else you have lined up for the night.'

'You do realise that I am inviting them around to talk interior design and colour schemes, don't you?' Lawson replied as he pulled out his cell phone.

'For real' Ward asked, surprised at the admission.

'No Ryan, not for real. But it is very reassuring that you can be dumb at times too,' Lawson replied.

'Well maybe when we get to the Baccarat Hotel you can find another receptionist to come and help with your interior design?' Ward said and smiled.

'That's the plan,' Lawson replied as Ward walked out of the suite.

THIRTY-EIGHT

28 West 53rd Street – New York

On the way over to the Baccarat Hotel, Ward had called
Eloisa and she had told him that she was just leaving
work and that she would rush home and prepare a meal
for them both. That put him in good spirits.
He was feeling focussed and energised by the way they
had systematically picked their way through the problem
that The Old Man had laid out in front of them, and
Darren Hughes was going to be the last member of the
committee to destroy.
He wondered if Centrepoint would be pleased at a job
well done, but then he reminded himself that he is more
than likely trying to get to the bottom of another mess
that the CIA had created.
They reached the hotel parking a hundred yards away
down a side street.

They walked down 53rd Street and in through the shiny entrance. He could feel as soon as he walked in that this was one of the most expensive hotels in all of Manhattan.

'I don't like their décor,' Lawson said as they approached the front desk, 'There is way too much chrome and glass and why are there so many mirrors here? You would have to have at least two full time cleaners working in my apartment if it was done in this style, they would have to be naked, so that they didn't smudge anything with their clothes,' he added.

Ward smiled.

Lawson was a genius at making people relaxed before the storm hit.

He saw that there were two women and one guy working behind the front desk, both of the women had already glanced up, and then taken the statutory second look at Lawson.

'Do your stuff Mike,' he said, 'I'll wait over here.' He walked over to a sofa in the lobby and sat down to observe Lawson in action.

He watched as Lawson had both the women playing with their hair and exaggerating their smiles to him in a matter of seconds. It was fascinating to watch. Lawson had an ability to affect women in a way that no other man he had ever known could.

He thought that maybe shooting Lawson and giving the rest of the male race an even playing field would be the decent thing to do, but then he concluded that the world's females would probably hunt him down and rip him to shreds if he did, and so he decided just to add it to the growing list of things that he admired about him.

A couple of minutes later, he was walking back over towards him, putting two folded bits of paper into his pocket.

'He's in the Baccarat suite, which actually costs nearly twenty-five thousand dollars a night,' Lawson said.

'And they needed to write that down on pieces of paper for you to remember did they?'

'Interior design help,' Lawson replied, as Ward stood up and they headed for the elevator.

Ward pressed the button that said 'Suites', which was on the top floor, and the elevator started to ascend.

'I bet there is a great view from up there,' Lawson said.

Ward instantly had an idea and smiled.

'What?' Lawson asked.

'Thanks for the idea Mike.'

'What Idea?'

'You'll see.'

The elevator eventually stopped after what seemed like an eternity, and the doors opened.

The floor had its own concierge, who was sitting at a desk at the end of the hall, which was positioned right outside the Baccarat Suite. He was a guy in his mid-fifties, and he had probably worked there for years. His role was more than likely to pamper to the needs of the super wealthy; women, drugs, anything they wanted, and he was probably a specialist at turning a blind eye.

'That's unfortunate,' Ward said as they approached the desk.

'How can I help you gentlemen?' the guy asked politely.

'We need to get in to see Mr Hughes in the Baccarat Suite,' he said, 'But we have a slight problem.'

Is it anything that I can help you with sir?' the concierge asked.

'Where does that lead to?' he asked, pointing to a door behind the guy that had 'Stairs' painted in the middle.

'Down into the lobby.'

'Not up onto the roof?'

'Not for guests, only for maintenance employees.'

Ward looked down on the desk and he could see a keyring, which was holding a number of access cards for the rooms.

'Can you render him unconscious but not kill him?' He whispered to Lawson.

'I'm pretty sure I can,' Lawson replied, and he lunged forward and grabbed hold of the guy's jacket, dragging him over the desk. In one swift movement, Lawson spun the guy's head around and pushed hard into his right temple with his thumbs. The guys' legs gave way and his eyes rolled back.

Ward had never seen anyone do that before.

'How long will he be out?' Ward asked.

'Fifteen minutes. He will just be groggy for a day or two but it's better than broken bones.'

'Put him in the stairwell out of sight for now,'

Ward said, as he leant over and picked up the access cards. He thumbed through them all and found one that said 'Baccarat Suite' he stepped across to the door and inserted the key into the slot. The light on the key pad went green and the door buzzed. He walked inside.

Hughes was nowhere to be seen, but he heard singing coming from the shower so turned to Lawson as he was closing the door.

'Bring him out here Mike,' he said and Lawson walked across the room into the bathroom.

He heard some inaudible shouting and a few moments later, Darren Hughes was staggering into the room naked, the result of a violent push into his back by Lawson.

'Sit down,' he said.

Hughes looked different to what he thought he would. He had thinning grey hair, and his body had started to head south a long time ago. With no clothes on, he looked weak and frail.

'You've been looking for us, I understand,' he said.

Hughes did not respond.

'Every single person that you sent for us is now dead. What do you think that says about how good we are? Two guys from Little Old Britain have destroyed everything that you have spent a lifetime building in a matter of days. Doesn't that make you feel kind of insignificant?' Ward asked with a smile, goading him as best he could.

'It would definitely make me feel kind of useless,' Lawson said, 'I mean, we have killed, what? twenty guys? We haven't even broken sweat. I would go as far as saying that this has been the most inadequate and hopeless bunch of bad guys that we have ever come across. You should be ashamed at just how pathetic you are,' he added, shaking his head as he finished speaking for added effect.

'Why do you think that we were hunting you, seriously, do you actually know,' Ward asked softly.

Hughes still said nothing so he raised his Glock and pointed it at his kneecap.

Panic consumed Hughes immediately.

'No. All I know is that the British government requested that you be allowed to work over here covertly, and that there was no record of you being here. I still don't know what it is that you think I have done,' Hughes replied.

'We don't work solely for the British government. In fact, most of our work is for the American government. You see, technically I am not British, I am as American as you, probably more so, because our government send me and my friend places to fix everything they want fixing, but don't want to get their hands dirty. We were sent by people way above the CIA or Lockhart. Who is this powerful friend that you claim to have?'

'What do you mean?'

'The person you bragged to Hasloff about?'

'I don't know who he is but he assured me that you would not harm me.'

'He pretty much let you down on that point, didn't he?' Ward asked and smiled, 'Because here's the thing, no one, and I really do mean no one, has any control over what we do. We make all of our own decisions, and then we leave it to people to sort out the mess we leave behind after we have gone. We killed Lockhart and his wife today, and it isn't the first time in the last couple of months that we have killed a sitting Senator, and the only person who we deal with has every single person in his pocket, probably even the President and most definitely the Vice President, they just have to suck it up and suffer in silence with the consequences of what we do. So you see, no one, no matter how powerful they might be convinced they are, can stop us from doing what the hell we chose to do to cowards like you.'

Hughes listened carefully to every word that Ward was saying and he realised that he was completely alone for the first time in his life.

'Another thing,' Lawson added, 'Whoever you think might have been able to help you, has probably run a long, long way away from us already. We have the best job in the world.'

Ward smiled at him. He had never thought of it like that, but Lawson was right, they did have the best job in the world.

Because they could do the things and address the moral dilemmas that normal people secretly would like the opportunity to address, but don't have it in them, then most importantly, they can stand up for the good people. They could fight back on behalf of the normal, honest, decent, working men and women of their two great nations.

'You know,' Ward said, 'I can see the only remorse you have over everything that you have done, is the fact that you got caught. Have you ever once thought of the misery that you have heaped on normal families, all of those people who have lost loved ones because you wanted to boost your profits?'

'It was not only about profits,' Hughes said defiantly.

'What else was it about?'

'Trying to bring a level of control to the way arms are handled in this country.'

'Control them by killing innocent people so that more people buy arms for protection. Is there a service you are doing for the country in there somewhere?' he asked, 'Because if there is I can't see it.'

'Once everyone is armed, balance and calm will be restored to the street. Some gangbangers are going to think twice about carjacking a car if they thought that the driver would more than likely be armed,' Hughes responded forcibly.

Ward laughed,

'You really are deluded, aren't you? I guess it is just a coincidence that you would be one of the main profiteers from your utopia?' he asked.

Before he could respond, Ward continued.

'You know, normally me and my colleague do this little role play thing about now, where we tell you that we have your family held hostage or that we have already killed them but to be honest, we have worn that a bit thin today, and I am pretty bored with it. Of course we would never really hurt innocent people, but we find it effective. It's our way of sending people to hell with hurt and anger burning its way through their entire body. But we aren't going to do that for you.'

Lawson raised an eyebrow,

'I'm glad you said it was wearing a bit thin, I was starting to become bored with your methods,' he quipped.

Ward smiled at him.

'Bring him with you Mike,' he said and he stood up and headed towards the door.

He walked out and checked the hall.

It was clear.

He beckoned for Lawson to follow him, and he stepped across the hall and opened the door with 'Stairs written on it, he held the door open for Lawson who was pushing Hughes forward with a vice-like grip on the back of his neck.

Lawson started to walk down the stairs and Ward said, 'Wrong way,' he turned to see Ward walking up the stairs.

He understood instantly.

Ward reached the door at the top of the stairs and pressed down on the safety bar, the door kicked open. He walked through the door and onto the roof.

Over forty-five floors up in the air.

Hughes started struggling as he realised what was going to happen, but Lawson just tightened his grip, he instantly felt like his bones were being crushed, and the pain immediately became too much for him to offer any resistance at all so he moved forward, feeling like he had no control over his body.

Ward walked to the edge of the roof and looked over the four foot wall around the edge.

There were cars and people milling around down below, he moved around to the side and saw there were parking spaces down below, where cars and vans were parked. It looked like the employee's and delivery entrance.

'Bring him here,' he said, and Lawson dragged him over to where he was standing.

'I have a question. Do you know who either Kyle Newson or Adam Ray are?

Hughes looked at him, desperation written all over his face.

'Please, don't,' he screamed, starting to kick his feet frantically, wedging them against the edge of the roof so that he couldn't be forced over.

So Ward pulled out his Glock and shot him in both kneecaps.

Hughes screamed and then vomited, just missing Ward's foot.

'Well if you can't remember who they are, think about it on the way down,' he said and nodded at Lawson, who pulled him into an upright position and tipped him, head first, over the edge of the rooftop.

Ward leant forward and watched Hughes' body fall, his head caught an air vent that was sticking out on the wall about ten floors down, and this made Hughes scream even louder.

His body gathered speed as it headed towards the sidewalk and then he hit the ground.

Even from the height they were at, they could see the blood spew from his body in every direction; it must have covered a twenty-foot radius.

'That is the first time I have thrown a guy from a roof,' Lawson said, 'I had no idea that the impact made the blood shoot that far.'

'So you've learnt something today,' Ward replied.

'Shall I call a clean-up crew?'

'Does he deserve one?'

'We'll leave him then. So, this is all done now?'

'Yes it is. But you need to be ready at 10:00pm.'

'I will. Because that is the bit that I have been waiting for all day since you told me about it,' Lawson replied, and they looked at each other and smiled.

THIRTY-NINE

DUMBO – New York

Ward arrived home just before six. The Old Man had tried calling him six times but he didn't answer. He was pleased with how things had worked out, and the only black mark from the whole operation was the death of Adam Ray. He opened the door to his apartment and saw Eloisa sitting at the table drinking a glass of wine, writing some notes down on a pad.

'Can you believe it,' she said, 'I have to go back into work at nine for a budget meeting. I was looking forward to a long night together.'

'That's OK, we still have three hours together and I'll be waiting here for you when you get back,' he replied, omitting to tell her that he had an appointment at ten that he was not going to miss, even for her.

'Have you finished what you were working on?' she asked as she stood up and walked over to him, before gently kissing him on the lips.

'Literally half an hour ago when we threw a guy off of the roof of the Baccarat Hotel.'

'Do you want to talk about it?' she asked, rubbing his arm gently.

'No, it's fine. It was a good operation where everything was achieved that we set out to achieve. But I do need a shower and to change my clothes, so if you want to order takeout, we can eat like normal people before you have to leave,' he said with a smile.

'Actually,' she said, wrapping her arms around his neck, 'I need to wash away my day to, can I join you?' she asked.

Three minutes later they were naked in the shower, lost in between kissing each other gently, and washing each other down. He pushed Eloisa back against the tiles and they made love for fifty minutes, the warm jet spray of the shower adding to the moment, like they were making love in the rain.

When they had finished, he washed Eloisa's hair for her. It was always an intimate moment that they both enjoyed when they shared a shower.

They climbed out of the shower and she wrapped a towel around her torso and said,

'Chinese?'

'I'm easy,' he replied.

'Chinese it is then,' she said, walking out into the kitchen to order from the takeout menu she had stored in a draw in the kitchen.

He started to dry himself and heard his phone vibrating on the bed and he picked it up.

It was Centrepoint.

He was going to ignore it, but then remembered that over the next few days he would be asking for his help dealing with the latest problem that Eloisa had asked him to solve.

So he answered it.

'If you are going to lecture me, can you save it until tomorrow, I've had a long few days,' he said as he answered.

'Actually, I was calling to say well done first of all,' he replied.

'Wow, very nearly a compliment!'

'You don't need my compliments Ryan; you know what a great job you have done. That committee had been running since the Second World War ended, and no one had been able to bring it down until you were set the challenge. So well done on that part,' The Old Man said, sounding uncharacteristically upbeat.

'But?' he asked, feeling uneasy at just how complimentary Centrepoint was being.

'Firstly, I have some bad news. The kid Adam Ray, his dad killed himself this afternoon. I guess guilt got the better of him.'

'I can't say I'm overly upset,' he replied, 'It was him who messed the poor kid up in the first place, he probably couldn't cope with feeling sorry for himself anymore, rather than guilt over what he did to that poor kid.'

'I'm glad you said that,' The Old Man replied, 'Because I have contacted our friends in the media, and they are going to run a story that he had a breakdown because his kid was mistakenly killed by a cop who thought he was a burglar, he flipped and found out that the CEOs of the biggest gun companies in the country were holding their annual convention, and he went in and killed five of them, so it all ties rather neatly together.'

'How convenient,' he replied, 'And Lockhart?'

'That's still a small issue, but I will have that resolved in the next couple of days, I just need to get the evidence fabricated, but the story will be that his wife discovered he had been having an affair for twenty years, the mistress has already come forward, and she went to shoot him, there was a struggle, he accidentally killed her, and in his despair over what he had done, he killed himself. So once again, everything will tie up rather nicely, so the whole operation was a resounding success.'

'Unless you went to school in Missouri or your name is Adam Ray,' Ward replied sarcastically.

The Old Man ignored him.

'But this Simone situation has escalated out of control,' The Old Man said with a sigh, 'The more that I discover about it, the more I am finding evidence that could alienate us, prompting the international community to turn their backs on us.'

'Why? What could be that bad?'

'Thousands of innocent women and children have died at his hand, we funded him and put him into power and we not only lost control of him, he turned against us,' he replied.

'So why can't you send in an elite team of Seals or borrow some of the SAS squadrons, to go in and take him out?'

'The big players are now fully aware of what has happened and they are avoiding it like the plague. The President has now dumped it on my lap to sort out.'

'And everyone keeps telling me to steer well clear of it. There must be a reason why everyone says this is a bad place to go?'

Eloisa walked back into the room and Ward said, 'Look, I can't talk now, I will call you tomorrow.'

'No you won't, but I will call you so make sure you answer,' Centrepoint replied and the line went dead.

'Everything OK?' she asked.

'The Old Man is getting in a panic about Samson Simone.'

'Everyone is Ryan,' she replied, 'What worries me is that everyone knows what is happening, but because of the politics involved, they are all pretending that the problem doesn't exist. We have created a monster and it's now almost like the very mention of his name at work is frowned upon. We have file after file of evidence of the atrocities that he commits, and yet because of the oil, natural resources and access that he provides for the big corporations, we just have to live with it,' she added, looking at the floor and imagining the suffering of the poor women and children as she spoke.

'So why don't you show the evidence to the world?' he asked.

'We can't because under instruction from way, way high above, all of the evidence has been removed to a secure location. I've seen what he does and it's heart-breaking.'

Ward shook his head in despair,
'Well I'll start dealing with this Zhang Wei guy in
Boston from tomorrow, so you will at least have
something to be positive about.'
'Let's get changed, the food will be here shortly,' she
said and kissed him gently on the lips once more.

Half an hour later they were sitting down at the table
laughing. He was explaining about Lawson's interior
design nightmare, and how he had all the female
receptionists at every hotel they had both visited eating
out of his hand.
'Mike makes light of a lot of things but how good do you
think he really is?' she asked, 'I mean take away the
looks and the humour what does he have?'
'Truthfully?' he replied, 'He has everything. He is tough,
loyal, ruthless, funny, compassionate, analytical, smart
and fearless. I don't think he has one weak link in his
armour. He plays this sexually obsessed card to dumb
himself down. It sticks out a mile. He doesn't want
people to take him too seriously, because then he will
have to be responsible for his actions. But the truth is he
is probably the best that I have ever worked directly
with, and that includes Mac and all of his team.'
She smiled at him.
'You think the world of him, don't you?'
'Yes. But if you ever tell him, I will have to shoot you,'
he replied with a smile.
The few hours that they had together went in the blink of
an eye. Before he knew it, Eloisa was putting her coat on
ready to leave.
'What time will you be back?' he asked.

'God knows, if it's too late when I finish, I will go back to my place, its closer and we can have tomorrow night together.'

'OK. But I won't be going to sleep until gone midnight, so let yourself in and join me if you aren't too late,' he replied.

She put her arms around his waist and said,

'I'm taking two weeks off next month, and I am going to book us a vacation away from everything. We will go somewhere secluded, and no matter what is going on in your world, you will be coming with me. Promise me that Ryan?'

'I promise,' he said and he kissed her gently.

'I'll be back as soon as I can,' she said as she walked out of the apartment.

He had an hour to kill, so he put his coat on and walked out of the building and hailed a cab over to Lawson's place.

38 W 31st Street – New York

'I'm outside,' he said as Lawson answered his cell phone, 'What number apartment are you?'

'I'm in forty-six. Come on up,' he said excitedly.

He walked into the building and climbed the stairs to the fourth floor, deciding against using the elevator as a group of women had already called it and were waiting for it.

He wondered how long it would be before they set eyes on Lawson, and they would be helping him with his interior design.

He reached the door and knocked.

A moment later, a beaming Lawson opened the door.

'Welcome to my new abode,' he said, as he bent down waving his arms dramatically for him to enter.

He walked inside and he stopped dead in his tracks.

He saw the receptionist Charlene; she was standing next to another girl who were both painting a wall at the back of the room.

They were both naked apart from large stripes of paint running across their bodies which he instantly suspected were the result of a paint fight, which Lawson had no doubt encouraged.

'Say hello to my friend Ryan ladies,' Lawson shouted out.

'Hello Ryan,' they said in unison, both waving at him frantically with such force that he had to make a conscious effort to avert his eyes away from their bouncing breasts.

'Hello,' he replied.

'He's cute,' Charlene's friend said.

He smiled to himself and shook his head.

'I did tell you,' Lawson said with a smile.

'Yes you did Mike.'

Apart from the naked women, the rest of the place looked surprisingly elegant.

The furniture was very modern, lots of prominent right angles, and the majority of it light wood in colour. Ward walked through to the kitchen, the women giggling together, convinced they had shocked him without knowing that he had seen and done things that they couldn't imagine.

The kitchen looked like something out of a catalogue. It was immaculate.

There were lots of chrome appliances and the walls were covered in a rustic tile which he had seen in most kitchens back in England.

'A taste of home?' he asked as he scanned around the room.

'Indeed it is.'

He saw a picture on the wall next to the gleaming refrigerator, and he walked across the kitchen for a closer look.

It was Lawson in full battle fatigues with a group of guys all sitting on a battered old Land Rover.

He studied the faces of the other men and one guy had a striking similarity to Lawson.

'This is your old unit and this guy here is your brother?' he asked, tapping his finger against a guy who looked every inch the same size as Lawson, and very nearly as handsome.

Lawson came across and stood next to him and looked at the picture for a few moments and then smiled to himself.

'They are all my brothers Ryan, but yes, that's John. He's still serving, and considered one of the best that the SAS have ever had,' he replied.

'Where was this picture taken?' he asked, noting the pride in Lawson's face as he spoke of his brother.

'It was on an operation in North Korea.'

'We actually sent people there?'

'No. We were in the south, and that guy there,' Lawson said, tapping his own finger against a guy standing behind him in the picture, 'He got kidnapped then taken over the border by their Special Forces team into the north. The government refused to sanction a recovery operation, so we went there and got him ourselves, no one ever gets left behind, you know that.'

Ward nodded his understanding,

'They are your family. No one deserts anyone, and you defend each other to the end, even if it means risking your own life. People who don't understand what we do can't really comprehend how we would lay down our life for someone who is not a blood relation,' he said.

Lawson looked at him and nodded.

'I would for you, and in spite of the little double act routine we have going, where you are the serious guy and I am the clown, I know that you would lay down your life for me too without hesitation. So sometimes, the false despair that you show, especially regarding my sexual endeavours, is wasted because I know it isn't genuine.'

Ward smiled at him, and just as he was about to say something serious, the door swung open and Charlene leant against the door frame and said,

'We've done Mike, come and look,' before turning around and deliberately dropping her paint brush and then bending over, much slower than was required, to pick it up.

Ward followed her movement every inch of the way, before turning his eyes away quickly when he found himself enjoying the view much more than he felt he should have.

'And let's face it Ryan, who wouldn't want that?'

He ignored the question but looked at his watch and then said,

'We need to go Mike; we need to be there at ten sharp.'

FORTY

'You know I'm not comfortable in large crowds,'
Tackler said to Nicole-Louise, as they stood outside of a
bar lazily called '230 Fifth', just before ten.
'I asked you to trust me more than you have ever trusted
me in your life, so I want you to come inside with me
and have one drink which you promised that you would,'
she replied.
'I don't like crowded rooms, you know that.'
'We aren't going to be standing in a room; there is a
party on the rooftop space which has a great view of the
Empire State Building. Just one drink,' she replied.
Tackler watched as a constant chain of financial district
workers streamed in and out of the bar, he felt as
uncomfortable as he used to feel when he was a teenager,
for the first time in years. He felt sick inside and his
knees felt weak.

'You can't ever break a promise to me Tackler.'

'I know,' he quietly replied.

'Then let's get it over and done with,' Nicole-Louise said before she took his hand in hers and walked into the bar.

They walked through the bar, it was difficult to see any décor because it was so packed, and they made their way up to the rooftop space.

When they reached it, they walked outside into the warm air, and discovered there were a good two hundred people milling about.

A fact that terrified Tackler, but made Nicole-Louise smile.

Tackler noticed a sign which said, 'Financial District Party Night' and Nicole-Louise squeezed his hand tightly and said,

'It will be OK; I swear to you.'

They walked across to the bar and she ordered two drinks, a beer for Tackler to calm his nerves, even though he rarely drank, and water for herself. She found two seats to the right of the bar and sat down.

She checked her watch; it was 10:00pm exactly.

She scanned the rooftop and her eyes rested on a group of about twenty guys who were leering at the women, laughing much louder than their attempts at humour warranted.

Then she saw him.

'Can you see that guy over there?' she asked Tackler, discreetly pointing towards the group of guys.

Tackler scanned the group and dropped his beer.

Francis Gollini was holding court, and his colleagues were gazing up at him, almost seeking his approval, like the kids used to do at high school.

'I want to leave now!' Tackler demanded.

'Sit yourself down right now Tackler,' Nicole-Louise said loudly, and squeezed his hand even tighter, 'I mean it, if you walk out I will never forgive you.'

Tackler sat down.

One of the guys in the group caught a glimpse of them, and he nudged Gollini and whispered something to him.

'That's Kevin Simpson; he was his running mate at school,' Tackler said nervously, he then started to shake as Gollini said something to the rest of the group they all scooped up their drinks and headed over towards them both.

'I want to go now,' Tackler demanded.

Gollini approached the table with every one of the group now following him. As he reached them, he looked at two guys sitting at the next table telling them to get lost. They promptly stood up and walked away.

'Do you remember me?' Gollini asked, 'Because I don't remember you, but Kev has just told me that you were one of the kids we used to take for a swim down the john, and who used to pee himself. Now I think of it, I can sort of remember you, Foxy isn't it?'

Tackler said nothing, he just looked at the floor and for a moment, he thought he was going to pass out.

'Hey everyone,' Gollini shouted at the top of his voice to the whole rooftop, 'Foxy is in the house and he has just peed himself again.'

A number of people laughed loudly.

'You shouldn't be here, and how have you got a bitch like that? Is she your carer or something?'

All of the men in the group laughed loudly.

'This place is for high achievers and rich guys, you aren't either so get lost before I take you to the bathroom,' Gollini said, he then pathetically downed the last half a bottle of beer he had in his hand to demonstrate what a man he was.

His followers lapped it up.

'You have ten seconds to leave or you're going to the bathroom Foxy boy,' Gollini said.

A couple of the guys in the group started chanting,

'Do it, do it, do it, do it,' when they were interrupted by a voice saying,

'He's going nowhere you pussy, he's with me.'

Gollini turned around, and the group and surrounding area fell into silence.

People weren't used to seeing anyone stand up to Francis Gollini.

Ward stood still, with Lawson by his side, a stare fixed on Gollini, just waiting for him to say or do the wrong thing.

Gollini stood up, he was a big guy, probably a handful in a fist fight, and so used to walking all over guys without any retribution, that he genuinely believed he was one of the toughest guys in the world.

'Then you can leave too,' he said, 'And take your pretty boy with you,' he added, pointing at Lawson.

'You insulted my friend, I won't be going anywhere until I've beat the crap out of you,' Ward replied calmly.

Gollini laughed a loud long laugh.

'Two of you against twenty of us Good luck with that pussy.'

Ward looked at the group, he knew that probably half of them would refuse to fight, but the other half would not risk the humiliation of abandoning a colleague, therefore they would half-heartedly join in.

By now, a lot of the rooftop had stopped what they were doing and had their eyes fixed firmly on the confrontation.

'There are not just two of them, there are nine of us,' a voice said over Ward's shoulder.

He recognised the voice immediately and smiled to himself.

Martin McDermott had responded to the call from Nicole-Louise immediately when she had told him what Ward had asked her to arrange, and now he was here, along with his entire team of his son Paul, Walsh, Wallace, Wired, Fuller and Fringe.

They were the most lethal team of mercenaries in the country, and among Ward's closest and only friends.

'So now you have a big problem,' McDermott continued, 'In fact, all of you girls do, because right now, you are faced with seven of the best Navy Seals that ever lived, an SAS warrior, and the best assassin this country has ever had. And guess what?' he asked Gollini.

'What?' Gollini asked, trying his best to not sound intimidated and frightened, but failing miserably.

'Our friend there is one of the most important people in our team whom we all admire and look up to. You want to threaten him; you have threatened us all. We aren't the kind of people who take an apology as a way of undoing a threat,' McDermott said.

Ward studied Gollini for a moment.

'I can see how frightened you are,' he said, and he turned to scan the group, 'I can see how frightened you all are.' he added.

To a man, every single one of them looked at the floor to avoid making eye contact with him.

'Throw this piece of trash off the roof Mike,' he said casually to Lawson, 'And if any of these girls make a sound, you can throw them off too.'

Lawson stepped forward.

'Someone call the cops!' Gollini screamed.

'The cops won't respond,' Lawson said.

Ward looked at him and raised an eyebrow.

'I cleared it with The Old Man,' Lawson said, 'We have a thirty-minute window where they will not respond. National security takes priority,' he added and smiled.

Wallace and Wired had somehow prevented the few people who wanted to leave from exiting the rooftop without using their guns, but the majority of the people stood still and watched. Everyone was waiting to see if these men really were going to throw Gollini from the roof, but the majority of the people stayed to watch in the hope that he was finally going to get his comeuppance.

With lightning quick speed, Lawson shot his arm forward and clamped his giant hand around Gollini's throat.

There were gasps from the people watching.

'Throw him off,' Ward demanded.

A number of people pulled out their cell phones and started recording the events from a distance, far enough away not to hear what was being said, so Wired, who was patrolling the back, decided to let it go.

This was going exactly as Ward had planned.

'You are a bully and a coward. Look around Gollini,' Ward said, much louder now so the rest of the audience could hear, 'For every action there has to be a consequence, and no matter how long it took, you tormenting our friend, has a price to pay.'

Gollini was desperately trying to scream but such was the force of Lawson's grip around his throat, no sound was coming out.

And then something happened which made this more perfect than Ward could have possibly wished for.

Gollini started to pee his pants.

And Tackler finally saw Gollini for the pathetic creature that he was after a lifetime of torment.

'Stop!' he shouted and he stood up, 'Put him down Mike, now!' he demanded.

Lawson let go immediately and Gollini fell to the floor.

'Back off Ryan, you won't be throwing anyone off of the roof,' he shouted.

'You know how we work Tackler. He picks on you; he picks on us. We can throw him off and there will be no come back on us at all, The Old Man will see to that, you know that,' Ward replied, deliberately trying to goad Tackler into an argument in front of the assembled mass.

'Killing people is not always the answer,' Tackler replied, and he walked over to Gollini who was now pulling himself up off the floor.

'I saw you in a coffee shop a while ago,' he said to him, you didn't even recognise me. You made my life hell at school and you ruined any chance of a childhood that I ever had. The fact that you didn't even recognise me is what hurt me the most; your hate towards me was unwarranted and directed at me only because I was not physically strong. Yet to you, I meant nothing, you couldn't even remember me.'

'It was only a bit of fun, we all did it,' Gollini stuttered in response.

'No, only you did it and these guys,' Tackler said, waving his hand towards Gollini's friends, 'They only stood by and watched because they were as physically inept as me, but they were afraid that you would pick on them if they didn't join in. Come on guys, how many of you actually like him and think he's a good person?' Tackler asked.

Not one person replied.

'He's an asshole,' someone shouted further back on the rooftop.

'You see Gollini. I've just realised that you are nothing but noise and threats. You have nothing about you that is endearing or remotely nice. I wasted so much of my life in fear of you, but now, the only anger I feel is at myself for not seeing what you really are. You are on the floor, you've peed your pants and you look pathetic. But that isn't the worse part for you.'

Gollini looked up at Tackler.

'Look around, there isn't one person here who has rushed to call the cops, or tried to defend you. They all feel as I do towards you, so that makes you the most pathetic and weakest person of all,' Tackler said shaking his head, 'I feel sorry for you,' he added.

Nicole-Louise stood up and put her hand on his arm.

'There will be no throwing anyone off of the roof Ryan, no killing, no hurting people, and no more threats. No matter how many people you have killed, you've never hurt an innocent person and you are not going to start now on my account,' he said loudly, 'We are leaving,' he said to Nicole-Louise, and took her hand and walked away from Gollini.

Then the most moving thing imaginable happened.

At the far end of the rooftop, a couple of people started clapping their hands together, softly and slowly at first.

The clapping got louder and more people joined in.

Then the people closest to Tackler started clapping.

It got quicker and louder, and by the time he was half way across the rooftop towards the exit door, he was receiving pats on the back and cheers.

By the time he had reached the door, literally the whole rooftop was clapping and cheering, and it went on for a good thirty seconds after they had disappeared out of sight.

Ward stood above Gollini and looked at him; Gollini was refusing to make eye contact with him.

He raised his foot quickly and stamped hard with his heel into Gollini's face,

'You aren't entirely innocent,' he said, and he turned and walked away, receiving a few cheers for his own actions.

On the street, all of them assembled together.

'How did you manage to arrange that?' Tackler asked Nicole-Louise, his voice full of energy and excitement, having finally lain to rest the ghost of Francis Gollini.
'Easy, I found out where he worked, hacked into their system, sent out an e-mail about a party night with free drinks, and allocated tickets for the bar and the rooftop for separate people, working through Gollini's e-mails and colleagues to make sure that maximum humiliation could be achieved.'
He smiled a big smile at her.
'Oh, and not only will him peeing his pants be all over YouTube by the morning, he will discover tomorrow that he has paid for the whole evening too when he checks his account,' she added.
He smiled broadly and shook his head.
'You are all amazing, every single one of you.'
'The night is young,' Ward said, 'We are all going for a burger on me,' he added, and he started to walk off down the street.

The burger became a pizza meal at Tackler's favourite restaurant, and they stayed out until gone midnight. They laughed loudly and Ward noticed a new confidence in Tackler that had never been there before.
'I know you instigated this Ryan, thank you,' Tackler said quietly to him while the rest of the table were engrossed in Lawson's theory as to why it is important to paint naked.
'No thanks needed. We are a family. You should have told me about him a long time ago then we could have fixed everything sooner.'

'I didn't trust you not to kill him back then,' Tackler replied.

'Who says we didn't kill him after you left?'

'You are joking, right?'

Ward smiled at him,

'You could always go back for an encore to check?' he said.

'Did you know that the situation was going to play out like that?'

'Don't I always?'

FORTY-ONE

Park Avenue – New York

Two days later Ward was sitting in Nicole-Louise and Tacklers apartment, watching them trying to arrange an appointment in Boston to view the product that Zhang Wei had for sale.

Nicole-Louise had established that the three restaurants that Wei owned were turning over just short of one and a half million dollars a year.

'The food must be expensive,' Tackler said, 'Because two of the restaurants only have enough tables for twenty people, the other only enough room for sixteen,'

Zhang Wei was originally from a place called Gansu in Northern China, a poverty stricken city where parents were unable to feed and clothe their children properly. There was little work, and even less help from the State. Capitalism had not had the positive affect on parts of

China that had been hoped for and now that greed had kicked in, the power hungry people were skimming money left, right and centre off the state sponsored businesses that were springing up everywhere. They had discovered that Wei got most of the children that he traded transported from his home city, and while they could find no definitive evidence as to how many young children he had smuggled into America, Nicole-Louise estimated it was well into the hundreds and her estimations were never far off the mark.

Wei's partner Yang Li seemed to be the brains behind the operation, an assumption reached by the fact that she had regular, and large, cash sums paid into her own personal bank account, amounts that were much larger than Wei's.

'So they get the children in and then sell them off, but that isn't all there is to it,' Nicole-Louise said.

'What else is there?' Ward asked.

'They profit from them twice.'

'How do they do that?'

'Once I had found them on the dark web, I enquired about the cost of a child, and how young they could be because I wanted my money's worth, I was told that for fifty-five thousand dollars they would provide me with an eleven-year-old girl. When I questioned the price, saying that it seemed very expensive, they said that either when the child was sixteen, or if I fancied an upgrade or a downgrade in age, that they would buy the child back for fifteen thousand dollars. When I said that the child might be damaged, they said it doesn't matter as they would be used for chores,' she said softly, her disgust and anger shining through in her voice.

'So I carried on searching,' she continued, 'I found a site that offered Chinese slaves for sale, and when I found the contact details, I managed to break through six different firewalls and establish that the messages were coming from the same address. They were selling the slaves for thirty thousand dollars. So fifteen thousand dollars paid out, eighty-five thousand coming in, and that is without the money they receive for trafficking those poor souls, so I estimate that they are making at least seventy-five thousand dollars on each victim.'

'What's my cover?' Ward asked Tackler.

'Your name is Reece Weldon and you are an investment banker. You live alone in London, and a check on your passport shows that you are a regular visitor to China, Cambodia and Thailand, all the hotbeds for the paedophiles, to give your cover some authenticity. You travel with your own personal bodyguard, which will be Lawson's cover, because you received death threats after an investment plan you sold, robbed people of millions of pounds. Your history and bank records will confirm your cover, and I have set up some fictitious news reports about your money dealings, and the threats to your life, which will be found with a simple name search on Google,' Tackler replied, in a matter of fact tone, expecting Ward to absorb all of the information that he had just received in one go.

'What am I aiming to purchase?' he asked Nicole-Louise.

'Two twelve-year-old girls, but you have asked to inspect them to see them at work before you buy,' she said solemnly.

'Why would I request that?' he asked, surprised at what she had just said.

'Because they must have brothels somewhere, and I can't find exactly where they are, no matter how hard I have been looking,' she replied.

Ward looked at the picture of Yang Li once again. She was actually much more beautiful than he had initially thought, Nicole-Louise had found some recent pictures of her through a social media post of pictures taken in one of their restaurants, and he was going to enjoy stripping her beauty away, bit by bit, with his bullets.

'So what are we waiting for now?' he asked Tackler.

'We are just waiting for the time and place to meet. They have already been going through your history, unless you have a friend in Quebec who knows that you are going undercover as a guy called Reece Weldon.'

'I had better call The Old Man,' Ward said as he walked out of the living area into the kitchen.

'So you must want something to be ringing me when you are on your downtime and this early in the morning?' Centrepoint said as he answered.

'I need the jet and The Optician. But you already know that no doubt.'

'Indeed I do. Of course I will make them both available Ryan.'

He noticed that The Old Man seemed perky, almost happy.

'What's put you in such a good mood,' he asked.

'Everything has been resolved from the fallout of the last few days. There is a panel that has taken over control of the five companies involved in the committee, so we can keep an eye on them at all times.'

Ward wasn't sure how he felt about that,

'That's assuming that the people you have controlling them don't get greedy like the others?' he said.

Centrepoint ignored the comment and said,

'But there is something else.'

'Isn't there always with you?'

'We have been tasked with sorting out this Simone mess. I don't know how we are going to approach it yet but we will have to think of something.'

'Invite him over for dinner,' he replied sarcastically.

'I see you are your usual helpful self.'

It was Ward's turn to ignore him.

'I will listen to what you say but I won't put anyone at risk. If I think it is too dangerous, I won't do it. Do you understand that? I'm serious on this.'

'I would never put you or the others in danger so cut me a bit of slack on this.'

'I'll speak to you when we have sorted this issue in Boston,' Ward said before he hung up the phone.

He walked back into the living area and Tackler was tapping away at his keyboard.

'They are satisfied that you are genuine. They have made contact and they are just trying to raise the price by five thousand dollars at the moment,' Nicole-Louise said to him.

'Don't do it,' he said quickly, 'They will be trying to work out if we are authentic still. If we agree to it, we will look too desperate to them. There are hundreds of these organisations operating; if we are genuine we would know that. Tell them that we will go elsewhere.'

'You're the boss,' Tackler said over his shoulder and he started to do as instructed.

'You won't have to wait for much longer than a minute, they won't turn away business,' Ward said.

As it was, they only had to wait for twenty seconds. A message came back saying that as a new client, and as a gesture of goodwill, they will fix the price at fifty-five thousand dollars.

'Tell them we are in the States now, and that we would like to make our purchase today, tell them that we can be in Boston within a couple of hours.'

Tackler did as he was instructed once again.

'How has he been since the other night?' he quietly asked Nicole-Louise.

'He's been a different animal all together,' she whispered, 'He seems happier, even stronger, but the most obvious thing is that he feels safe. It was mainly me who popped out to get us coffee's or food because he hates crowds, but he has offered to go out more over these past two days than he has in the past two years, so I'm sure that the ghost of Francis Gollini has gone forever.'

'You did well Nicole-Louis,' he said, and he smiled at her squeezing her arm.

'They will collect you from Boston Common by the statue of Paul Revere at 1:00pm. That's all that they will give us at the moment,' Tackler said.

'The common is close to Chinatown if I remember?' Ward asked.

'I believe it is,' Nicole-Louise said.

'So wherever they will be taking us, it will be within walking distance,' he said.

He pulled out his cell phone.

'Ready?' The Optician said as he answered.

'I need you in Boston, by the statue of Paul Rivera at 1:00pm. I will call you on the way if anything changes, but I can't give you a definite place on where to set up, because I don't actually know where I will be going. I'll get the information on the people that we are hunting sent to you, and if anything changes between now and then, I will let you know. Remember, this is not official, you have a choice.'

'I don't really my friend. The Old Man won't be happy if anything happens to you, so to make my life easier, I'll be there as usual.'

'I knew I could rely on you. Can you tell The Old Man that we need the jet in the air within the hour?'

'I will. By the way, you should have had Lawson throw that guy off of the roof the other night,' The Optician said and the line went dead.

Ward smiled to himself, The Optician really was everywhere.

He then pressed speed dial again.

'Hello?' Lawson said wearily.

'You need to be up and out of the house within half an hour, to collect me from Nicole-Louise's and Tackler's apartment,' Ward said.

'For real? This is my day off,' Lawson protested.

'Yes for real,' he replied, 'Tell your interior designers, or whoever you have there with you right now, that you have to go so they will have to leave,' he said and hung up the phone.

Twenty-five minutes later, a fresh looking Lawson was walking into the apartment, drinking a coffee.
'Morning all,' he said happily.
'You got rid of them quick,' Ward said.
'Rid of them? I've left them painting the spare room and the hall,' he replied with a smile.
Ward shook his head,
'Let's get to the airport,' he said as he picked his coat up, 'If anything changes, let me know immediately please. And keep digging to see if you can find where they might be holding these children,' he said over his shoulder to Nicole-Louise and Tackler as he walked out of the apartment.

They arrived at JFK and entered through the secure entrance at the back of the airport. Lawson pulled the car to a stop fifty yards away from the jet. They climbed out of the car, and Ward hurriedly walked to the plane, like every second was of high importance. He climbed up the steps and glanced at the pilot who nodded at him, the co-pilot did not turn around to look at him.
The co-pilot never did.
But the co-pilot, or rather The Optician, didn't need to look around, he always knew exactly where Ryan Ward was.

Five minutes later, they were in the air. Lawson seemed less inclined to flirt with the pretty flight attendant Karen, than he usually did, simply because Ward decided that he had probably been exhausted by his interior designers, and the fact that he leant back into his seat and closed his eyes, only confirmed this point to him.

He leant back into his own chair and looked at the pictures of Zhang Wei and Yang Li. He etched their faces into his mind, and pictured killing them, and the look of fear that he wanted to see in their eyes before he ended their lives.

He was clear on what he was going to do and that made him feel in control. He closed his eyes, he thought of Kyle Newson and Adam Ray, and how fate had been a real bitch to them both, but Kyle now had an opportunity to live a happy life and he felt confident that he was going to grab it with both hands.

He lived in a world of death, deceit and horror, but he saw enough goodness in human nature in the people he defended, to know that he wasn't fighting a lost cause and that is what inspired him to keep going at the pace that he did.

Ryan Ward still had many rivers to cross. He still had many things to learn about the people closest to him, and everything was getting closer to unravelling in devastating and heart-breaking fashion.

But for now, he was happy to continue being a ghost.

To Be Continued

PART FIVE

Warlord

They marched the villagers out onto the dusty square which acted as the focal point for their community. Everyone was there. The men, women, and children, who lived in fear of the moment that the soldiers would visit them and accuse them of crimes they had not committed.

That moment had come today.

They were made to line up, the men to the left, the women to the right, and the children in the middle. The soldiers walked up and down the lines making sure that no one spoke.

A loud rumble filled the distance and five open top vehicles came into view, and everyone immediately looked down at the floor. By the time the vehicles had pulled to a stop twenty feet away from them, every one of the villagers was kneeling on the floor, an order given by the soldiers to show respect to their king.

Samson Simone stepped out of his vehicle and walked across to where the men were lined up, and looked along the line with contempt. One of the men dared to look up at him and so he removed his gun from his holster and shot the man in the head. He died instantly.

A woman on the other side screamed and so he walked across to her and kicked her, hard in the face, his huge, military grade boots destroying her face upon impact.

Everyone else continued looking at the floor.
'Prepare the boys,' he barked.

His soldiers marched across to where the children were kneeling and screamed at all the boys to stand on their feet. The boys responded quickly, almost as if they were playing a game, and they were all upright in a matter of seconds.

Simone studied them, most of the boys looked under the age of ten, apart from two boys who were much taller than the rest of the group. He stamped across the dirt and looked closer at them.

They were definitely too old.

He pulled his gun out of the holster again and shot the two boys he did not need in the head from close range. The rest of the children did not make a sound, they were too afraid.

'You are now enlisted to my army,' he said loudly, pacing up and down as he spoke, fixing his eyes firmly on the terrified boys, 'And to prove your loyalty to me, I am going to give you your first command,' he added, looking for a reaction that would indicate the slightest sign of disobedience in his new charges.

All of the boys stood still. No tears, no noise and no movement.

'Bring them over,' he barked as he strode across to where the men were kneeling.

The soldiers shuffled the boys over, prodding them in the back with their machine guns which had been willingly supplied by the CIA, and the boys lined up in front of their grandfathers, fathers, brothers, uncles and cousins.

The soldiers relinquished their machine guns, placing them in the hands of the boys and then they pulled out their own handguns from their holsters, and to a man, planted the barrels of their weapons firmly against the back of the heads of the boys.

'You are with my army, or you are our enemy,' Simone shouted, his deep, hollow voice echoing around the square, 'I will count to three. On three, those of you that fail to pull your trigger and kill the men in front of you will die, and so will your mothers and sisters. If you show your loyalty and kill the man before you, your women will live and you will be welcomed into my army with open arms.'

The boys, the majority of them eight or nine years old, felt the tears filling their eyes.

'Do it Sadio, save your sister and mother,' one desperate father whispered to his son, who had been unfortunate enough to be lined up in front of his own father.

'One, two, three,' Simone shouted, without a pause or build-up. He didn't want to drag this out; they had three other villages to visit that day as part of their latest recruitment drive.

On three, all but one of the boys fired their machine guns at the men kneeling in front of them, the kick of the guns sending over half of the small, weak boys onto the floor. The nine year old boy, who could not bring himself to kill his father, had been shot in the back of his head by his charge before the echo of the gunfire had drifted away.

'You have proved your worth,' Simone shouted, 'Welcome to my army. Load them up.'

The boys were all marched to a waiting truck and loaded onto it in silence. There were twenty seven of them, all of them in tears and struggling not to let the soldiers see their devastation and tiny, broken hearts.

The women and girls watched the truck roll out of sight, their sons and brothers gone forever.

The soldiers lined up in front of Simone, awaiting their next command, excitement building among them, hoping that their reward would be fitting for the recruitment of twenty seven new warriors. He walked across to his waiting jeep, climbed in and his driver started the engine.

'You have one hour. Rape and enjoy the women and girls, and then burn their village and their bodies to the ground,' he shouted, and then Samson Simone was gone.

Printed in Great Britain
by Amazon